Dear Reader:

In HarperPaperbacks's continuing effort to publish the best romantic fiction at the best value, we have taken the unusual step of pricing nine of our summer Monogram titles at the affordable cost of $3.99. Written by some of the most popular and bestselling romance writers today, these are magical and exciting stories that we hope you will take to your hearts and treasure for a long time.

Open the pages of these wonderful books and give yourself the gift of a reading experience like no other. HarperPaperbacks is delighted to present nine extraordinary novels—at a very attractive price—by favorite authors who can bring the world of love alive for you.

Sincerely,

Carolyn Marino

Carolyn Marino
Editorial Director
HarperPaperbacks

TEMPTATION

Griffin raised his head and looked down at Cicely's upturned face. Her rich chestnut lashes formed twin crescents on peach-blushed cheeks. Her parted lips were moist and swollen from his kisses.

He wanted her. Hot blood hammered through his veins. His hands trembled with his need.

She opened her eyes. There, in those wide, amber-brown depths, he saw something unexpected. Something that left him more shaken than his raging desire. Something that filled him with a curious humility.

This woman was no common wench to be tumbled in a field, nor was she a pedigreed ewe to be bargained for as her father had done. Cicely was someone special. Someone who deserved to be wooed. Patiently. Tenderly.

She was the woman he wanted for his wife.

"*A Hidden Magic* is a sensational story! The romance, the adventure . . . are all marvelous and highly enjoyable!"

—*The Paperback Forum*

Books by Terri Lynn Wilhelm

A Hidden Magic
Fool of Hearts
Shadow Prince

Published by HarperPaperbacks

A Hidden Magic

 TERRI LYNN WILHELM

HarperPaperbacks
A Division of HarperCollinsPublishers

HarperPaperbacks   *A Division of* HarperCollins*Publishers*
10 East 53rd Street, New York, N.Y. 10022

Cover illustration by John Ennis

First printing: June 1996

Printed in the United States of America

HarperPaperbacks, HarperMonogram, and colophon are
trademarks of HarperCollins*Publishers*

❖ 10 9 8 7 6 5 4 3 2 1

To Carolyn Marino,
who shines with the magic of books.

1

England, 1763

He'd robbed the widow Honeysett.

Griffin Tyrrell shifted in his place on the hard wooden bench, trying to ease the ache in his right leg. After five days in the saddle, the wound he'd received several months ago pained him. Determinedly, he tried to ignore it, turning his thoughts to this venture that excited him beyond words.

He knew he should be ashamed to have taken such advantage of a woman's ignorance, but he couldn't help smiling as he absently gazed around the common room of the inn where he'd spent the night. After twelve years of riding to the king's pipes and drums, he was a free man. And now, thanks to the widow Honeysett's lack of good judgment, he had a fine house.

This summer morning saw the large stone fireplace standing empty, save for a pile of old ashes. The room smelled of stale beer, onions, and spent tobacco. At this hour only one other guest occupied the room, a young fellow who snored softly as he slumped on his bench, his head resting on the age-darkened oak table in front of him, his mouth gaping, his wig askew.

The inn's front door opened and the gray light of dawn almost pierced the smoky interior. Digby Prither entered. Stocky, in his early thirties, he wore his dun brown hair pulled back in a stubby workingman's queue. Griffin had hired him in London before undertaking the journey south to Sussex to claim his estate.

"Horses have been fed, Cap'n, and they're rarin' to go."

"Come," Griffin said, motioning Digby to the bench on the opposite side of his table. "We'll eat before we saddle them."

With a short nod, Digby swept off his three-cornered hat and strode to his seat.

Griffin ordered them ale, cheese, bread, and sausage from the pretty little serving wench.

"You're right cheerful this morning," Digby observed.

"That I am."

Today Griffin started his new life. Today he would see his new home for the first time.

He'd spent years fighting and bleeding in the king's service. He'd often lived under hard, primitive conditions. He'd seen friends fall, one after another, on forest trails and on smoky battlefields in the New World. In America he'd come close to dying of his wounds after an ambush and had even been reported dead. In Cuba, a Spaniard had driven a bayonet into his leg. Now, in his thirtieth year, he was ready for peace, and one month ago, he'd resigned his commission.

"Tell me again, Cap'n, about Cranwick Abbey," Digby said, and for the first time, Griffin realized that the place would be Digby's home, too.

"It was an abbey, but during the time of Henry VIII, it was made into a private residence. I've bought the furnishings from the previous owner." The foolish widow Honeysett. "Now those acres are mine to farm or rent. The closest neighbor is the estate of Blekton, which hasn't been occupied in years. The gentleman who owns it has a condition of the stomach that confines him to his bed in Crawley."

The terms for the purchase of Cranwick Abbey had been so generous that Griffin's agent, Mr. Zacchaeus Fremlin, had almost been overtaken by an apoplexy of ecstasy. That gentleman had been to see the property himself and had found the manor, the stable, and the outbuildings all in acceptable repair. The acreage seemed vast compared to what Griffin had expected his savings would purchase. Cranwick Abbey was a dream come true.

"Why?" he had asked Fremlin. "Why is she all but giving it away?"

"She does not wish to live there anymore. She desires to travel." Fremlin had shrugged. "Who can account for the vagaries of women? I've been told the widow is rich. She can do as she pleases."

This pleased Griffin considerably. He worked at squashing the guilt that nagged him. He'd taken advantage of a woman. Worse, of a grieving widow. But she was wealthy, he reasoned. She did not want Cranwick Abbey. He, on the other hand, was not wealthy, but he greatly desired a place of his own.

He had been free of his enemy's attentions for above half a year now. It was finally safe to put down roots.

"And Cranwick is in Sussex."

"The village of Alwyn is situated not far from the estate."

"Never heard of it."

"I shouldn't wonder that you've never heard of either place. A tiny coastal village and a modest estate. Hardly likely to gain attention in London."

The wench brought their platters of food and tankards of ale, setting them on the table with a flirtatious smile at Griffin, flashing him a generous view of her cleavage. He grinned and paid her, including something extra for her trouble. She moved still closer to him, slipping an arm around his shoulders.

"Not now, my little rose," he said. "I've business to attend." He patted her on her backside, and she giggled as she swished away across the room through the doorway that led to the kitchen.

As soon as the men finished breaking their fast, they went out to saddle the horses. Griffin had been so eager to see Cranwick Abbey, that he'd packed a kit, a few changes of clothes, and arranged for his possessions to follow.

The sun was rising as, limping slightly, he led his handsome sorrel stallion, Apollo, out of the inn's stable. Iron horseshoes rang on the courtyard cobbles. Behind him, Digby led his own sturdy, if less elegant, mount. Griffin's spirits soared. Tonight he'd sleep in his own bed, in his own house, on his own manor. Damned if he would feel a farthing's worth of guilt over the silly widow Honeysett.

"Quickly, Hannah, I wish to be well away from the abbey before the new owner arrives." Lady Cicely Ann Honeysett tied the ribbons of her straw milkmaid's hat under her chin as she swept out the front door to the waiting carriage, determinedly squashing a spurt of guilt.

"Yes, m'lady." The maid scurried down the hall after her mistress, her arms loaded with a large basket containing meat pasties, a wedge of cheese, berry tarts, and a bottle of smuggled French wine. "I just thought we should take some nourishment-like. We don't know what them Frenchies might try ter serve us. Mightn't agree with us, you know." She hoisted the basket up onto a seat inside the coach, sliding through the door sideways to accommodate the oval hoop–enhanced shape of her hips and skirts, then plopped down on the seat next to the basket.

Cicely laughed, feeling gay and lighthearted for the first time since her girlhood. At long last she was going to have the adventure she'd only dreamed about until returning home from poor Edmund's funeral. Tomorrow the ship would take them across the Channel where, at long last, she would actually see with her own eyes the wonders of the world. The architecture, the countrysides, the people. And she would capture it all with her pastels, stroking shape and color onto the thick, rough paper. After being first the dutiful daughter, then the dutiful wife, she was at last free to glory in the sights, smells, and sounds of new places.

There was no one to ridicule her now.

"Hannah, I cannot comprehend how you stay so slim when you always seem to concern yourself with food."

Hannah smiled, and the expression lighted her plain features almost to prettiness. "Someone has to think of it, m'lady, else you'd never eat proper."

Suddenly Cicely leaned forward and clasped her maid's hands in hers. "Oh, Hannah, we're going to see such sights!" she said earnestly, excitement bubbling up inside her. "We shall be ladies of the world. Bold adventuresses! We'll drink the wines of France and sample exotic Italian dishes to our hearts' content. I have read of it all in Sir Thomas Nugent's book, *The Grand Tour*, and taken those precautions he suggested. I have packed among my belongings a map made of linen, a prospective glass, my pastel crayons and paper, of course, a pocketknife—oh, and many other items suggested to me in my reading. Monsieur Mission's book was also a treasury of sound advice." Cicely frowned, vaguely uneasy. "Although I fear I was unable to procure the inflatable bath with bellows. The device proved most elusive."

Hannah cast Cicely an uncertain look. "As you say, m'lady."

Cicely's confidence rebounded as she thought of all the other precautions she had taken on the authors' instructions. "Never fear, Hannah. We'll make do without the inflatable bath."

A weathered face appeared at the coach door window. "All's ready, Lady Cicely," Will Allcorn said. "You take care o' yourself now." He nodded toward Hannah. "Keep a sharp eye on this wench, too. She's the apple of Mark's and Nan's eyes."

"I'll do my best, Will."

His mouth curved up at the corners. "I know you will, m'lady. You've always tried ter do right by the folk in Alwyn."

Cicely felt her cheeks warm under what was, for Will Allcorn, high praise. "Are you certain you wouldn't like to continue on at the abbey? I'm sure the new owner will be in need of help. I did have my agent stipulate that he keep you on if you wanted to work for him."

Will slowly shook his head. "No. You know I was never easy here. None of us really were. I only stayed on for your sake, and now I'm free ter leave."

Cicely swallowed, willing back tears that suddenly threatened to make a mess of this difficult parting. There was little chance of her ever returning. Cranwick Abbey had a new owner now, one who had paid an exorbitant price, considering.

Despite herself, Cicely reached for Will's hand and grasped it between her own. Like the man, it was warm and rugged. Like the man, it had served her and comforted her. She would miss Will. In the past six years he had helped to alleviate the soul-withering loneliness.

She pressed her lips together as tears rolled down her cheeks.

"Here now," Will said gruffly, "let's have none o' this."

Cicely wiped her eyes with the back of one hand. "Quite right," she agreed, sniffling. "It only makes things worse."

"I won't say I won't a-miss you, Lady Cicely, 'cause I will. But you're well away from this dark place. Your husband, may God take mercy on his soul, was wicked ter have kept you here."

Reluctantly, Cicely relinquished Will's hand, and he lightly thumped the coach door with it and stepped back.

With the handle of her parasol, Cicely rapped the ceiling of the passenger compartment. She lurched back against the squabs as the hired coachman wheeled the team of horses around the curve of the drive in front of the abbey, and down the straight carriage approach, toward the country lane that fronted the estate. It seemed he'd taken to heart the orders she'd given him earlier regarding haste.

She straightened in her seat, rearranging her hat, smoothing her skirts, and retrieving her dog-eared book of Celtic myths from the floor. She resisted the urge to look back at Cranwick Abbey. No, from this day on, she would look only forward. Tonight she and Hannah would stay at the inn where she'd reserved rooms, and tomorrow, when the ship sailed out of Portsmouth, their great adventure would begin.

*   *   *

Quickly, Griffin pulled his horse over to the side of the road, making way for the coach that rumbled past them at breakneck speed, sending out behind it a billowing cloud of dust. He fanned the gritty air in front of his face. Someone was in a very great hurry.

Digby coughed. "Some people have no manners," he protested, glaring over his shoulder at the coach.

"So it would seem." Griffin eagerly searched for the landmarks his agent had given him. *Home*, he thought. It had been so long since he'd had one to claim.

With the danger of being run over past, he nudged Apollo with his bootheels, and the big sorrel stallion resumed its stately pace. Digby rode almost next to Griffin, but not quite. His horse ignored most of his incessant urging for more speed, maintaining a slower, plodding gait.

Then Griffin spied the drive that opened between the two lichen-covered stone pillars. "We're here," he said, abandoning any attempt to preserve his dignity. "Come, Digby, let's inspect our new home!" At his silent command, Apollo galloped down the drive to the house. Griffin gloried in the feel of the sea-tinged wind in his face that threatened to tear off his three-cornered hat. In the distance, he saw cottages and knew them to be his tenant farmers' from the description given him by Fremlin.

What held his attention was the stately three-storied house of age-darkened stone. Mullioned oriel windows, their small, rectangular panes winking in the midsummer light, punctuated the wide length of the building with elegant symmetry. The hard-packed earthen drive widened to form a circle in front of the house.

Griffin reined in his mount and sat for a moment,

drinking in the sight of his new home. It was quite grand—much grander than he'd ever expected to possess. But possess it he did, land, buildings, chattel, and all for a ridiculously low sum: the bulk of his savings and a small mortgage. He'd kept back what he had estimated he would need to live and to purchase animals and to keep the estate productive. Fremlin had told him that the lands of Cranwick Abbey were already bringing in revenue. The agent had shown Griffin the manor's account books. Griffin shook his head in wonder. Why had she given it up? Edmund Honeysett must be thrashing in his grave at what his irresponsible wife had done.

Leather creaked as Griffin swung stiffly down from the saddle, favoring his leg. He looked back to see Digby and his steady steed approaching at a saunter. The look of stormy resignation on Digby's face caused Griffin to grin.

"Well, what do you think?" Griffin asked, gathering Apollo's reins in the fingers of one hand and gesturing with the other to indicate the abbey and the lands surrounding it.

"'Tis a right fair palace, Cap'n. Right fair indeed. It's as good as anything King Georgie's got, I'll warrant."

Griffin laughed. "Well, perhaps not quite that palatial, but it will do very nicely for my less noble needs." He walked closer to the building, towing Apollo behind him, seeking to round the side of the mansion in search of the stables.

Suddenly Apollo reared his head, almost jerking the reins out of Griffin's hand. Surprised, Griffin turned to see what the matter was. The stallion backed away, eyes wide, and Griffin quickly scanned the ground for a snake, but found none. He sniffed the air, thinking an unfamiliar smell might have set off the creature, but all he could detect was the faint salty scent of the Channel a mile away. He found no reason for the horse's alarm.

He moved slowly toward Apollo. "Come, now, old fellow, what has you so disturbed?" he asked in a soothing voice. Did the horse hear something he could not? He stroked the red-brown neck and Apollo calmed under his touch.

Digby slid off his dobbin and led the beast toward Griffin and Apollo. No sooner had the dobbin passed Apollo than he pulled back, nostrils flaring, eyes rolling. He tried to break free of Digby's grip on the reins, but the little man hung on with indignant determination. When the horse had backed up several feet, the gelding steadied to his usual stolid self.

"What the devil has gotten into the beasts?" Griffin muttered, frowning. As an experiment, he led Apollo parallel to where they stood in front of the house, and the stallion followed him quietly. Then he moved closer to the building.

Abruptly, Apollo pulled back, a sharp neigh rumbling in his chest.

Griffin and Digby looked at each other in surprise. "Try it with your animal," Griffin said.

Dutifully, Digby walked the bay gelding in a course parallel to the front of the manor from where they now stood. Dobbin walked docilely along behind him. But when Digby changed direction to take them closer to the house, the horse pulled up sharply, vigorously shaking his head and snorting.

Digby cast the silent manor house a worried glance before he directed his gaze to Griffin. "It's the house, Cap'n."

Griffin caressed Apollo's velvety nose as he considered the situation. "At least this part of it. There must be something in one of these rooms that they smell or hear." But he read the doubt in Digby's face. "Come," he said impatiently. "We'll see how they react to the rest of the building on our way to the stables."

The men found the stables around the back of the towering Jacobean structure. The trip gave them additional opportunities to test the reaction of the horses to the building itself, but each time, the results were the same. The animals wanted nothing to do with the building.

Griffin drew one of his flintlock pistols from its place on his saddle and held it at the ready as he cautiously led Apollo into the clean stables. New straw had been laid down, and he found a day's supply of hay and oats. The water in the troughs was fresh. All compliments of the previous owner.

Griffin and Digby set about pulling the saddles and saddlebags off the horses and seeing to the beasts' welfare. It didn't take long. They had traveled lightly, for speed, so anxious had been Griffin to see his new home. The wagon with their possessions would arrive in two days. Until then, they'd packed enough in the way of clothing in their saddlebags to see them through. Anything else they might need could be purchased in the village.

Griffin took the other pistol from its holster. He slipped it into the waist of his buckskin breeches and held the other. It was time to explore the house.

Digby eyed the weapons. "Expectin' trouble, Cap'n?"

"Let's just say I wish to be ready if trouble is expecting *me*."

The servant nodded and pulled a pitchfork from its place on the wall. "It'll have to take us both on, then."

The place was silent as they quietly walked through a courtyard toward the back of the house. Griffin saw no sign to indicate that anyone but he and Digby were there. A bird's trilled song suggested that they were alone.

Finding the door locked, Griffin withdrew from his coat pocket the large brass key his agent had given him. It turned in the keyhole with an audible *click*, and under his hand, the door opened.

They entered a kitchen, with a high, beamed ceiling and white plaster walls. No fire burned in the enormous fireplace. The widow had left the old oak worktables, he noticed, as well as the kettles, pans, and molds, which hung on the walls. He walked softly to keep his boots from ringing against the flagstone floor. As with the stables, the kitchen and stillroom, pantry and scullery were all clean and orderly.

"Looks like the widow was right tidy-like," Digby observed in a low voice.

Griffin hushed him with a narrowed look, then proceeded quietly down a corridor. One by one, Griffin checked each room on the ground floor, finding no intruders or any reason that he could see for the horses' odd behavior. What he did see was a comfortable, well-cared-for house that any man would be proud to call home.

Sunshine streamed through the myriad small panes of the bay windows to gleam upon the mellow, amber-colored oak of the linen-fold paneling that covered the walls. The white, lime-washed ceiling, with its pendants and intricate, low-relief vines so popular more than a century earlier, seemed to glow in that natural light. As per their agreement, the widow Honeysett had left her furnishings, which, to his pleasure, included costly Turkish carpets, excellent-quality wing chairs, couches covered in French brocades, and finely crafted tables. In all rooms, elegant overmantels topped handsome fireplaces. Everywhere he looked, taste in colors and materials had been employed, and nothing other than the building itself looked above five or six years old.

The more he saw of Cranwick Abbey, the more paltry his price for it seemed. Many years of good fortune and hard labor would have been required before he could have afforded to furnish the abbey in this manner on his own.

Clearly, the widow had more gold than sense.

Digby at his heels, Griffin mounted the impressive wooden staircase, impatient with the insistent stiffness in his leg. He marveled at the elaborately turned newel posts, each of which was topped by a gilded wyvern. On every one of the six posts, the two-legged dragon held its wings back and erect. The creature's long, scaled tail wound around the post.

At the top of the staircase, Griffin paused to listen, and Digby ran into the back of him. The servant teetered backward, arms windmilling wildly. The pitchfork clattered down the stairs. Only Griffin's quick grip saved Digby from following the farm tool back down to the ground floor.

"Blast it, man, watch where you're going!" Griffin whispered sternly.

Digby's homely face grew dark red, but he nodded, his gaze sliding longingly down the stairs to the pitchfork.

Griffin sighed. "Go get it. But be *quiet* about it."

Digby scrambled almost silently down the steps to retrieve his weapon, then back up again to stand next to Griffin, but well away from the staircase.

This whole business was probably pointless, anyway, Griffin thought, beginning to feel foolish creeping through his own house like a thief. But he remembered the horses and decided it was wiser to complete his stealthy tour.

They went from room to room of the east wing first, and encountered a grand salon—converted, no doubt, from the high great chamber—two dining chambers, and three bedchambers with antechambers, a drawing room, and a long gallery. All were elegantly furnished, all impeccably clean and nicely arranged. As Griffin rounded the corner into the west wing, he stopped short in amazement and was again buffeted by Digby.

"Gadzooks!" Digby exclaimed, peering around Griffin, into the drafty, wide corridor that marched the length of the wing.

Cobwebs hung like ghostly draperies from the ceiling, from portraits, from old-style girandoles and sconces bearing candles that surely had not been lighted within Griffin's lifetime. Dust formed a thick gray pall over side tables and chairs, carpets and floor.

"What the devil happened here?" Griffin asked, expecting no answer. A shiver of foreboding traveled down his spine.

"No good, I'll warrant," Digby said in a hushed voice, making no move to leave his place behind Griffin. "'Tisn't natural, this place. It has the feel of witchery about it."

Uneasy over the eerie atmosphere of the place, impatient with such superstitious rot, Griffin said dryly, "Rather it has the feel of sinful neglect. I'd wager a guinea this wing wasn't used, so no one bothered to clean it." But even as he spoke the words, he couldn't accept them. The rest of the house was too flawlessly spotless. He looked over his shoulder to see Digby shake his head. "The death of a loved one, then," Griffin suggested, trying again to put a comfortingly logical reason to this strange place of neglect. "I've heard of parents refusing to touch the room of a favorite child who has died. Or a widow who greatly loved her husband." Griffin fastened on that excuse with a sense of relief. "The previous owner of this estate was a widow."

Digby gave him a doubtful look. "Aye, Cap'n, but didn't you say Mr. Honeysett died two months ago? This looks more like generations o' dust."

Griffin had to admit that was true. "Two months. She certainly did not stay to mourn her unfortunate spouse long, did she?"

"No, but then the Quality seldom marry for love."

Also true, Griffin thought, struggling to hold the old, burning bitterness at bay.

He straightened and drew in a long breath of inexplicably cold air. What he had, he'd earned by his own wits and skill. His enemy had not stalked him for half a year now. After so long, it seemed to Griffin that he must finally be free. An unswept corridor posed no threat to a man who had withstood the horrors he had known.

"Come, enough of this dithering," he said. "A couple of skittish horses and a few cobwebs are not a menace to grown men." He glanced back at Digby, who clutched the skirt of Griffin's leather riding coat.

"Release me," Griffin commanded, and, with obvious reluctance, Digby obeyed. "Now, stay or go as you please, but I intend to investigate this place." And with that, Griffin stepped into the corridor.

A chilling breeze immediately swirled through the hall, setting the draperies of webs and dust dancing and raising gooseflesh on Griffin's neck for more reason than just temperature. No open window was responsible for this wind. It was summer, and outside it was warm. Refusing to give ground to the unknown, he continued on his path to the first closed door.

It opened under his urging, the screech of long-unoiled hinges echoing in the corridor. Here the furniture was of a different age than that he'd seen in the rest of the house. This heavy, dark stuff, with its trailing cobwebs and rotting upholstery, hailed from an earlier century. Like the house, this furniture had come from the time when Elizabeth or James Stuart had ruled the kingdom.

He opened the next door. Like the last, the bed of this chamber was hung with trailing cobwebs and tattered red damask, which undulated in the growing wind. Before Griffin could close the door, it jerked from his fingers and slammed shut. He looked behind to find Digby still standing at the entrance of the corridor, eyes wide with fright, clutching the pitchfork in white-knuckled fists.

"Cap'n, come back! Something wicked is in this place, I can feel it. *Please*, Cap'n!"

Suddenly, deep, hollow, spine-chilling laughter boomed through the hall. Griffin spun around, trying to locate the source, but he found nothing. Then, directly in front of him, a towering death's-head materialized with a blast of freezing air. Its bony jaws clattered with each gale of the horrible sound.

Digby shrieked. Griffin heard bootsteps thunder down the stairs. They faded into the distance.

The skull grew larger and more gruesome, until its bottom jaw was equal to Griffin in height. "BEGONE," the thing rumbled. Panes in the windows rattled. Figurines clattered on the tables.

It didn't need to speak twice.

Griffin had faced cannon fire, musket fire, swords, starvation, and exposure and taken it all in stride as a soldier's lot. He'd fought Frenchmen, Spaniards, red Indians, and men whose skin was the blue-black of polished jet. But never in his life had he come against a talking human skull the size of a cottage.

He raced down the stairs, his game leg nearly tripping him up and sending him sprawling. He ran back through the manor the way he'd come. He lurched through the kitchen door into the warm clasp of the summer's late morning. He didn't stop until he crossed the courtyard. When it was apparent that the monster did not pursue him out of the house, he leaned over, hands braced on thighs, and waited for his heart to stop hammering. He bunched fingers into a fist and slammed it against his damaged leg in furious frustration, intensified by his alarm.

Christ Almighty, what was that thing in the hall?

As his panic gradually subsided, his thoughts cleared. Whatever it was, it did not appear to be inclined to follow him outside the manor house. But that didn't mean it could not, should it choose to do so. Griffin straightened and shoved a shaking hand through his hair, managing to pull a hank of it out of his queue. The next order of action was to find out about the grisly inhabitant of the house that belonged to *him*, to Griffin Nelvington Tyrrell.

Before he resaddled Apollo, Griffin looked around for Digby, but it appeared the man had deserted and taken Dobbin with him.

All the way to the village, Griffin brooded. His agent had not adequately performed his duties. Clearly the man had never gone into the house. And dear old Widow Honeysett. Likely she was cackling right now over the price she'd received for that house of horror. Griffin ground his teeth. There was no getting around it.

He'd been swindled.

2

The thought rankled. It gnawed at him with every step of Apollo's iron-shod hooves.

She'd made a fool of him.

He'd given his hard-earned guineas for a house where another ruled. Another that he could not oust by any means he knew, being unacquainted with the ways of hellish monsters.

As he rode into Alwyn, Griffin grew aware of the smothered smirks, the averted smiles of the men and women walking or riding by him on the street. Heat gathered in his neck, in his face. They knew! The villagers knew he'd been made a fool. But then, how could they not know? Now that he thought on the matter, it seemed inconceivable that everyone in the parish would not know of the demon that dwelled in Cranwick Abbey. And as neighbors to the treacherous Honeysett female, they would also know that she'd managed to unload the abbey on some unsuspecting dolt.

Griffin stabled Apollo with the liveryman, who barely

managed to contain his merriment, then struck out to shop for his dinner and the meal for the next morning. As he strode down the street, he grew more and more resentful of being so obviously considered a gull by the populace. Oh, no one said anything. No one actually sniggered or laughed. In fact, all were polite and as courteous as one might wish. But their satisfaction and amusement were there, bubbling just beneath the surface.

That knowledge burned inside Griffin like a red-hot coal. No man enjoyed being made to look a greedy blockhead. But the last laugh would be on that conniving Honeysett woman. He would find a way to rid his home of the monster.

To that end, he smiled and remained ever the pleasant new resident. Despite the sorry offerings in the baker's store and the cheese shop, he made his purchases with good grace, reminding himself that in the past he'd often had to settle for worse. As he eyed the scrawny carcasses that hung in the butcher's shop while waiting for that worthy to wrap the chops he'd bought for dinner, it occurred to Griffin that the fare offered in the shops was likely directly related to the many brown, withered fields he'd passed on the way to his manor.

Even if Fremlin had neglected to mention the demon in the west wing of Cranwick Abbey, he had not failed to mention the blight that had affected many of the crops in the area. That and the fact that local fishermen struggled with poor catches.

As Griffin accepted the neatly packaged chops, he thanked the butcher, a muscular man with bright red hair named Uriah Coppard.

"How does Cranwick Abbey agree with you, Mr. Tyrrell?" Though the butcher inquired politely enough, Griffin did not miss the twinkle in the man's eyes.

"Quite well, thank you," he replied. "The manor and house are ideal for my needs."

"And what needs might those be, if you don't mind me asking?"

Griffin saw the question as a quest for information on his intentions, the most direct one to be put to him. Landlords that absented themselves from their manors brought little or no trade to the local towns, and seldom took an interest in the welfare of the people there.

"I intend to live in the manor and farm the land."

Coppard regarded Griffin steadily. "What of the families already on your lands?"

Griffin smiled mildly. "You are an impertinent fellow, aren't you?"

"Some might say."

Griffin considered the information he wanted, weighing his chances of getting it by bartering his paltry bit of news with the butcher. He'd already noticed the fondness and respect in which the people of Alwyn seemed to hold the treacherous widow Honeysett. Apparently it was only strangers who should beware of the female. But he intended to set the score aright.

"Direct speaking is always best, don't you agree?" he asked the burly Coppard.

"That I do."

"Then I will tell you that any man who is clearly trying, who is not afraid to work, and is willing to accept my guidance when I deem it prudent, will have no cause for concern."

Coppard nodded slowly, his massive arms folded over his chest.

"Now I have a question to put to you," Griffin said. "I was hoping to have the privilege of meeting Mrs. Honeysett in person, but it seems I missed her by only hours. Where did she go?"

A shuttered look instantly came over Uriah Coppard's face. "I wouldn't know, sir. The gentry don't confide in a humble butcher."

Ha, Griffin thought. There is nothing humble about this butcher. No, the wily widow is too popular with the villagers for Coppard not to be informed as to the details of her destination.

"I doubt that," Griffin said. "I imagine little occurs here that you do not know."

Color appeared in Coppard's cheeks. "Mayhap that's so."

"Oh, I believe it is," Griffin continued, not above using blatant flattery to get what he wanted—his hands around the Honeysett woman's swindling throat. "That is why I have not troubled to speak to anyone else of my desire to meet my benefactress. You see, Cranwick Abbey is what I have always wanted as a home. Even when I was fighting the French and the Huron Indians in America—"

"You were in the army?" Coppard asked, suddenly interested. "You've seen action against the frog-eaters?"

"Yes, as I said." The effect of his careful revelation had won an even greater effect than he could have hoped.

"My cousin, he took the king's pence and fought the Frenchies and their savages." Coppard straightened and lifted his chin proudly. "He were with Braddock. Died in a forest by the Monongahela River."

A North American forest. The thought had the power to cast a dark pall over Griffin. He'd failed to protect Jeremy. Dear God, never had he failed so horribly.

"I was in that battle," he said quietly.

Coppard regarded him for a moment, then, as if sensing the past was best left to silence, he nodded.

With an effort, Griffin turned away from the dark

memories. "Yes. Well. So you understand how a man would appreciate a property as comfortable as Cranwick Abbey. But I cannot thank her if I cannot find her."

"And what would you do if you found her?" Coppard inquired, running his forefinger along the handle of his largest knife.

"I would tell the lady how I esteem her kindness. What man come into a prize like Cranwick Abbey would not wish to make his true feelings known to the person responsible?" Oh, he'd make his true feelings quite clear to the scheming female. "I cannot rest until I have expressed my gratitude."

Coppard's finger hesitated. He stared down at the knife handle. "Lady Cicely will be leaving for Le Havre from Portsmouth tomorrow." He lifted his gaze and fixed Griffin with a stern eye. "She's a good sort, is our Lady Cicely, and if you harm a hair on her head, you'll have ter answer ter me."

Griffin widened his eyes. "What possible reason could I have for wishing to harm the widow?"

Again color flashed in the fair-skinned cheeks of the butcher. Then he scowled. "Just you mind my words, Mr. Tyrrell."

"I shall keep them next to my heart, sir." Griffin grinned as he picked up his parcel of chops. "My thanks to you." And with that, he swept out of the butcher's shop.

He strode impatiently down the walkway, past the narrow doorways of the shops, and the occasional display window, then crossed the cobbled street to the livery. He paid for Apollo's hour stay, stuffed his packages in a saddlebag, and swung up into the saddle.

As the stallion's long legs ate up the distance heading west, away from Cranwick Abbey, his hooves pounded a strong rhythm on the dirt road.

So the kindly widow Honeysett was taking a trip to France, was she? Fleeing England, no doubt.

Just before dusk, he reached the bustling port town. The streets were filled with the racket of iron-shod hooves and wagon and carriage wheels ringing against the cobbles, the continuous flood of voices from sailors, shopkeepers, and patrons. The singsong cries of the vendors hawking the last of their day's wares rose above the cries of wheeling seabirds. Docked along the waterfront, fishing boats and luggers rose and dipped gently with the gray-green water. Offshore, the furled sails of the frigates and corvettes, East Indiamen and tea clippers gradually turned from bright white to rose and orange as the sun set, throwing its purple and pink and gold across the land and sea.

As he breathed in the sharp tang of salt water and the oily smell of fish, Griffin thought about the monstrous death's-head in the west wing of his new home. A grim elation rose within him.

Here is where he would find the widow Honeysett.

The following morning dawned bright and clear. Anticipation bubbled inside Cicely, as she eagerly watched through the carriage window for the docks to come into view. Cicely smiled. Le Havre. Her doorway to the wonders of the world, to adventures, to . . . freedom.

To Cicely's amazement, it didn't take long to unload, and by the time she'd settled with the driver, half of their luggage had already been taken aboard the ship.

As she swept up the plank, Hannah close behind her, she was stopped by a short, barrel-chested fellow of middle years.

"Where's your man?" he demanded.

Not wanting to begin her new life with unpleasantness, Cicely returned his rudeness with civility. Smiling, she held out her gloved hand to him. Distractedly, he took it, and sketched a brief bow over it.

"Good morning to you," she said. "We have not been introduced, but I am Lady Cicely Honeysett. And you are . . . ?"

"The captain of this vessel," the man announced so forcefully Cicely thought he must expect someone to deny it.

"I'm sure," she murmured reassuringly, suppressing the silly urge to pat his tanned, weathered hand. "Perhaps you might be so good as to tell me your name."

He started, as if realizing he'd forgotten his manners in the presence of a lady. "Francis Miller, madam. *Captain* Francis Miller."

Cicely inclined her head. "I am so very pleased to make your acquaintance, Captain Miller."

"Uh, yes. As you say. Enchanted to meet you, Lady Cicely. Where is, uh, Lord Honeysett?" he asked with an inflection that could only be described as hopeful.

"I am Mr. Honeysett's widow." Well, he really couldn't be expected to know that, since she'd decided to forgo mourning black. In truth, she could not even say that she mourned her late husband. He had been barely civil to her during the six years of their arranged marriage, leaving her a prisoner of his rural Sussex property while he spent his time in London or Paris with his sporting cronies.

The captain cleared his throat. "Please accept my condolences."

"Thank you, Captain Miller. You are most kind." Why had he gestured to his men to stop loading her and Hannah's trunks on the ship?

"There is still the problem of your man."

Cicely clung to her patience with determination.

"*What* man? I plan to hire a guide and bodyguards when I arrive in Le Havre, but they'll not trouble you here."

"The man who is traveling with you, Lady Cicely. Where is he? No unescorted woman is coming aboard *my* ship." Captain Miller's face grew dark red.

By now a small crowd had gathered around them. On the deck, surrounding the captain, stood some of the crew. Tanned and tough-looking, they growled their assent. "'Tis bad luck," one of them declared.

Miller shot the man a glare. "Less luck than lust, I'm thinking." He turned back to Cicely. "I'll not be responsible for the welfare of an unescorted female." His gaze flicked over Hannah, who peered over Cicely's shoulder. "*Two* unescorted females." He crossed his arms over his barrel chest, as if the matter was now settled.

Cicely stared at him in disbelief. "But this is absurd! We seek passage only across the Channel, not the Atlantic!"

"Things happen," the man insisted stubbornly.

"Quite right," a deep, male voice rumbled behind her. "Things do happen."

Cicely stiffened. Slowly—because to move suddenly might overbalance Hannah, sending them both tumbling off the plank into the dirty water of the harbor—she turned to see who sought to interfere. Hannah's hat prohibited a clear view of the busybody. All Cicely could see was a bit of his gray waistcoat.

"I will thank you, sir," she said, annoyed that her precarious position on the plank robbed her icy tone of some of its effect, "to tend to your own affairs, and allow me to tend to mine."

Captain Miller eyed the person behind her. "Do you know this woman?"

"I do," the deep, masculine voice replied. "I have

been on her trail since yesterday, when she escaped from the bosom of her family."

Indignation swelled in Cicely. She tried to turn the rest of the way, but first had to pry loose Hannah's grip. Impatiently she curled aside the brim of Hannah's milk-maid hat, giving her a clear view of the madman.

He was tall, broad-shouldered, and lean. His thick, black hair was pulled back into a neat queue and secured with a black ribbon at his nape. Below his dark gray three-cornered hat, black eyebrows slanted like the outspread wings of a raven over slightly uptilted eyes of silvery gray. High, elegant cheekbones, a straight, finely sculpted nose, and a sensual mouth completed the picture.

Even in her quick perusal, Cicely was struck with his rare good looks. No man should possess such masculine beauty, she thought. It belonged to some rebellious angel. And it was clear from that light in his eye, he was no angel.

She was disappointed to find no revealing details about his person. He was dressed for traveling in well-cut, if somber, clothing. His riding coat was of a good-quality leather and had seen both service and care, as had his buckskin breeches and his top boots. His neck-cloth was simply tied. His cambric shirt sported no embroidery nor excessive lace at his wrists. Even his waistcoat was plain gray. His only indulgence appeared to be the watch, hidden away in his breeches' fob pocket except for its black ribbon, upon which hung its key and one seal.

"You are unknown to me," Cicely stated flatly. She looked at Captain Miller. "I do not know this man."

The stranger shook his head sadly. "That's the way it often is," he said to the captain. He looked to either side, ignoring the surrounding crowd, which had grown larger and more avid. "She's quite mad, you see," he confided in the captain. "Wanders off continually."

Cicely stared at the tall man, speechless with outrage. Carefully turning, she found the captain regarding her and Hannah, rolling his lips out and in.

"Why don't they lock 'er up?" he asked the stranger.

The fellow sighed. "Oh, they've considered confining her and this cork-brained abigail she insists on keeping with her—"

"Cork-brained!" Hannah yelped indignantly.

"I am *not* mad!" Cicely declared, having recovered the power of speech. "Sirrah, I have never met you before." She minced around to face the captain. "I have never met this—this *person* before in my life! Please have him removed at once."

Captain Miller seemed to consider her demand for a moment. He stared down into the water as he scratched the side of his nose. Then he directed his gaze to the stranger. "What is your name?"

"Griffin Nelvington Tyrrell at your service, sir." He swept his arm out in a gesture that encompassed the women. "And this is my dear cousin Cicely Honeysett and her faithful, if simple, maid."

The blood drained from Cicely's face. Griffin Tyrrell! Dear God, it was the man who had bought Cranwick Abbey! He wasn't supposed to be here—no, there—yet. His agent had told her Mr. Tyrrell would be unable to arrive at the abbey before this evening. She darted a wary glance at her victim's face.

The gleam of revenge sparkled deep in his eyes.

"This man is not my cousin!"

"I'm not simple," Hannah protested.

"And now, without further ado," Mr. Tyrrell said to the captain, "I would like to remove my poor cousin from the public notice before she commits one of her favorite pranks." The stranger moved forward, coming up the plank toward Cicely and Hannah.

An expression of uncertainty had settled on Miller's face until he heard Griffin Tyrrell's last words. "Prank?"

Panic and fury warred inside Cicely as she backed up the plank, hauling Hannah with her, away from the new owner of Cranwick Abbey. "Captain, I protest. I call on your protection! Help us!"

Tyrrell shook his head sadly. "When she becomes disturbed, as she is now, she often exposes herself."

"God's hooks," the captain muttered, turning vivid pink. "Get her out of here, Mr. Tyrrell," he snapped. "I have passengers to consider."

Panic won out, and Cicely clutched at the captain's coat, desperately struggling against his efforts to pry her fingers loose of him.

"*I* am one of those passengers," she insisted.

Miller finally managed to win free of her grasp. "No, madam, you are not. You did not have an escort. Now, be a good girl and go quietly with your cousin. Look how you've upset your maid," he said slowly, as if addressing an imbecile.

Hannah drew her foot back and kicked the captain, calling him a name Cicely had never before heard her use.

"You cod's head," Cicely shouted at the man, knowing her cause for a lost one as she watched him hop around the head of the plank, holding his injured shin. *"The man is not my cousin."* Furious, determined to take some satisfaction before having to turn and face the music of her deception, Cicely reached out and tugged Captain Miller's neckcloth, sending him off-balance.

He tumbled into the harbor with a loud splash. Laughter rose from the mob on the dock, but when angry crewmen swarmed off the ship's deck and down the plank toward Cicely, Griffin Tyrrell scooped her up in his arms. He tossed her over his shoulder like a sack of millet.

"Quite mad," he told the closest crewman. "Not responsible for her actions, you understand." And with that, he strode down the docks, Hannah scurrying to keep up with him. The crowd parted to make way for him, calling out encouragement to the loathsome beast. Cicely braced her arms against his back, trying to keep her head upright, burning with humiliation. His gait was not smooth, but had a slight hitch to one side, causing her to roll a little, back and forth.

How *dare* he tote her about as if she were no more than a bag of flour?

Then she caught sight of the hillock of trunks that rested near the bottom of the plank with other, similar piles. "My luggage," she wailed.

"I'll send someone for it," he growled, catching Hannah's arm as she stumbled, steadying her and helping her keep pace without so much as breaking his stride. "Unless you wish to face the captain's men?"

"No! No, that won't be necessary," Cicely said hastily.

"Who is this gentleman, Lady Cicely?" Hannah panted, dodging dogcarts, horse dung, and urchins.

"Surely you can see, this man is no gentleman, Hannah." Cicely thumped him on his broad, hard back. "Put me down!"

Instead of complying, Griffin Tyrrell swatted her on her rump, stunning her into inarticulate outrage.

"I'll put you down when I feel it is safe to do so," he said.

"How—how *dare* you, sirrah! I will not tolerate such liberties with my person. Put me down this instant!" She pounded his back with her fists.

He swatted her again. Although it did not hurt, cushioned as it was by ells of petticoat and underskirts, it shocked her. Never before in her adult life had she been struck by anyone, and now this Tyrrell person had done it twice!

"I'll put you down when I deem it safe," he repeated firmly. "You nearly started a riot back there."

"You will not strike me again."

His brisk stride was rapidly setting distance between them and the angry crewmen. "Then cease beating on me."

Dizzy and uncomfortable, watching her chances of boarding a ship to France dwindle away, Cicely wilted against his back. "You're a cad."

"And you, madam, are a cheat and a thief."

His words struck a harder blow than his hand ever could.

"You'll not speak ter Lady Cicely so," Hannah informed him hotly. "She's as fine a lady as ever you'd want ter meet."

He stepped off the dock, onto the walk. "I'd set my sights a bit higher if I were you, my girl. Fine ladies do not swindle persons who buy their properties."

Sick with guilt, filled with self-pity that she should have been caught in her one indiscretion, Cicely half-heartedly hoped that nothing of a personal nature was being revealed to one and all in the street as she dangled over this man's sturdy shoulder.

"Where are you taking us?" she asked dully.

"I'm taking *you* back to Cranwick Abbey. Your maid will stay at an inn here with that mountain you call your belongings until I send someone to fetch them." He hailed a hackney carriage that rattled down the street.

The shabbily dressed driver blithely maneuvered his team over to the walk, infuriating a costermonger, a liveried coachman, and a brawny, foulmouthed wagoner in the process. The driver lifted his hat to Tyrrell with a bright smile. His eyes darted to Cicely then back to her captor. "Lovely day, eh, m'lord?"

"Yes it is," the fiend Tyrrell answered amiably, as if he carried off females every day. He opened the door of the vehicle and deftly unloaded Cicely onto one of the cracked leather seats without so much as loosening the ribbons of her hat. Quickly he handed Hannah inside. "Do you know the Golden Lion Inn?" he asked the driver, who owned that he did.

The new master of Cranwick Abbey got in the carriage and closed the door. Immediately the carriage lurched forward, into motion, sending Hannah and Cicely back against the ancient squabs.

Cicely regarded the tall, dark-haired man who sat across from her, trying to take his measure. He was angry, of course. Maybe he had a right to be. But he had embarrassed her unforgivably, even if he had saved her and Hannah from what likely would have become an ugly situation. He confused her, and she resented that, too. "Why the Golden Lion?" she asked sullenly.

He shifted his gaze away from the window to her. For the first time, she caught the full, stunning impact of those silver eyes.

"It was where you stayed last night," he said. He neither smiled nor frowned, but she somehow drew the impression that he missed nothing. No detail escaped him.

She found his knowledge distressing. "How did you know that?" she demanded.

He shrugged one shoulder and looked out the window again, as if her disquiet bored him. "I asked about."

His indifference, his self-confident power over her infuriated her anew. "I won't go with you." She glared at him.

He settled back against the squabs. A slight smile curved that beautiful mouth. "Yes, you will, my dear mad cousin. If you wish, we shall place a wager on just how quickly the innkeeper and his wife trundle you off into my tender care."

Cicely's fingers tightened on her reticule in impotent anger and anxiety. She'd already seen how eagerly proprietors delivered a lone woman into the clutches of any man claiming her. "You are upset over the abbey. Stop at my bank, and I shall buy it back from you." She had spent some of his money on equipment for her travels, on tickets for passage across the Channel, and for Hannah's dowry, though Hannah had no idea yet. "Just . . . just let me go. Free Hannah and me and I'll free you of ownership, if you will be a little patient. I spent some of the money, but I will find a way to make the debt good. Then you may go on your merry way and find another manor more to your liking."

He stretched his long legs as far as he could in the cramped interior of the carriage. "No, that will not do. That will not do at all. You see, I want Cranwick Abbey. And you, fine lady that you are, are going to help me."

She frowned. "Help you how? I sold it to you."

That infuriating smile grew slightly more pronounced. "A fact with which we are both well acquainted." He folded his clasped hands over his flat belly. "No, your service to me shall go beyond that."

Cicely sat bolt upright in her seat. "Service? There will be none of that, sir! I am a respectable woman!"

"Becalm yourself, Lady Cicely. As delectable a body as you may possess, I have no designs on it. I find my sport among those who are willing. And when I take a wife, she will not only be respectable, but honest. You are unqualified on both counts."

Mortified heat burned Cicely's cheeks. She did not

deserve to be compared to a demirep. She had been with only one man in her life, and that had been her husband. As to his other slur . . . well, she could not object that it even was a slur. She had rooked him, and now she must face the consequences.

"So"—she cleared her throat—"what task is it you wish me to perform?"

He laughed, revealing even, white teeth. The sound was deep and richly masculine, and, had it not been at her expense, Cicely would have taken pleasure in it. "Ah," he said, "not so difficult a task, surely, for such a resourceful female."

"What is the task?" Hannah demanded impatiently.

"Lady Cicely is to rid Cranwick Abbey of the creature."

Now it was Cicely's turn to laugh. "You kidnapped me to banish the ghost from the abbey?"

Griffin Tyrrell observed her through narrowed eyes. "Yes."

"I cannot do it."

"And why is that?"

Hannah answered. "Only a Honeysett can drive the spirit away."

"How fortunate, since our scrupulous lady is such a one."

"I'm a Honeysett by marriage," Cicely pointed out triumphantly. "Legend has it that only a true Honeysett can free the abbey of its possession."

The evil smile that curved Mr. Tyrrell's mouth sent a shiver of foreboding through Cicely. "Be that as it may," he said softly. "You're the only Honeysett I have. You will have to do."

Her eyes widened. "You're mad!"

"No, dear cousin, I'm afraid that part falls to you."

"But-but-but I can't banish the ghost! I just told you—"

"Have you ever tried?"

"Well . . . no."

"Then how do you know? Legends are often wanting in accuracy."

"I . . . that is to say . . . legends . . . "

"You have said that you cannot return all my money."

Cicely nodded, unable to speak for her choking fury—at Edmund, at fate, at this wretched man. At herself.

"Then purchasing another property cannot be a consideration for me."

"Can't you just . . ." She felt her courage dwindling away. "Can't you just live there?"

He looked at her as if she were indeed a lunatic. "Live there? With *that?*"

"I did."

"I applaud you, madam. Your acquaintance with the thing will aid you in ridding the place of it."

"I cannot. I do not have the power. Perhaps no one does."

"A jolly thought," he said, considering the mended leather ceiling. He remained silent for a few moments. Hannah looked in question at Cicely, who shrugged. Abruptly he directed his attention back toward her. "Here is another one. If you do not banish the spirit from its haunt of my house, I shall inform the authorities that the good people of Alwyn are engaged in smuggling."

Cicely went numb. From the corner of her eye, she glimpsed Hannah's pale face.

How had he found out?

"I-I don't know what you mean," she lied.

His mouth curved into a slight smile. "I think you do."

"The very idea of Alwyn being a smuggler's haven is

quite ludicrous." Her heart beat rapidly as she thought of the king's dragoons going through the village in search of untaxed goods from France. The penalties would be severe.

"Ludicrous? With their very fine little cove—what is its name?"

"Maresmouth," she supplied dully.

"Yes, Maresmouth. Ideal for hiding a ship fresh from France while it is being unloaded. Midnight rendezvous are so intriguing, don't you think?" When she didn't answer, the curve of his lips increased. "That's right, you don't know what I mean. But the customs men would. So would the king's men who aid them."

The thought of what could happen to the people of Alwyn if this man went to the authorities made her sick with anxiety. How could he sit there smiling when he knew the carnage that would result?

"Very well," she said, hating the quaver in her voice. "I shall endeavor to evict the spirit from Cranwick Abbey."

"I thought you might."

"I-I . . . It's just that I feel responsible for your unhappiness with the abbey, you understand." Her gaze slid away from his, unwilling to meet those knowing, quicksilver eyes. "Perhaps I was not as forthcoming with your agent as I might have been." And it had shamed her. Only desperation to be away could ever have prompted her to do anything so dishonest. "However, your accusations against the people of Alwyn are unfounded and therefore have no bearing on my decision to assist you." She attempted to summon up a measure of indignation, but she was such a poor liar that she feared her effort was not entirely convincing.

Griffin Tyrrell tossed his handsome head back and laughed, a deep, humorless sound that did nothing to ease her anxiety. "Not as forthcoming as you might have been? Madam, please! That get of hell lurking in the west wing would be impossible to forget. Indeed, on such brief acquaintance as I've had with the thing, it's already run off my servant." He shook his head. "No, you will excuse me if I fail to believe such an absurd tale. Your pretty lips issued a bold lie that would shame the most dishonest horse trader."

"Here, now—" Hannah began, inching forward on the seat, as if making ready to launch herself at the man.

"You are no gentleman," Cicely told him frostily, placing her hand firmly on Hannah's arm. Never before had anyone spoken to her in such a rude manner. Not even Edmund.

"I stand—or sit, if you may—chastened." He gracefully bowed his head in a mocking gesture of penance. "After all, everyone knows 'tis perfectly acceptable for a woman to swindle a man yet retain her status as a lady. It's done all the time, though, I own, their business usually takes place in a bedroom."

Cicely gasped. Hannah swung her reticule, and her horde of coins clinked as it collided with his shoulder.

"Begad, woman, what have you in there? An anvil?" he demanded, rubbing the place she had struck.

"'Twould serve you right if I did," Hannah informed him furiously. "You learn ter mind your manners around Lady Cicely, you hear?"

The carriage lurched to a halt, and Cicely saw they had arrived at the Golden Lion. Immediately, Tyrrell paid the driver and arranged for the retrieval of her and Hannah's belongings with the lad who came out of the inn to assist them. When that was done, he swept the two of them along before him into the inn, where he ordered a guest room for Hannah until he sent someone from Alwyn to retrieve her and the baggage. To Cicely's surprise, he took aside the innkeeper and his wife and asked them to watch over Hannah, telling them that the maid was an innocent, godly young woman. Just as Cicely was about to commend him on his show of consideration, she heard him add that normally he would never have considered leaving Hannah alone, but he must rush Cousin Cicely home before she had another fit. During such fits, he confided in a low voice, she was prone to violence. He allowed his words to trail off, favoring the woman with a look of sad hopelessness. Cicely's jaw snapped shut on her kind words, her lips forming a tight line.

"Wretch!" she hissed at Tyrrell as soon as they were alone. "I told you I would return with you. Why must you insist on telling people I'm mad?"

He smiled, and she was startled at his transformation. For an instant his oblique, silvery eyes, his upswept raven brows, his high elegant cheekbones and sensual mouth brought to mind the tales she'd read about ancient, unmatched warriors, members of a magical race that had long ago inhabited the Isles. Magical . . .

"You're right of course," he said, wicked light gleaming in his eyes. "Telling people is quite unnecessary."

The aura of magic vanished. Hoping to put him in his place, she scathingly raked him up and down with her frigid gaze, then turned on her heel and went to join Hannah in the room he had paid for.

There she seethed for half an hour, listening to Hannah alternately berate the man and grumble over Cicely's omission in telling the agent about the ghost. Cicely, however, did not need Hannah's remonstrations. Guilt already ate at her like acid. She'd known she was wrong to have neglected mentioning the detail that the abbey was haunted. It was just that she'd wanted so badly to see the wonders of the world, to savor her freedom. Her parents and her duty to them had been her first master. Niggardly, complaining, capricious Edmund had been her second. She wanted no other.

Most especially, she did not wish the arrogant Mr. Tyrrell to exercise power over her. Cicely sighed heavily and walked over to the window, absently staring down at the traffic in the street.

A surge of anger boiled through her. It wasn't fair! She'd been a dutiful daughter and married the man her father had decided upon, a stranger to Cicely. She'd struggled to be a good wife to Edmund, despite his complete lack of interest in her or even in getting an heir. Despite his abandoning her at Cranwick Abbey, his least favorite property.

Through it all, she had been good! She had been obedient! And what had been her portion? Years of poverty and loneliness.

Did a lifetime of doing what she should count for nothing? Now, when she was so close to tasting the glory of freedom, to living adventures of her own instead of through books, now, when she might capture the rare beauty of an Italian sunset with her pastels, with no one to deride her, one small error, born out of desperation, had jerked it all from her grasp.

It wasn't right! It wasn't just!

And if Griffin Tyrrell conceived that she was just another woman to be easily manipulated, he was in for a rude surprise.

3

A knock sounded at the door. When Hannah opened it, the innkeeper's wife smiled at her. "Mr. Tyrrell sends his respects and asks if Lady Cicely will join him downstairs. He sends to say your good-byes now, my lady, that it's time to leave." With a bobbed curtsy, the woman left.

Cicely frowned. "I don't like leaving you like this, Hannah."

Hannah hugged her. "Never you worry about me," she said. "You just take care o' yourself. Mr. Tyrrell seems a mite high-handed, but I don't believe he'll bring you harm. I'll soon see you at the abbey."

As Cicely swept down the hall with a militant step, she struggled to be reasonable. She should try to make the best of the situation. As unpleasant as Mr. Tyrrell had been so far, she had to confess that his behavior was not entirely unwarranted. At least he had not involved the authorities in the matter, and for that, she supposed, she ought to be thankful.

He rose as she entered the common room.

"I am all amazement you were capable of procuring transportation so quickly," she said, striving for calm and civility. "Did you rent me a horse?"

Griffin Tyrrell smiled. "And have you gallop off?" He shook his head. "No."

"I told you I would return with you," she said stiffly, reminding herself that she'd given him little reason to trust her.

He offered her his hand, and, after a slight hesitation, she laid her palm upon it. "Let's just say that I did not desire you to change your mind and do something about it." He guided them out of the inn, toward the courtyard that fronted the inn's stables. The area was empty.

"Were you able to buy us tickets on the stagecoach?" she inquired, her curiosity growing.

"I did inquire, but none were available."

"Oh."

The rumble of wooden wheels on cobblestone filled the air as a stable boy drove a ramshackle farm wagon drawn by an aging nag into the courtyard. Following behind, tethered to the back of the wagon, pranced a handsome sorrel stallion. After a brief glance, Cicely continued to wait for their transportation to arrive. She flicked open her fan and restrained her hand to a leisurely movement—so at odds with the tightening knot in her stomach.

"I had a hamper of food packed for us," Tyrrell said. "Enough for luncheon and a bit besides."

"Excellent," she murmured. She managed the facade for a few interminable seconds before her calm broke under the weight of her impatience. She snapped her fan closed. Now that she had accepted her immediate fate, she wished to get it over with. "Where is our carriage?"

He bowed solemnly, sweeping an arm out toward the rickety farm wagon. "Your coach awaits, madam."

Cicely stared at the dilapidated wagon. "This *conveyance*? You jest, of course." But as she studied his face, she saw by his wicked smile that he did not.

"This is outrageous!" she stormed. "You cannot expect me to ride in this awful thing." She gestured with her fan. "Why there's still straw in it, and"—she eyed the hard wooden seat and the straw-cushioned bed uneasily—"heaven knows what else."

"I just swept it clean, m'lady, 'n' laid down fresh straw," the boy said. "Scrubbed the seats, I did. See? They're still wet."

Tyrrell grinned and flipped the lad a silver coin. "That's yours if you can bring a cover to protect your nice clean seat from our dry clothing."

The boy examined the coin with delight. "Aye, Cap'n!" He dashed into the inn.

"'Twas all that I could procure immediately. Seems a herd of the Quality have arrived in town for some purpose or other. There was not a carriage to be had."

She eyed the rig. "Indeed. A horse for me to ride would have been considerable less bother and expense."

"I have neither the energy nor the inclination to chase after you."

Her fingers clenched on her fan. "For the last time, I have said I would return with you."

He looked over the wagon and horse. "So you have. A bit too easily for my complete comfort, if you will pardon my saying so." He turned his head to regard her with a hooded gaze. The thick, black lashes, which partially concealed his silver-gray eyes, created a contrast of light and dark that fascinated Cicely despite herself. "Unless," he continued in a lower voice, "you are simply too naive for your own good."

Despite the warmth of the bright morning, a chill shimmered up her back. "Do I have cause to worry with you, Mr. Tyrrell? Are you . . . a danger to me?"

His raven-wing brows drew down a little, but still she could not fully see his eyes. Then, suddenly, he raised his lashes and his gaze collided with hers. A shock rushed through her, stealing her breath.

Confused at her reaction, embarrassed by her confusion, she looked away. With a whisper of silk, she slid open her fan again and employed a tempo intended to distract from the color she knew must show in her cheeks.

"I am no danger to you, Lady Cicely," he said softly.

Cicely very much doubted that. Yet for some reason beyond her ken, she believed that he would not intentionally hurt her. And that was all a woman could ever expect of a man. Careful not to slide a glance back at his solemn, dark-angel face, she continued to fan herself.

The stable boy raced out the inn's back door to present Tyrrell with a sheet of oilcloth, a length of coarse-woven cotton, and a dingy, yellowish pillow that Cicely suspected harbored a collection of unwanted inhabitants. Her own pillow was locked in one of her trunks on the dock. She mustered a smile for the boy and added her thanks to those of Tyrrell, who promptly placed the oilcloth over the seat, and the fabric over that. To her relief, as soon as the boy was out of sight, he discarded the pillow. Then he assisted her up to the hard, plank seat and joined her there, gathering the reins in his hands. He flicked the leather lines and clucked to the horse, who started up, trudging toward the narrow lane out of the courtyard, into the busy street.

Cicely looked back at the inn to see Hannah at the

room window, waving to her, a fretful expression on her face.

"I don't like leaving her alone like this."

"Someone must stay until the rest of your trunks are retrieved from the ship. I've paid the innkeeper well to see to her needs and watch over her. Several captains I spoke with on the waterfront assured me that the Golden Lion is an honest establishment, clean as inns go. I'll send someone from Alwyn to fetch her as soon as we arrive there." He watched the busy traffic in the street. "Before we continue on to Cranwick Abbey."

She refused to think about that now.

They said no more as he negotiated the crowded streets, taking them out of Portsmouth.

The mare surprised her by showing unexpected energy, though progress remained slower than she would have liked. Cicely's teeth jarred as the wheels of the wagon banged against cobbles. Clearly this contraption had no springs.

Finally, they plodded out of the port town. Except for the echoing cries of the seabirds in the near distance and the rattle and thump of wheels on the dirt road, the noise abated. Cicely breathed in the salty sea air. She had almost won free, she thought. She'd come so close. So very close.

Suddenly tears welled up in her eyes. Angrily she blinked them away. She'd erred, and now she must make things right. That was simply justice, not the end of her dream.

Minutes dragged on, edging toward an hour, and neither Mr. Tyrrell nor she spoke. Faced with riding all the way back to Cranwick Abbey, with this dilapidated wagon shaking up every bone in her body, sitting next to the man she'd tried to swindle, Cicely cast about for a topic of conversation. Anything was better than considering her immediate future. "Mr. Fremlin mentioned you had spent time in the army, and the boy at the inn addressed you as 'captain.' May I assume that was your rank?"

He continued to look straight ahead. "You may."

Cicely nodded. There was a hard competency about the man that seemed to her to suggest he had survived danger more than once. He certainly seemed more like a "captain" than a "mister."

She persisted, her curiosity aroused. He'd likely traveled and seen some of the world. Certainly he'd had adventures. "Was it exciting?"

Slowly he turned his head to look at her, observing her with that hooded, soot-and-silver gaze, which concealed his thoughts. She shifted on the hard seat, feeling that her innocent question had taken on a meaning to him she'd never intended. Without speaking a word, he turned his attention back to the rutted country road that stretched before them. In the northerly distance ran the smooth, undulating line of the South Downs.

Sitting next to him in the stony quiet, Cicely surreptitiously studied him. His profile was at once elegant and masculine. The nostrils of his straight nose possessed an almost imperceptible flare. His mouth was sensual, slightly sulky. Only a sculptor with a gifted hand could have chiseled that angular jaw and the clean, strong, columnar lines of his neck. She moved her eyes down to his broad shoulders. Between them hung his queue, heavy and glossy black against the tobacco-hued leather of his riding coat.

As she drew her gaze up, she noticed for the first time a scar that ran along his temple hairline to brush the edge of his left cheekbone. In the shadow cast by his hat, that pale line was easy to miss, even as starkly contrasted as it was against the unfashionable sun-darkened bronze of his skin.

Quickly she looked away, feeling, for some inexplicable reason, as if she were prying. From the corner of her eye, she glimpsed his fingers tighten on the reins.

Awkwardly, she cleared her throat. "What I meant was . . . did you go many interesting places? Did you see new things?"

He didn't respond immediately, but appeared to consider what she'd said. "I was ordered to America, to fight the French and their Indian allies. 'Tis a majestic land. There I saw . . ." He scowled down at the rump of the horse. "Trees." He lifted his eyes to meet hers, and Cicely knew that was not what he had been going to say. "Taller than I've ever seen before," he continued. "Dark, dense forests. I met men who wore bone breast-plates, who shaved their heads save for a single plume of hair that they dressed to stand erect. Most of the forts I visited were naught like the ones here in England, which are built of proper stone. Many there were no more than clusters of huts surrounded by wood stockades. Their doors were tanned animal hides. It becomes bitter cold there. So bitter . . ."

She waited for him to go on, but he seemed disinclined to speak further, and they traveled on in silence, sitting side by side, yet worlds apart.

Cicely had never felt so alone.

Griffin finished his task of binding together the mare's hind legs to keep her from wandering. Slowly, he walked back to the wagon, watching the widow Honeysett rummage through the food hamper.

She sat in the straw in the wagon bed, her skirts spread around her like a blue silk lily pad. Her milkmaid's hat lay on the seat, along with her fan and gloves. Now the night concealed the vivid colors of her chestnut hair and her golden brandy brown eyes. Moonlight poured silver over her, transforming the warmth of her peach-blushed skin to cool alabaster, shadowing her cheeks and her full, sweetly formed lips, changing her into a being of mystery.

Or perhaps this was her true nature. Griffin had already discovered she was not at all what he'd expected to find. This female was no sly beldam. She was young and beautiful, and seemed to be all alone in the world except for one cheeky maid. She'd had with her no man, which had surprised him, considering she'd been embarking to the Continent, where no unescorted woman was safe. Indeed, even in England a woman needed a man's protection against predators.

If she was rich, she did not flaunt her wealth. Oh, she dressed well enough, but more like prosperous landed gentry than a rich widow with no husband's firm hand to restrain her expenditures.

He'd been surprised when she'd not put up a greater resistance to returning to the place she'd seemed so eager to escape that she'd been willing to cheat him. She should have feared him, or at least been more wary. After all, he was a stranger to her.

A stranger, it seemed to him as he watched her pick and poke about in the basket, who was strangely susceptible to this unusual woman. Her artless questions had drawn from him honest, if incomplete, answers, when usually he avoided discussing his time in the New World altogether. Perhaps it was the memory of what a fool, a callow fool, he'd been, thinking to escape the unceasing scythe of his enemy and actually believing in glory, king, and country. Hardship, fear, and squandered lives had reminded him of the former and cured him of the latter.

Frozen in his memory forever was the sight of Jeremy's body sprawled in the snow, his dark red blood bright against the dirty white. Where his sandy hair had grown full and thick, there was only raw, pulpy flesh. His blue eyes stared at Griffin, dull and devoid of life, accusing. Griffin shook his head, as if that could ever throw off the nightmare vision. He had failed. Failed horribly. And again his enemy had proved his power over him.

"There is naught left in there," he pointed out to Lady Cicely, determined to thrust his memories back into their dark cave. He rested his arms along the side rail of the wagon. "That's why I brought the tarts and meat pasties back from the tavern when I returned from the smith's."

She set the hamper aside and sighed. "I know. I just kept hoping we might have missed a bit of cheese, a plum—*something*."

Mare in tow, he'd ridden two miles back to a tiny village they'd passed. There the blacksmith, who doubled as the area cooper, had promised to fix the wagon wheel and bring it to them tomorrow morning, along with food prepared by his wife, to break their fast.

The one tavern in the hamlet had been swarming with drunken dragoons. The place was not fit to house a lady even for a single night. So Griffin had purchased their dinner and hurried back to the wagon and Cicely, whom he'd given orders to stay out of sight. To his relief, she had been there when he returned. More, she'd been unharmed. With dragoons roaming coastal villages, Griffin did not like to think of the possibilities.

"The smith agreed to bring us food tomorrow morning," he assured her, wishing he had something to give her to ease her hunger. He studied her moon-silvered face. It was too easy to forget she'd tried to swindle him. As crazy as it seemed, she possessed a sort of innocence that repeatedly slipped by his world-weary defenses to work an unexpected charm on him. He would have to take better care. Perhaps what he took as innocence was in fact skillfully employed art.

In the light of the full moon, he saw slender eyebrows draw down over her small, elegant nose. "Oh," she said, "'tis not as if I'm starving. I desire a small bite only." Her lips curved up. "In the evening I am accustomed to having a cup of chocolate and a biscuit or two with Hannah. We often read to each other, or play at cards, or chat as we work at our stitchery."

Griffin recalled Digby's reaction to the thing in the hall. "Does the monster not bother you? Or your servants?"

She dropped her gaze to her hands that rested in her lap. "Of course. As for servants . . . well, until last year when Hannah arrived, there were none. Once in a while Kitty and Nan gather their courage and come to help with the cleaning or with the preserving when fruits or vegetables are to be put up." She smiled sadly.

No servants? The woman must have worked herself near to death, trying to do everything herself. "What of your husband? Did he never try to rid the place of that presence?"

She glanced up at Griffin then looked away. "Oh, Edmund seldom visited Cranwick Abbey." Her words were lightly spoken, but through them thrummed an edge.

He thought of her alone in that large old house, and a flash of anger shot through him. What manner of man would abandon his wife to the mercies of that abomination in the manor house? "Was Mr. Honeysett a military man?"

"No."

"He traveled, then, seeing to his other properties, perhaps? Or his business?" What the deuce did it matter? Griffin thought, suddenly annoyed with himself. This woman's relationship with her husband did not concern him.

"He traveled with his many friends. He had a house in London and another in Paris." One of her hands curled into a fist. As if catching herself, she quickly straightened her fingers, spreading them out on her skirts. "Edmund craved excitement, you see," she said in a low voice Griffin had to strain to hear. "He believed there was little of that at Cranwick." As he studied her bowed head, he glimpsed a sparkle on her cheek. Looking closer, he saw that a single tear glimmered in the moonlight.

She turned away from him. "I fear I am feeling quite fatigued, Captain Tyrrell. I think I shall try to take what sleep I may, if you will excuse me."

"Of course." Griffin stepped back from the side of the wagon. "Sweet dreams."

"And to you, Captain."

When he saw that she lay quiet, nestled in the fresh straw, he shrugged off his coat, using it as a pillow when he stretched out on the grass beneath the wagon. He glanced over to make certain the mare and Apollo were nearby, then closed his eyes.

He went to sleep thinking of her tear.

Bright and early the next morning, the smith made good his word. He brought them the repaired wagon wheel and reattached it.

As he wiped his hands on a rag he'd brought, the big man nodded. "'Twas wise o' you ter keep your lady here, away from those soldiers. They caused a right ruckus in the tavern last night. Celebratin' their big catch, they said."

"Big catch?" Cicely asked, eyeing the slices of bread, cheese, and chicken he'd brought for her and the captain.

"Heard some high-and-mighty lord has a bug in his ear about smuggling in these here parts. Seems he means ter cause us all misery, he does." The smith shook his head. "Small village west o' here were raided by the king's men. Nabbed a goodly number of the village men and some o' their women and little ones. 'Tis enough ter put the fear o' the devil in a soul, it is."

Cicely listened to his report with growing alarm. She doubted there were many villages on the coast that were not in some way involved with smuggling in untaxed goods from the Continent. Gangs of smugglers brought brandy, wine, silk, and tea in by way of the Channel, and paid local people to stash the contraband about the hamlets. Later, other smugglers gathered the goods and took them inland to buyers who appreciated luxuries acquired at a bargain. To many families, the money paid by the smugglers meant the difference between eating and starving. Alwyn depended on her midnight traders and their cargo, and more than once Cicely had watched from the abbey's banqueting tower as the villagers carted the uncustomed goods up from the beach at night.

The penalty for apprehension was severe. No official had ever bothered with tiny Alwyn before, but she had heard of those who had been caught. They had been sentenced to transportation. While waiting for a ship, they were kept in the hellish hulks, prison ships rotting on the Thames near London. Without money to bribe their jailers, prisoners too often died in those wet, dark, airless pits. If they did survive, they were transported to lands far away from England, where they labored for ten to eighteen years. For most, a swift hanging would have been a kinder penalty.

She fell silent and remained so even after the smith left and through the meal she shared with Captain Tyrrell, her thoughts occupied by the increased danger to those she'd come to know in her six years at Cranwick.

The captain ate the last bit of cheese and brushed his hands together, for want of a napkin or towel. "Are you contemplating how you shall drive away the ghost?"

Cicely looked up to see he had risen to his feet. He offered her his hand, which she reluctantly accepted. "I cannot conceive how to *un*haunt the abbey," she said. "Besides, 'tis most inhospitable. You're the newcomer, you know. He has roamed Cranwick for a long time." When she saw Captain Tyrrell's jaw tighten, she added, "I've searched before and never found anything, but I'll search again. Perhaps there is a journal I've overlooked in the abbey library which will provide the answer. I shall endeavor to locate one."

He tethered the stallion to the back of the wagon. Cicely untied the mare's legs, then led her over to the captain. "Is it not something of a disgrace that poor old Octavia should be required to pull such a heavy conveyance?" she mused. "After all, she is a female of some years. We should have a care for her age, for her dignity."

Captain Tyrrell took the reins from Cicely and led the mare to the front of the wagon. "Octavia, is it?" He set about hitching up the horse.

Cicely's cheeks warmed slightly. "It seems to fit her. She possesses a certain important address, and we can't continue to call her just 'horse,' now, can we?"

"Unthinkable," he agreed solemnly as he handed her up to her seat.

"I believe you are funning me, Captain."

The light of amusement twinkled in his eyes. "Never."

Cicely lifted an eyebrow with what she hoped was a

regal air to let him know she did not believe his denial. "As I was saying, I worry about poor Octavia having to pull this big wagon. Is the weight too much for her, do you think?"

The wagon dipped and creaked as the tall captain mounted. He took up the reins, then flicked them, calling to the horse. "This wagon is empty save for straw, an empty hamper, you, and me. It is light enough for the beast. Be assured, she's sturdy, in good health, and not so old. You'll see a difference when she has had better food and care, I promise. I thought she might be a suitable mount for you."

Cicely blinked in surprise. "Me?" Edmund had never permitted her a horse. She'd always thought it likely that he feared she would run away. Not that he'd have actually have minded her absence, since they were seldom in one another's company. No, he would have found her desertion an embarrassment before his peers.

"You'll need a horse during your stay at the abbey." His sensual mouth curved up. "I'd be foolish to give you a young, spirited beast which could take you away from Cranwick before I could catch you. You can ride, can you not?"

"Of course," she informed him briskly, annoyed that his temporary gift of Octavia touched her so deeply. "I'm an excellent horsewoman." Or rather, she had been before she'd wed. It had been six years since she'd ridden.

"Then you should have no problems with, uh, Octavia. She has a smooth gait."

Cicely busied herself drawing on her gloves. He'd slung her over his shoulder in front of everyone on the dock. He'd kidnapped her and forced her to ride in this decrepit wagon, to spend the night in the rough thing!

And now he had given her a gentle mare. She swallowed against the lump in her throat. Wretched man.

She attempted to don her hat, struggling to keep it in place with the interference of the slight breeze created by Octavia's sedate pace. Finally, in a fit of pique, Cicely pulled the ribbons tight under her chin and wadded the ends into what must pass for a bow. She tapped the end of her fan against one palm. "I think you presume I will be staying a goodly time at the abbey, but I assure you, sir, that shall not be the case. I intend to solve your small problem and go about my own business."

A bark of laughter burst from Captain Tyrrell's throat. "My *small* problem? Madam, I think you make too little of this concern. If it is easy to vanquish some entrenched hellhound, why have you never done so before?"

Cicely regarded him with a haughty air. "It never occurred to me to be so rude."

"Oh, quite."

She tried to maintain her aloof demeanor. Why, everyone knew one could not drive off a ghost from its own house. A lesson she feared Captain Tyrrell would soon learn. Then she would have to take back the abbey, and all her dreams of adventure, of seeing the sun set over the Parthenon or the way the morning light fell on Mount Vesuvius, would be lost forever.

"I thought you liked Octavia," he said.

"I do. I simply do not intend to stay long."

He shrugged. "If you can complete the exorcism quickly, it will suit me well. In fact, I shall personally escort you back to Portsmouth, where you may board the next ship to France—if you can."

She glared at him. "Oh, be assured that I shall bring with me a male. One would not wish to fret another beef-witted ship's captain and his crew of clod-pates. Perhaps one of the village lads will desire to accompany Hannah and me. And he'll be large enough to prevent anyone else from declaring me mad and absconding with me."

The captain made no reply. Instead, he simply watched the road ahead. Feeling she'd gotten the better of him for once, she contentedly settled down to consider how she might approach her daunting task. But when she glanced at him from beneath the cover of her lashes she saw that he was smiling.

When they reached Alwyn, Griffin arranged with Uriah Coppard for a reliable man to be sent to retrieve Hannah and the luggage. The butcher expressed surprise at seeing Lady Cicely. He sent a sharp look toward Griffin, but seemed to accept her explanation that she had decided to try to find a way to put to rest the spirit that haunted Cranwick.

Griffin had to admire her composure. She managed to reassure Coppard and make the whole thing look as if she'd decided on her own to return.

From the butcher's shop she directed Griffin to a small, neatly kept cottage, which was the home of Hannah's parents, Nan and Mark Boulden. Griffin managed to calm them with assurances that he'd provided their daughter with a room of her own at the inn, under the care of the innkeeper and his wife, who could be trusted. When he added that he'd just sent a young man to retrieve her, Nan would hear nothing but that she accompany Lady Cicely and Griffin to the abbey.

"'Tisn't fitting for the two o' you ter be alone together like, and well you know it. Lady Cicely has a fine reputation." The capable-looking woman fixed him with a knowing eye that communicated clearly her opinion on what *he* was likely to do to that reputation.

"Mrs. Boulden, Lady Cicely is a widow, not some babe stolen from the nursery. I'm certain she knows very well how to behave. And I would like to believe that I am a gentleman." At the lift of Lady Cicely's eyebrow, he returned her silent rebuttal with a pointed look and amended, "Or can be one when called upon. Which, of course, would be when I am in the presence of a lady."

Mrs. Boulden looked him up and down, and Griffin bore the inspection silently. "Young, good-lookin' fellow like you might try ter resist a woman as comely as our Lady Cicely, but in the end, you'll yield ter temptation."

Mr. Boulden nodded sagely. "'Tis nature's way. And Lady Cicely, she might be a widow, but she's an innocent. Not worldly, if you take my meanin'."

Out of the corner of his eye he glimpsed high color in the fair Cicely's cheeks. "I'm not certain I do, but perhaps we may save that particular discussion for another time."

The older woman clucked over Lady Cicely. Mark Boulden went to a crockery jar that sat upon the clean-swept wooden floor and ladled up two cups of a golden liquid. The sweet, appley scent of cider burst into the air of the small cottage. As his wife quickly set about packing, Mr. Boulden served his guests their refreshment.

The cider slid down Griffin's dry throat like a sharp, sweet balm, washing away miles of Octavia's dust. His manor possessed a small orchard, he knew, of old trees. He smiled. Next year he would drink cider from his own press. His smile faded. But first there was the matter of that hellspawn.

A few minutes later, he, Lady Cicely, and Nan Boulden were on their way. No one spoke as the wagon creaked down the dusty country road. As he turned into the unfashionable shaded lane, he caught the troubled glance that passed between the two women.

Octavia shied away from the house, and Griffin allowed her greater distance from it. In the yard at the back he helped Lady Cicely and Mrs. Boulden out of the wagon, instructing them to wait while he tended the horses. When he was finished, he opened the back door and led the way into the still house.

They had no more progressed from the kitchen than a blast of icy air struck them. A terrible moan gradually grew louder until it filled the house. There in the parlor, the death's-head took form, looming huge and grisly. Mrs. Boulden swooned, hitting the carpet with a soft thud before Griffin could catch her.

His first instinct was to protect Cicely. He placed his hand on Lady Cicely's shoulder, about to propel her back, toward the kitchen and the door, when her words halted him.

"Stop that, Alasdair," she said sharply to the enormous skull.

Gradually, the death's-head began to alter. It shrank and changed form until a tall man who looked to be approximately Griffin's age stood before them. His blond hair was long, and he wore a white shirt and a wide length of plaid wool fabric, the bottom portion of which was belted and pleated at his waist. The top section was draped across his chest and looped around his shoulder. His soft boots, upon closer study, were actually buskins, likely made from deer hide. But the most astonishing thing about the fellow was his disconcerting translucency.

"I'd be ashamed," Lady Cicely scolded. "You show very poor manners."

"So. Ye've returned." The apparition smirked. "I knew ye would."

Griffin stared at the . . . He groped for an accurate word.

"Alasdair," she scolded, "you promised. You assured me you wouldn't pull your pranks on the new owner of Cranwick."

Alasdair sniffed in disdain. "*I* am the owner of Cranwick Abbey."

"You promised."

The ghost scornfully studied Griffin. "I dinna like him," he announced. "I'm no bound to a promise I dinna wish to make in the first place if I dinna like the man."

Griffin's annoyance got the better of his fear. "The feeling is quite mutual, I assure you."

Lady Cicely sighed. "Captain Tyrrell, I would like to present Mr. Alasdair MacNab. He is an . . . er . . . former owner of Cranwick."

Griffin and the ghost eyed each other in silent hostility.

"I'm the new owner," he informed the ghost.

Alasdair puffed up with indignation. "*I've* been here for near two hundred years." His r's rolled off his tongue.

Two hundred years? It might be more difficult to rid the place of this spirit than Griffin had anticipated. "Some people don't know when to gracefully exit."

Suddenly the temperature in the room plummeted. Alasdair glared at Griffin. "I dinna like him," he informed Lady Cicely.

Then, with a *pop*, the ghost vanished.

4

Griffin muttered an oath as he stared at the spot where the ghost had stood. He looked at Lady Cicely, feeling like an idiot for having blathered on and on about the demon, the creature, the hellspawn. "*That* was the monster?"

Lady Cicely lifted an eyebrow. "I would not make light of Alasdair. I've seen him make life most unpleasant for those he doesn't like. And it's plain he doesn't like you."

"I don't know why," Griffin said indignantly, stepping around her to the supine form of Mrs. Boulden. "I've never done anything to him. It." He frowned. "Him," he conceded as he went down on one knee to check the woman's pulse and satisfy himself that she had not damaged herself when she'd hit the thick carpet.

Cicely withdrew a small vial from the embroidered reticule that hung at her wrist. She joined Griffin on the floor. "Here, try this." She unstoppered the container, releasing the sharp, eye-watering smell of hartshorn.

He waved the stuff under Mrs. Boulden's nose. On the second pass, she jerked her face away, coughing. Her eyes fluttered open. Griffin handed the container back to Lady Cicely. She was careful, he noticed, not to touch his fingers when she took it from him.

"Dear me," Mrs. Boulden said chokingly. Griffin assisted her in rising to her feet. "Oh, dear me."

Griffin led her to a wing armchair. "Rest yourself a moment, Mrs. Boulden."

She refused to sit. "I'd just as soon not be anyplace near where that Scottish demon has been. 'Tisn't natural. 'Tisn't natural, and that's what I say."

"He's gone now, madam."

A high note of hysteria infected Mrs. Boulden's short laugh. "He'll be back, never you think he won't. This manor is his place, and he don't let anyone believe otherwise."

Griffin sent Lady Cicely an accusing look, and she dropped her gaze to a small table, picking up a porcelain figure of a shepherdess to examine, as if she suddenly found it of riveting interest.

"His days here are numbered, Mrs. Boulden," Griffin said firmly. "Are they not, Lady Cicely?"

Not taking her gaze from the delicate figurine, she replied, "That remains to be seen, Captain Tyrrell."

"Oh? Have you lost interest in your journey to France?"

The corners of her full, sweetly shaped mouth turned down. "No."

Griffin allowed his threat to hang silent in the air between them. From the rebellious glance she shot him, he knew she understood.

"Are you up to working in the kitchen, Mrs. Boulden?" Cicely inquired. "Perhaps we should prepare dinner."

Mrs. Boulden bustled toward the kitchen, obviously relieved at escaping the place where she'd seen the ghost. "A very good idea, indeed, m'lady." Lady Cicely followed, not looking at Griffin as she passed him.

He thought of something. "Mrs. Boulden . . . "

That woman turned. "Yes, sir?"

"Have you ever seen the ghost before?"

Her gaze darted nervously about the room, as if speaking of the spirit might recall him. "I have, sir. Many have."

He nodded. "Thank you, Mrs. Boulden."

She scurried away, clearly eager to be gone. She disappeared through the arch that led to the passage into the kitchen. Before Lady Cicely could reach it he said, "Did Zacchaeus Fremlin see the ghost?"

She stopped and slowly turned to face him. "No. Alasdair appears when it pleases him. The house is large, and Mr. Fremlin is infirm. His leg frequently pains him. He tires so easily."

"Yes?" he prompted, his voice dangerously soft.

"I showed him through the house." She cleared her throat. "Well, you know with all the stairs in the abbey, the long hallways, the many rooms . . ." Her voice died away.

"He never saw Alasdair's wing of the place, did he, Lady Cicely?"

She hesitated, catching her bottom lip between her teeth. "No."

"I see."

"Yes," she said gloomily. "I fear you do."

Her blushing guilt, her artless misery found a chink in his carefully tended armor. She had stayed in this house for six years, he thought. From the villagers he'd learned that she'd come to Cranwick Abbey only days after her wedding to the eldest son of a wealthy merchant family. More than that, they had refused to divulge to the newcomer.

What manner of man would drag his wife off to this haunted place? Alasdair claimed to have lived in the abbey for two hundred years. His garb and the architecture of the buildings gave credence to his claim. Griffin could not believe Edmund Honeysett had not known of the ghost if, as Fremlin had stated, the abbey had been in the Honeysett family for the past century, give or take a few years.

And what business of his was it anyway? a strident voice within Griffin demanded. He had plans of his own—none of which involved a conniving widow.

"Go prepare our dinner, if you will," he said flatly. "I shall tend the horses."

From the corner of his eye he caught the instant her fingers tightened, almost concealed among the folds of her skirts. Just as quickly, she eased her hands open, smoothing the crushed silk in a single motion as, without a word, she turned to sweep through the Tudor arch, after Mrs. Boulden. Silently, Griffin followed, but as he continued through the vast, high-ceilinged room and out the door into the kitchen yard, with its gardens for vegetables and herbs, a vague dissatisfaction plagued him.

It followed him about his work like an unseen cloud as he put away the wagon, then groomed and fed both horses.

Dusk saw the arrival of Hannah and the luggage. She explained that she had persuaded the innkeepers to allow her to leave when the trunks arrived at the inn, but only under the condition that their stolid, burly son escort her. The young man Mr. Coppard had sent met them on the road. When Griffin started to shoulder a leather-bound trunk off the wagon sitting in front of the house, Mrs. Boulden hurried out to stop him.

"No need for that," she informed him, bustling about like an officious hen. "These trunks are a-going ter the dower house."

"Dower house?" Griffin echoed as he eased his burden back down onto the wagon.

"Dower house," Nan Boulden repeated firmly. "Or didn't you know about that neither?" She chuckled.

Griffin bristled. Buy one haunted house and you were marked forever as a fool. "I'm quite aware that this property includes a building on the west boundary which is referred to as the dower house. As yet I've had no opportunity to inspect it."

"'Tis in good order," Hannah said, "else we would not have Lady Cicely a-go there. Bigger 'n most dower houses, so I've been told. It's got five bedchambers, all in order, it does, and a kitchen almost as large as the one in the manor house. Has two proper parlors and—"

"Just why, may I ask, are you set on moving into the dower house?"

All three women turned to stare at him as if he'd gone quite mad.

"I cannot stay here with you," Lady Cicely said. "A widow sleeping under the same roof as a bachelor?"

"I should say not!" Mrs. Boulden exclaimed. "'Tis most improper, most improper indeed!"

Hannah hitched herself up to sit on the wagon bed's rear edge, her feet dangling. "Shockin', it is, that you supposed Lady Cicely were planning ter stay with you in the house."

"Not *with* me. Egad, woman, I'm not a seducer." No, all the women he'd bedded had come to him willingly. Enthusiastically.

"The dower house is fine and cozy," Mrs. Boulden said. "A good house in all ways."

Lady Cicely accepted the assistance of the village lad Coppard had sent as she climbed up onto the wagon's seat. "Never fear, Captain. I shall be comfortable there."

"A great weight off my mind," Griffin drawled.

Lady Cicely smiled and, unexpectedly, Griffin found himself entranced. Her delightfully formed mouth curved up, revealing dimples in her cheeks. Her amber eyes, framed lavishly with lashes, twinkled merrily. "I knew you would be relieved."

He caught himself staring. "Uh . . . certainly." He met her gaze. "You will not forget why you have returned?"

She sobered, but made no attempt to look away. "I shall not."

He helped Mrs. Boulden up onto the seat of the wagon, then he stepped back to allow the lad to turn the horses. "I'll call upon you," he shouted over the noise of the wagon wheels, suddenly unwilling to have Lady Cicely out of his sight.

She turned on the wagon's bench, looking back at him. "At your convenience, sir," she called. She re-garded him for a moment longer, then settled back onto the seat. The wagon and its passengers rattled out of view, obscured by the dusk-shadowed swath of beech trees and poplars that formed the woods between the houses.

Reluctantly, Griffin walked back into the abbey alone.

Cicely found the dower house just as she'd left it when she and Hannah had made their regular cleaning trip two weeks ago. All the rooms were neat and orderly. All the furniture was draped in holland. Only a fine film of dust told of the passage of time.

She chose a bedchamber from among the five available. Hannah had not spoken in jest; this was a quite large residence to be a dower house. Apparently some Honeysett dowager had been possessed of a social nature.

Hannah insisted on taking the largest of the servant's rooms, claiming that it wasn't fitting for her to take over a finer chamber, that it might give her notions, at which Cicely could only roll her eyes. What uncontrollable notions it might give her she refused to make clear, so Cicely let her have her way.

Benjamin Smith, who had encountered Hannah and the hillock of trunks on the road from Portsmouth, unloaded those same trunks into the designated chambers. When he finished, he joined the women in their portion of the dinner they had prepared and brought with them from the manor house. Afterward, Mrs. Boulden rode back to the village with him, leaving Cicely and Hannah on their own.

"Tomorrow," Cicely said as Hannah helped her undress, "I must go into Alwyn. Please make a list of things we need."

In a matter of minutes, Cicely changed into her night shift and dressing gown. Hannah lighted the bedside candle in its brass holder, then took up her own and started toward the door. She stopped and turned to face Cicely, her expression troubled.

"How long do you reckon it will take for you ter get rid of that wicked ghost?"

Cicely knew what the villagers thought of Alasdair. She'd heard them call him the devil's minion, and some of the same names Captain Tyrrell had used for him, but she wasn't easy with the prospect of "ridding" Cranwick of a spirit who had dwelled there for two hundred years. A spirit who, over the past six years, had often been her only companion. Oh, he was temperamental, and he played pranks, but she'd never found him to be evil or in the least devillike.

"I don't know, Hannah," she said. "I just don't know."

Hannah nodded, then quietly let herself out of the room.

Cicely crawled into the massive canopied bed hung with blue damask silk. The sheets were faintly cool against her skin. Melting beeswax scented the chamber. A mellow glow from the single candle danced against the blue silk-covered walls, flicking its warm light over the walnut bedside table, the deeply carved wardrobe, the fireplace with its classics-inspired white marble mantelpiece. Beyond the reach of the single candle flame loomed shifting shadows.

She stared into the darkness and wondered about Griffin Tyrrell. Who was this stranger who had given her her first real taste of adventure?

When Griffin entered his house, he was greeted by an icy blast of wind, and an eerie, echoing moaning. He knew what—rather *who*—was causing these things now, and hot mortification surged through him again.

Ignoring the discomfort of the annoying racket and the cold, he made his way into the kitchen, where he discovered Lady Cicely and her protectors had laid out his dinner. Ale, pigeon pie, pickled red cabbage, bread, and even stewed damsons for his dessert. A simple but hearty meal for a hungry man.

He sat down at the table, took up his napkin—

—Alasdair appeared. He floated in the air, sitting

cross-legged a foot above the dishes, in the middle of the table, his kilted plaid hanging down.

"Bringin' Lady Cicely back to Cranwick Abbey was likely the most intelligent act ye've ever committed," the ghost said. "And what have ye done, but driven her away again." His mouth turned down.

Griffin studied the apparition for a moment. Alasdair was tall and well built. Doubtless women found him handsome. Although the ghost's translucence made it difficult to be certain, Griffin thought the supernatural Scotsman's eyes were blue. "I've done no such thing."

"Och, so ye say, but I know ye'd say anything to persuade me to go away." Alasdair smirked. "Ye should have seen yer face when first I appeared to ye. Tremblin' in yer shoes, ye were. And that other fellow—what's his name?—Digby." He hooted his amusement. "Now there's a brave man, one to have at yer back."

Remembering his own behavior when he'd first encountered Alasdair, Griffin flushed hotly. "I imagine Digby had never seen a ghost either. Certainly not an enormous death's-head floating in a deserted-looking corridor."

"Aye," Alasdair said fondly. "'Tis one of my most effective forms. I thought your servant would soil himself."

Griffin glowered at the chuckling ghost. "You're quite amused with all this, aren't you?"

"Aye, that I am. There are few enough pleasures given a spirit." His smile faded, his face took on an expression of powerful longing. "Few enough," he muttered.

As he viewed the ghost's unhappiness, Griffin felt as if he were intruding on Alasdair's privacy. He brought himself up short. Alasdair's *privacy?* What of his own? The last thing he wanted in his house was a damnable ghost.

"Where is Lady Cicely now?" Alasdair demanded.

"If you're so all-knowing, perhaps you should tell me." He was done answering to this wretch.

"Ye bold poltroon!" Alasdair roared in a voice so deep, so loud it shook the windows.

Griffin swallowed heavily and stiffened his spine. He'd not back down to this skirt-wearing vapor!

The ghost exited into thin air. Griffin half expected his meal to exit, too, but the room remained the same as before Alasdair had made his startling appearance. With a sigh of relief, Griffin picked up his knife and fork.

Dishes began to dance around the kitchen. To his dismay, there went his stewed damsons—*splat!*—onto the stone floor. Uttering a curse, Griffin lunged for his pigeon pie. The dish dragged him halfway across the table before it stopped. Quickly he forked up a mouthful. As he hastily chewed, he ducked out of the path of a flying bowl. He watched helplessly as the pickled red cabbage twirled through the air with the grace of an opera dancer, flinging bits of vegetable everywhere. A gob thumped against the back of Griffin's head. The sharp smell of vinegar reached his nostrils as moisture seeped through his hair to his scalp. The pewter ale mug whirled about the room in a crazy dance. It struck his shoulder, slopping malty brew all down his chest, drenching waistcoat, shirt, and skin.

Furious but determined, Griffin took another bite of pie, glaring about the kitchen in search of Alasdair's hovering form as he chewed. He managed to get a few more swallows of food before the plate containing the last remnant of his dinner was jerked from his fingers and went hurtling into the cavernous fireplace. At once, the objects twirling in the air crashed to the floor. Dishes shattered. The mug clanged, bounced, and rolled to a stop.

Laughter echoed eerily in the kitchen.

Griffin's hands curled into fists. Bloody ghost! He scoured his brain, trying to come up with a satisfying revenge he might have on the creature, but his mind could supply nothing. Alasdair would go unpunished for demolishing an excellent meal, not to mention the breakage and the mess.

Stalking out of the kitchen, Griffin headed toward the chamber he'd chosen for his own, where he'd stored the few articles of fresh clothing that must hold him until his trunks arrived from London with all the worldly goods he'd owned previous to purchasing Cranwick Abbey. Oh, he thought angrily, and a wise purchase that had been. What a cod's head he'd been not to ride to Sussex himself to inspect the property, to hell with the fact that Mr. Fremlin had come highly recommended. Clearly a man could trust no one these days.

When Griffin placed his hand on the latch of the dark oak door, he found it would not move. The door was not locked, yet it was frozen in place. He tried again, to no avail. Only one being he knew of might have the power to keep this unlocked door so firmly closed. Sopping with ale and pickled cabbage juice, Griffin ground his teeth in frustration.

"Leave off, ghost!" he roared. He doubted his command would persuade the spirit to open the door, but the force with which he issued it provided some small release for his pounding fury. He glared at the closed door. Very small release.

His only answer was a cool breeze through the corridor.

Swearing under his breath, Griffin strode to the door of another bedchamber. That door also remained fixed tight against his entry. And the next, and also the door beyond that. Entry to every one was denied him.

The second floor and the long-unused third floor provided the same results. Griffin wanted no part of Alasdair's wing. He had no intention of putting himself at an even greater disadvantage than he was now.

Which was considerable. He could not gain admittance to any room in the manor house save those without doors. Wait, he thought, the kitchen had a door. He tried that and found it opened to him. Across the wide stone floor there stood one more door that would quite probably open to him—the door to outside.

Oh, so that was the bastard's game, was it? Herd the intruder out of the house. Well, Griffin thought grimly, he had no intention of playing.

Suddenly, a piercing shriek filled the air. It grew higher and higher in pitch, stabbing a stiletto of pain through Griffin's ears. He clapped his palms over them, but the noise intensified, and with it the searing agony in his head.

The kitchen door opened.

Beyond anger now, wanting only to escape the driving pressure, the searing torture, he staggered across the room and outside.

Abruptly the sound and pressure ceased. The door slammed shut behind him.

He stood there in the kitchen yard for a moment, breathing hard, waiting for the pain to subside. Without testing the latch, he knew the door would not open to him, but he tried it anyway. It didn't budge.

The manor house loomed huge and dark before him. No light shone in any window. Moonlight poured silver over the ivy covering the age-darkened walls and gleamed on polished glass panes. It revealed the neat rows of greenery in the gardens. A night bird cried in the distance. In the stables, one of the horses snorted softly.

Cast out of his own house by an owner who'd died almost two hundred years ago. This was not at all what Griffin had planned. He'd thought to move in, to make the manor even more productive, find a wife, and sire a flock of children. Boys and girls, he wanted both. He wanted a wife who wanted both.

He wanted peace. Quiet. Serenity.

He had none of these things.

What he had was an empty stomach, a crashing headache, a ringing in his ears. His hair and clothing had come into closer contact with his dinner than his teeth had managed. He reeked of vinegar and ale. And it looked as if he'd be spending the night in the stables.

With a low growl of disgust, Griffin looked around for the well, which, by all rights, should have been located in the kitchen yard. As he turned, he saw one, its bucket dangling on the rope wound neatly around the shaft.

There was no splash when he lowered the rope, only the thump of the stout wooden bucket striking limestone. Griffin swore foully.

He cranked the pail back up. Tonight he'd have to endure the discomfort of wearing a portion of his meal. It was too dark, and he was too unfamiliar with the layout of the manor to conduct a search for fresh water now.

The stable door creaked as he opened it, casting a slice of moonlight into the absolute darkness. He heard the restive stamp of hooves and murmured assurances to the horses as he cautiously groped his way toward the empty stall, where he remembered a newly pitched layer of straw.

His boot struck something solid.

"Ow!" a man hollered. "Here, what are you doing in these stables? They belongs to Captain Tyrrell, and he don't take kindly to trespassers."

Griffin recognized the indignant voice. "Digby?"

"Uh . . . Cap'n?"

Griffin heard rustling in the straw. A solid weight collided with him. Digby muttered under his breath, then asked, "Did you bring a lantern or candle, Cap'n? There ain't any in the stables."

"There are still none. My exit from the house was somewhat hurried. And what, may I ask, are you doing here? I thought I'd seen the last of you when you fled." Griffin felt his way around to a corner of the stable box, then eased down onto the prickly bedding.

"Aw, don't hold that against me," Digby implored, his voice saturated with humiliation. "'Tis just that I've never seen a giant talking skull before. Never want to again," he added fervently. "But I came back right soon after, only you was already gone."

Griffin leaned back against the wooden wall. He sighed heavily. Blast. Could he really expect courage from the man, when he, a trained soldier, had turned tail? "If you stay in my employ, Digby, you must know that you will likely be called upon to go into the presence of the spirit again. It is much to ask, but there you are. Until Lady Cicely can find a way to rid Cranwick of the thing, it seems we are stuck."

Digby settled back down on the straw, from the sound of it. "I was off in the woods, trying to trap a squirrel for dinner when you returned, Cap'n. Did you see the monster again?"

Griffin sat up. "Squirrel?" His stomach rumbled at the thought of food. "Did you catch one?"

"No. 'Twere only berries and onions from the garden

for supper tonight. Had a rabbit yestereve though," he said proudly.

"A resourceful fellow. Tonight we'll both go without, I suppose."

"Seems so," Digby agreed glumly.

"To answer your question, I have indeed seen the monster again. I've even learned his name."

Digby emitted a low whistle of admiration. "What is it, then? Lucifer? Beelzebub?"

"Alasdair."

There was a second of silence. "Alasdair?"

"That fiend on earth is a Scotsman named Alasdair MacNab. Or, rather, was a Scotsman named Alasdair MacNab. Now he's a ghost."

"A Scotsman."

"Yes. An ill-tempered Scotsman at that." One rude enough to deprive a man of his dinner. "He owned Cranwick Abbey almost two hundred years ago."

"How did he die?"

"I didn't have time to find out. Maybe Lady Cicely will know."

"Lady Cicely. Did she come back?"

"So to speak. She's agreed to rid the estate of Alasdair MacNab."

"As well she should," Digby exclaimed indignantly. At his tone of voice, Apollo snorted and stamped a hoof.

Griffin heard Digby rustle around in the straw. "Good-night, Cap'n."

"Rest well, Digby."

A few minutes of sweet silence passed. Griffin tried to get comfortable in his bed of straw. This must be what it was like to sleep on a giant pincushion, he thought irritably. Inside the manor house was his bed. And—he peeled the damp shirt away from his skin—

soap and water. He'd been dirtier than this before. Many times he'd been covered with mud and blood and gunpowder. The smoke on the battlefield had burned his eyes and coated his skin, his hair, and his uniform. This stuff he wore now—mellow ale and the juice of pickled red cabbage—was, by comparison, frivolous and infuriatingly ludicrous. But it was the tangible evidence of Alasdair's insult, and it festered on him like a canker.

A tearing snore erupted from Digby's throat. It was followed by another. And another. And another. The deafening noise formed a tortured seesaw rhythm that, by all rights, should have sent the horses into a stampede.

Excellent, Griffin thought savagely. All that was wanting was a call to battle on a rusty bugle. He flopped over onto his back and was rewarded by being pierced in several places by needles of straw.

Digby snored on.

Stiff-jawed, Griffin tried to summon less violent thoughts than the ones forming in his head. Something—anything—to relax him and help him get beyond Digby's thunderous serenade. He thought of a chuckling brook, golden in the sunlight. He thought of a starry midnight sky over a quiet country road.

He thought of Cicely.

Her brandy brown eyes golden in the sunshine. Her skin luminous in the moonlight. The woman was not at all what he had expected to find when he went after her. Instead of being middle-aged and jaded and sly, she was saucy-tempered and delectable. He thought again of her full, tempting lips, her graceful, peach-blushed throat, her slim ankles.

She was young, too young to be a widow. Married six years, and she looked not a day above eighteen. Not unusual, he knew. Often girls were married at twelve and thirteen. It was the way of wealthy families. Children were traded to consolidate holdings, to firm alliances, to form islands of stability in an unstable world.

Did she mourn her husband? Was that the reason for the single, crystal tear he'd seen on her cheek? Or was he, Griffin, responsible for making her weep? The thought made him cringe inwardly. His actions had been inexcusable. He'd taken her captive and dragged her across two counties, yet he'd seen none of the fear and little of the anger that he might have expected from her. If he hadn't known better, he would have thought she was not entirely disagreeable to the escapade, but that seemed too outrageous an idea to entertain.

Digby snuffled, mumbled, and resumed snoring at greater volume.

Griffin raised his head to glare at his peacefully slumbering servant. The devil take this racket! At this rate he'd never get any sleep. He brushed a piece of straw off his cheek. When he'd sold out of his regiment, Griffin had promised himself that he'd sleep in a real bed the rest of his days. Ha! This damnable pallet of nails next to the bellowing Digby certainly did *not* qualify as a real bed.

He sat up sharply as memory struck. What was he doing here anyway? He owned a bed other than the one in Alasdair's lair. Indeed, he owned several beds besides the ones the ghost held hostage. By God, Griffin didn't intend to lie here when he could spend the night in comfort and quiet.

Abruptly he stood. Groping around, he found Apollo's bridle and slipped it on the animal. He led the horse out of the stables. Moonlight shone on the stallion's sleek bare back.

The lovely Cicely would be asleep now, Griffin thought, gathering the reins in his fingers. She'd be soft and warm, lying there alone in the deep, still darkness of her canopied bed.

Griffin swung himself up onto Apollo, then headed out of the stable yard, toward the dower house.

5

Cicely woke to the pounding at the front door. Sleepily, she turned toward the mantel clock. In the dim glow from the candle stub it revealed the late hour. Who could be calling now? Anxiety spurted up through the layers of slumberous fog, clearing her brain. *Crisis.*

She scrambled off the bed and pulled on her voluminous embroidered shawl, jamming her feet into her yellow kid mules. Snatching up the candlestick with its nubbin of wax, she hurried out of her room, into the hall, where she was nearly knocked over by Hannah, who bustled down the corridor, dragging on her own shawl as she went. From her worried expression, Cicely knew Hannah, too, was concerned.

They raced through the house to the modest entrance hall, where, at the last second, caution asserted itself.

"Who are you?" Cicely called through the door.

"The master of Cranwick Abbey," returned a deep, masculine voice.

Cicely and Hannah looked at each other in consternation. What could he want at such an hour?

"Open the door, ladies," he said, the blade of strained patience running through his tone. "I mean you no harm."

Cicely considered for a moment. That voice belonged to the captain, there was no denying that. She'd have recognized that commanding baritone anywhere. But why was he here now? He didn't sound corned. His words didn't possess the hated slur that had so often infected her father's. She nodded, and Hannah reluctantly opened the door.

They stared at the unsmiling man who stood on the porch. The strong odor of ale slammed into her. She wrinkled her nose in distaste. "You're in your cups," she accused.

Hannah quickly tried to shut the door on him, but he snapped out an arm to hold it firmly open. "I'm not so fortunate," he said tightly. "Rather I am wearing my ale."

Something else assailed her nose. Frowning, she leaned a little closer, trying to detect the source. "You reek of pickled cabbage."

"Ah, a most discerning sense of smell, dear lady, though I own it would be difficult to mistake this fragrance. Do you intend that I stand on this blasted porch all night?"

"What happened?" Cicely asked as she stepped aside, but she suspected she already knew.

The captain strode inside. If ever a man looked like a ruffled hawk, it was Griffin Tyrrell. His high cheekbones wore the color of embarrassment. Locks of ink black hair had pulled free from the ribbon that bound his queue and stood out at all angles. There were bits of shredded cabbage on the back of his head. He wore no coat. His neckcloth was pulled awry, and his once-spotless white shirt was stained. He bristled with spikes of straw, which clung to his clothing and hair. Cicely smothed a smile. A quick glance to Hannah revealed she, also, struggled to maintain a solemn expression.

"I apologize for rousing you from your beds, Lady Cicely, Hannah, but I could not even find the well in the dark."

"Pray tell us what happened," Cicely repeated.

The captain drew in a sharp breath, paused, then huffed it out, as if he struggled to control his temper. "That foul Alasdair. The demon set my dinner to dancing about the kitchen. The dish with the pickled cabbage *threw* the stuff. I think he aimed it at me," Captain Tyrrell said darkly. "Indeed, I'm certain of it. Just as he aimed the mug of ale—perfectly good ale!—at me. Hit my shoulder and spilled down my front." His eyes narrowed at the memory.

"What happened then?" Hannah asked, clearly enthralled with his story.

"He drove me out of my house!" he exclaimed indignantly. "First he locked me out of my chamber, then the fiend set up a scream so shrill I thought my head would burst." He began to pace back and forth. "He drove me out of my house—*my own house*—and locked the door after me." He growled low in his throat. "If I could get my hands around his miserable, vaporous neck, I'd wring it!"

Just as she'd suspected, Cicely thought with a sigh. Alasdair had decided to make the captain's life difficult.

"I see by the evidence"—she nipped a piece of straw off his sleeve—"that you then retired to the stables."

"Yes, only to discover Digby, my servant. He's

stayed there during my trip to fetch you, run off by that wretched Scottish phantom when we saw him upstairs the day we arrived."

"Allow me to venture a guess," Cicely said. "Alasdair appeared to you as a vast death's-head."

"As he did this afternoon. But the first time I was not prepared for such an encounter."

"I fear 'tis one of his favorite tricks."

"I've lost count of the times he's done it ter me," Hannah said. "Likes ter sneak up, he does, and pop into the air, all big 'n' horrible."

The captain's mouth tightened. "So he's not above terrorizing women."

Cicely and Hannah stared at him in astonishment. Just what did he think *he'd* done, when he, a stranger, had arrived on the dock, proclaimed Cicely mad, and made off with her slung over his shoulder with no thought to her feelings or dignity? Why, Hannah had been forced to trot alongside him, afraid to go for help lest she lose her mistress forever.

As if reading their thoughts, he had the grace to flush. "You may find it difficult to believe, but I seldom accost women."

Cicely tactfully refrained from comment.

The flush darkened considerably, but he made no further effort to apologize for his actions.

"Why have you come here, Captain Tyrrell?" she asked.

He looked surprised. "I thought 'twas obvious. I need someplace to live until I have access to the abbey. There are bedchambers going in want of occupants in this house. This house belongs to me. Ergo, I shall live here."

The sheer audacity of his proposal caused Cicely to blink. "You can't stay *here*. A single man and a new widow? Why, our reputations would be ruined in no time at all. I'm—I'm in mourning," she blurted, seizing on the next excuse that came to mind.

The captain studied Cicely's jade green shawl. "Odd, isn't it, that I've not once seen you wear black? Your gown yesterday was blue. Not so much as a black ribbon have I seen on you, Widow Honeysett."

"She's got a black dress," Hannah informed him heatedly. "That's enough for the likes o' Mr. Edmund Honeysett."

Cicely wished she could feel the loss of her husband more than she did, but even though she tried to summon some good, honest wifely grief, she felt none. When she cast about within herself, searching for the name of the emotion she'd felt at learning of Edmund's death, she was ashamed to admit that it was relief. She'd felt hollow for too long. Hollow and useless and unwanted. Behind her relief followed a distant sadness. She experienced the feeling with her mind, not her heart, and that knowledge had brought a more penetrating melancholy. Edmund had meant nothing to her but loneliness, anger, and a rending helplessness that she'd taken care to hide from the world. "Please, Hannah. Let us not speak ill of the dead."

Hannah opened her mouth to say more, but at the warning lift of Captain Tyrrell's eyebrow, she remained silent.

"I will have a care for your reputation, Lady Cicely," Captain Tyrrell said. "It's not my wish to cause you harm in any way."

"I cannot help but feel, sir, that a gentleman would make room for himself in the stable."

The tall captain stiffened. "Had a *lady*"—he fixed her with a pointed look—"not omitted the intelligence that Cranwick Abbey is already inhabited, I would presently be living the comfortable life of a gentleman farmer on a nice property in Buckinghamshire. Its house was somewhat smaller than the abbey, but it was quite empty. I know this because *I* visited the place."

"May I ask why you did not visit Cranwick Abbey?" Cicely asked.

"Clearly I should have, but I had business in London. It's not unusual for a person to rely upon his agent to make a purchase."

"Yes. Yes, of course," Cicely agreed, eager that the subject of her perfidy be dropped. The knowledge of her dishonesty bothered her greatly. She had sinned and now must pay the price. Tomorrow she must begin the task Griffin Tyrrell demanded of her.

"Now," the captain said, "I require soap, water, a towel, and a bed."

Hannah rebuilt the fire in the kitchen and set a kettle over it to warm enough water for a washstand basin. Cicely accompanied the captain as he chose one of the unoccupied bedchambers, then saw to the provisioning of the room.

"You have no fresh clothing," she pointed out, trying to concentrate on the practical necessities and not think of how tall he was, of how broad his shoulders were. Of how his breeches fit his narrow hips and the taut curve of his buttocks. He was certainly nothing like Edmund!

"I'll get them in the morning." A steel undernote in his voice told her that, ghost or no, he would retrieve his clothing from the abbey.

"But you'll have no nightshirt for tonight."

He shrugged, unconcerned. "I never wear one."

"Oh." Heat rushed to her cheeks, prompted more from her own envisioning than his four simple words. Quickly she pushed aside the arousing images in her mind.

She gave the colorful quilt a final tug to straighten it,

then plumped the goose-down pillows and laid them in place. All these things now belonged to the new owner of Cranwick Abbey. She had never expected to handle them again.

When Captain Tyrrell made no reply, she glanced toward him and found him observing her. That hooded gaze seemed to take in everything about her. Nervously, she smoothed her hands down the silken front of her shawl. "I'm sure your water will be heated quite soon. Hannah will bring it."

She turned and hurried out of the room, closing the door behind her, but in the corridor her steps slowed.

This was all her fault, she thought. Captain Tyrrell had purchased Cranwick Abbey in good faith, and now here he was, soaked in vinegar and ale and covered with bits of straw, unable to sleep in his own house. And tomorrow he would have to don his reeking clothing and return to the battle for his home. It hardly seemed right. The least she could do was retrieve his fresh clothing for him.

In her own bedchamber, she explained her intention to Hannah, who was already dressed. Quickly the maid helped Cicely to pull on a plain short jacket and skirt, stockings and shoes. Hannah rapidly pinned up her hair, and Cicely put on a Mary Queen of Scots cap of lace. One needed to maintain appearances, even with ghosts. Maybe especially with ghosts.

"Say nothing of my errand to the captain," she instructed Hannah. The man's pride had taken sufficient battering for one day. She would simply place his fresh clothing outside his door, then knock. By the time he opened the door, she would be out of sight, on her way back to her bed.

Outside the dower house, Cicely did not stop to saddle the single horse in the small stables, but rather ran down the lane, through the woods. Moonlight filtered through the crooked branches of the trees. Here she heard an owl call. There she saw a pair of eyes gleam yellow. She continued on her way. This place no longer frightened her, as it had when she'd first arrived. Over the years she'd learned to appreciate its beauty, learned its secret hideaways. She'd made this place hers.

When she came to the front door of the manor house, she paused to catch her breath. Here, all was still. Not so much as a breeze stirred. Under her hand, the latch opened, and she stepped inside. The room was ink dark, and Cicely turned in the direction of a drawer where she'd kept steel and flint and the stuff to create a lighted candle. Before she reached the drawer, flames sprang to life on a branched candlestick on a table to her right.

"Thank you, Alasdair," she said, and, picking up the candlestick, she headed toward the rooms she thought Captain Tyrrell most likely to choose as his.

Suddenly the ghost appeared, walking at her side. "'Tis surprised I am to see ye here, lassie."

"You shouldn't be," she said.

"Och, the *Sasannach* came cryin' to ye like a spoiled wean, did he no? I should have expected as much." He smirked. "I will say he's more entertainin' than the rest o' the so-called owners o' my house—not so easily run off. Stubborn as a stone, I'd say. Aye, he's provided some good sport already."

"I very much doubt that Captain Tyrrell wishes to provide you anything but a hasty exit from this house."

"Ha! Let him try! A captain, ye say?"

Cicely nodded absently, holding the candle aloft, trying to decide which room might appeal the most to the broad-shouldered man now washing off the smell of ale and pickled cabbage back in the dower house. She decided on trying the closest door first. "A captain who has fought against the French in His Majesty's service."

Alasdair made a rude noise. "What do Englishmen know about fightin'? If it's fightin' ye want, give me a handful o' Highlanders any day. Ah, the savagery of a Highlander when his blood is up—"

"Englishmen, even soldiers, aren't savages, Alasdair," she informed him pertly as she gazed about the shadowed room, finding no sign of habitation. She went to the wardrobe, but when she swung wide the doors she found it empty. Sweeping around Alasdair— unwilling to pass through him, as she knew she certainly could—Cicely headed toward the next bedchamber.

"Och, they're savages all right, and dinna ever forget that. Just because a man wears a uniform instead of a kilt woven by his womenfolk doesna mean he's a gentleman. War does things, terrible things, to a man. It changes him forever." A distant sadness drifted over his translucent features. "It . . . violates him. Ye canna see all scars with yer eyes, lassie."

Cicely paused at the next door, her hand on the latch. She dropped her gaze to the Savonnerie carpet beneath her feet. "Is that what happened to you, Alasdair?" she asked softly.

He didn't respond immediately, and she expected him to vanish, as he did whenever a question was put to him that he did not wish to answer. To her surprise, he did not. "Perhaps that was a part of it," he said. "'Tis of no import now."

She wanted to question him further, to ask yet again how he'd become a ghost. But he had never answered that question, and she decided that she'd pushed as far as she decently could for the moment. It was not her wish to hurt him by dredging up painful memories. For years, Alasdair had been her only companion after she'd been abandoned here by Edmund and deserted by frightened servants, before Hannah—blunt, practical, loyal Hannah—had come to stay, albeit sometimes nervously.

Opening the door, she saw immediately that this was the captain's room. His empty saddlebags sat on the floor. In the wardrobe his riding coat hung neatly on pegs. In the chest of drawers she found a fresh shirt, stockings, breeches, and liners. Nowhere was there a nightshirt.

Clearly he must be expecting additional clothing to be delivered, for this was too inadequate to sustain him for long. But that was not her worry, she reminded herself.

She draped his riding coat over her arm. Shrugging the heavy saddlebags over her shoulder, Cicely picked up the branch of candles and left the room.

"I ask that you cease plaguing Captain Tyrrell, Alasdair. Perhaps he would content himself with sharing the house with you if you behaved as a gentleman should. Even ghosts can be gentlemen, surely."

Alasdair grinned impishly. "And just what do ye know of gentlemen ghosts?"

"Well, little, 'tis true."

"Likely good, sweet-natured, honorable souls are no consigned to walk the face o' the earth for all eternity," he pointed out.

She sighed. "True. But I cannot conceive how you came to this state. You're not an evil man, er, spirit."

His handsome face broke into a smile—for her sake, she had no doubt. "Dinna worrit yer fair head over me. Perhaps 'tis wean-hearted Tyrrell ye should pity. Thinks he's the new master of Cranwick Abbey, does he?" Alasdair vanished, but his laughter echoed behind him.

Cicely deposited the candlestick on the table by the

door as she left, setting off toward the dower house and a tall, broad-shouldered man who needed these clothes.

Tomorrow she would go get Octavia, she thought as she retraced her way through the moonlit woods. Transportation. Something she'd never had when she'd been a prisoner here. Edmund had doled out a trickle of funds so that she had clothes on her back and food, but he'd taken care never to allow her a swift method of escape. Not that she'd probably have taken that route. No, she'd always been too dutiful. Too predictably, tediously dutiful. A dunce, that's what she'd been, foolishly attempting to honor her marriage vows to a man who did not want her.

He'd formed a disgust for her. And what husband would not have? She'd humiliated herself and him by trying every means to lure him to her bed to give her a child. She'd bungled the single time she'd succeeded. And there had been no children.

But now at least she had a horse of her own. The cozy stable by the dower house would be Octavia's home—at least until Cicely found a way to ease Alasdair from the abbey.

She flinched at that thought, feeling like a traitor. She didn't want to ease him out. The great pile of stone erected in the time of Henry Tudor belonged to him, as did the manor he roamed at will. If only she could persuade Alasdair to temper his pranks and allow Captain Tyrrell to live in peace in the house he'd paid for, perhaps all would be settled. She could be off on her adventure in good conscience. Alasdair would continue as he had for almost two centuries. And the captain would no longer hold her in contempt.

Not that his opinion of her truly mattered, she told herself stoutly. She reached the kitchen door and hurried inside.

As she passed through, intent on making her way to

his room, she noticed the faint glow of candlelight under the door of the small room in back of the kitchen. She heard no sound. Doubtless Hannah had washed out the captain's clothing, and, in her fatigue, forgotten to put out the candle.

Cicely unloaded the saddlebags on the flagstone floor, then opened the door of the small room—

—To find a naked Griffin Tyrrell standing by the tin tub of bathwater, reaching for the towel draped over the back of a wooden chair.

"Oh!" Quickly she spun around, turning her back to him. Fire scorched her cheeks. "I-I do apologize, Captain. You had said . . . I mean . . . " Mortified, indignant, fascinated, Cicely searched for words to cover her agitation. "You were going to bathe in your chamber!"

"I was," he replied calmly. "But there was too much damage done to get clean with a simple sponge bath. So I sent Hannah to her bed, and fetched the water to fill this tub. I warmed a few kettlefuls over the fire and used your soap."

"Most resourceful," she muttered, wondering what to do now.

"You may turn around if you wish. I'm decently covered with this towel. I doubt you'll see anything you have not seen before with your husband."

Cicely shuddered. What she had seen of her rotund, hirsute husband she did not wish to see again. Wet, shiny lips that never ceased to remind her of fat garden slugs. His pale, pink skin so much like that of a pig. He'd grunted like a pig the one time he'd— She swallowed hard and slammed an inner door against those memories. No, she had no wish to see anything that resembled Edmund ever again.

But curiosity gnawed at her. From what she'd glimpsed of Captain Tyrrell, he appeared nothing at all like the man she'd been forced to marry. Hesitantly, she turned around. Her eyes widened.

In the flickering candlelight, he stood tall and impressive. His gleaming raven-dark hair clung wetly to his bare, broad shoulders. Crisp, black, curling hair was scattered in a light mat over his deep chest, narrowing as it passed down his ridged abdomen, disappearing below the linen towel he'd wrapped around his narrow hips and which fell to mid-thigh of his long, well-muscled legs. On his right thigh, a scar extended below the bottom edge of the towel to just above mid-calf. It was the bright pink of a healed wound.

She lifted her gaze to find that he had folded his arms over his chest.

"Do I pass inspection?" he inquired.

She realized with dismay that she'd been staring. "I do apologize, Captain Tyrrell." Averting her gaze from him, she pressed her palms to blazing cheeks. "I . . . It is not my custom to ogle gentlemen at their baths, I assure you."

He came to stand close behind her back, yet he made no move to touch her. He did not have to, she thought, finding it difficult to breathe normally. The heat of his body pressed its brand down the length of her. What was wrong with her? she wondered distractedly. Edmund had never set her heart hammering like this.

"Cicely?" he asked.

"Y—" Her voice cracked. She cleared her throat and tried again. "Yes?" He was so masculine. His maleness vibrated against every fiber in her body. She breathed in the crisp, clean smell of pine balsam soap and the more unfamiliar warm scent of healthy male skin.

"What are you doing here?" he asked, his voice low and slightly husky. "I thought you had gone to your bed."

"Mmm?" She knew he'd spoken, yet she was bound by a peculiar spell.

"Why are you here?"

She edged away from him, certain that a little distance between them would make clear thinking easier. And when her brain did start to function more normally, she realized that her plan to deliver his clothes to him anonymously was no longer feasible. But before relinquishing her scheme, she tried to save it. Instead of answering him, she asked a question of her own. "Where are your dirty clothes?"

"On the line here." He stepped aside, and in the shadows behind him, Cicely saw his things hanging from the line suspended for the purpose. "Hannah kindly washed them for me—muttering under her breath all the while."

"And what did you plan to wear back to your room?"

"I thought you were in your room, asleep, just like Hannah."

She eyed his towel and fixed him with a stern look, quite sure that he'd planned to return to his room in naught but what he had on. "Well, I'm not."

"So I see." He reached over to twitch his shirt off the line.

She plucked the wet garment from his fingers. "And just what do you think you're doing with the things Hannah slaved over?"

"Madam, if I am to guard your good name, I will need to do it in more than a towel."

"I brought you your change of clothes." She hastened out of the small room, of which he seemed to take so much space, so much air, and snatched up the saddlebags. Refusing to look on him again, she shoved them at him, then hastily removed herself to the kitchen.

Silence filled the house as she stood there, excruciatingly aware of his presence in her domain.

There had been no one in Cicely's life who compared to that impossible man dressing in the next room—which left her adrift without bearings. Surely this awareness of him, of his physical presence, could not be normal. She'd experienced no such preoccupation with Edmund, and he had been her husband.

She could hardly expect Captain Tyrrell to sleep in the stables, and until she convinced Alasdair to come to a truce, or persuaded him to leave the manor house altogether, it seemed the captain could not live there, either. If she moved to the abbey and left the captain in the dower house, she had no doubt that Alasdair would haunt here. She was amazed that he'd, so far, shown unusual restraint, since she knew he considered the entire manor and all its buildings still his. Well, it had only been one day.

The captain strode into the kitchen, fully clothed. Only his hair was not dressed. Thick, dark, and heavy, it hung, unbound, past his shoulders. He deposited the saddlebags next to the back door.

"Though I would not have had you go alone to the manor house, I thank you for your assistance."

"A pleasure, Captain," she said politely.

He took the lantern from her unresisting fingers and led the way through the house. At her door, he halted. "My name is Griffin Tyrrell," he said. "I would take it kindly if you chose to call me by my Christian name. 'Tis not as though we are perfect strangers."

"I would venture to say our perfections are few."

He chuckled softly. "*Touché*, Cicely."

She lifted her chin. The bold rogue. It was much too early in their hopefully short acquaintance to be addressing one another by their first names. "I'll consider it."

He gave her a single, short nod, then walked into her bedchamber, leaving her speechless with shock.

"Really, sir! You will leave my chamber at once!"

He lighted the candle on her mantel with the one in the lantern, then returned to the hall where she stood. "I intended to," he said. "'Tis only that I knew you would not wish to stumble around in the dark."

Her cheeks warmed in embarrassment over her ludicrous presumption. As if any man would be interested in her that way. "Yes," she muttered. "Quite so."

He smiled. "Good-night, Cicely."

"Good-night, Captain." She stepped into her room and shut the door. When she heard him leave, she immediately opened the door a crack, peering into the darkened hall, watching as he strode away, surrounded by the golden glow from the lantern. His shadow trailed behind him, impossibly tall, prowling the walls, rippling over gilt-framed paintings, small console tables, and alabaster busts on their pedestals. In a moment, he was gone. Out of sight, if not out of mind.

Cicely closed her door and leaned back against it, feeling suddenly limp-limbed. Dear heavens, how was she ever going to get through this?

The next morning, in the cozy dining room, the three of them broke their fast with porridge. There was nothing more substantial than oats left in the pantry. When Captain Tyrrell discovered the teapot, he asked if there was any coffee.

"No," Cicely answered, setting down her teacup. "Neither Hannah nor I have ever acquired a taste for it, but I will be going into the village today and shall make a point of purchasing a packet for you."

"Thank you. What business takes you to the village?"

A familiar chill spread through her, clenching around her stomach. Did he mistrust her to leave the manor?

She lifted her china cup of watery tea, relieved that her hand did not tremble. "Captain, were I intent on escape from you, I would not tell you I wished to go into the village," she said in a light, flippant tone manufactured to conceal an old panic. "I would simply go—and keep on going."

He smiled, holding up his palm in a mock gesture of warding her off. "'Twas curiosity only, madam. I have little knowledge of the place and wish to learn more, that is all."

She drew in a quiet breath of relief. Would he have given her Octavia if that were his intention? she reasoned. Of course not. She, Cicely, had come back of her own will to right a wrong she had committed. She was no longer a prisoner. Never again. "I plan to inquire of certain persons in Alwyn what they know of Alasdair, and how he came to such a pass." Years ago she had asked Cranwick's tenant families, and the owners of the surrounding manors. She'd asked almost everyone she knew, except the two most obvious possibilities. Why she'd neglected inquiring of them, she wasn't certain.

"Do you wish me to accompany you?" he asked as he eyed the contents of his cup.

She shook her head. "I'm certain you have things you wish to do at Cranwick. I'll make my inquiries, buy supplies, and visit for a bit. Do you require luncheon?"

His eyes widened slightly in surprise. "That would be nice."

Cicely calculated the time it would take to accomplish her tasks and for her and Hannah to prepare a noon meal with meat pasties from the shop of Samuel Ginger, the baker. Since she'd sold all the livestock, thinking to be off on her grand tour, there were no fowl to slaughter and prepare. As of this morning's breakfast, the last of the oats and tea were gone, and

Alasdair's pranks had seen to it that there was nothing left of the pigeon pie Hannah's mother had brought, so Cicely would need to purchase food.

"I found an old chaise in the stables. I'll hitch up Octavia so that Hannah may accompany you," the captain said. "I didn't wake Digby when I left last night. Likely the poor fellow is hungry now. Would you mind if I brought him the last of this porridge? And perhaps a bit of tea?"

"Who's Digby?" Hannah asked, rising from the table.

"My servant. He came with me from London, but I thought he'd deserted when he ran off after seeing Alasdair in all his grisly glory. He returned shortly after, but I had already gone. I found him in the stables last night." Captain Tyrrell stirred his spoon through the dregs of his porridge, gazing down at it as if the task required his full attention. Thick, black lashes kept his eyes from Cicely's view. "He needs some kind of accommodation until this matter of Alasdair is settled and he can move into the abbey." He slanted her a guileless look.

Cicely drew in a deep, resigned breath. In for a penny, in for a pound. "There is another vacant bed-chamber here."

Carrying a warmed pot of tea, Hannah entered the room just in time to hear the captain's last comment and Cicely's response. "Oh, and wouldn't that look lovely?" Hannah asked, scowling. "Two unmarried women and two unwed men, all a-living together in the same house. 'What's going on there?' people will say. 'Must be having an orgy.'"

"You are welcome to save your reputation and move out, Hannah," the captain said with deceptive softness. "There will be room in the stables for you."

She stared at him in shock for a moment. Then she went about her business of placing the porcelain teapot on the table. "As if I ever would desert Lady Cicely ter such a turn. And her the only woman with two men." She sniffed in disdain. "Not likely."

"The choice is yours," he said, "so we'll hear no more about it."

"Yes, sir," she muttered, and started for the door.

Having finished his food, the captain tossed his napkin onto the table. "No one will learn I am here if we all exercise discretion. Digby, I might add, is the soul of discretion. He is a man who understands a lady's honor."

Finally, Cicely came to the point of what had been bothering her about the task he'd given her. "Is it really necessary for me to try to rid the abbey of Alasdair?"

"It is. Why?"

She worried her linen napkin between her fingers. "'Tis so severe. He's inhabited this manor for more years than anyone. It is his *home*. Perhaps I could persuade him to fewer pranks. If he would withdraw to his wing of the house, would you be satisfied?"

He leaned back in his chair, crossing his arms over his chest. "No. I'll not be satisfied until the damnable fellow is gone completely."

Cicely's brow creased with consternation. "Can you not find it in your heart to forgive him?"

The captain studied her face for a moment. "Cicely, did you never think that he might wish to find his rest?"

She drew back, struck by the realization of her own selfishness. Always she had found in Alasdair companionship. It had never occurred to her that he might long for peace. She thought how she might feel, consigned to live beyond the years of all she loved, of times she knew. Pity for Alasdair filled her. She had not considered beyond her own needs. Shame burned inside her.

"I'll deliver Digby his breakfast and hitch up your Octavia," Captain Tyrrell said, seeming to sense her turmoil. Quietly, he left the table.

A few minutes later, Cicely paused at the back door, donning her straw milkmaid's hat, its yellow ribbons fluttering in the breeze. Her embroidered reticule dangled from her wrist. "I will wait for you at the abbey, Hannah. Please don't be long."

Hannah smiled as she dried her hands on a towel used in the scullery. The washed dishes sparkled in the sunlight that poured in through the window. "I'll be there straightaway."

Cicely walked the lane that cut through the cooling woods. Birds called to one another. A squirrel darted up a tree trunk. Here and there, glowing in shafts of light filtering through the leafy canopy, she spied the purple petals of sweet violet and dainty sunshine-hued yellow pimpernel.

When she reached the front door of the great manor house, she hesitated. If only things could be left as they were. If her marriage agreement had not stipulated that Cranwick Abbey should go to her upon the death of her husband, it would have gone to one of Edmund's equally disinterested brothers, and everything would have remained the same for Alasdair as it had for centuries.

She pulled the latch, and the heavy, nail-studded oak door swung open on silent hinges. Dust motes danced in the morning light that shone through the leaded windows. Cicely regarded them absently, making a note that she and Hannah must continue to clean the abbey, or it would soon be a disgrace.

A breeze wafted over her cheeks, and she smiled. "Good morn to you, Alasdair. I have come to ask a question."

With the familiar *pop* that was little more than a burst of air, Alasdair materialized, sitting in one of the wing chairs arranged in front of the fireplace. "Is it an important question?" he asked with a lift of his fair eyebrows.

"To me it is."

"Och, but is it to *me*?" He grinned, looking to Cicely like a Celtic warrior of old. Which, of course, was probably what he had been.

Looking at him, remembering all her lonely days and nights, when Alasdair's teasing and his pranks served to make her forget her misery for a while, Cicely's throat tightened. "It could be."

Alasdair sobered and floated up out of his chair. "What is it, lassie? Ye dinna often seem so pensive these days."

Cicely took a steadying breath and released it. "Alasdair, do you . . ." Tears burned at the back of her eyes. "Do you ever think . . . Would you like to be at peace?"

He went stock-still. His gaze lifted from her to focus somewhere in the distance. His face took the stark expression of a yearning so intense, so filled with soul-wrenching melancholy that it hurt her to look on it. She had never seen him like this before, and it stirred in her a vague panic.

"Yes," he whispered. He faded until he vanished.

"Alasdair?" She found she wanted his reassurance that he was well. But, as she had seen, he could not, in truth, give her that assurance.

The house remained silent.

She whirled and rushed out the door, almost running into the captain, who caught her in his arms to steady her. "What is it, Cicely? What's wrong?" he demanded, concern vibrating through his words.

"Nothing," she lied chokingly. "Nothing at all."

His eyes narrowed, and she felt he must be able to see her falsehood branded on her forehead.

"I asked him," she said.

6

There in the drive that curved around the front of the house, Griffin cradled Cicely close to his body. "What did you ask him?" His voice was deep and gentle.

She knew she should refuse his comforting, but it had been so long since anyone had thought to offer her his strength, that she'd forgotten how good it felt. Only for a minute, she told herself. She'd let him hold her only for a minute, then get back to the business of standing on her own two feet. "I asked him if he wanted to find peace." Recalling that fierce longing so clear in Alasdair's translucent features, she swallowed and pressed her forehead against the captain's chest, knocking her hat askew. When she made no move to right it, he gently tugged loose the ribbon, and slipped the hat from her head.

"What did Alasdair say?" he asked as he stroked a stray wisp of hair back from her temple.

"He said yes." She hated the quaver in her voice. She hated even more that somehow, some way, she must send Alasdair to his rest. Despite his contrariness, despite the many wicked tricks he'd played on her over the years, she owed him much. She chewed her lip. Would she never be free to do what *she* wanted?

"I wonder that news does not make you feel better."

She lifted her head from his chest. "I don't know how to do it!" she cried. "He's the only spirit I know, Captain Tyrrell."

He sighed. "You call the spirit 'Alasdair,' yet you refuse to address me as 'Griffin.'"

"I have known him longer, and there were times when—" But she had said too much already. She pulled away from her comforter's strong arms, and he released her, but when she tried to retrieve her hat from his fingers it did not budge. Agitated, frustrated, she faced him squarely. "Do not toy with me, sir. I am no demirep to be teased and dallied with."

"I have never thought you were. A swindler, perhaps, but not a woman of dubious morals." His moon silver eyes met hers, and an unfamiliar ripple of shock passed through her. He placed her hat upon her head and tied the ribbon. His fingers accidentally brushed the sensitive skin of her nape, stopping the breath in her throat. "Never that," he said, his voice low and solemn. "I know I've treated you roughly. For that I ask your forgiveness."

Looking into his eyes, so strikingly vivid against the soot black of his thick lashes, at his sensual mouth that wore no smile, she found herself believing him. But she refused to allow him to forget his shocking behavior so soon. She wasn't quite ready to forgive him. "I am all relief, sir—"

"—Griffin—"

"—That you accept I am not a harlot looking for a patron. Nor am I a desperate female seeking a husband to protect her from the supposedly wicked world." Oh, she'd already seen exactly how well a husband protected his wife. As Edmund had protected her. As her father had protected her mother. "I'm seeking no man's protection. I wish only to be left alone. Do that and we shall get on tolerably well."

Midnight eyebrows drew down in a scowl. "*Supposedly* wicked world? Madam, you have indeed been sheltered if you doubt the world is choked with evil. It is. Evil comes in many disguises, the better to prey on the unsuspecting." His gaze bored into her, driving home the point he wished her to take. "Sometimes it is large and loud and terrible, but you cannot get out of its way. Sometimes it comes cloaked as kith or kin, and, when you least expect it, cuts you to ribbons. For a man it is difficult enough. For a beautiful woman it would be worse."

The picture he painted, the way he spoke it, as if he had personal experience, frightened her. She would not believe him. Nothing could be so horrible. Defiant, determined to overcome her fear, she lifted her chin and glared up at him. "I'm certain you would prefer I believe that. Men will always wish to keep women ignorant of the excitement of adventure. Of the wondrous sights there are to be seen. It is to their advantage to keep us in terror so that we will always be at their beck and call when *they* return from their play in the world outside the borders of their garden or manor. Call it town house or country house—for women, it is still their prison!"

He drew slightly back from her, as if confronted by a viper. "By God, woman, is that what you truly believe?"

His reaction took her by surprise. For the first time, a sliver of doubt crept in, but she did her best to dismiss it. "Yes. Yes, it is."

For a long moment, he studied her. His face, striking in its light-and-shadow masculine beauty, revealed nothing of his feelings. She found that very impenetrability unnerving. It was as if he had learned long ago to harbor his thoughts behind a mask of neutrality.

Then he inclined his head and swept out an arm to indicate Octavia and the chaise. "Your coach, Lady Cicely."

Why, she could not say, but it pricked her, his use of her title. Gone was plain, ordinary, intimate Cicely, and in its place the cool distance of formality.

"Thank you. Hannah will be here soon. Until then, I thought I would search the library for some clue as to Alasdair's condition."

He indicated that Octavia's reins were secured. Then he gave her a single, short nod. "Madam." He strode away, toward the stables.

Trying to shrug off the unsettling impression that she'd come down in his estimation, Cicely reentered the quiet house and went straight to the large library. The chamber was filled, floor to ceiling, with leather-bound volumes collected over the past two centuries. This was one of her favorite rooms in the abbey.

Knowing she had only a little time before leaving for Alwyn, she began once again a methodical search of the shelves for journals or logs dated around the time she calculated Alasdair had begun his haunting. She started with a portion of the library that held little interest for her. The books were too old-fashioned.

Before she progressed more than a few shelves her attention was caught by two large tomes she'd never noticed before. They were bound in red morocco, their spines each embossed with a gold rose. The books sat too high for her to reach, but that problem was easily solved. She glanced around the room until she spotted the stepladder Tom Sparke had made her, complete with wheels and brakes. Under her hand, it moved easily across the wooden floor to the shelf.

"Lady Cicely!"

She recognized the voice as belonging to Hannah, who seemed to be calling her from the entry hall. Hannah, she knew, would not willingly come farther into the house. Though she had stayed with Cicely at Cranwick Abbey this past year, when no one else but Will or Mrs. Boulden would enter, she, like the rest of the villagers, feared the place. Only for Cicely's sake had she struggled with her fright and remained. And now an odd note sounded in the young woman's voice. Was Alasdair indulging in his ghostly tactics again? Cicely hurried to see what was amiss.

She found no sign of Alasdair. There was only Hannah, standing in the open doorway, one foot inside, and the other firmly planted outside, ready to take flight. As if Alasdair could not leave the manor house.

"What is it, Hannah?" Cicely asked immediately. "Is there something wrong?"

"Not so as you'd say, Lady Cicely. 'Tis only that I knew you'd want me ter let you know when I arrived and"—she turned to point at a disheveled man standing next to the chaise, with straw sticking out of his hair and clinging to his clothes—"is this the captain's man?"

The fellow swept off his three-cornered hat, scattering bits of straw around him. "Digby Prither, ladies. Your servant."

"The captain's servant, more like," Hannah muttered.

"Enchanted, Mr. Prither," Cicely said. "Have you broken your fast?"

"That I have, Lady Cicely," he replied. "My thanks for your generosity."

"We'll do better tomorrow. You are invited to take your meals in the house." She removed her gloves from her reticule and pulled them on. "We must be on our way now. There is much to do." If she was ever to see the sun rise over the Parthenon or set on the Rhine, she must help one blustering, teasing ghost find peace.

She placed her foot on the step of the two-wheeled, one-horse carriage, and instantly Digby offered her his hand. He assisted her up onto the seat, then helped Hannah, who regarded him from under her lashes. The man might not send maidens swooning with his beauty, Cicely thought, but there was in his homeliness a certain aspect that suggested a good nature. Perhaps it was his smile. It was a very nice sort of smile. She looked at Hannah and saw that her maid, too, had noticed.

"Thank you, Mr. Prither," Cicely said.

"It's Digby, m'lady. It's what the cap'n calls me. It's how most o' my acquaintances in London know me."

"Very well. Digby it shall be."

He turned his gaze to Hannah. "How may I be privileged to address you?"

"Miss Boulden."

His smile warmed. "Ah, a shy flower."

To Cicely's astonishment, practical, no-nonsense Hannah blushed.

He stepped away from the chaise. "Have a safe journey."

"We're only going into Alwyn, Digby," Cicely said.

"Highwaymen, m'lady. They're everywhere."

Cicely had never heard of a highwayman plying the road to Alwyn. She clucked her tongue at Octavia as she twitched the reins. The chaise jerked into motion. What would there be for a bandit to steal? From this direction to the cliffs that ran along this section of the coast, there were only two estates, and no other houses. Blekton had stood empty for years, save for a bilious old caretaker and his family, and, while Edmund had purchased fine furnishings for the abbey, he had given Cicely no jewels or furs, nothing of value. He'd habitually shorted her allowance, the amount agreed upon in their marriage contract. Her letters to her father, to her ever-absent husband, Edmund, and his father, and to the one solicitor she had been bold enough to write went unanswered. She had remained a prisoner of Edmund's isolated estate, entombed before her time.

She looked up the lane bordered by fields of leafy, green hops that climbed the tall poles set at each small hill. Here she saw an apple orchard, there an orchard of plum trees.

Most of the villagers' livings came from the sea. Prawns, lobsters, and crabs drawn from this section of the coast were of especially excellent flavor, and an Alwyn cockle was superior to even a Selsey cockle any day. Oysters were always in demand and were easily kept alive in pails of brackish water during transport up the rivers. This year, however, the fishermen had taken fewer catches than usual and those dramatically smaller in size.

There was, of course, the occasional midnight rendezvous in Maresmouth Cove with a black-painted lugger. Its cargo was casks of rich wines and brandy, and parcels of delicate silks and tea. On none of this had the English tax been paid.

No, highwaymen had never been a problem on this country road. A greater concern might be dragoons, but they had never come here either. So for now, mud was the worst fate this track suffered. She wouldn't worry for her safety here.

Besides, she had more pressing problems than highwaymen or dragoons. She had tall, handsome, disturbing Griffin Tyrrell living under the same roof as she and Hannah, and if that were not difficult enough, she must find a way to bring Alasdair his rest. Oh, she could ask him how, but she strongly doubted he would give her the answer. He'd never been forthcoming with information about himself. Perhaps he could not remember. Ghosts clearly lived by different rules than mortals, but she had no inkling what those rules might be.

Hannah's silence finally worked its way through Cicely's preoccupation. "You're unusually quiet, Hannah. Is something amiss?"

"'Tis naught amiss, m'lady."

Cicely smiled, enjoying the mildness of the morning weather before the heat of the afternoon set in. "Is it Digby that bothers you?"

"The cheeky baggage," Hannah declared, even as she blushed again. "It's clear to see that he isn't a proper gentleman."

"It seems we are burdened with two men who fall somewhat short of that ideal."

Hannah nodded solemnly. "Seems so." She was silent a moment. Only the rattle of the chaise's wheels on the bumpy road and the steady thud of Octavia's hooves sounded in the country stillness. Then Hannah's lips curved fractionally upward. "Still, he's a pretty fellow, ain't he?"

Cicely almost laughed aloud. *Pretty?* Digby? The man had a good-natured charm but she doubted anyone had ever called him pretty before. Plain, perhaps, if they were feeling generous. She suspected the man was a charmer and a rogue. Likely he had never wanted for feminine companionship, but if he thought to play fast and light with Miss Hannah Boulden, Cicely knew he would soon learn his mistake. "I'm not certain I noticed him well enough to rightly say. With so much on my mind, Hannah, I fear I sometimes don't pay the attention to things I should. Pretty, you say?"

Hannah considered for a moment. "Pretty in his own way. He's got lots of nice brown hair. Like as not he'll always have hair. I fancy a man with thick hair, don't you?"

"Why, uh, yes." Cicely hadn't considered the matter until that moment.

"Lovely eyes, too. Like a hound's, they are, all big and trusting-like." Hannah's ash brown eyebrows drew down slightly. "A man like that could easily fall victim to a scheming female."

A man like that probably was able to outscheme any schemers, Cicely thought, amused at this new side of Hannah. "Without question."

Hannah was silent for several minutes, her gaze trained on the road ahead. For all the world, she appeared to be serenely enjoying the ride, but Cicely believed the gears and cogs of mental machinery were turning.

"Well, there are few such females hereabouts," Hannah said. "He'll be safe enough."

"Perhaps."

Cicely's first stop was on the outskirts of Alwyn, at the neat little lime-washed cottage of Dame Eliza Ingate, the oldest living person in the parish. Still spry and acerbic at ninety-five, that good lady was much revered by those in the village and the surrounding area. In her younger days, she had pulled downed fishermen from the waves. More than one victim of the sea owed his life to her. She'd hauled a plow, a net, and contraband. No one could ever accuse Dame Ingate of being a shirker. She'd borne sixteen children, buried three husbands, and still lived in the same cottage to which she'd come as a bride of sixteen. The surrounding cottages were inhabited by her staunchly loyal family.

At Cicely's knock, one of the twenty-six adult great-grandsons showed her and Hannah to the tiny garden in back, where the old woman sat in a homemade wooden chair. A needle flashed in the sunlight as she mended a tear in the pair of breeches draped on her lap.

She looked up as their feet crunched on the oyster-shell gravel that covered the garden path. When she saw who it was her wrinkled face glowed with a welcoming smile. "Good morn, Lady Cicely, Hannah. I confess I am surprised ter see you. I'd thought you would be a-sketching the Italian countryside with your crayons by now." She shook a mock-scolding finger at Cicely. "You did promise me a pretty picture of a villa."

Pleasure in Dame Ingate's encouragement bloomed warm in Cicely's chest. This lady had always encouraged her gift, as had the few other villagers who knew about it, much unlike her father or Edmund. They had ridiculed her love of capturing landscapes and people with strokes of her chalky pastel crayons, until she'd learned to hide her work.

"I have not forgotten," Cicely assured her. "As to my being here, instead of Italy . . ." She cleared her throat. "The new owner of Cranwick Abbey took exception to Alasdair."

Amusement twinkled in Dame Ingate's faded blue eyes. "Are you surprised?"

Cicely sighed. "I suppose not. It's only justice for not having been completely honest with the agent. My eagerness to be free overshadowed my conscience."

Dame Ingate leaned over and gently patted Cicely's hand. "It always catches up with us, sooner or later, in one way or another. 'Tis wisest, you know, ter try ter live the way our Lord taught us. In the end, the evil are always consumed by their own deeds. You're an innocent in this world, though you be a woman grown, so your wickedness was a small one. But look what has come of it."

Cicely reluctantly nodded. "Captain Tyrrell is most unhappy with Alasdair, and Alasdair has formed a vast dislike of the captain. Now it is left to me to find a way to put Alasdair to rest. He has told me that he, also, wishes it. But I have no idea how to begin." With a forefinger she absently stroked a smooth ivory stick of her closed fan. "I hoped you might be able to tell me. Or even how Alasdair came to his present state."

The good dame sat quiet for a moment, as if searching the long tracks of her memories for an answer. A light breeze caught the lappets of her white muslin cap, fluttering them against her lined, rosy cheeks. "I cannot tell you how to help the ghost find peace. The story of how he came to his present state was lost long before I was born. I have heard only that he was a selfish man in life. Whether or not that was so . . ." She shrugged. "Perhaps the vicar will know more of the matter."

After Cicely and Hannah made their farewells, Cicely headed Octavia to the vicarage, where she found Mrs. Lambert Joyes, the vicar's wife, digging in her garden.

"How delightful to have you back," Sally Joyes exclaimed as she pulled off her earth-smudged gloves. "I'd heard from Mr. Coppard that you'd returned to Cranwick Abbey."

"Yes. Alasdair is causing the new owner distress. It seems the only satisfactory solution for both Alasdair and Captain Tyrrell is to find how to send Alasdair to his proper peace."

Mrs. Joyes shook her head. "I could never understand how you tolerated the ghost. I know it would frighten me to death! It must have been quite wicked in life to have incurred such a fate. You are very kind to want to set matters right. Come, Mr. Joyes is in his library, working on his sermon."

She led them through the vicarage, which was little bigger than Dame Ingate's modest cottage. Mr. Joyes's "library" consisted of a writing table and chair set in a corner of the parlor and surrounded by shelves filled to overflowing with books.

As the three of them approached tall, gangly Mr. Joyes, he seemed unaware of them. His hand swept across the sheet of foolscap before him, writing furiously. They waited to be noticed, the only sound in the room the scratch of his quill upon the cheap paper.

Finally, Mrs. Joyes moved closer to him. "Lambert," she said softly. "We have guests."

He looked up, and the expression he wore reminded Cicely of someone awakening from an enthralling dream. He blinked up at his wife. "Guests?" Then he saw Cicely and Hannah. His boyish-looking, snub-nosed face burst into a smile. "Why, an excellent surprise!" he proclaimed, rising from his chair, pushing an unruly lock of blond hair out of his eyes. "How good to see you, Lady Cicely, Miss Boulden. I hope you will excuse my preoccupation, ladies. I was working on Sunday's sermon."

Mrs. Joyes ushered everyone to the cozy arrangement of chairs and couch in another corner of the parlor. "I'll just go make a nice pot of tea." Smiling, she left her guests to discuss their business with her husband.

When Cicely had finished explaining her quest, Mr. Joyes sat for a minute, looking thoughtful.

"As to the story behind the Cranwick ghost, one hears rumors. There always are about such things." He frowned in concentration. "I've heard two of them. Now . . . what was it I heard?" He brightened. "Ah, now I remember. One tale is told of how Alasdair MacNab was always chasing people away. He was a recluse, as the story goes, and hated for anyone to come near his house, where he kept a king's ransom of gold and jewels that he'd gathered as a pirate. One night a traveler became lost and wandered onto the manor. He thought the traveler had come to rob him and slew the fellow with his pirate's sword. Just before the man died, he laid a curse on MacNab."

Cicely sat there, stunned to think of Alasdair murdering an innocent traveler. She knew him as quarrelsome and blustering, a prankster with a peculiar sense of humor. But a murderer? She could not, would not, believe it of him. "And the second story?"

"If I recall aright, it had MacNab as a traitor to the Crown, some sort of spy in the cause of Mary Stuart. He fled London, and hid at Cranwick. It was there he was discovered by the queen's men. A battle ensued and he was killed."

Although Cicely was certainly no Stuart sympathizer, she much preferred the second story. "I find it curious that there is no one legend regarding Alasdair. Well-known ghosts always have equally well-known myths attached. Why, do you suppose, are there none about Alasdair? Even Dame Ingate doesn't know of any such stories. I certainly do not, nor does Hannah. I would be surprised to find that anyone else in the countryside knew even as much as you."

At that moment, Mrs. Joyes entered the parlor, bearing a tray loaded with a fat brown teapot, four cups, and a plate of biscuits. She set it down on the table next to the couch. In a matter of minutes everyone held steaming cups of tea and one of her delicious, buttery biscuits.

"Now that you have mentioned the matter," Mr. Joyes said, "it is rather unusual that there is no horrific legend surrounding MacNab. Perhaps he was indeed a hermit. If that was so, it's possible no one really knows what he did to cause his ungodly unrest."

"'Twas that very unrest I wished to talk to you about," Cicely said.

"Yes, of course, so you said, Lady Cicely." The vicar went to one of the bookshelves and withdrew a volume. "There is a provision for exorcism, but, I must confess, I have never used it, nor know any minister who has."

He leafed through the pages, presumably searching for the rite of exorcism.

Cicely shifted uneasily in her place on the couch. "I quite dislike the word 'exorcism.' It has a nasty sound to it."

"It is, of necessity, a nasty sort of procedure. Dealing with evil is never pleasant."

Could anyone describe Alasdair as evil? Difficult, yes. But evil? "I would not call Alasdair iniquitous, precisely. Whatever his crime, I can only believe it must have been a little one. He has no grisly aspect. Well, hardly ever. The only time he moans and clanks chains is if he feels he's been ignored. He's quite sensitive, you know. Certainly not your common sort of ghost."

Mr. Joyes closed the book and slid it back into its place. "I would not know what a common sort of ghost is, having little experience with phantasms," he said soberly. "My only experience with any such being was MacNab. While I would not call having a chamber pot dumped on my head truly evil, I would not say it showed a contrite heart."

Hannah ceased nibbling on her biscuit. "Do spirits have hearts?"

"I was speaking in the figurative sense, Miss Boulden, and I would presume they must have something akin to a heart if they are to suffer torment so that, ultimately, they may repent."

"Do you think that repentance alone will give him rest?" Cicely asked, finding a sudden ray of hope.

"I wish I could give you a certain answer, my lady, but, as I say, my experience in such matters is limited. If you wish for an exorcism to be performed, I will be happy to speak with the bishop."

"Would an exorcism be . . . painful? Would it hurt Alasdair?"

"Possibly. Its purpose is not to make him comfortable, but to extinguish him."

"Extinguish," Cicely echoed faintly. She knew Alasdair wished to find eternal peace, but she doubted very much that he desired anything so unpleasant, so positively dreadful-sounding as this. No, exorcism would not do at all. "Perhaps further research is warranted, Mr. Joyes."

"You are wisdom itself, Lady Cicely," the vicar said, looking distinctly relieved.

The four of them chatted for a while after that, but the subject of ghosts and exorcism was never resurrected. Fifteen minutes later, Cicely and Hannah took their leave.

From the vicarage, they went to Uriah Coppard's butcher shop, where Cicely viewed the meat hanging on display from the low ceiling beams with dismay. There was little choice, and even that was of poor quality. Mr. Coppard usually offered only the best.

"I had hoped to find a nice, plump capon," she told him.

"I wish I could sell you a nice, plump capon, Lady Cicely," he replied. "I wish I could sell you a nice, plump anything. 'Tis the blight, you know. It sickened many of the crops and so much of the grasslands. The farmers had ter slaughter many of their cattle and their sheep earlier or be left with starvin' beasts, so now there are few left." He shook his head. "Many folk are in dire straits."

Numbly, Cicely settled on two thin rabbits. Cranwick and its tenants had escaped the blight, and she'd been so involved first with Edmund's death and funeral, then her plans to leave and the subsequent sale of the property, that she hadn't realized what was going on in the lives of her neighbors.

Isolated as she had been at Cranwick, which supplied all her food, she had suffered no deprivation. Now she realized others had.

"Mr. Coppard, I fear I have been so concerned with the events in my own life that I neglected those in the lives of others. Which families suffer most?" She felt safe that Hannah's parents were secure. What they'd planted in their small plot seemed not to have attracted the blight, and the excellent woolen blankets Mark Boulden wove always found buyers. The only problem for him that she could see would be if there were not enough sheep left for a good shearing.

Uriah Coppard told her the families hardest hit. When she heard the names of Kitty and Tom Sparke, Cicely's alarm increased. Kitty was expecting their first child. But now, when she should be eating well, Tom's fishing nets had stayed nearly empty.

Cicely bought the best of Mr. Coppard's meager offerings, thanking him for his information. From there she and Hannah went to the baker's shop, and, after procuring meat pasties for the noon meal, and bread for their own needs, she purchased bread for the families she planned to visit. By visiting the homes of those she knew were likely to have a bit of surplus from their gardens and orchards, Cicely was able to buy enough to fill the baskets she and Hannah carried.

"You'll not be able ter carry all this by yourself, Lady Cicely," Hannah said. "I'll go with you."

"I would not have you miss your visit with your parents. I'm certain I can find some young lad to help me."

Hannah made a face. "Lad, indeed. Likely he'd drop the lot and then where would the hungry folk be? I'll see my mum on the next trip."

Cicely smiled. "Thank you, Hannah. In truth, I will feel better to have you with me. Seeing our neighbors in such distress will not be easy."

They called on several of the families Mr. Coppard had mentioned, leaving with them food enough for at least one meal. Finally, Cicely briskly led the way down the sunny lane toward the cottage belonging to Tom and Kitty Sparke. Oyster-shell gravel crunched under their shoes.

The Sparkes' place was clean, well tended, and snug. Stones the size of Cicely's hand neatly lined the short, white oyster-shell path from the road. Small, cheerful beds of daisies grew by the front door.

According to Uriah Coppard, despite Tom's herculean efforts, there was often not enough to provide more than a poor dinner for the young man and his breeding wife, Kitty, leaving them without breakfast or luncheon. Cicely worried that Kitty might sicken, as might the babe she carried. Both needed their strength for the coming ordeal.

When the door opened, the sight that greeted Cicely's eyes shocked her. Kitty—pretty, blond, blue-eyed Kitty—stood there, hollow-cheeked and pale, thin but for the bulging belly that announced her advanced state of pregnancy. Her clothes hung loosely on her shoulders and arms.

Immediately, Cicely and Hannah swept into the cottage, fussing over Kitty, all but carrying the girl to a stool, urging her to sit down, causing her to laugh—a pale echo of her usual joyful sound.

"I'm not sick, you know."

"And we wish to keep you that way," Cicely said. "Mr. Coppard offered me an excellent bargain on rabbits. He practically gave them to me, so I have brought two for you and Tom." She withdrew from her basket the skinny, undersized carcasses that were the best rabbits the butcher had to offer. She hung them on a wall peg. "And here are some carrots, some cabbage, and some cheese. Oh, and a rather nice, big onion."

A hungry gleam shone in Kitty's eyes as she stared at the food Cicely had taken from her wicker market basket. "You know we cannot accept such gifts, Lady Cicely." Wistfully, she dragged her gaze from the rabbits. "I know Mr. Coppard's meat is very dear, and what with the blight and the fishing hauls so poor 'tis bound ter grow dearer still." She gave Cicely and Hannah a smile that anyone could see was meant to reassure. "We have no way of knowing when fishing will improve, so we could not repay you. As for the blight . . . well, I'll just have ter replant our plot." She wearily shrugged one shoulder. "It's not so very large. Mayhap a new crop will be healthy and have time ter ripen before the cold sets in."

Cicely's stomach clenched. If people were starving now, in summer, winter was sure to see the death of many.

Her eyes swept over the gaunt figure of Kitty, and something tight and hard grew in her chest. She discovered her gloved fingers had curled into a fist. She thought of the others Hannah and she had visited that day. Good people suffering. It pained her to see it.

Surely there was something to be done to keep starvation at bay. She considered speaking to Captain Tyrrell about the matter, since he was now an important member of the community. Quickly she discarded the idea. He had threatened to inform the authorities on Alwyn—not the act of a man who could be trusted with the villagers' welfare.

"You *can* accept my gift," Cicely told Kitty firmly, "and you will. Else I shall be sorely offended."

Kitty ducked her head. Sun shining through the open window glimmered on the golden strands of her simply styled hair. So fair. Too fair, and too young, to bear the loss that would surely come if she did not receive proper nourishment.

"It's Tom you're a-worrying over, isn't it, Kitty?" Hannah asked.

Kitty nodded.

Hannah made a disapproving noise in her throat. "Just like a man ter be so prideful."

Cicely absently withdrew her fan from her reticule. In her agitation she needed something to occupy her hands. With a practiced flip of her wrist, she flicked open the ivory sticks covered with painted silk. "He is also a man with a breeding wife." Idly she fanned Kitty's face. "I cannot imagine that Tom would risk your welfare for the sake of his consequence. He's a good man, and you're dear to him. Tell him"—Cicely smiled—"tell him that when your babe is born, I shall make a portrait of the child."

Kitty's face lit with pleasure. "Will you? Oh, I would treasure a picture of my baby! So would Tom, I know he would."

Feeling suddenly self-conscious at Kitty's enthusiasm over her offer, Cicely cleared her throat. "Yes. Well. You must eat so that I may draw a plump, healthy baby. And Tom must eat because he is the head of the household, and his family relies upon him."

After Cicely and Hannah took their leave of Kitty, they finished the rest of their shopping, then walked back to the vicarage, where Cicely had left Octavia and the chaise. The ride back to the dower house was a quiet one. Neither woman had much to say. The hunger and misery they'd seen among their neighbors hung over them like a pall.

Food was desperately needed, Cicely thought. Since there was so little available in this area, it must be brought in from elsewhere, which meant a goodly amount of silver was needed.

And for Alwyn, there was only one way to obtain that much silver.

7

Cicely and Hannah arrived back at the dower house in time to warm the meat pasties on a shelf in the kitchen fireplace, moisten some dried fruit with brandy and water, slice some of the bread and cheese, and set the table. Just as Hannah started out the back door to look for the men, they tramped in, hanging their hats on wooden pegs on the wall.

In the heat of the summer day, they had removed their coats and waistcoats, leaving Griffin and Digby in their shirts. Although Cicely accorded Digby a smile of welcome, it was Griffin who commanded her attention. He stood so tall and broad-shouldered, his flowing white cambric shirt open at the throat, his sleeves rolled up, revealing his strong, sun-bronzed forearms dusted with raven black hair. No ring adorned his freshly scrubbed long-fingered hands.

Her sharp awareness of him unsettled her. It thrummed under her skin, along her nerves, into her bones. He walked by where she stood at the fireplace, her back to the room, and her attention followed him, though she refused to turn around. He drew out a chair at one end of the kitchen table. Cicely had reasoned it was silly to take their noon meal in the dining room, where the chairs were covered in brocade. Why, all of them would be much too busy with their tasks to wish to take the time to change out of their work clothes into fresh garments. The sturdy oak kitchen table was a more sensible choice.

When she saw that Griffin waited, holding the chair for her, she placed the platter of meat pasties with the other dishes already on the board. She accepted Griffin's thoughtful courtesy, surprised to find how much it pleased her. As he moved her chair in, the back of his hand lightly grazed the back of her upper arm. Despite the light, serviceable cloth of her sleeve, a sparkling shock rushed through her, stilling the breath in her throat.

Apparently unaware of the contact, he moved to the head of the table, which everyone had instinctively left to him. As hostess of the house, she sat at the opposite end.

Griffin said grace, and, in the silence that followed, the clatter and clink of dishes and utensils were the only sounds in the kitchen.

Determined to thrust Griffin back from her too-immediate consciousness, Cicely employed the magic her mother had taught her. She used those little phrases and small services of a good hostess that helped ease others so that there might be good company for all. Subtlety was everything in such delicate manipulation.

She had been given little opportunity to put her mother's lessons to use before today. Never had she been allowed to be a hostess. Edmund had brought no visitors home to meet her on his few brief visits, and the villagers and surrounding gentry avoided Cranwick Abbey, inventing excuses to escape invitation.

"So you have been inspecting your manor this morning, Grif—" Instantly she caught her mistake. "What have you discovered?" she asked smoothly. Slowly, one corner of his mouth curled up, and she knew he'd caught her slip.

"I have discovered you made a valiant effort to make this manor prosper," he said, "but that you did not have enough men and women to do the work needed."

Cicely stiffened. "I have done what I could do. Alasdair refuses to have strangers on his domain and has always done his best to chase them off. For the most part, he succeeded."

Griffin slowly chewed a bit of pasty and swallowed, looking thoughtful. Since the pasty was not up to the baker's wife's usual quality, Cicely doubted he was savoring the taste.

"Has Alasdair ever hurt anyone?" he asked.

Cicely frowned slightly, trying to recall anything she'd heard. She looked at Hannah, who shook her head and shrugged. "I do not recollect ever hearing such a thing," Cicely said, "aside from the old fable Mr. Joyes told us about Alasdair as a pirate hiding his treasure in the abbey."

"My mother cut her head once when Alasdair appeared in front of her," Hannah offered. "Walking up the drive she was, when he popped into the air in front of her. She swooned and struck a stone when she fell."

"Does your mother swoon whenever she sees him, Hannah?" Griffin asked.

"She does."

"Do you know how many times she's seen him?"

Hannah considered a moment. "About twelve."

"Twelve!" Digby exclaimed incredulously. Everyone

at the table turned to look at him. "I mean, 'twelve,'" he hastily amended, correcting his surprised tone of voice to one of crooning sympathy. "Poor woman."

Griffin polished off his meal with a swallow of ale. "So. Even though the ghost has never hurt anyone, the villagers refuse to work at Cranwick."

Put like that, Cicely had to admit the people of Alwyn sounded like a cowardly lot. But she knew fears of the unknown and superstitions were not a measurement of an individual's true bravery. The same man who ran from a wailing apparition might unhesitatingly risk his life to rescue a drowning friend.

From under her lashes, she studied Griffin, accepting with grudging honesty that she liked his name, that she preferred it over the more formal—though proper—mode of address. Yet now he did not seem so distant, so intimidating as he had yesterday. Her gaze moved over his beautiful face. How had he acquired the pale, thin scar that licked at his cheekbone? A war wound? She lowered her eyes, unwilling to risk staring.

He intrigued her. He was as unlike Edmund or her father as the powerful, mysterious moon was unlike the petty pebbles strewn along the road. It frightened her a little, that difference. With a small sigh, Cicely told herself none of it mattered.

Soon she would be gone.

"Did you have a pleasant trip to the village?" Griffin asked.

She looked up and met his eyes. When she saw the sincerity and genuine interest, she almost blurted out the villagers' troubles. The words trembled there, on her tongue, but she closed her lips on them. He had threatened the villagers.

She gave him the answer she thought he wanted to

hear. "Quite pleasant. Thank you for hitching Octavia to the chaise."

He regarded her for a moment, and she felt as if those argent eyes of his could see deep inside her, right down to the truth. "You're welcome," he said. His neutral tone told her that he knew she wasn't being honest with him.

That bothered her. It bothered her that he saw her as a woman who easily resorted to lying. It bothered her even more that she had given him reason for such belief.

Before she could correct her falsehood, Griffin excused himself, saying he must return to his work. There was a scraping of wooden chair legs on the flagstone floor as Griffin and Digby pushed away from the table. A second later, the back door closed behind them.

Hannah stood and started picking up dirty dishes to clear away. "That captain, he doesn't miss much, does he?"

Feeling defeated, annoyed, and frustrated, Cicely began helping Hannah collect the dishes. "No, he doesn't."

"Why didn't you just tell him folk are starving? I could see you wanted to."

It was a testimony to the sturdy construction of the pewter ale mug that the handle didn't break off when she thumped it down on the table in the small scullery. "He threatened to inform the authorities of their smuggling."

Hannah's hands wedged on her hips. "So you don't tell him they suffer?"

Cicely abruptly turned to the big basin of water. "I know," she muttered, exasperated more with herself than with Hannah's questioning. Instantly she regretted her outburst. Hannah was right. Cicely sighed. "I know."

"Well, he's been in the butcher's shop, so he'll know all's not right."

Cicely nodded. "Come, Hannah, I'll help you with the dishes first. Then I'll go find the captain and tell him the truth."

Griffin was talking with a tenant farmer he'd discovered was wise in the ways of nature, when he saw Cicely striding toward them across the fallow field. He stopped to watch her, enjoying the sight. She wore no hoops to hide her natural womanly shape. The breeze from the Channel blew her skirts around her long legs, now outlining them, now concealing them, occasionally flipping up the edge of the garment to reveal a glimpse of slim, pink-stockinged ankle. The lace lappets of her small white cap streamed back from her face.

"A fair sight she is," said the farmer, John Longley.

"Yes," Griffin agreed, not taking his gaze away from Cicely. "Very fair indeed."

"I have a daughter of her years living in Rye with her husband and three children. 'Twould be good ter see Lady Cicely as happy as my Meg."

"She was married six years," Griffin said absently, enjoying her sure grace. No affected, mincing steps for Cicely Honeysett.

John snorted. "Six years and the fellow come here not but four times. Didn't stay but a day or so at longest. 'Twas his valet kept him away, I'll warrant."

Valet? Reluctantly Griffin turned from the lovely vision of Cicely to look at John. "How could a man's valet keep him away from his wife?"

"Threw a proper fit, the valet did, last time the two was here, above a year ago. Didn't like Mr. Honeysett having anything to do with Mrs. Honeysett. And Mr.

Honeysett set great store by his valet, if you know what I mean." John lifted his eyebrows meaningfully. "A right couple were Mr. Honeysett and his valet. No one ever let on ter Lady Cicely about it, though. A married woman she may have been, but an innocent like her don't need ter know about all the wickedness in the world. Helps the rest o' us ter believe 'tis not all so corrupt."

Before Griffin could respond, Cicely arrived. She brushed the breeze-tossed lappets out of her face and smiled.

"Good day to you, John," she said. She looked at Griffin, sharing her angelic smile with him, too. "I hope I'm not interrupting?"

Griffin smiled back, knowing he should feel suspicion at her cheerfulness, but unable to feel anything but the upward rush of pleasure. "John was just sharing with me some of his valuable wisdom about the land."

"A veritable font of knowledge in such things is our John," Cicely said, her words suffused with sincerity. "I've always relied upon his advice in matters of husbandry."

John's broad, weathered face flushed a bright red. "You're very kind, Lady Cicely."

Cicely reached over and lightly touched John's arm. "You know very well 'tis true."

John's face grew an even brighter hue. Taking pity on the man's discomfort, she turned to Griffin.

"A word, if you please, Captain Tyrrell."

"As you wish."

"I'll only keep him a moment," she assured John Longley.

Despite the vivid shade of his face, John inclined his head in a dignified manner.

Cicely looked up at Griffin. "Walk with me," she said, making of the three words an invitation.

He matched his pace to hers, and, leading them in the direction of an old, elm-lined path, waited for her to speak. Until they entered the shade under the green, leafy canopy she remained silent. Whatever she had come to tell him clearly was not easy for her.

"You asked me if my trip to the village had been pleasant," she finally said.

"Yes."

"It was not pleasant. Not at all. The blight and the poor fishing have taken their toll. Many in the parish suffer, and it is yet only summer."

As they walked, he studied her. Her eyebrows were drawn slightly down as she looked at the ground. He detected tension between her slim shoulders. "You are concerned for them," he said.

Her gaze flew to his face, her eyes wide with surprise. "Of course."

"Many would not be."

"Who?" she demanded. "Who around here would not be moved by their plight?"

Griffin weighed his words before he spoke, not wishing to be too harsh, yet needing to know for his own peace of mind. "You did leave."

Her soft lips pressed tightly together, and she looked away. "I didn't know."

"You were neighbors, how could you not know?"

Now she stopped and turned to him. Overhead, leaves rustled and sighed in the summer breeze. When she spoke, her voice was low and husky with misery.

"I was selfish. I knew about the blight, even about the poor fishing, but the death of my husband distracted me. After his funeral, my only wish was to leave. I never thought to inquire after anyone's welfare."

"What would you have me do?" he asked, touched

by her anguish at having neglected the hungry of the village. Who else among the local landed gentry concerned themselves with the less fortunate? He reached across the space between them and tucked a stray wisp of chestnut hair back under the lace cap. Her eyes followed his hand, and to his surprise, she made no movement to avoid his light touch.

"Help them," she said, her voice barely audible. Her large, brandy brown eyes searched his face.

As they stood together in the cool shade of the great elms, surrounded by the soft, murmurous rustle of their summer green leaves, Griffin was struck by the innocence in her. It was a rare quality in one full grown, and he suspected it had as much to do with what was in her heart as her long isolation here. That artlessness that opened to him now was not due to childishness or dearth of wit. Rather, he thought, it came of a basic decency intrinsic to Cicely's character, a profound resistance to relinquishing . . . hope.

Rare, so piercingly, beguilingly rare that in his life Griffin had known only one other who possessed that heart-tugging innocence. His younger cousin, Jeremy Edman. Gifted, trusting Jeremy, who had joined the army over Griffin's protests, laughingly claiming that he knew Griffin would protect him from harm. And Griffin had tried. God in heaven, he had tried.

He had failed. The cost of that failure had been the life of the one person in the world Griffin had permitted himself to love.

The memory of his failure dried Griffin's mouth with old bitterness. He dropped his hand away from Cicely. "How?" he asked dully. "How can I help the villagers?"

The light of hope brightened in her eyes. "If anyone can help, 'tis you. Cranwick was spared when the blight swept through the area. You have said that the beasts you bought to start your own flocks and herds—sheep and goats, chickens and ducks—"

"—And three fine mares," he added absently, caught by the way the color heightened in her cheeks.

"—and mares—should be here any day now. Milk and eggs would help feed the starving. Share what you can from your kitchen garden. 'Tis large and bountiful." In her ardor she laid her hand upon his upper arm and leaned toward him. "The crops here were harvested and sold months ago, and nothing replanted, so there is no help in that. But there is one more thing you could do to help."

He watched her sweet, full lips move, and listened with half his attention to what they spoke. Here was a woman who took her responsibilities seriously. A woman who had earned the respect of her neighbors, gentry and villager alike. Here also was a woman who was made as females should be made, with fine skin and lustrous hair. Slim and lovely, she fired a man's imagination as to what it would be like to hold her in his arms, and remove the layers of clothing.

Ever since he'd spent the night sleeping beneath her, under the wagon, she had occupied Griffin's thoughts more than he would have liked. After all, she'd tried to bilk him. He knew that should bother him more than it did now. But since this morning he'd already discovered two things about her. One: She was a poor liar. And two: She had been abandoned here—more or less—by her husband. Reason enough to want to leave.

From the corner of his eye he saw her bosom rise and fall with her every breath. Between her stomacher, corset, and the lace handkerchief, secured by a bow, any trace of her breasts was effectively concealed, firing his imagination.

She was unscrupulous, he tried to tell himself, but he didn't really believe it anymore.

"Are you listening?" she asked.

"Yes—" He caught himself. He would not lie to her. "Well . . . no," he admitted. "My mind was wandering to other things."

Cicely's eyebrows drew down slightly in exasperation. "Just what were you thinking of that was so important?"

Griffin stepped toward her, closing the distance between them. "This," he said, tipping back her head with a fingertip beneath her chin.

He kissed her.

Taking her gently into his arms, he softly, slowly, brushed his open lips across hers. Her eyes widened at first, but when she made no move to pull away, he slanted his mouth to hers and deepened the kiss, strumming her bottom lip with the tip of his tongue.

Tentatively, like hesitant butterflies, her hands settled on his chest. Her shy acceptance encouraged him. His palm and spread fingers coursed up and down her back, feeling the dip that centered between the smooth muscles. She seemed so small, so startlingly fragile. Then she tilted her head and awkwardly touched the tip of her tongue to his.

His body ignited like a fiery rocket. He cupped her face between his hands and surged into her mouth with his tongue, sleeking over the interior walls of her cheeks, over her teeth, to rub against her tongue.

A small moan rose in her throat, and her hands moved restlessly on his chest.

His blood pounding through his veins, his body hard with desire, Griffin found coherent thought almost impossible. Only steel-strong discipline forged through years of danger and hardship allowed him to release Cicely when what he wanted to do—*needed* to do—was back her against a tree, pull up her skirts, and take her right there.

He stepped back. Dragging in air through his nostrils, he fought to regain his composure. *Christ.* No woman had ever driven him so hard, so quickly, with so simple a response.

Even now, as the thunder of his heartbeat gradually slowed, he wanted her. Time and some distance, he thought. That's what he needed to regain his balance.

She lifted her fingertips to her lips as she stared up into his face. Slowly the color drained from her lovely face—a sight that rammed into Griffin's gut with the force of a bayonet. He had done this to her.

He reached out to touch her cheek, then thought better of it, curling his fingers into a loose fist that he dropped to his side. "Cicely?"

Her hands fluttered around her hair, patting it and poking it under the edges of her cap, but succeeding more in pulling tendrils loose than putting them in order. "I'm quite all right, Captain. Quite all right. 'Tis-'tis not as if I'm some y-young unmarried miss—" She broke off, her lips trembling, her eyes filled with distress.

Guilt and regret twisted in Griffin's stomach. He wanted to reassure her, comfort her, but to apologize now might sound as though he regretted the kiss, and he would not on any account have her believe that. "I will dine with you this evening and we'll discuss how to help the people of Alwyn through their troubles," he said, his voice low and soft, the only comfort he felt she would accept from him. "Until tonight, then?"

Pressing her lips firmly together to still their trembling, she gave him two jerking nods, then turned on her heel and strode off. He watched her walk away, a slim, solitary figure surrounded on either side by towering elms. Then, as he watched, she began to run.

Cicely ran until she reached the woods between the abbey and the dower house. There she crept into her secret place—an alcove formed by the trunks of several close-growing poplar trees. She pressed her forehead to her knees and let flow the tears that she'd tried so hard to hide from Griffin.

Why hadn't she had these feelings—these heart-racing, soaring, confusing feelings—with Edmund? Why hadn't his few kisses thrilled her and sent that hot achy tingling through her body like Griffin's kiss had?

Wasted. Six years she had wasted here. Had she repulsed Edmund so in her single bumbling attempt to beget a child that he had withheld this experience from her? And now, after being imprisoned here for so long, now that her freedom was close at hand, a man came along who made her feel like . . . feel like . . . well, like nothing she'd ever felt before.

Cicely lifted her head and touched her tear-wet lips with her fingertips. They felt slightly swollen. She remembered how her heart had raced, how the ground had seemed to spin away from her feet. Griffin had touched her tongue with his. Was he supposed to do that? No one had ever said. Her mother had refused to discuss relations between men and women, and her sisters had been too young to know. Closing her eyes, she thought again of how being held in Griffin's arms had made her feel, of how his lips and tongue had made her feel. She decided that whether or not he was supposed to do that, she liked it.

With the heels of her hands, she wiped the wet of her tears away. What a ninnyhammer he must think her, babbling on as she had about not being an unmarried miss. Her cheeks burned with embarrassment. He was a man of the world. Why, he'd probably kissed hundreds of women. Thousands, maybe. She doubted any of the others had ever made such a dunce of herself. With a heavy sigh, Cicely climbed to her feet. Well, she thought, as she brushed bits of humus from her skirts and apron, she was new to this kissing business. Perhaps with Griffin's help, she would learn more about it.

And she would carry with her more worldly experience when she left Cranwick the second time.

8

For the rest of the day, Griffin found it difficult to concentrate on his work. After he left John Longley, he visited two other tenant farmers, walking over the fields with them, listening to them detail how they worked the land or left it fallow. How they grazed their sheep or cultivated their hops or wheat, how they brought water to this field or drained that one. He came with his head filled with the latest discoveries in animal husbandry, obtained through journals and correspondence, and he was ready to advise his tenants if he saw room for improvement. But he also came to learn. Once that was established, he found the farmers willing to share their experiences.

As he worked, thoughts of Cicely haunted him. Her nurturing nature pleased him. Even he had benefited from her soft heart last night, when she'd gone to retrieve his clothing. She was sensible of her responsibilities as lady of Cranwick and strove to fulfill them.

Again and again, through the afternoon, Griffin was

forced to thrust away the memory of Cicely's soft, feminine curves, all too aware of his body's rampant reaction to her. Releasing Cicely had taken all his willpower. No woman had ever excited him like that.

When he had bought Cranwick, he'd had it in mind to take a wife. After all, he was a man with roots now. A man with roots, no matter how new they were, needed a helpmate, a woman to share the good times and the bad. A woman to have his children. The thought of sharing the master's bed with Cicely sent a molten fever burning through him. Yes, Lady Cicely might make him an excellent wife.

As he rode away from the last farm he'd visited, twilight had fallen, bringing with it lusher colors and softer air—and Alasdair.

A whirlwind of cold breeze spun toward him, spinning leaves and dust up into a funnel shape. Apollo nervously sidestepped the thing, which emitted a loud howl that sounded like nothing so much as a man in a temper.

Working to keep Apollo under control, Griffin snapped, "What are you doing here, Alasdair?"

Keeping his distance from the stallion, the spirit materialized, hovering at eye level with Griffin. "Ye sent yer damnable possessions to *my* house, *Sasannach*, without so much as a by-yer-leave."

Griffin regarded Alasdair evenly. "I have a valid deed that would dispute ownership with you, ghost, but 'tis pointless to argue the matter since you seem cursed to walk this particular patch of earth for the time being."

Alasdair's eyes narrowed. "And just what is *that* supposed to mean, ye coxcomb? A fiddlin' piece o' parchment is naught compared to almost two centuries of residence."

"It means that your time here is limited. Now, where are the wagons?"

Blond eyebrows lifted. "Och, so it's lord o' the manor are ye? Well, the wagons have come and gone, and all ye own is now locked in my house. Get it if ye can!"

Griffin nudged his bootheels into Apollo's sides and directed the horse toward the manor house.

Alasdair followed him, floating beside him, leaving some distance between him and the horse. "Ye kissed her!" he bellowed. "Ye put yer great hairy paws on that sweet lassie and kissed her!"

And he longed to do it again, Griffin thought. "She's a woman, Alasdair, and a beautiful one at that."

The ghost scowled at Griffin. "Aye, she's a woman right enough, and bonnier than most—"

"Then we agree."

Alasdair glared fiercely at Griffin. Abruptly he vanished.

Judging he had plenty of time before he need present himself for his dinner with Cicely, Griffin rode leisurely to the abbey, then placed Apollo in the stables with a manger of fresh hay. That done, Griffin walked to the house and lifted the latch to the kitchen door.

The unlocked door remained fixed in place.

"Alasdair, open the door," he said quietly to the air around him.

Silence answered him.

"Alasdair, do not push me," Griffin warned. "I would rather allow Lady Cicely to find a decent way to send you to your rest, but if you persist in keeping me from my house, I promise you, I will ride to Chichester and bring back the bishop himself *to exorcise you.*" He waited a minute for a response, the kitchen courtyard silent but for the occasional twittering from a sparrow.

The door slowly swung open.

Secretly elated with the success of his bluff, Griffin strode into the vast kitchen. He didn't really believe an exorcism would work. But then, he didn't really believe in ghosts. At least, he hadn't until he'd entered the west wing of Cranwick Abbey.

Despite the evidence, he still found himself denying the existence of phantasms—except Alasdair. That vaporous scoundrel was proving damnably difficult to ignore. Still, Griffin had no intention of getting the church involved. They had supported his enemy without even considering Griffin's claim, bought off with a substantial donation to the bishop's pet building project. No, Griffin would hire a warty witch to spell Alasdair away before he'd bring in one of them. First, however, he would let Cicely try to find a way to bring her friend to peace.

For the moment, he had gotten the better of the ghost. He'd enjoy his triumph while it lasted. With that thought in mind, Griffin made his way to the room he'd chosen as his own. The master's room. With an ear-splitting, echoing creak that he recognized as one of Alasdair's effects, the door to the chamber opened when he lifted the latch. A cold wind swirled in after him.

Stacked neatly at the end of the bed were his two trunks.

"Where is Digby's trunk, Alasdair?" he asked, knowing full well the ghost was present.

The spirit of the Scotsman materialized, leaning against a heavily carved post of the damask-draped tester bed. "In the stable," he said sullenly.

"It doesn't go in the stable."

"Ye may stuff it up yer arse for all I care."

Griffin studied Alasdair for a moment. The clothes

were the same he'd worn the day of Cicely's return. The white shirt. The length of woolen plaid made into a kilt. The soft leather buskins. Perhaps he couldn't change his garments. Perhaps his attire, like his soul, had been condemned to roam the earth. Griffin made a rude noise in his throat. His fancies were getting the better of him. He had more important matters to think on.

"Brave talk considering you could easily become nothing more than a memory—a very old, very tedious memory. Is exorcism painful, do you think?"

Alasdair's jaw snapped shut as he glared at Griffin and winked out of view.

Griffin grinned as he set about unpacking. Maybe he should move back to the abbey. As if sensing the direction of his thoughts, Alasdair sent a curl of cool air wafting across the back of Griffin's neck. Very well. The ghost had made his point. He would not give up without a fight. Not that Griffin had ever thought he would. Still, it was nice to know Alasdair's weak points. There were two that Griffin had seen. Cicely and exorcism.

Now, where was Digby? There was much to be done. As Griffin headed out the door of the bedchamber, he nearly collided with his servant, who ran full tilt into the room.

Digby thumped his hat to his chest, breathing hard with surprise. "'Struth, Cap'n, you near startled me to death! For a minute there I thought you was the ghost. Like as not I've lost ten years of growth."

"I was just going to look for you."

"I was feeding the horses and saw you enter the house. Feared for you, I did. Thought you might need some help." Color flooded his still-pale face. "I don't always run, you see." He bent to pick up the pitchfork he'd dropped.

"Any man would run from a giant death's-head, Digby." Griffin clapped the shorter man on the shoulder as he led the way out of the chamber, heading toward the small room behind the hearth where Cicely kept the tub.

"*You* don't."

Griffin laughed as he picked up his kit. "I did the first time. Thought my end had come. Now, my good fellow, I need a bath and a shave. I'm going to dine with the widow Honeysett and discuss the plight of the villagers."

A spark of interest lighted Digby's brown eyes. "A right pretty lady is the widow. Any man would want to discuss the plight of the villagers with her."

"Any man is not invited." The thought of another man calling on Cicely nettled Griffin. "My bathwater, if you please, Digby. I would not keep Lady Cicely waiting."

Digby left the kitchen grumbling and several minutes later was still grumbling as he reentered, carrying a pail of water from the well. "In my opinion, you take altogether too many baths. 'Tain't good for you. 'Tain't good for you at all." He poured the water into a large, blackened kettle and hung it on the equally blackened iron hook in the kitchen fireplace. He lighted the fire, then went back outside, empty pail in hand. "Bathing so much will sicken you, take my word on it," he said over his shoulder before Griffin swung the door closed.

With a smile, he shook his head and proceeded to sharpen his razor on the strop he carried in his kit.

"I could easily move that verra sharp razor across yer throat," Alasdair said. He floated a few inches above the seat of a wooden chair next to Griffin.

Startled by the ghost's sudden appearance, Griffin almost cut his hand. Only years of discipline kept his face schooled to cool neutrality. "Oh? Are you a murderer?"

"Nay. I've never killed a man that dinna need killin'. 'Twas no murder, though."

Griffin examined the fine edge of his blade. "If you've killed, but it was not murder, were you an executioner?"

Alasdair regarded Griffin with ghostly pale eyes. "Executioner is it? Aye, some might say that. But at the time I thought 'twas done for honor."

Griffin slowly lowered his razor to the worktable before him. "You were a soldier."

"Aye."

"I've killed for honor," Griffin said in a low voice.

Alasdair nodded. "Only it doesna feel so honorable when ye sink yer sword into the heart of a lad who's only left his mother's knee."

"Yes." His sword had cleaved the breasts of too many such lads. Yet he had failed to save the one boy who had looked to him for protection. Jeremy . . .

"I murdered in the name of Queen Mary. Ye murdered in the name of King George. Honor leaves a long, bloody trail."

Griffin stared at the deadly blade in his hand. Honor. There were times when he wondered if he had any left.

The door banged open and Digby stamped in lugging a sloshing pail. Muttering to himself, he poured the water into the kettle. Griffin looked to where Alasdair had been floating an instant earlier. The ghost was gone.

All through his bath, and through the close, even shave Digby gave him, Griffin wondered about Alasdair. Who was he? What crime had he committed that was so foul it kept his soul tethered between heaven and hell?

When Digby held up the small looking glass for Griffin's approval of the shave, Griffin firmly set aside thoughts of the ghost. Tonight there would be no thoughts of death. There was room only for the prospect of life.

He had survived twelve years of persecution, most of them in a succession of desperate battles. He'd come so close to death he'd heard its seductive call. Now, at last, he had freedom, he had peace, he had a home to call his own, though that claim might temporarily be disputed by the former occupant.

It was time to take a wife.

After looking deep into Cicely's wide, brandy brown eyes this afternoon, after holding her in his arms and kissing her ripe, responsive lips, he knew a likely candidate.

She was no crafty swindler. She had made no attempt to escape when he'd caught up with her in Portsmouth. She'd given her word to return with him—and abided by it. Now, after hearing what John Longley had said of her husband, Griffin could understand why she'd been so eager to be free of Cranwick Abbey that she'd failed to mention to the agent that a ghost haunted the manor. How well he understood that blinding, panicky need to be free of entrapment.

She'd been alone for almost six years, save the company of a Scottish ghost. Unloved, untouched by her husband, without even the benefit of children. Griffin shook his head as he climbed the staircase, on his way to his chamber. How could any man wish to leave Cicely for even a night?

As he gazed into the wall mirror in his room, his fingers manipulating his white lawn neckcloth, he recalled the single, crystal tear he had seen slip down her cheek the night they spent under the stars. His hands paused. How could the tear have been for her husband? That bastard deserved to be reviled, not mourned. But he could not reach her now. So, for the first time since she had grown to womanhood, she had taken flight, soaring toward the warm land of France, away from her prison.

Until Griffin had clipped her wings and dragged her back.

His hands hesitated in their task. Regret clenched in his gut. He had returned her to her gaol. God, he knew that choking hopeless feeling. It clawed at your insides. It drove you to cry out in the lonely night. His gaol had possessed no manor's boundaries, no ancient walls or slate-tiled roof. His gaol had been the disbelief of others and his enemy's wealth and power.

In the mirror, Griffin regarded himself with brutal honesty. What could he offer Cicely Honeysett that she might want? Well . . . he wasn't too bad to look at, if you discounted scars. He limped, but he did have a strong back and a quick wit. He could offer a comfortable house with which she was familiar, and acres of rich land. And children. He would do his best to see that she had all the children she might want.

The prospect of making those children with Cicely sent a surge of desire burning through him. As he remembered her sweet response in his arms, he mistied his neckcloth. Children. Sons and daughters with brandy brown eyes.

Feeling lighter of mood, Griffin cheerfully hummed a fragment of tune from an old Handel oratorio as he loosened his error and rearranged it correctly.

An icy wind swept through his room, stirring the draperies on the bed. Alasdair had come to call.

He stood next to Griffin, scowling. "Ye're goin' to her."

Griffin shrugged into his coat, strode across the

room, and picked up his black felt three-cornered hat from the seat of a chair. "That I am."

Alasdair followed him. "Ye've no respect for the lass!"

"I've great respect for Lady Cicely."

"Here ye are, all dressed up and struttin' about like a prize cock," Alasdair blustered. He fixed a sharp look on Griffin. "Ye're lustin' after her, ye are, and don't deny it."

Settling his hat in place, Griffin gave its crown a pat for good measure. He grinned at the nearly apoplectic Alasdair, refusing to let anyone spoil his good mood. "Yes, I am. Any man worth his salt would find Lady Cicely desirable. She's a beautiful woman with a kind nature any man would admire. And now I must wish you a pleasant evening, sir, for I really must be going. No gentleman keeps a lady waiting." He walked out the door of his chamber and down the hall as the temperature in the house plummeted. Alasdair howled through the air, whirling above Griffin's head in a wide circle. Griffin continued on his way, unable to keep the grin from his lips.

Cicely paced the parlor floor, the train of her yellow taffeta sack gown a weight behind her. Hysterical butterflies battered the inside of her stomach. Her fingers gripped her closed fan dangerously tightly. As the edge of the mother-of-pearl sticks bit into her skin, she absently eased her hold.

She jumped when a light knock sounded at the door. "Come." It couldn't be Griffin yet. Or could it?

The door opened and Digby, attired in a somber dark suit, entered bearing a lighted branched candlestick. "He likely left the big house shortly after I did," he said, setting down his candlestick on a side table and picking up the one with the low-burning tapers. "I thank you again for making me welcome in your house, m'lady. You won't regret your generosity."

"Captain Tyrrell has every faith in your discretion, Digby, and I'm certain his faith is well placed."

A smile lit Digby's face. "The captain don't place his faith lightly, that's a fact. Now don't you go fretting over this evening. Your Hannah has prepared a meal fit for the king."

"Fretting? I'm not fretting." At Digby's knowing look, she flushed. "Well, maybe just a little. Captain Tyrrell and I did not meet under ideal conditions, you see, and I would like to amend those first impressions."

Digby nodded sagely. "First impressions are important. 'Tis easy to come away filled with wrong ideas."

Cicely pounced on the opportunity to direct the conversation away from her. "Exactly. Since we shall all be together here until I'm able to find a way to place Alasdair's spirit at rest, it's important that we maintain amiable relations."

"Truer words couldn't be spoken, m'lady." He stood there a moment, with an expectant air about him, but she couldn't think what he expected. Finally he said, "Will there be anything else, m'lady?"

"Not at this moment, Digby. Don't let me detain you from your duties."

With a dignified inclination of his head, Digby silently withdrew from the room. Cicely stared at the closed door for a few seconds, then returned to her pacing, now in a more brightly lighted room. She stopped and frowned. This evening promised to be awkward at best, as she sat across from Griffin, trying not to think of their kiss. Trying not to recall all those exciting sensations he had aroused in her. The way his lips had felt against hers . . .

She stared unseeing out the night-dark window, remembering. He had touched her as no man ever had before. Oh, Edmund had kissed her, of course, but she tried not to think of that experience. Then there had been that awful night when, determined to get a baby from him, Cicely had squeezed her eyes shut and darted her face toward his, lips puckered, praying passion would ignite and nature would take its course.

She'd taken him unawares and nearly broken his nose with her chin. All her effort had gotten her was banishment to her bedchamber while Edmund's valet tenderly plied him with cool wet cloths and soothing words. Given the opportunity, she would have applied the cloths and murmured the words, but, as usual, he had not wanted her near. It was difficult to be a dutiful wife when your husband could not bear your touch.

Griffin bore her touch very well, she thought, applying her fan to cool the warmth that memory brought to her face.

The door to the parlor opened, and Griffin Tyrrell entered.

Tonight he wore a coat of black velvet, lined with oyster gray satin. His grosgrain waistcoat was of the same gray hue, embroidered with black silk. Snug, black breeches hugged muscular thighs and oyster gray stockings covered well-developed calves—calves she had seen bare. Quickly she lowered her eyes, noticing absently that he wore black, polished shoes with gleaming silver buckles instead of his usual boots. Lifting her gaze, she saw that his ink black hair caught the glow of candlelight. As he turned his head to glance out the dark window, she caught a glimpse of his unfashionably long queue, which hung down between his shoulders, secured by a black ribbon.

He approached her, and to her consternation, she found his limp more pronounced this evening.

"You have hurt yourself," she said, frowning with concern. "Pray sit down, Captain Tyrrell."

Color tinged his high cheekbones. "'Tis only an old wound." He made no move to take a seat.

"Which you have aggravated with all your labors these past two days," she scolded lightly, boldly taking his hand and drawing him to a chair. "Now do sit down. I'll not hear otherwise."

He scowled. "I'm quite well, thank you."

And goats can fly, she thought. This man was in pain but too stubborn to admit it. "As you wish," she said airily, as if it mattered not one whit to her. "May I offer you some porter or claret?"

"Porter, if you please."

As she stood at the cabinet and poured out a glass of the heavy, dark beer, she felt his gaze on her. It flustered her, making her glad she'd taken special pains with her hair. Hannah had arranged it in a chignon high on the head, with a ringlet above each ear. A lunette-shaped comb, ornamented with pink flowers, had been placed in her hair just behind her temple. She'd tied a black velvet ribbon around her throat, with a bow in back. Now the exposed back of her neck felt warm. She turned and moved across the room to him, the soft rustle of her taffeta skirts the only sound in the room.

He accepted the glass from her with a murmur of thanks. As he took a drink, she continued to study him. Even the dark color of his well-fitted coat could not diminish the broadness of his shoulders. He was tall and long-limbed and impossibly beauti-

ful. The fine scar that curved from temple hairline
to elegant cheekbone did nothing to detract from his
looks.

Cicely snapped open her fan, a sharp reminder to her
overactive imagination that this man had no place in
her future. She refused to sigh over him like some
moonstruck miss. "You have had a chance to speak
with the tenants now, and you've seen the land. What
do you think of Cranwick, sir? Is it all you'd hoped
for?"

He smiled. "Aside from Alasdair, I'm pleased with
the manor. The tenants are earnest, hardworking folk,
and the soil is rich. I couldn't ask for more."

Something twisted in the region of her heart. Here
she had known loneliness that no man or woman
should have to endure. Here she had known humiliation and abandonment. He might not ask for more, but
she did. She asked for her freedom. She yearned to see
what lay beyond the boundaries of this manor, this
parish, this shore. The captain had already seen more of
the world than most. He would never understand her
need.

After a few light taps, Digby opened the door. "Dinner is ready to be served at your convenience," he
announced.

"Thank you, Digby, we'll eat now," Cicely said,
relieved to have some action open to her.

Digby withdrew, and Griffin offered Cicely his hand.
Reluctantly, she placed her palm on the back of it, and
they walked together down the corridor to the dining
room.

The table had been covered with a white damask
cloth, then laid with polished silver, sparkling cut glass,
and delicate imported china. On the blue-painted wall,
the candles in the girandoles had been lighted. The hon-

eyed scent of beeswax wafted through the high-ceilinged room.

Griffin pulled out Cicely's chair for her, and as she swept her voluminous skirts out to her sides and accepted the seat he offered, it seemed as if his presence enfolded her. She could hear him breathing behind her. His warmth caressed her, carrying with it the clean, crisp pine balsam scent of the soap he'd used. Then he moved away to take his own chair.

Their places, she noted, had not been arranged at each end of the table, but rather on each side, across from each other, where the distance was least. She must remember to show Digby the correct way to set a table. Suddenly it occurred to her that Griffin might think *she* had placed their settings so close together. Glancing up at him through her lashes, she tried to gauge his reaction, but his features revealed nothing of his thoughts.

Digby poured the wine, brought out the first course which Hannah had prepared, then retreated back to the kitchen. Griffin took a sip of his Spanish Green Pottage.

He smiled. "This has an excellent flavor, Lady Cicely."

Intrigued by the rare beauty of his smile, she found herself answering it. "You're too kind, sir. 'Tis a receipt given me by my mother."

"Ah. A family secret handed down through generations." His silvery eyes lit with an inviting mischief.

She felt compelled to join him in the fun. "Oh, quite. Two very long generations. Likely she smuggled it out of an alehouse in exotic London."

Griffin laughed. "Exotic London! Does she think that?"

Cold, gray memories seeped through Cicely's carefully constructed inner shields. There had been a lesson to be learned from the way her parents lived, and she had learned it well, long before its inevitable end.

"She reveled in London. She loved everything about it. The colors, the sounds, the excitement. All of it thrilled her."

"You speak as if your mother is no longer living."

"She isn't." And that was the end to it. The captain was here to discuss what could be done for the villagers, not her family.

"I'm sorry," he said softly.

"It was years ago." Wasted years.

After that, conversation grew more stilted. Long silences accompanied the removes. Cicely kept waiting for Griffin to introduce the subject that was the purpose of this dinner, but he continued to keep what conversation there was impersonal.

Finally, after a simple dessert of sliced fruit taken from Cranwick's orchards, Griffin complimented her on the meal, rose stiffly from his chair, and walked over to a small table which bore the few liquors and some of the wines Cicely had been able to find in the abbey. "I hope you will excuse my making myself at home," he said with only a trace of dryness. "Would you care for a glass of sack?"

She watched him move. His limp was still pronounced, though he was trying to disguise it. "This is your home after all, Captain," she pointed out. "Digby will bring tea to the parlor, so I shall have that, thank you."

One corner of his mouth lifted as he poured himself a whiskey. "Hannah is in the kitchen cooking. Digby is serving. One might almost believe they were servants."

Cicely couldn't help smiling. "I doubt that will ever happen."

He came around the table and helped Cicely with her chair. "Perhaps we should not keep Digby waiting on us." He offered her his free hand, and, as she took it, she noticed the white brackets of pain around the tense line of his lips.

Casually, she opened her fan. The stubborn man seemed to do nothing for the improvement of his leg. Seemed, in fact, determined to ignore the whole thing. Well, she had seen the pink scar ridges of his wound. She had seen him bend his knee, which had been largely untouched by the scar.

She slowly moved her fan. "Will you please excuse me a moment, Captain? I'll join you in the parlor." At the courtly inclination of his head, she swept away, through the house to the stillroom. Quickly inspecting the labels on the smaller stone jars, she located the one she wanted, then snatched up a clean towel. Her skirts rustled in the dimly lighted quiet of the halls that led back to the parlor. Outside the towering, white-paneled door she paused to draw in a deep, fortifying breath, then twisted the doorknob and breezed in. Griffin turned to smile at her as she entered and carefully closed the doors behind her.

He eyed the towel and the stone jar she held with curiosity. "What have we here?"

He will not like this one bit, Cicely thought. She summoned up a bright smile. "Please be seated, Captain. In this chair here, I think," she said, directing him to an unupholstered wooden chair.

He looked at her as if she'd gone quite odd, but did as she asked, clearly trying not to favor his right leg as he eased down. The white lines around his mouth deepened. "Very well. Now what?"

Cicely set her jar on a side table and pried off the wax cap. "Now," she said briskly, "please roll down your right stocking and pull up the right leg of your breeches."

9

His eyes widened. "What?"

Cicely hesitated under that woodsmoke stare, then made up her mind. She was not going to be a timid mouse anymore. She'd been obedient and dutiful, and just look where it had gotten her. Well, as of this moment, she was a woman of action. Yes, a woman of action, and the first action she'd take was to do something about this stubborn man's leg.

Setting her jaw, she picked up the stone jar and towel, arranged her skirts, and knelt in front of Griffin.

"What do you think you're doing?" he growled, trying to get to his feet. "Stand up. Or sit down, if you will, but for God's sake, do it in a chair."

With a tug on his coat, Cicely succeeded in unbalancing him. He sat down hard with a thump and a strangled groan.

Instantly she felt contrite, but reminded herself women of action did not shirk unpleasant tasks. "I'm sorry, but I did ask you to sit down." She unfastened the knee buttons on the right leg of his breeches, and began rolling the cloth up his thigh.

"I believe you're opening the wrong part of my breeches," he ground out, his fingers gripping the seat of his chair. "You need only have asked, Cicely. I would have been more than happy to oblige you."

Ignoring his sarcasm, she finished with his breeches, raising the fabric above the tight-drawn, pink scar that she knew extended down the inside of his leg, from mid-thigh to mid-calf. She shoved his neat gray stockings out of the way, revealing the rest of it.

"How did you come by this?" she asked as she reached for the jar and poured a dollop of yellow, aromatic oil into her palm.

Griffin glared at her and tried to stand up without knocking her over. Taking advantage of his awkward position, she planted her free palm against his hard stomach and pushed. He went down like a stone.

"Bloody hell!" he sputtered. "Get out of my way."

"No," she said, feeling a lot less composed than she sounded. "Left to your own devices you'd dawdle about until this muscle tightens up beyond hope."

He opened his mouth to retort, but she interrupted. "Oh, I've seen you, trying to pretend nothing was amiss. I've also seen that when you've been riding Apollo all day, or working in fields for hour upon hour, when you're tired, your limp becomes more noticeable. If you don't take care of this leg now, you'll end with a permanent limp."

He regarded first her, then the lotion she cupped in her palm, through narrowed eyes. "A bayonet."

"Pardon?"

"You asked me how it happened. A bayonet. In Cuba. Some months ago." A muscle in his jaw jumped. "The surgeon told me I'd always walk badly."

She met his gaze levelly. "The surgeon was a horse's posterior. Now, do I apply this oil on the chance that—with work—your leg might mend more nearly normal? Or do you enjoy your disability?"

Anger flared in his eyes. His mouth tightened to a hard line.

Satisfied she had won, at least for the moment, Cicely smoothed the golden oil over the long ridges of scar. Beneath her fingers she felt hard, tight sinew. Slowly, gently at first, she began to massage his leg.

It was more than a little intimidating, being so close to Griffin. His size far outstripped hers. Why, his very knee was as big as both of hers together. But it was an exceptionally nice knee, she reflected. Muscular and flush with the rest of his leg. Not knobby like many men's. She kept her gaze locked to the area she worked, unwilling to meet his eyes. Many would consider what she was doing quite improper.

The fragrant oil warmed beneath her hands. She felt the roughness of hair as it was drawn under the silken influence of the balm. Gradually she applied more pressure.

Finally Griffin broke the long, strained silence. "Smells like olive oil," he observed, grunting a little as she pressed her thumbs deeper into his flesh.

"It is. Olive oil infused with marjoram."

"What does the marjoram do?"

"It's for relief of pain. I've found it especially effective for sore joints."

"'Tis not my joint that's sore."

She looked up from her work. "No, but—" Her words died in her throat when she saw the swelling in the front of his breeches.

Cicely couldn't help staring. She recognized this sign of a man's arousal, having observed Edmund in such a state once or twice. It had been when his valet was applying rouge and lip color to her husband. Thus she had assumed that the cheeks and lips of a man must be especially sensitive, if even the touch of a valet could induce such a response. But, merciful heavens, the bump in Edmund's breeches could not begin to compare to the massive swelling in Griffin's!

"You are stroking my bare skin," Griffin explained, his voice gruffly gentle. "A natural reaction. Don't be frightened."

She tore her gaze away from Griffin's monument to manhood and met his eyes. "I'm not afraid. Only . . . surprised."

"Surprised?"

"I feared I was causing you pain, but 'tis unavoidable. Does pain . . . arouse you?"

He frowned. "No, of course not. But your hands on my naked thigh, touching me, caressing me—" He broke off and his jaw tightened. "The pain is not great enough to obliterate the feel of your hands on me. In God's name, woman, you are on your knees before me, touching me as a wife might touch her husband."

Warmth tinged Cicely's cheeks, as confusion and curiosity flooded through her. And something else. Something new and unfamiliar to her. The feeling of power.

She had evoked this strong response in this man. She, a woman who could not even entice her husband to her bedchamber, much less her bed, had excited a manly response from tall, strong, beautiful Griffin Tyrrell.

As a wife might touch her husband. But he was not her husband. Embarrassed, she dropped her gaze and withdrew her hands from him. "I wished only to help. Will Allcorn was not my husband, yet I massaged his leg every night for weeks after he was cut by a scythe."

"Will Allcorn?" She heard the displeasure in his voice. "Who is Will Allcorn?"

She refused to look at him, sick with shame that she had behaved so brazenly with Griffin. She had expected resistance, but not like this. Rather she had thought he would refuse and protest that her help was not necessary—not that her help aroused him, pointing out that she touched him too intimately. Quickly she began wiping her hands on the towel. "You should wrap your leg to keep it warm for the rest of the night," she mumbled.

"Who is Will Allcorn?" he repeated.

"A man from the village. He was the only one who put up with Alasdair to help me."

"Why did he help you?"

The true meaning of his sharply spoken question was all too clear. It stung her. She snapped her narrowed gaze up to meet his. "He was not my lover, sir," she said, matching her tone to Griffin's. "He is a kind, brave soul who did not like seeing me struggle to work this estate by myself."

Griffin regarded her for a moment, then nodded. "Where is this fellow now?"

Annoyed that he had not bothered to apologize for his unpleasant question, Cicely stood. "He went down the coast to Cinderlea, where his cousin has a smithy."

"What? You mean this strapping young man so casually uprooted his wife?" he asked blandly.

Cicely frowned. "Will Allcorn? He's not—" She stopped. Griffin seemed a bit more interested in Will than was warranted. Of course, it was ludicrous to imagine Griffin could be jealous. More likely he wanted to see if it might be worth his while to offer Will a job. Yes, she supposed, that was it. Griffin needed strong, healthy men to work the manor. Mayhap he thought he could use the homesickness of a wife to entice Will back.

"Will's Margaret died six years ago. He's not young, but he is strong enough to help you a great deal, and a more dependable man you'll never meet. He has a kind heart."

Griffin smiled, and once again Cicely was struck with his dark-and-crystal-light masculine beauty. Rather than superfine or leather, she thought it more fitting that he be suited in armor of silver and mounted on a fire-breathing steed of gleaming black. A magical warrior from a misty time before the rise of mortals.

And he had kissed her. There beneath the spreading elms, he had kissed her, and magic had glimmered in his touch. Were she honest with herself, she must admit that she wanted that experience again.

"Although I'm not a rich man," Griffin said, "I can employ men and women from Alwyn, and I will pay a fair wage. I need help for the manor, and for the manor house and here. It was never my intention that you should cook and wash. Perhaps I can send to buy hens and wheat more reasonably than the folk of Alwyn may find around here. Famine drives up food prices." He removed his shoe and peeled down his stocking the rest of the way. With the towel, he wiped the oil off his leg.

Cicely remembered the years she had struggled by with only Will's help, and once in a while the assistance of Nan Boulden. Alasdair had harassed them occasionally, but that had been enough to keep everyone else away. When she'd asked Alasdair why he'd never pestered the tenants, he'd drawn back, horrified. "They put silver in my pocket!" he'd exclaimed. She'd refrained from pointing out that it had been nearly two centuries since tenants had paid their rents to him. She already discovered that sometimes Alasdair's interpretations of events seemed to come from another plane.

"I should be surprised if your plan succeeded," she told Griffin. "The village folk are afraid to set foot on the manor."

"Alasdair has not injured anyone." He straightened in his seat. "You said so yourself."

"That's true, but it matters not what I know, rather what the villagers believe. And they believe Alasdair is a demon. They fear him."

Griffin shrugged one shoulder. "Perhaps hunger will cure their fear. I can offer honest work for fair wages. More than that I cannot do. The king is not so generous with his captains that they may return to England and live like lords."

Cicely sighed. It was a widely known fact that an army captain's pay was not overgenerous. Judging from the few trunks that had been delivered to the abbey, Griffin would continue to live as simply as he did now. All things considered, his offer was magnanimous. Many would have offered employment at low wages in such circumstances, profiting from the desperation of others.

He levered himself out of the chair, the pain brackets back around his mouth.

"You must keep that leg wrapped and warm tonight," she instructed him, not taking offense at his ignoring her outstretched hand. His uncooperative limb must grate on his pride. "I saw that you had the trunks delivered to the manor house and that you changed clothes there. Does this mean that you have come to an understanding with Alasdair and will be moving into the abbey?" Alasdair's tolerance of the captain after all the antagonism puzzled her.

A smile flickered across Griffin's lips. "You could say we have arrived at an understanding of sorts. But I'll not be moving there until he is gone. I don't fancy trying to sleep in a freezing room—or worse."

"He may come here," she pointed out, studying the stone jar in an attempt not to stare at his breathtakingly beautiful face. She wanted him to kiss her again.

"But he hasn't. A matter of courtesy to you, I suppose. But since he takes exception to my being here, he may pay me a call." He handed her the towel and she took it, restraining her desire to brush his fingers with hers.

"I can't conceive why he hasn't called on you yet," she said as she turned away.

"One of the mysteries that remains to be solved."

He followed her out of the parlor and to the quiet, deserted kitchen, where embers glowed in the fireplace. The hour was late and Digby and Hannah would have retired by now.

Cicely replaced the cap on the jar, pressing the softened wax to re-form the seal, then deposited the towel in the scullery. She selected a length of new muslin intended for making more towels.

"Now what torture do you plan?" Griffin asked, eyeing the fabric in her hands.

She smiled. "This is for you to wrap around your injury so that the heat may work while you sleep tonight. Tomorrow we shall repeat the massage. I know it hurts now, but, God willing, you will eventually gain better use of your leg."

From their candles a soft amber halo enveloped them, staving off the surrounding darkness. The only sound in the kitchen was the occasional pop from the burned wood in the fireplace.

The two of them regarded each other. Anticipation curled inside Cicely, making it difficult to breathe.

"Do you like children, Cicely?" he asked softly.

"Children?" His question was far from what she had expected in that moment. Her cheeks burned as she recalled how difficult it had been to lure Edmund to her bed, but she had yearned for a babe. Oh, how she had wanted a little one to fill the empty place in her heart. On the one occasion she'd succeeded in coaxing her husband to her, the procedure had been embarrassing, painful, but blessedly brief. Edmund had seemed as unsettled by the whole business as she. And there had been no baby. Cicely swallowed against the tightness in her throat. Her fault. Somehow she had done something wrong, but she could not fathom what. "I like children very much," she said, her voice a hoarse whisper.

Griffin nodded. "Come," he said, gently placing her right palm atop the back of his left hand and leading her from the kitchen. "I've kept you from your sleep overlong."

Together they made their way down the halls that took them to the corridor onto which all the bedchambers opened. At her door, Cicely's heart began to pound more rapidly. Would he kiss her? In the dancing candlelight, his eyes darkened. She held her breath, ready.

Instead of dipping his head and covering her lips with his, he softly stroked his fingertips across her cheek.

"Sweet dreams, Cicely," he murmured.

Disappointment plummeted in her like a gray stone. She turned and slipped inside her chamber, closing the door behind her. She stood there. After a moment, she heard him leave, his footsteps echoing hollowly down the hall until their sound faded.

She struggled out of her gown. It had not been in her to insist Hannah wait up to assist. Seldom had there been occasions since her marriage that had required she wear any but the most practical clothing. She'd grown used to undressing herself. Now her disappointment frayed into annoyance as the difficult-to-reach fastenings eluded her fingers.

What had she been thinking, moping over the lack of his kiss? she thought, prizing the last of many hooks from its loop, the joints of her shoulders protesting the abuse. Wasn't it enough that he pushed his way into her house, where he insisted upon staying, no thought to her reputation? Ha! The last thing she needed from that man was a kiss!

Heaving a sigh of relief over freeing the last of the hooks, she quickly finished undressing. Finally, clothed in her night shift, she wriggled under the bedcovers and reached for the first of the three old journals she'd taken from the abbey's library.

She would keep her word and find a way to give Alasdair his rest. As soon as she succeeded, she planned to fly from this place that had been her prison, leaving Griffin Tyrrell and his kisses far behind.

In his chamber, Griffin absently stared out the window at the black velvet sky littered with diamond-chip stars.

He had wanted to kiss Cicely. He'd sensed she'd been ready. But there had been something about her expression when he'd asked her if she liked children . . . a yearning that touched him. In her shadowed eyes he'd seen a vulnerability that had given him pause.

He knew this lovely flower of a woman with her peculiar brand of honesty had suffered. She had been forced to endure a soul-devouring loneliness Griffin knew too well.

Despite that mutual loneliness, their lives seemed to have taken them on separate courses. Cicely had retained an intrinsic innocence that mingled intriguingly with her womanly ways. His own circumstances had hardened him. His survival had so often depended

on his wits that sharp caution had become second
nature.

Griffin turned away from the window, thinking of
Cicely, of her expressive eyes and her soft lips, of her
innocence and her quiet courage.

Where was his caution now?

The following morning at breakfast Cicely broke the
initial silence that sat at the table between her and
Griffin like a gloating guest.

"I discovered something about Alasdair in one of the
old journals from the abbey's library."

Griffin set his cup of coffee down. "Excellent. What
did you learn?"

"According to the entry, which was made in 1589 by
Richard Cranston, the man who bought and resided on
the property after Alasdair died, Alasdair's spirit is
restricted to the bounds of the manor. If he leaves the
property, his soul will be lost forever."

"How did Cranston come to know this?"

"He asked."

With more force than necessary, Griffin speared a
small square of cheese with his fork. "A novel idea.
Perhaps you should try it."

"Do you think I never asked such questions in the
time I've lived with Alasdair?"

"Since you seem to know nothing about him, I have
wondered."

"Well, I've asked him many questions."

"And?"

Cicely eyed a spoonful of her watery porridge.
Hannah usually made good porridge. "He doesn't
answer them. He either changes the subject or van-
ishes."

"He answered Cranston's question," Griffin pointed out.

"True, but he was new at being a ghost then. Perhaps he'd not yet become accustomed to his new form."

He lifted an eyebrow. "What has that to do with the matter?"

"Consider, if you will, Griffin"—his name slipped so naturally from her lips that she didn't catch her error until she saw him smile. Oh, lud, she thought peevishly. Well, she wasn't going to worry over it. The man was living with her, for heaven's sake. What was in a name, after all? She cleared her throat and continued. "How disorienting it must be to awake and find you've assumed another form. One goes through one's whole life accepting certain rules, and suddenly everything changes."

"What rules?" he asked, his warming gaze never leaving hers.

"Rules," she echoed, feeling unaccountably flustered. The man was only looking at her, but the way he was looking at her made her feel heated and flushed, as though she'd been standing too long in the sunshine. "Uh, rules. Yes. You know—rules." She drew in a deep breath and quietly let it out. "Universal laws. Law number one, you cannot walk through walls. Law number two, 'tis impossible to vanish, especially at will. Law number three, no growing into a huge death's-head—"

His sensual mouth moved from a smile to a grin, revealing even, white teeth. "I perceive your meaning."

"Then you comprehend what an enormous adjustment such a change would require. But that is not the greatest difficulty that faced Alasdair, I feel certain."

"No?"

She shook her head. "No. He was the only one of his kind here. He has no ghostly wife, no spirit children. He was all alone." It was his loneliness that had first touched her. "Perhaps after two hundred years he does not feel obliged to answer other people's questions."

"Especially if the questions concern something he did, something that makes him ashamed."

"Pure speculation." A speculation she preferred not to make, though a part of her understood the probability that, whatever Alasdair had done to incur such a fate, it had not been an act of goodwill.

"More like a reasonable assumption." Griffin finished his coffee and placed his napkin on the table.

"When will your beasts arrive?" she asked, changing to a more constructive subject.

Griffin lounged back in his chair, his legs stretched out, one booted ankle crossed over the other. "I expect the hens and cocks within the next few days. The rest will come by ship from various places over the next fortnight." He brightened. "Did I tell you that I've purchased goats? My father used to keep goats on the lawn in front of the house. Brown-and-white ones from the East."

His reference to his father immediately caught her attention. This was the first time she'd heard him speak of his family. But before she could learn more, he rose stiffly from the table.

She observed his movement with interest. "How fares your leg this morning?"

"Devilish sore," he informed her peevishly.

She ignored his ill temper. "It will be for a while. It requires several sessions of massage before you see it start to improve."

"I'll have Digby attend to it."

Cicely rose to her feet. "I shall do it." Her determination rang in her voice.

All her life she'd been taught that as a female, she must be meek and obedient, bending like a willow before the will of the superior male. She had spent so much time bending it was a wonder she had not acquired a permanent stoop. She'd practiced meekness and obedience so diligently she'd almost forgotten she had a will of her own. Now she eyed the latest man to lumber into her path. Griffin Tyrrell was as intelligent and as beautiful as the *sidhe* described in her book, those mythical ancient gods who had once walked these isles, but he was still stubbornly, undeniably, humanly male. Now here he was going on about having Digby care for that neglected leg of his, a leg that needed expert attention if it was to recover. And she was the closest thing he had to an expert in this remote bit of Sussex. If men are the superior gender, she thought, God help us all.

Griffin scowled. "Digby—"

"I've seen trained apes show more grace than you are showing now, Captain."

"I doubt they would behave so well if some female were digging her fingers into them," he grumbled.

Surprised, Cicely laughed. "Come, now. I am not merely 'some female.' We share our meals. We share the common cause of bringing Alasdair to his rest, though I own for different reasons. I wish only to give you relief from the pain that plagues you. Why not indulge me? What is there to lose?"

They passed out the back door, into the small kitchen courtyard, and Griffin firmly closed the door behind them, turning to face her.

"Your reputation, madam, if we are discovered. And my dignity."

Cicely scowled up at him. "*Your* dignity? What of *mine? You* were not the one kneeling—" As soon as the words left her lips she realized how scandalously provocative they sounded. Her jaw snapped shut and her face flamed with embarrassment.

A slow smile stole over Griffin's face. "No, but in my heart I was." A sensual light burned in his silvery eyes. "As I sat in that quiet room, with you on your knees before me, your lips parted, your white breasts displayed for my enjoyment, I took my mind off the pain by imagining you sitting in that chair, instead of me. Your legs were spread."

Cicely's mouth went dry. Unfamiliar heat pulsed through her body as the image he'd described insinuated itself vividly into her mind. Her blood seemed to slow and thicken into something molten. Her breath quickened, grew more difficult to draw. She knew she should be ashamed of her behavior, but she could not seem to help herself. Never before had she been possessed by such peculiar, such delectable sensations. She wanted to experience them a little longer.

She hesitated, but the warm, coiling, languorous sensations that possessed her urged her on. She saw the pulse in the side of his strong neck beat more rapidly.

He moved closer to her, stopping just before his body brushed hers. The heat of him pressed against her, as intimate as a caress. The scent of him, that mingling of starched linen, pine balsam soap, and freshly turned earth, seemed to heighten her perception. She inhaled deeply, drawing that part of him into her.

"Yes," he said, his low voice thrumming with an unfamiliar intensity. "I'm on my knees. Then . . . I place my palms on your knees. I can feel the shape of you through your skirts."

Her knees warmed as she imagined the scene.

"Slowly, I draw up your skirts and petticoat, slipping them up until your calves are revealed to me. Your pretty calves, covered with pink stockings tied with garters of white satin ribbon."

Cicely felt her eyelids growing heavy as that coiling,

flushed feeling called forth an aching swelling in her breasts. "You see my . . . legs?" She should put an end to this shocking exploration. Her mind told her it could lead to no good. Her body refused to care.

"Only part of them. I need to see more." He lifted a lappet of her cap and brushed his lips softly along the outer rim of her ear, and she shivered with pleasure. "I lift your skirts higher," he whispered next to her ear. "Your legs are as smooth and white as the finest cream. The sight inflames me."

"It does?" Was that her voice sounding so breathless?

"Mmm-hmm." His fingertips skimmed lightly over the pulse point at the base of her throat. "I spread your knees wider. Inch your skirts higher. My hands are on your naked flesh." Gently, he cupped her jaw in one hand and lifted her face. "I confess," he murmured, "I'm surprised you haven't slapped me for my boldness."

She took his words as a reprimand, and, as mild as it had been, her own conscience gave it the power of a stinging slap. Stricken, she lowered her eyes. "I—It's just that . . ." Mortified, she pressed her lips together before she could do more damage.

"What?" he asked softly, his voice little more than a whisper, inviting her to confide the truth.

She fixed her gaze on a loose pebble near the toe of her kid shoe. "No man has ever wished to be on his knees before me or—" She broke off. Was it not terrible enough that she had repelled her husband? Must she also drag her failing out for inspection by the one man she wished to think well of her? Shame burned in her.

"Tell me," Griffin whispered, his lips moving against her forehead.

She squeezed her eyes closed, against the memory of

the disgust she'd seen in Edmund's face. "Touch me." The words came hard through the tightness in her throat. "No man has ever wished to . . . touch me."

There. She'd said it. Now Griffin will hold her in contempt just as her husband had done. Tears burned at the back of her eyes. Dear God, she'd thought she'd grown hardened to feeling this tearing rejection. Hadn't six years of it been enough to build a callus on her heart?

Griffin cupped her jaw in his palms and gently nudged her face up. "Look at me."

Reluctantly, she did as he bade. In his solemn face she saw no amusement or anger.

"You are a beautiful and desirable woman, Cicely," he said, his voice like velvet. "But you do not always see the darker sides of a man's nature. In your life, I swear to you, men have wished to touch you, but they knew they should not."

Edmund had possessed the right to do with her what he had pleased, yet he could barely bring himself to look on her. But Edmund was not whom she thought of now. Edmund had not stirred her with his kiss. Thoughts of him had never tugged at her consciousness as they did for Griffin. And the only reason she had endured her husband's groping was to get a child, not because she longed for him, for his nearness.

She met Griffin's eyes. Despite her silence, her question hung in the air between them. His eyes darkened, and she knew he understood.

Do you wish to touch me?

10

"Yes." He expelled a long breath and sharply drew in another. "Yes, I want to touch you." God, how he wanted to touch her. He hungered to take her right here, to brand her with his body, with the pleasure he longed to give her until she would never again doubt herself—or wonder who might wish to touch her.

But he could not. Not now. Not here. The time must be right. Damn it all, the time must be perfect. For all that she'd been married, he suspected that in the ways of love, she was essentially a virgin. Dark anger boiled through him. Her bloody, buggering husband had injured her deeply.

Now it was up to Griffin to help her heal.

He read the question in her gaze and did his best to answer it, struggling against his ill-timed desire for her. "God in heaven, I want to do more than just touch you. But in these matters . . ." He scoured his brain for the proper words. "Timing is important. If some . . . delicacy were not employed, why, we'd . . . uh . . . we'd be no better than . . . cattle in the fields." No, no, no! That was not the right direction at all!

She stared at him, clearly confused.

He tried again, clearing his throat to gain him time. This would all be so much simpler if he could just make love to her here and now. "A man approaches a woman— That is to say—"

An icy chill settled over her features. "I think you have said quite enough, sir. I'll detain you no longer."

"No, you don't understand—"

"I think I do. Please allow me at least my pride—"

Oh, damn and blast! Giving up on diplomacy, Griffin slanted his mouth across hers. Into his kiss he poured his towering desire, his volcanic need, and a nascent, less familiar emotion that refused to be denied.

She stiffened for an instant. Then, as his lips moved over hers, she melted against him. Her hands drifted up to lie upon his chest, feeding the flames that blazed inside him. Her eyes fluttered shut.

Finally, with heroic will, he forced himself to release her. His heart thundered in his ears.

She blinked at him, looking stunned. She swayed, then straightened abruptly, casting him what likely would have been a stern look, had her pretty eyes not been out of focus.

Ruthlessly he crushed the impulse to reach for her. He dare not touch her now for fear his good intentions would go up in smoke. Not yet, he told himself, gritting his teeth. Not yet.

"I have to go now," she informed him loftily.

He nodded.

Cicely walked away, toward the abbey, weaving only slightly.

*   *   *

Neither of them brought up their encounter again, but Cicely thought of it often over the next ten days. She had never known any man like Griffin. He was charming and stubborn by turns, considerate and arrogant, as usual. But she had become even more aware of him, as if his kiss had infused in her a sensitivity to his presence, to every change in his expression or tone of his voice.

Cicely stood on the roof of the abbey, in the old Elizabethan banqueting tower, and stared out over the morning-misted lands of the manor. Cranwick's green pastures were dotted with grazing sheep. The pond there had become the favorite place of the white ducks that had arrived squawking in their cages four days ago. Closer in were the three elegant mares. Even the brown-and-white goats had a place of their own, as did the hens and those two contentious cocks. She sighed. This was the way Cranwick should always look. Lush and serene.

A soft pop of air announced Alasdair's arrival. He stood next to her for a moment, gazing out over the land with his ghostly eyes.

She smiled. "It's lovely, isn't it?"

"Aye. 'Tis a bonny place, and no mistake. It has a gentleness about it that always appealed to me."

That very quality had also touched her. "Gentleness. Yes."

"Ye could have had a worse prison, lass."

"I suppose." Cicely turned and left the tower, stepping carefully until she came to the door that led from the roof. Alasdair floated beside her, his plaid drifting around him. "But for all its beauty, Alasdair, a cage is still a cage."

"Aye." The simple word was laden with centuries of regret and anguish.

Cicely stopped short in her descent of the stairs. She reached out to him, even though she knew her fingers would pass through his translucent form if she tried to touch him. "Please let me help you," she pleaded. "I know you aren't happy. You're every bit as much a prisoner as I've been. Indeed, even more. My sentence was six years. Yours was eternity. Do you love this place so well that you wish to remain here forever?"

Alasdair's face twisted in terrible sorrow. A long, low moan issued from his lips. Instead of replying to her, or vanishing, he floated ahead of her. She sensed he wanted her to follow him.

He led her out of the manor house, through the kitchen courtyard and well beyond, into a place that had been allowed to grow wild. It was one of those patches, here and there around the manor, that had escaped clearing. She'd never had time to do anything about the areas, so she'd simply ignored them.

Cicely ducked thorny limbs. Weeds caught at her skirts and stuck to her stockings. Brambles pricked at her apron.

The ancient, weathered headstone canted to one side, as if overcome by its burden of twisted brier boughs and nettles.

Cicely stared at it, surprised to find a grave so far from consecrated ground. Picking her way to the stone, she used her apron to protect her hands as she pulled away dead vines and nettle branches to read the time-darkened inscription.

Alasdair MacNab

Died 1581

No more than that. Nothing of his birth or life, only his death.

"Oh, Alasdair," she choked, her throat tight with grief.

"'Twas no a hero's death," he whispered hollowly, sounding like a dirge on a winter wind. "I fell down an auld well while chasin' some travelers from my land." His face spasmed with misery. "Ye canna help me, lass. No one can. I'm cursed. Cursed for all time." His final words rose into a wail so mournful tears stung Cicely's eyes. The tormented notes lingered in the air as he faded from sight.

She ran her scratched hand over the grimy, lichen-spotted surface of the headstone. *Cursed for all time.* "No," she said. "I don't believe it." She knew there had to be more to the story.

Reluctantly she left the solitary grave and returned to the dower house, where earlier that morning she had assembled the foodstuffs she planned to take to the village. Griffin had generously allowed her to harvest a bit from the garden and take several eggs, though he'd drawn the line at taking a hen. "The hunger is going to get worse, Cicely," he'd cautioned. "If we kill the hens now, what will anyone eat later? Take the eggs."

As she drove Octavia into Alwyn, she glanced in the baskets that sat by her on the cracked leather seat of the chaise. There seemed pitiful little in them, yet it was all she could manage.

Just as she'd predicted, no one had come to take Griffin up on his offer of employment, she thought, annoyed. He needed help if he were to make of the manor what he hoped. Two men couldn't do it all.

Yet Griffin gave up almost all the milk and eggs from his beasts. She had always carefully managed the household food supplies, but now she was finding that she must strictly ration them if there was to be enough to share. There had been no complaints from Hannah or Digby or Griffin, and suddenly she saw the matter as unfair.

She left Octavia at the livery stables and walked to the Sparkes' cottage, where she strode briskly up the neat oyster-shell path to rap on the door.

Kitty's face lit when she saw who called. "The mid-wife said as how the baby will be coming soon," she confided as she welcomed Cicely and showed her to the best seat in the modest cottage, a pretty little stool Tom had built and carved two winters ago.

"Good news, surely," Cicely said as she watched Kitty lumber to another stool and pull it over to the small table to join Cicely.

"Indeed," Kitty agreed, carefully attempting to lower herself to the seat.

Cicely leaped up to assist Kitty before the poor girl's knees gave out under the weight of her burgeoning belly. With a soft grunt that served to expel the breath she had held, Kitty settled on the hard wooden surface.

"You look as if you've filled out a bit," Cicely said, studying the young, too-thin face. "But not enough for my peace of mind. Here. I've brought you two more eggs"—she removed them from the basket, setting them on the table—"some fresh milk, and some greens from the garden." A crockery jar and the greens themselves followed out of the basket. Cicely smiled encouragingly, excited about the impending birth, yet worried about the strength of the mother and babe.

Kitty gratefully accepted the gifts.

"Have you spoken to Tom about working for Captain Tyrrell?" Cicely asked.

Kitty looked away. "I have. And his answer remains the same."

Cicely frowned, but before she could speak, she heard Tom's voice outside the window. It was low and secretive. She recognized the other voice as belonging to Henry Diplock, who had lost his left hand in a fishing accident two years ago.

Tom said, "'Tis overlong since last she came."

"Mayhap it only seems overlong since we've been so hungry," Henry said, "but she's comin' right enough."

"Thank God. Lady Cicely has been bringing food, but it isn't enough. Few have enough ter eat these days."

"The black lugger will take care of that. She'll be anchoring in Maresmouth Cove."

Cicely could almost see Tom's impatience with Henry's unrealistic optimism. "It will take more than one visit from the black lugger ter see us all fed and through the winter safely."

"It's a start. And the lugger will be back soon with the biggest cargo ever, so's I've heard. It'll be her last visit before spring."

"When does she come first?"

"No one knows yet. I'll tell you as soon as I hear."

The two men bade each other good-bye, and Tom entered the cottage. His eyes widened when he saw Cicely.

"Hello, Tom," she said.

He inclined his head respectfully. "Lady Cicely. I didn't expect ter find you here."

"That's rather obvious."

"You know we've always tried ter keep you out of this."

"I know. I've also known about the black lugger for some time. You can see everything on the beach from the banqueting tower at the abbey. And I've often observed the activity from the cliffs."

Tom raked his hand through his brown hair. "'Tis a foolish risk if you have no need ter take it."

"The soldiers have never come here before. But as I've told Kitty and Mr. Coppard and anyone else who will listen to me, they might come here now. The king will have his taxes to pay for the war. The dragoons have visited other villages of this coast. Tom, men have been hanged."

His mouth pulled down at the corners. "'Twould be a faster death than starvation."

"Faster and a great deal surer." She leaned forward

on her stool. "Work for Captain Tyrrell. He has need of reliable men to help him improve Cranwick, and you'd be breaking no law. You've never been afraid of hard work. The captain is a fair man."

Tom's broad-boned face took on a mulish expression. "And have the demon lay a curse on my manhood? I'd as soon die at the end of a rope with chains on."

Cicely blinked. "What? A curse on your— I've never heard such a thing. It's ridiculous!"

"'Tis a well-known fact," Tom insisted.

Cicely stood. She brushed her skirts smooth, struggling to restrain her exasperation. "There are few well-known facts about Alasdair, but that is not one of them."

Tom scowled and opened his mouth to reply, but Kitty struggled to get up. Immediately, he lent her his arm to lean on. "Who can say what is true and untrue where the demon is concerned?" she said breathlessly. "Even you cannot be certain, Lady Cicely, you have said so yourself."

"Kitty, in the six years I have lived at the abbey, Alasdair has done nothing more than frighten people. And make them uncomfortable, upon occasion," she added. But to her knowledge, the freezing breezes, high-pitched shrieks, and hail had never permanently affected any man's . . . uh . . . capabilities. Of course, the only men she knew of who had encountered those things had been Edmund and Pierre, his valet, Mr. Joyes and Will Allcorn, Digby and Griffin.

Had that been why Edmund had experienced such mortifying difficulties? And what of Griffin? What effect had the ghost-induced cold had on him? She shook her head. Rumor, merely rumor. And able-bodied men were allowing it to keep them from honest work. She said as much to Tom.

He stiffened. "You said yourself I'm not afraid ter

work, and I'm not. But I'll take no chances with something so important. I've a wife and future children ter think of."

"But you're willing to gamble with their starvation?"

Dark red moved up the large, young fisherman's neck. "Who are you ter accuse me of risking my family?"

"A friend," Kitty said firmly, fixing first her husband, then Cicely with a stern eye. "Lady Cicely is a friend, and she worries for us both. For all *three* of us. Can you deny that, Tom Sparke?"

Tom stood resolute for a moment, then huffed out a sharp breath. "No. I cannot, nor would I. My apologies ter you, Lady Cicely. I know you mean us well."

"And you," Kitty said to Cicely, "know very well that everyone fears setting foot on Cranwick. 'Tis been so for more years than any of us have lived. Can you expect such dire fear ter be forgotten for something like hunger? We *know* hunger. 'Tis more familiar than a demon from the Pit."

Cicely sighed. Kitty was right. The fear of Alasdair was long-standing and extreme. Perhaps the people's hunger would never get so bad that they would be willing to work at the manor. Not for the first time, it occurred to her that the manor's tenants had not complained to her about Alasdair.

She tapped her closed fan against her palm. "So you choose smuggling over working at Cranwick. How will you carry enough goods without Kitty?"

As Tom sat on the edge of the bed, Cicely noticed that not only had he lost weight, but new, premature lines had etched themselves into his face. "I already thought of that," he said, "but there's no help for it."

"I can still work," Kitty insisted.

Tom turned his gaze to her, and Cicely saw his eyes soften as he looked at his wife. "No, you cannot. I'll not endanger you or our babe. The black lugger will return. It always does."

Mr. Coppard had once told Cicely that it took at least two to carry enough contraband to earn decent money. Many families had their children unload, working alongside the adults. She knew Tom's effort would be valiant, but reality had an ugly way of ignoring valor.

Kitty and Tom were young. They were in love. In Cicely's darkest moments of loneliness, their bond to each other had been her proof that in this world, true affection and fidelity did exist.

She could not let them starve.

"I'll help," she said. "I'll take Kitty's place."

"Cap'n, I think you ought to see this," Digby said as he held out a ladle of fresh water.

Griffin looked up from the irrigation ditch he was digging. He drove the blade of the shovel into the freshly exposed earth, leaving it to stand upright as he leaped out of the swale to accept the wooden dipper. The water swept cool and wet into his parched mouth. He swallowed thirstily, and when he'd emptied the ladle, he handed it back. "See what?"

Digby dropped the dipper back into the bucket he'd just filled at the manor house well. "You need to see it for yourself."

With a gesture, Griffin indicated he would follow Digby.

When they'd walked for ten minutes, Griffin grew impatient. "Where the devil is this thing I should see?"

"Not much farther, Cap'n."

They approached a tangled wooded area. Griffin had never seen so many thorns in one place.

"I just seen that ghost and Lady Cicely come here," Digby said. "I was drawing water, you see, and just caught sight o' them afore they came in here. Sometime later, Lady Cicely came out. She were by herself and lookin' unhappy and upset, like."

Griffin studied the recently torn path through the brier wood. What had happened here to distress Cicely? "You're right, Digby. I do want to see this."

He followed the path, Digby close on his heels. Griffin's leather work gloves helped avoid the worst of the vicious thorns as he expanded the tunnel to accommodate his greater size, but the fresh smear of blood he noticed on a broken-thorned stem testified that Cicely had worked with bare hands. His grudge against Alasdair expanded.

When he came to the center of the wood, an old limestone monument caught his eye. Nettles all but covered the tilting, weatherworn thing. It looked to Griffin as if no one had ever tended this grave. And what was it doing here, so far from a churchyard?

Even before he saw the name chiseled into the stone, he guessed to whom this burial place belonged.

Digby stared at the headstone. "So this is where Alasdair was buried," he muttered.

"His crime must have been terrible indeed."

"Who would come to tend his grave, when the folk here 'bout are so terrified of him that they won't even come here to work for you?"

"True enough," Griffin granted, studying the bramble-grown grave and its marker.

"This place gives me the shivers, Cap'n. 'Tain't natural-like. Best we leave."

"You said Lady Cicely was upset?"

"Yes. C'mon, Cap'n."

She had not known of this grave before. Griffin was

willing to wager a milk cow on that. The path to the grave site was freshly made.

As the two men made their way back out of the small patch of brier wood, Griffin thought of how distressed Cicely must have been at finding her ghostly friend's grave in such condition.

"The place is cursed," Digby said as they won free of the wood. "Nothing good grows there."

Cicely had gone into the village, that much Griffin knew. There she would be faced with the hunger of her neighbors. So much for her to bear . . .

Griffin struck off in the direction of the byre to retrieve the scythe.

Digby jogged to keep up with him. "What are we doing now?"

"Lady Cicely has a tender heart and too much has happened lately to tear at it. I'll not have her disturbed over anything so easily rectified as an unkept grave."

Digby's eyes widened. "You don't mean to try to clear that area?"

"I do."

Color drained from his homely face. "That's not a good idea, Cap'n."

"Help me or not, as you please."

"It's cursed!"

Griffin turned a steely look on Digby, determined not to discuss the matter further. He was uneasy enough as it was at the thought of hacking away at the wickedly barbed growth that concealed the grave. The place had an eerie, unnatural feel to it. Maybe Digby was right. Maybe it was cursed. But he could not let that signify. "I'll not have her unhappy over it."

With a long-suffering sigh, Digby trotted after Griffin.

They got their tools and strode back to the brier wood. In the few hours Cicely was likely to be gone,

Griffin knew the entire woods could not possibly be cleared, but a wide path could be cut, the headstone set aright, and the grave site cleaned.

Despite Digby's grumbling and nervous glances over his shoulder, they accomplished that much with time left over to make a little more progress on the irrigation ditch. The rest of the woods could be cleared a bit at a time. Now, at least, Cicely would not return to the wretched sight of that overgrown burial place.

If only Alasdair could be gotten rid of as easily as the nettles that had hidden his grave.

Once the chaise left the high street and struck the packed dirt of the country road, Cicely urged Octavia into a canter. She didn't know why she was in such a hurry. She knew only that she wanted to go home, and Cranwick was as close to a home as she possessed.

Suddenly a rabbit darted out into the road. Hard on its heels dashed a brown-and-white puppy.

Cicely pulled back on the reins, unwilling to see the mongrel pup trampled by Octavia's iron-shod hooves. The mare responded, tossing her head in protest at the strain on her mouth. Cicely spoke to her softly, soothing and reassuring. The rabbit and its pursuer vanished into the fields that bounded the road.

Securing the reins, Cicely quickly climbed down from the little carriage and went around to gently take Octavia's bridle in her hand. "There we are," she crooned, checking the mare's tender mouth. "I know. You don't deserve such treatment." Satisfied that no damage had been done, she stroked Octavia's velvety nose. "Such a good girl."

The mare nodded, as if agreeing, then dipped her head to nuzzle Cicely's jaw, unconcernedly knocking her hat crooked. Chuckling at Octavia's antics, Cicely tried to straighten her hat with one hand as she scratched the mare's ear. At this moment, the black lugger didn't seem so threatening a risk.

A high-pitched puppy bark sounded from the ground near her feet, and she looked down to see the puppy gazing up at her, pink tongue lolling, and white, brown-tipped tail wagging.

Octavia lowered her head to investigate the source of the noise, and received, on her nose, a lolloping swipe from the small tongue.

"My, aren't you a bold one?" Cicely told the puppy, who jumped around in a frenzy of exuberance, then stood on his hind legs, dirty front paws placed above the hem of her long apron.

The small creature was white with a brown spot encircling one eye, a brown tip on his never-still tail, and four brown paws. It was difficult to resist such open friendliness, and Cicely didn't try. She scooped him up. He weighed too little, she thought, her fingers encountering the prominent outlines of his ribs.

"Where are your brothers and sisters?" she asked the wiggling little bundle. She knew of no one who had bred such a pup.

She studied him as he nestled contentedly in her arms, settling to lick her wrist. "What shall I do with you, little fellow?" After seeing his injudicious bolt across the road, Cicely found herself reluctant to simply leave him. His next tangle with traffic might find him not so lucky.

Octavia nudged her shoulder.

"Yes, I know. We must be on our way. And I suppose this pup must come with us." So, cradling the puppy in one arm, and balancing herself against the carriage with the other, Cicely climbed onto her seat and flicked the reins.

*   *   *

As Cicely passed the farm of John Longley, she suddenly remembered the question she had wanted to ask him. Slowing Octavia, she turned into the drive that led to his modest, well-kept cottage. As she pulled Octavia to a halt, she heard John's cheerful hail, and turned to see him striding past the avenue of elms, toward her. She waved back, even as the vivid memory of being in Griffin's arms, of feeling his lips moving over hers, flooded in.

"A fair day, is it not, Lady Cicely?" John said, smiling up at her.

"Yes, it is."

"You heard that the dragoons moved on Cinderlea, didn't you?"

A stone thumped against her heart. "No, I had not. Have you had news of Will Allcorn?"

"Yes. His cousin was caught. Hauled off for transportation. Will has stayed ter take care of the fellow's wife and children."

Cicely offered up a silent prayer in thanks for Will's safety. "I've come to ask you a question, John. Likely it's a question I should have asked you years ago, but, in truth, I've only thought of it since I've moved to the dower house."

"I'll do my best ter answer, Lady Cicely."

She smiled. "I know that. What I would like to know is this: Have you or any of the other tenants been bothered by Alasdair?"

"No. He never comes here."

"Why is that?"

John grinned. "Have you asked the spirit?"

"Yes. He said it was because your rent put gold in his pocket."

"Well, what can you expect from a Scotsman? A Scotsman who's a ghost at that?" John laughed. "But this land, and that rented by your other tenants, was not part of the manor when he owned it. This was all purchased much later, in my grandfather's time."

"So you believe he doesn't annoy you and the other tenants because he cannot enter lands that weren't actually owned by him when the curse was laid?"

"Seems likely, don't you think?"

"Hmm. Yes. Yes, it does. The dower house and its buildings were built not quite fifty years ago." She sighed. "I should know all this."

"How, I'd like ter know?" John patted her hand. "Who was there ter tell you? Your mister? That slippery demon, Alasdair?"

"I should have known you would have all the answers."

John laughed again, this time a deep, rolling laugh. "May you always believe that ter be so, lady!"

"What else do you know about Alasdair, John?"

He shook his head. "You have the sum of it."

"Oh."

"Dame Ingate's boy, Marcus, told me that you're looking to put the demon to rest."

Cicely nodded, stroking the puppy's sun-warmed fur. "I am, but I can find so little to aid me. No one seems to knows anything about him, and he will not—or cannot—tell me how to bring him peace."

John scratched his head as he glanced down at the ground, then back up at her. "I've heard tell of an old, blind hermit that lives north o' the ruins. A wise man, they say. Learned in the lore of strange things. Mayhap he'd know something of the demon."

What did she have to lose in seeking the help of this hermit? As it stood now, she had no idea how to help Alasdair. "Thank you, John."

line. His dark hair had been brushed into its usual queue, and secured with a black velvet ribbon. He looked every inch the lord of the manor. Indeed, with those startling silver eyes, that straight nose with its slightly flared nostrils, and that sensual, sulky mouth, he had the look, and exuded the aura, of power more common to a prince than to an untitled country gentleman.

"A blind hermit," he said, and she found herself paying particular attention to his mouth, to the motion of his lips. "Why am I not surprised?"

"Surprised?" she echoed, forcing her gaze up to his eyes, unwilling for him to notice her fascination.

He dipped his spoon into the blancmange on the plate before him. "Yes. A blind hermit is, after all, an unusual character. Though, in truth, I would not have been surprised to hear we must consult three witches and their cauldron regarding Alasdair."

Cicely focused on her own blancmange and frowned. The bland white stuff was no substitute for Griffin's intriguing face. "I would imagine few persons know much about the habits of ghosts."

"True. And if he is old, we'd be well advised to call on him at once." He ate another bite of his dessert. "We'll go tomorrow."

A curious reluctance to settle the matter of Alasdair so soon wormed its way into Cicely. Which, of course, was ridiculous. She *wanted* to help him find peace. She wanted her freedom. Too much of her life had already been wasted at Cranwick.

"Tomorrow it is, then," she agreed briskly. "Perhaps this expedition shall put an end to your dissatisfaction with the manor, and I'll be on my way."

11

Griffin's mouth tightened for an instant. "I see you've not abandoned this folly of yours to go off on your own."

"No. And I do not consider it folly in the least. This time I shall hire a big, strong guard who will save Hannah and me from curmudgeonly sea captains and outraged landowners." She smiled at him, inviting him to enjoy her small joke, but his sullen look told her he found her wit lacking in amusement.

"'Tis madness."

"Perhaps. But, for the first time, my life will be ruled by *my* madness."

He regarded her a minute, his fine mouth unsmiling, his lashes an inky fringe partially concealing the silver of his uptilted eyes. "Not all men are like Edmund Honeysett."

No, many more were like her father—strong when disciplining his wife, weak when it came to protecting her.

"I know that," she said.

"I would not have you harmed."

She felt herself soften. "I know that, too."

He tossed his bunched napkin onto the table. "The world is a hard place, Cicely."

"So you have said."

"You are not a hard woman."

She smiled, hoping to tease him from this serious address of a subject that she considered closed to discussion. "No, but I am clever. Perhaps my wits shall save me from bandits and other nefarious sorts who mean me no good. My wits and a large, muscular guard."

"I wouldn't count on it."

Exasperated, Cicely rose. "Come, it's time to massage your leg."

"Digby can do it."

She swept around the table to where he sat. "You have said that every night since first I began almost three weeks ago. Look at me and deny you find improvement in the use of your leg."

He was slow to turn his head and look at her. "I'll not deny the truth."

"There, you see?" she said triumphantly. "Let Digby help Hannah with the dishes and the kitchen."

Griffin pushed back his chair and got up. "I don't know, is it safe? The way those two squabble over every little thing, you'd think they'd been born enemies." He followed her into the parlor, where he poured her a small glass of hock and himself a whiskey as she opened the crockery jar and spread the towels to warm on the hearth. When she straightened, he handed her the drink.

"Rather I think they might be fated to be together," she said, accepting the glass. "But Hannah is suspicious of Digby's flowery compliments."

Griffin set his drink on the table next to his chair and proceeded to unbutton the right knee of his breeches. He rolled it up out of the way and pushed down his stocking, then sprawled back in his seat.

Cicely knelt and arranged her skirts. Then she poured a dollop of the fragrant, herb-infused oil into her palm. Slowly she spread this over the tracery of scars on the inside of his leg. Beneath her fingers she felt the warmth of his skin, and below that, the hard resistance of muscle and bone.

He took a sip of the golden liquid in his glass and stiffened slightly as her fingers worked deeper. She'd noticed that the brackets of pain around his mouth at the end of the day were not as pronounced as they had been when she'd first insisted he allow her to attend his leg, nor was his limp as noticeable. Perhaps this, more than freeing him from Alasdair, would be her legacy to him and give him cause to remember her.

The thought of his no longer being a part of her everyday life left a hollow feeling in her chest. Eager to drive it away, she paused to take a swallow of her wine. She would not think of leaving now. Not tonight as they shared the peace of the parlor in an intimacy that had become the focal point of her days.

She raised her eyes to his and smiled. "You cleared Alasdair's grave."

"No man's grave should be overgrown."

"It took time away from your other work. A great deal of it, I would say. Work for which you're desperately shorthanded."

He made no reply.

"Cutting through the brier wood had to be difficult labor."

He took a swallow of whiskey.

"Hours in the hot sun."

Finally he looked at her. "And your point is?"

As her hands worked, she studied his face, loving every beautiful, stubborn-set detail. "Thank you. You are a decent man."

He made a harsh noise in his throat and took another swallow.

Silence settled between them. The crackling of the small fire in the fireplace was all that saved the room from tomblike quiet.

She moved her hands slightly lower, to concentrate on the scarred side of his knee. "I still say it would be more practical for us to do this at lunchtime, when we're both in our working clothes."

He regarded her from beneath lowered eyelids. His mouth curved into a faint smile. "That would never do."

Her fingers encountered stiff muscle, and she pressed deeper to loosen it. His breath hissed sharply between his teeth.

"Why would it never do?" she asked.

"Because then I would not see you by the golden glow of firelight," he said tightly.

Surprised, she paused in her work. "Really?"

He released a strained breath. "Really."

Aware of her neglect, she continued massaging, reaching for the deeper, drawn-up sinew. Griffin tensed.

"Is that all?" she asked shyly, warmth rising to her face for her boldness.

"I would not get to see your swanlike throat," he gritted between set teeth.

Cicely blushed with pleasure. Swanlike throat? No one had ever said anything like that before. During the day she did wear the voluminous handkerchief around her neck, like most countrywomen with work to do, but she didn't think it covered all that much of her throat.

Still . . . She looked up at him expectantly, hoping for another compliment.

His fingers gripped the arms of the chair. "Nor would I see so much of your milk white breasts."

She snatched her hands away from his leg. "Is that all you care about?" she snapped. "Seeing my breasts?"

Temper flashed in his quicksilver eyes. "Christ Almighty, woman, I'm not a stone saint!" He leaned down until they were almost nose to nose. "Every night you insist on sinking your claws into my leg and—"

"Claws, is it?" Outraged, she tried to rise to her feet to exert her dignity, but he clasped her wrists in his iron hands, keeping her where she was. *"Claws?"*

"Dainty hands," he amended grimly. "Dainty, rosy-fingered hands."

"Too late, sir. Your pretty words are wasted." She struggled to free herself, but his hold remained firm, incensing her to greater efforts. "I know very well now what you think of me. *Let me go!*"

He tugged her closer. "Listen to me, Cicely."

She stopped her struggles, but knelt there glaring at him.

"First of all, I want to thank you."

Her eyes narrowed in suspicion. "Thank me?"

"Despite my grumbling and show of bad grace, you always take care of my leg. And now it is stronger and more supple. Before you ordered me to accept your ministrations"—he smiled—"I was certain this leg would plague me the rest of my life. I no longer believe that. It may never be as it was before that bayonet did its work, but it will be considerably closer than if I hadn't obeyed you."

"You make me sound like a shrew," she muttered.

He chuckled. "No, not that. Never that. Rather an

angel who does not like to see someone suffer for his own stupidity."

"I would not call you stupid, precisely," she objected.

"Not precisely. Secondly, I must insist that I meant every word I said about liking to see your swanlike throat." He lowered his head to place a soft kiss on the area under discussion.

Cicely's heart bolted into double time. "You . . . you do?"

He nodded. "Umm-hmm."

"Oh."

"And only a fool would not find your breasts"—he brushed his lips across the top of first one, then the other breast—"delectable, incomparable, and very, very"—he bent to slip his tongue along that pale, sensitive skin above the edge of her gown's low neckline, just an inch above her nipples—"arousing."

Throbbing heat filled Cicely. Her breasts felt swollen and her nipples tingly and sensitive. "Arousing?" she whispered, unable to care that he was taking improper liberties. She wanted to know more, feel more, and she wanted Griffin to be the one to teach her.

He eased from the edge of his chair, down to his knees. His hands smoothed roughly over the silk and lace of her sleeves. He palmed her shoulders. All the while, his gaze burned into hers. She found herself waiting . . . wanting. . . .

"God, yes, arousing," he murmured, his lips brushing kisses over her upturned face with growing intensity. "I'm probably insane for telling you this, but you have power over me."

She clung to him, her fingers curled into the cloth of his coat. "I do?"

"Such power. You're like the honeycomb just taken from the bees. Golden and fragrant and drenched with sweetness. But it's a sweetness that comes from rare flowers. It doesn't overpower."

"It doesn't?" She found it difficult to concentrate on his words when his fingertips lightly stroked the shell of her ear.

"No. You're like that. Golden, sweet, and rare."

"Rare," she echoed, feeling as if something within her was gradually coiling, tightening.

His forefinger slipped beneath her satin neckline to stroke over the hard pebble of her nipple.

It was as if he'd plucked a taut harp string that ran through her body. Dazzling vibrations struck fireworks of sensation within her, driving a startled gasp from her lips.

For a moment, Griffin searched her face, combing his gaze over what must be each minute detail. Then he cradled her head between his hands and lowered his mouth to hers.

He burned her with his parted lips, seared her with his ardent tongue. She squeezed her eyes shut and absorbed the volcanic power of his passion, taking it inside, allowing it to fill that empty, echoing place in her that had once held only loneliness.

She lifted her hands and laced her fingers through his thick, dark hair, loosing locks of it from his queue. Tentatively, she placed slow kisses up the side of his throat. Drawing confidence with each touch of her lips to him, she breathed in the mingled scents of pine balsam soap and warm man's skin that she was coming to associate solely with Griffin. She would never forget the subtle scent that was warm and intoxicating and his alone.

Gradually, he grew still, save for the rapid rise and fall of his chest. In the quiet parlor, his short, sharp breathing sounded suddenly loud.

"What's wrong?" she asked.

He softly touched his fingertips to her cheek. "Nothing." He dropped his hand. "Everything." He heaved a sigh and jammed his hand through his hair, leaving his queue disheveled. Then he looked at her, his startlingly light eyes reduced to narrow bands of silver around polished obsidian pupils in the glow of the candles and the embers which were all that was left in the fireplace. "Me."

"I don't understand."

One side of his mouth lifted in a half smile. "Nor do I. I only know how I feel when you're near me." He laid his cheek on the crown of her head. "Never worry that no man wishes to touch you, sweetheart."

She smiled, wishing she could stay there in his arms forever.

But her wish was not to be granted. Dropping a kiss on her forehead, Griffin released her. Before she knew what was happening, he'd wrapped his bared, oily leg in the heated towel, stood up, and reached down to assist her to her feet.

Disappointed, she brushed out the larger wrinkles from her skirts, only to discover she still had a trace of oil on her hands. She glanced over at Griffin and enjoyed the small satisfaction of seeing the oil from her hands on his face, his ears, his neck and coat. It gleamed in his tousled hair.

"If we're to visit the hermit and have time to return home, we must make an early start tomorrow," he said.

She nodded. True enough.

He saw her to the door of her bedchamber, and bade her good-night. Without so much as a kiss, he left her there.

He had changed his mind about her, she thought as she entered, torn between hurt and indignation.

"Well, aren't you a sight for sore eyes," Hannah said, hands on her hips.

Cicely jumped, startled. "Hannah, I thought you'd be in bed by now."

"I remembered the hooks on this gown you're wearing are impossible for you to reach." She eyed her mistress. "From the looks o' your hair and the state o' your gown, I'd say you was in quite a wrestlin' match with Cap'n Tyrrell."

Only too aware of the picture she must present, Cicely resisted the urge to smooth back the lock of hair that was hanging in front of her left eye. "As you know, Hannah, I massage the captain's leg."

Hannah began unhooking Cicely's stomacher. "As you may not have noticed, when you was massaging his leg, you got oil on your skirts."

"Yes, I know." She held out her arms, turning this way and that to facilitate Hannah's efforts.

"Like as not his foot got caught in your hair."

Cicely pressed her lips firmly together, embarrassed and annoyed.

Nothing was said for a minute. There was only the weighty *tock* of the clock on the mantel.

"The dinner was excellent, Hannah."

"Considering what I had to work with, 'tis a miracle."

As irritating as it was to find Hannah in such a mood, Cicely could not help but wonder what had caused it. "What's bothering you, Hannah? Is it my appearance?"

Hannah heaved a long-suffering sigh. "Judging from the way you an' the captain have been looking at each other when you think the other's not aware, 'twas only a matter of time before ye got ter rollin' around together."

Shocked at the implication she heard in those words, Cicely whirled to face the other woman. "Hannah! Captain Tyrrell and I did not— There was no— That is to say we didn't . . . Well, we just *didn't*."

Hannah's eyebrows rose in disbelief. "You didn't kiss 'n' cuddle?"

If she'd been standing there wearing blancmange on her face, Cicely would not have felt any more foolish. "Well . . . yes. In a way."

"What did you think I meant?"

Red-faced, Cicely cleared her throat.

"Oh, that." Hannah waved away that possibility. "The captain is a lusty man, or I don't know peas from cabbage. I've seen his eyes when he looks at you sometimes—"

"How does he look at me?"

"Oh, his eyes go darker and all *smoldering*-like," Hannah declared dreamily, draping the ells of gown over a chair.

"They do?" Cicely asked from the depths of the night shift she pulled over her head.

"Oh, yes. Why, any woman would give her best corset busks to have such a man look at her like that." Hannah steered an unresisting Cicely over to the upholstered bench in front of the dressing table.

"I thought you didn't like Captain Tyrrell."

Hannah removed the pins from Cicely's hair, placing them in their ivory box. "I don't," she said. "Well, not much," she added grudgingly. "But there he goes and asks me if my mum and da were getting enough to eat. You know how he gives up almost all the eggs and milk ter the folk what's starving. And him a-working himself to the bone, needing help. Don't seem quite fair, now, does it?"

Cicely brushed out her hair. "That very thought

occurred to me this afternoon. And do you know what I found out?"

"No, what?"

"People believe that a man setting foot on Cranwick will be cursed by Alasdair."

Hannah sat down on the bed, Cicely's gown draped across her lap. "What kind of curse?"

Indignantly, Cicely set down the brush, and turned to look at Hannah. "'Tis the most preposterous thing! They think Alasdair will curse their—their manhood. As if Alasdair could give a fig about their manhoods! Isn't that ridiculous?"

Hannah looked thoughtful. "A demon's curse on your husband's manhood might explain why you never conceived."

Cicely ran her palm back and forth over the stiff bristles of her brush. She could not bring herself to reveal that her husband had formed a disgust for her, and so only once had forced himself to have congress with her. "You know he seldom came to Cranwick," she muttered.

Edmund's absence had always been common knowledge. Edmund himself had never failed to divulge his easy absence from his wife to every coach driver, liveryman, and innkeep between here and London. In doing so, he'd opened her to countless humiliating smirks and half-veiled jests.

She'd never understood his active dislike of her. He had not wished to marry her, but, then, she had not wanted him, either. At fifteen she had yearned for someone handsome and clever, not the dull, toadlike Edmund. But at fifteen she had also understood her duty to her family, and so she had wed her father's choice.

"Besides," she said, unwilling to consider the misery she'd suffered at Edmund's hands a moment longer,

"Richard Cranston and his wife had twelve children in the years they lived here."

"Well, I suppose that leaves out any manhood curses. Does everyone in Alwyn know about Cranston?"

Cicely sighed. "Likely not. I'll take Cranston's journal to the vicar, and perhaps he and Mrs. Joyes can help me put the lie to that outrageous belief."

Hannah stood and picked up her pewter candlestick, the ivory-colored candle in it burning halfway low. "I'll leave you ter your sleep, then. Tomorrow will be a long day for you."

After Hannah had gone, Cicely lay in her bed, the draperies tied back on this late summer's night to reveal the moon through the window's thick panes. If only she'd been wed to Griffin instead of Edmund. Everything would have been different. If only . . .

Early the next morning, Hannah and Digby came out to see Cicely and Griffin off on their quest to find the hermit. Hannah reached up to secure their basket lunch to the back of Cicely's sidesaddle.

Digby gallantly stepped in to lend Hannah a hand, taking the weight of her burden so she could fasten the small cinch. He immediately received a sharp look from her, which he blithely ignored.

"I can do this," Hannah insisted in a furious whisper that was audible to all.

"Of course you can, my flower," Digby gallantly agreed, making no move to let go of the basket. "Anyone can see that by your shapely, muscular arms. But no gentleman would ever let such a lovely lady strain herself."

"It's *no* strain."

Digby clucked his tongue in gentle disapproval.

"Being in such excellent womanly form, you simply don't feel it. Other women would, you know. Less fit women."

Hannah directed attention to quickly finishing the task while Digby continued to hold up the basket. As soon as she was finished, she lifted her skirts and hurried back into the house, calling back her good wishes for the journey. Digby bade Cicely and Griffin a good trip, then strolled off toward the stables, whistling.

Cicely's eyebrows drew down in concern. "Perhaps I should send Hannah to her parents while we are gone."

Griffin grinned and shook his head. "She's safe with Digby. I've never seen a man so smitten." He nudged Apollo into motion.

"Are you certain? One minute they're fighting, the next she's pushing him away, while he's being persistently good-natured and flattering."

"Sounds like a courtship to me."

Intrigued, Cicely caught up with Griffin. Her only experience with courtship was through observation of others. Tom's courtship of Kitty had been considerably different from what she saw going on between Hannah and Digby. Kitty had openly adored Tom, and her regard had been just as openly returned.

"Hannah doesn't seem to truly dislike Digby," she mused aloud.

"Cease fretting over it. They are best left alone to sort things out as they will."

"I suppose," she said.

"I doubt Hannah would welcome interference in this matter. But she might welcome a friendly ear."

True enough, Cicely thought. She would remind Hannah that she had an ally if she needed one.

"Not many ladies would concern themselves with the happiness of their maids," Griffin said. His black three-cornered hat cast a shadow across the upper part of his face. A playful breeze stirred the gleaming ebony queue that hung down between his shoulders.

Cicely studied him as he looked down the road in front of them. Tall, broad-shouldered, and lean, he sat straight in the saddle, his hips accommodating Apollo's rhythmic sway. He wore his leather riding coat, a blue waistcoat embroidered with black dragons, and buckskin breeches. And, as ever, his black top boots.

She wondered if he was looking forward to finding the hermit. Did Griffin care that Cicely would leave when Alasdair was safely at rest? Would he miss her?

It was foolish to consider such things, she knew. It should not matter to her if he would miss her or not. Either way, she would leave.

She turned her thoughts to the more cheerful prospect of sketching imposing Stor fjord. Uriah Coppard had related to her the descriptions a cousin visiting Norway had sent him in a letter. The country had captured her imagination, especially Stor fjord, which sounded wild and majestic, a subject to be captured with her pastels. Cicely smoothed away a nonexistent wrinkle in the skirt of her brown superfine riding habit. She had been taken with this rich color, she remembered, along with the leaf green of her gold galloon–trimmed waistcoat. Mayhap she would wear it on a ride through a park in Oslo. Her eyebrows drew down in puzzled uncertainty. That is, if there were parks in Oslo.

"Why the frown?" Griffin asked.

"I was merely considering taking a ride through a park in Oslo. Is there a park in Oslo?"

A corner of his mouth curved up slightly. "Yes, a quite excellent one."

"Have you been there?"

"Yes."

"What is it like?"

He shrugged. "'Tis a pretty park, like many others. Where there are towns, there are parks. Even in America, where the towns are surrounded by parklands of a sort, though they're much too wild for a lady's leisurely ride."

"Then I'll visit more civilized places, like Norway and Italy. Being eaten by a bear is not an ambition of mine."

Griffin was silent a while. "What do you seek in your travels?" he asked.

She glanced at him to determine if he was teasing her, but she saw no sign of amusement. "Why does anyone travel? To see things. Exotic things. To see new places." To capture these places with her pastels and paper.

"Is that all? To see new sights?"

She leaned over and patted Octavia's neck as she considered his question. In three words, he had managed to reduce her dreams to the mundane. But what she felt inside, what burned like a beacon, was not mundane. It was . . . essential.

"I seek to be free," she said. "Truly free, for the first time in my life. I shall go where I like, when I like and, once there, do what I like. Perhaps you cannot understand such a desire. You're a man. You've always had freedom."

He looked away, off into the distance for a moment. Then he turned back to regard her. Thick lashes almost concealed his silver eyes. "Being a man does not guarantee freedom."

She met his gaze. Her spiked words died on her tongue.

Edmund had wallowed in freedom. Her father had abused it. But Griffin was different. Despite his initial arrogance, which, she had to admit, might have been warranted, he had shown her a regard she had never received from the other two men. Unlike either of them, he concerned himself with the preservation of her reputation, and with those things he knew were important to her, often at expense to himself. He labored diligently, and his tenants respected him, though he had owned Cranwick manor not quite two months. She had never seen Edmund do an hour's work, much less a day's. As for her father, his idea of work was an evening spent at the gaming table.

As she looked into Griffin's gaze, she sensed that he was a man whose freedom had come at a dear price.

"What do you want in life?" she asked. He had offered little about himself, and she found herself thirsting to know more.

He broke the connection of their eyes and looked down the narrow dirt road lined with elms and hedgerows. A faint smile curved his lips. "I want peace."

She nodded. Perfectly understandable for a man who had just come home from a long war. She, on the other hand, had endured more peace in these past six years than anyone could ever want.

"I want a place where my children and their children can count themselves a part of its fabric."

Once, she had wanted the same thing. Once, she had been astonishingly naive. Griffin, however, was not naive. But then, things were different for men. She thought about him living at Cranwick without her, about him taking a wife, marrying her, perhaps, in the old Norman church in Alwyn. Later he would kiss his new bride. He would take her to his bed. And the babies she bore would have black hair and startlingly light gray eyes.

Quickly she shoved aside those thoughts. She didn't like to think of Griffin taking another woman to wife, or another woman rocking his child in her arms.

"Well," she said brightly, "I fear you'll not have your wish until Alasdair is put to rest. Perhaps the hermit will tell us how."

Griffin nodded. "Yes. The hermit."

She tilted her head and looked at him questioningly. "You sound unconvinced."

"Why would a man who lives well away from Cranwick Abbey know about Alasdair, when no one in Alwyn even knows?" Slanting raven eyebrows drew down. "It smacks too much of witchery for me to feel easy in the matter. 'Tis all unnatural."

"Love apples were once thought unnatural."

"They were thought an aphrodisiac, not unnatural."

His correction robbed her of her comparison. She frowned, trying to line up another, but failed.

He smiled, and she found herself entranced. Soot and silver. Dark and light. Pain and joy. It was easy to allow her imagination to take flight and see him wearing gleaming mail armor, his dark hair streaming in the wind. He'd carry a famed sword and ride a fire-breathing stallion with ruby eyes. An enchanted warrior returned from beyond the mists of time.

Cicely shook her head. She'd been alone too long! Enchanted warriors didn't settle for being farmers. They had battles to fight, giants to slay. Digging irrigation ditches and examining the muddy hooves of sheep would not interest the *sidhe*.

Griffin palmed the crown of his hat and adjusted it on his head. "We come from different directions on the matter of Alasdair. For me, he is a nuisance. He bars the way to my full possession of Cranwick. To you, he is a companion. I respect your defense of him, Cicely. I, however, find his behavior indefensible. But then, he does not nurture an affection for me."

Birds sang in the trees that spotted the landscape,

and in the fields and hedgerows. The syncopated thud of hooves gradually took on a soothing cadence. Cicely decided now was a good time to change the subject.

"You should go to Alwyn more often," she said. "The people need to meet you. And you need to meet them."

"I need to work. In case it has escaped your notice, there are only Digby and me to work the manor. Besides, you do very well in representing Cranwick Abbey to our neighbors."

Our neighbors. The two words, spoken so casually, sent a warm flutter through Cicely. As if their residing together had created a special bond between them. Now that she considered the matter, she saw that it had done just that.

She wasn't certain how that made her feel. Her head and her heart sent conflicting messages. *Run*, said her brain. But like a starved wild thing, her heart urged her a little closer to Griffin's shelter.

"Thank you," she said, impatient with her ambivalence. There was only one path for her, and it led away from Cranwick Abbey. "I cannot, however, take the place of the new master of the manor. Your position in the parish is one of importance, being one of the largest landowners on one of the oldest manors. I know you are desperately understaffed. With Digby acting as shepherd now, you're left to do everything else by yourself. But that may change soon."

Griffin's eyebrows lifted in surprise. "May it?"

"I hope so."

"Ah." That one syllable conveyed an ocean of implication.

"Well," she said defensively, feeling foolish over her inability to solve the situation at Cranwick. "I do hope. Most ardently. Do you think I enjoy knowing that I'm responsible for your inconvenience?"

"Inconvenience, is it? Madam, you have a gift for the understatement."

Heat rushed to her face. She held her silence. He was right, of course. She had loaded him with a property no one but him would work. Without workers, it could not be properly maintained, sufficient crops could not be planted or harvested to meet his payments to the bank.

Without workers, Griffin would lose Cranwick.

She had done this to him.

"Perhaps the hermit will enlighten us," she said. For Griffin's sake, she hoped so.

Griffin squinted up against the brightness of the sunny sky. "We live in hope," he muttered.

At noon they stopped to eat their meal. Cicely spread the cloth on the ground amid the ruins of a Norman castle. Only vine-draped stone walls stood now. Shafts of sunlight poured through window holes high above, spearing downward into the refreshing shade. Daisies mingled with deep violet bellflowers and dainty white clover blooms in the green carpet of grass. As Cicely laid out the dishes and napkins, Griffin watered the horses at a tiny brook that flowed nearby, then led them back among the ruins. There he hobbled their hind legs and turned them out to graze.

"Ah, and what have we here?" Griffin asked, rubbing his hands together. "Hmm. Smells like"—he sniffed the air and his eyes grew wide in feigned astonishment— "chicken."

Cicely laughed. "A considerable surprise." They'd had chicken frequently, since the sides of beef and pork curing in the smokehouse he'd built were for their winter meals. Both Hannah and Cicely had learned several new receipts for chicken and eggs—and were thankful to do so. Griffin kept them from hunger.

"Let's see, what kind of chicken do we eat today?" He peered under the cloth that covered the heaped platter. "Ah, roast chicken. My favorite kind."

"Every kind is your favorite kind," she teased.

He sat down cross-legged next to her. "Lucky for me, wouldn't you say?"

Cicely served up a plate to him bearing two pieces of roast chicken and helpings of each of the two other dishes. She pulled the cork from one of the bottles, and the sweet smell of homemade cherry wine drifted up to make her smile. She'd forgotten all about this wine. Hannah must have found it on the back of a shelf in the stillroom.

"What prompts such a pleasant smile?" Griffin asked.

"Oh, just a silly thing."

"Can you speak of it?"

She poured the fragrant wine into a pewter cup, which she handed to Griffin. "I was but remembering how I came to make this wine from Kentish cherries." She watched as he inhaled the fruity perfume, then took a sip.

"'Tis different," he said, judiciously. "I've not tasted cherry wine before." He sampled a swallow more. Then he smiled. "I like it. And you say you made this?"

She nodded as she poured a cup for herself. "I did."

"You are indeed a woman of unexpected talents."

A spark of mischief twinkled up in her. "Yes, I am."

Griffin laughed, and his baritone echoed through the ancient castle, lifting Cicely's spirits, charming her as no other man's laughter ever had before.

Delight danced in his eyes. "You are a saucy wench, aren't you?"

Feeling a heady freedom that was new to her, Cicely

plucked up a piece of chicken with her fork, and popped it in her mouth. Her silent laughter bubbled at the edges of her lips, causing them to twitch.

Griffin leaned over and lightly tugged a curling tendril of hair that had escaped her chignon to find its way from under her three-cornered riding hat. Then he leaned back and tended to his meal in earnest.

They laughed and teased throughout the meal. It was the most pleasant repast Cicely could remember. When they were finished, she packed the cloth, dishes, and utensils back into the basket, except their cups and the almost-empty bottle of cherry wine.

They strolled through the sunlight-dappled shade of the ruins. The day had grown warmer, but here they found the cooling lushness of verdant quiet. She breathed in the mingled scents of old stone, rich earth, and—she smiled—dark, sweet cherry wine.

"Where did you live as a boy?" she asked, straying beyond that invisible, unmentioned line that seemed to exist between them.

"Hereford."

When he did not elaborate, she tried again. "Are your parents still living there?"

"No. They died years ago."

He tugged a leaf off the green mass of vine that cloaked much of the wall. His gaze dropped to the splash of emerald between his thumb and finger. Cicely sensed he did not see the leaf at all, but rather some scene from the past that played out in his head. Something about his stillness left her with the impression of unfinished business in the matter of his mother and father.

"You miss them," she said.

His mouth curved up. "Yes. I do miss them sometimes." He twirled the leaf by its stem. "My parents were unfashionably besotted with one another. Theirs was a love match. One could only look at them together and wish for such happiness." His lips curved more. "Do you know, what I remember most clearly about them was their laughter?"

His smile unconsciously coaxed one from her. "Have you any brothers or sisters?"

Griffin's smile vanished abruptly. "No." He tossed away the leaf. "What of your family?"

"I have two younger sisters. My family's lineage is old and glorious, but I fear the glory took place long ago."

"How did you meet your husband?"

"Years of ill-advised financial decisions and my father's refusal to economize placed us deeply in debt. As did my mother's gambling. Edmund's father had made a vast fortune in shipping, and he wished to elevate his family's social standing by allying it with the name of a peer. My father was an earl who needed money. Edmund's father had money to spend. So terms were agreed upon and a marriage arranged." Her fingers tightened on her pewter cup. "It was a bargain that seemed to profit everyone."

"Everyone, it seems, but the bride," Griffin said softly.

She remembered when her father had informed her that she was to marry Edmund Honeysett. At the age of fifteen, she had received his announcement with bowed head, silent as a dutiful daughter should be. Dread and resentment had churned in her stomach. After her father had left her room, she had given in to tears. Weeping as she had lived her life after the stiff wedding ceremony—alone.

Griffin turned to her. Gently he pried the cup from her fingers and dropped it to the soft earth. His eyes searched her face, and there was about them an expression she'd never seen.

Before she could think further, she felt his thumbs stroke her cheeks. Then he lowered his head, dodging the brim of her hat, and gently brushed his parted lips back and forth across hers, stilling her breath in her throat.

His fingers lifted the galloon-trimmed three-cornered hat from her head.

"Oh," she murmured, reaching up to self-consciously touch her bared head.

He smiled. "Yes. Oh." Then he gathered her into his arms, hat still in his hand, and kissed her again.

His mouth moved over hers, coaxing, teasing, searing, until she willingly parted her lips for his entry. With sensual progress, his tongue moved toward hers. His free hand roamed restlessly over her back.

She wound her arms around his waist, leaning into him. The hard shape of his arousal pressed against her. Automatically, she drew away. He gathered her back to him, nuzzling her ear. "There's nothing to fear, sweetheart," he whispered. "'Tis natural for a man's body to react so when he's kissing the most desirable woman in England."

Heat rushed to Cicely's cheeks, and she shoved at him ineffectually. "Cruelty does not become you, sir. You know very well I'm not the most desirable woman in England." If she had been, Edmund would not have been so repulsed. "Likely I'm not even the most desirable woman on the manor."

Griffin cocked an eyebrow. "Who is the better judge of female desirability here? You or I? To me, you are"—he dropped a tender kiss on the lid of an eye that had been glaring at him—"the most beautiful"—he placed a kiss on her other eyelid—"and desirable woman"—his lips planted a kiss on the crown of her right cheekbone—"in"—another kiss on her other cheekbone—"all"—his lips caressed her chin, then

moved up to her mouth—"England." The final word
was spoken against her lips, an enchanting tracery of
movement against her firmly closed mouth.

She breathed in the leather, horse, and pine balsam
scent of him, and his breath redolent with cherry wine.
Lifting her gaze to his, she searched for the lie, the joke
that would mock her. But all she found was the truth.
Or, rather, she amended, *his* truth.

That was good enough for her.

She pressed her lips to his.

His arms tightened around her. "Cicely." The word
was a benediction and a supplication whispered against
her lips. In answer, she raised her arms and twined
them about his neck.

He dropped her hat. Though she could feel the rigid
tension in him, his lips touched hers with tender sensuality, stealing her breath. His gentle hands heated her
through her clothing. Never before had she experienced
such feelings. The thunder in her heart. The singing in
her heart. It was a kind of magic.

Griffin raised his head and looked down at Cicely's
upturned face. Her rich chestnut lashes formed twin
crescents on peach-blushed cheeks. Her parted lips
were moist and swollen from his kisses.

He wanted her. Hot blood hammered through his
veins. His hands trembled with his need.

She opened her eyes. There, in those wide, amber-
brown depths, he saw something unexpected. Something
that left him more shaken than his raging desire. Something that filled him with a curious humility.

He saw . . . wonder.

Griffin knew he could take her now, here among the
wildflowers. She would give herself to him willingly, of

that he was certain. Temptation seared him, whispered
to him.

It was defeated by her innocence, by her wonder that
shone from her eyes.

This woman was no common wench to be tumbled in
a field, nor was she a pedigreed ewe to be bargained for
as her father had done. Cicely was someone special.
Someone who deserved to be wooed. Patiently. Tenderly.

She was the woman he wanted for his wife.

12

Gently he drew away. "One last kiss." He smiled. "But we must keep it quick, or we'll never get 'round to see the hermit."

Her mouth curved up as she lifted her face toward his, and he found himself charmed again by the loveliness of her. He joined their lips in a lingering kiss that sent his heart pounding into triple time.

Finally, he dragged in a deep breath and let it out sharply. "Come, sweetheart. Best we go *now*."

She nodded bemusedly and, with his hand at the small of her back to guide her, they went to find the horses.

He'd ask her to wed him tonight, he thought. The decision fit into place like the final piece of an incomplete puzzle, and he knew at once it was right. More right than anything had been in his life for too long.

As he untied the rope around Octavia's back legs, Griffin considered how much his life had changed in a span of months. He had a home now, and land. And soon, he hoped, he would have a wife. Suddenly he grinned.

Life was good.

Despite a delay for turning back to retrieve Cicely's hat and cup, they found the hermit's cottage with little trouble. All the farm folk in the area knew of the old man. Indeed, they seemed to hold him in reverence.

He dwelled in an oak forest, and his tiny cottage blended so well with the land that only Griffin's experience in tracking kept them from riding past it.

Echoes of birdcalls and the rustling of small, unseen creatures rooting through the humus endowed the deeply shadowed forest with an eerie, haunted quality. On edge, Griffin glanced over his shoulder. It had been in a forest similar to this one that he'd nearly lost his life.

"Stay mounted," he instructed Cicely. "I'll see about the hermit." He fixed her with a stern look. "If I don't come back out, or if you hear any strange noises from inside that house, you *ride*, do you hear me? Ride like the devil was on your coattails."

"An intriguing picture, I'm sure," said an unfamiliar voice from the house.

Griffin whirled, his flintlock cocked and ready.

"You may put your weapon away, my boy." A small, wizened man with long, flowing white hair and an equally long beard stood in the doorway, leaning on a staff of gnarled wood. He smiled, and his rosy-cheeked face lit, reminding Griffin of paintings of angels he'd seen in his father's collection.

Griffin regarded him warily. "We were told the one who lives here is blind."

The bent little gnome smiled. "And so he is. So he is, indeed."

Griffin cast a sidelong glance at Cicely, who regarded the fellow with interest. He'd have felt better if she'd looked more cautious.

"My name is Griffin Tyrrell, and I come seeking information."

"I am Dunstan. Welcome." With a regal wave of his arm, he indicated four beautifully carved stools arranged outside his front door. "Come, Griffin Tyrrell. Sit." He looked up, directly at Cicely, who had been sitting quietly. "You, also, my dear. There's no need for you to stay on your horse. Pray, be seated, and I shall fetch the nice apricot cordial I've opened for your visit." Wearing the smile of a wise cherub, he turned and hobbled back into the cottage.

Griffin frowned at his retreating back. Out of the corner of his eye, he saw Cicely dismounting, and he strode over to assist her, enjoying the opportunity to feel her slim waist between his hands.

She looked away, blushing. "There are proper ways of helping a lady down from her horse," she murmured.

"I know," he said, delighted by her shy modesty. "I enjoy doing it this way."

They sat on the stools carved with strange patterns, and a few minutes later Dunstan returned with a tray bearing three small, carved-horn cups and an earthenware jar.

He set it unerringly on the fourth stool, then turned clouded, pale blue eyes toward Cicely. "My dear, would you please attend the honors for me?"

Cicely smiled. "Yes, of course." She carefully tipped the jar to pour, releasing the heavy golden liquid into the cups.

She handed the first to their host, who thanked her. The second cup went to Griffin, who touched her fingers as he accepted it from her. Color glowed in her cheeks.

Dunstan turned to her. "I don't believe we were introduced, child."

"Lady Cicely Honeysett," Griffin said, "may I make known to you Dunstan of the forest?"

"I am so pleased to meet you, Dunstan."

"You flatter an old man, my dear, but I am quite gratified finally to make your acquaintance." He leaned slightly closer to her, his unseeing eyes crinkling at the corners in amusement. "I think this fellow is most cautious where your welfare is concerned."

Cicely's eyelashes lowered, and a bright peach-tinted blush bloomed in her cheeks.

Griffin smiled, then took a swallow of cordial. The sharp, fruity perfume of apricots and brandy filled his nostrils.

"Which brings us to the purpose of your visit, does it not?" Dunstan suggested gently.

"Yes," Cicely said.

Dunstan set his cup on the tray. "I wondered how long it would be until someone tried to help him find peace."

Griffin lifted a suspicious brow. "Who?"

An angelic smile lit Dunstan's face. "Why, Alasdair, of course."

"How did you know?" Cicely asked.

"Oh, I'm familiar with the spirit of Alasdair MacNab. The presence of that unhappy soul can be felt all the way to this cottage."

Griffin studied the old man closely. "How do you know that's why we've come?"

Dunstan shrugged. "Some things are given to me."

Griffin eyed the remainder of golden cordial in the cup. He found the hermit's answer unsatisfyingly vague, yet oddly acceptable. Clearly he'd been living with a ghost too long.

Cicely leaned toward Dunstan, her face glowing with earnest intensity. "I do wish to help Alasdair find peace, Dunstan. I've asked him, and he told me that he desires his final rest. But he does not believe it can be done. And he cannot, or will not, tell me how his present state was brought about."

The old man turned his face, and Griffin could have sworn Dunstan saw something perhaps so distant that their more ordinary eyes could not glimpse it.

"Near the end of his mortal days," Dunstan said quietly, "Alasdair was reclusive and evil-tempered.

"One night, there was a terrible storm. The thunder crashed and the dark sky poured down a driving rain. Just outside the gate of Cranwick, there was an accident. The carriage of a traveler, a woman dressed all in green, broke a wheel. Alasdair refused to leave his manor to assist her, which sent her into a fury. Unfortunately for Alasdair, this woman was different from other travelers. She wasn't mortal, you see, but rather from the realm of Faerie. And Alasdair's lack of charity angered her.

"She placed a bane on him: He would die a foolish death, and his spirit would be chained to his precious land for all eternity."

Griffin received the story with skeptical reservation. Cicely's solemn expression told him that she accepted Dunstan's tale with the innocence of one who believes there are powers beyond her reckoning. He sighed, swirling the cordial around in his cup. Then he smiled. Her innocence, her willingness to believe, were just two of the many things about her that enchanted him.

She placed her fingertips on the brown sleeve of the old man's robe. "Dunstan, what must we do to release Alasdair's soul to his eternal peace? Does it require magic?"

"Of a sort." The old man turned his blind face directly to her, and his lips curved in a smile lit with secret knowledge. "But there is more magic at your Cranwick than merely a Scotsman's spirit."

Her eyebrows drew down in puzzlement. "What do you mean?"

Dunstan patted her hand, but gave her no answer.

With a frown, Griffin set his cup down. He disliked mysteries. "What do you mean by that?" he asked impatiently.

Dunstan rose to his feet with the help of his gnarled staff and Cicely's instant assistance.

Griffin stood. "How do we put the ghost to rest?" he asked again, worried that the old fellow would go into his cottage and leave their most important question unanswered.

Dunstan turned back to them. "The time is not right to tell you. Return to me after the passing of the moon cycle." He hobbled into the dark interior of the cottage and closed the door.

Griffin brooded over Dunstan's evasiveness most of the way home. Cicely seemed inclined toward silence. Occupied, he imagined, with thoughts of what had passed at the forest cottage. He'd much rather she'd been thinking of him than a mad hermit and a vile-tempered ghost.

The moon was high in the sky by the time they arrived at Cranwick. As if summoned by Griffin's thoughts of him, Alasdair appeared.

"A fine thing it is, keepin' Cicely from her sleep," he thundered, feet planted wide, hands propped on narrow, wool-clad hips. He floated along-side Griffin. "Ye cauldhearted poltroon! If ye have no care for yer own reputation, at least have a care for hers." His face soft-ened as he looked across at Cicely. "Are ye sore weary, then, lass?" he asked, his voice gentled by concern.

Cicely smiled tiredly. "Yes, I'm weary, Alasdair, but a night's sleep will remedy that."

"Och, and it's exhausted ye'll be tomorrow, for ye'll no have a full night's sleep this night. Too much of it is already spent." He glared at Griffin.

Griffin bristled. "I'll not be scolded as if I were some truant apprentice. Especially not by a vaporous harpy."

The ever-present cool breeze that circulated around Alasdair grew more agitated. "Vaporous harpy, am I?"

Griffin glared at him. "You heard me."

Alasdair ominously lifted a hand.

"Stop it!" Cicely ordered. "Stop it this minute. Alasdair, don't you dare call down anything on Griffin. And Griffin, Alasdair's only showing his concern for my wel-fare. It *is* late." She directed her words to Alasdair now. "We've been to see a blind hermit to consult him on how you can find your rest. He gave us no answer today, but told us to return after the next moon cycle. Which we shall do. Alasdair, I'll tell you all about it later, if that's agreeable."

He inclined his head. "At your convenience, sweet Cicely." He vanished.

"Bloody arrogance," Griffin muttered, shooting a narrowed glance at the air where Alasdair had been the second before.

They made their way to the dower house stable, where they tended the horses, then let themselves into the house. In the kitchen they found a small fire burn-ing in the fireplace and a pot of stew warming in the ashes. Griffin blessed Hannah's thoughtfulness.

He took two bowls from the cupboard shelf and spoons from their case, and Cicely dished up the stew.

They ate their late-night meal accompanied by warm ale and the occasional popping ember in the fireplace.

"What do you think he meant, 'There's more magic at Cranwick Abbey than just a Scotsman's spirit'?" Cicely asked abruptly, her voice breaking the silence like a pebble plunked into still water.

Griffin shrugged. "More of his mystic's nonsense, I expect. I would not be astonished to arrive there again, only to have him tell us that we must return yet another time."

"You didn't believe him?"

"Do you mean his tale of the Green Lady?" She nodded. "Well—" He broke off as he noticed her serious expression. Quickly he rephrased what he had been about to say. "I find it difficult to believe," he admitted, "but I'm trying. 'Tis hard not to be skeptical of things you've been told all your life don't exist."

Cicely reached across the table to pat his hand understandingly. "Perhaps it is easier for me because I have been around Alasdair so long. After seeing him float in the air, change shapes, and vanish again and again for so long, it becomes quite easy to believe almost anything."

Griffin chuckled. "I suppose that must be true."

"I couldn't help but notice how uneasy you were when we entered the forest near Dunstan's place."

Dark memories rushed through him. His muscles knotted with sudden tension. "I was nearly killed in a forest much like that one. I was leading a scouting party. We were ambushed."

He looked away. "I was left for dead by my retreating men, shoved under a bank of ferns in hopes my carcass wouldn't be scalped. My young cousin, Jeremy Edman, wasn't so lucky." The muscles in his jaw jumped. "I *told* him to get out of the regiment, to resign his commission when it became clear we wouldn't be sent to India. He actually laughed when I tried to persuade him to stay home. 'I know I'm safe with you, Cousin,' he said.'" Griffin stared down into his mug, struggling to hold the guilt and rage at bay.

Cicely leaned across the table and touched her fingers to the back of his hand. "Griffin, even I can perceive how impossible that would be. It was war. Even generals are killed in battle, and they have entire regiments around them. Jeremy was a soldier. He had to have understood the risk."

"He was young. Only seventeen."

"His parents could have withheld their consent."

"They trusted me."

"Enough to turn over their son to an enemy's bullets? I doubt that very much. It was an indulgence on their part, an abdication of responsibility. Perhaps he was headstrong, I cannot say. But no one could have actually expected you to 'keep him safe' in battle."

They ate their meal in silence while Griffin pushed back his memories of that ambush. When they were finished, they took the dishes to the scullery. As they walked through the dark house, toward the corridor where their bedchambers were located, he caught Cicely studying him.

"Your limp is worse," she said.

"I've spent hours in the saddle. Considering that, the muscles aren't nearly so cramped as they used to be when I'd spent the day riding." He was charmed by the way her lovely face lit up.

"I'm delighted to hear you feel your leg is improving."

He took her hand. "If you would not mind stepping into the parlor, there is something I would like to say to you."

"Very well." In the light of their candles, her silhouette danced along the walls, into the towering parlor.

As Griffin closed the door behind them, a spurt of nervousness shot through him. He was getting ready to ask this woman to wed him. How well did he know her? Could he make her happy? Could he be happy with her? For the rest of their lives?

Then she turned around to face him, and he felt his panicked doubt melt away. She was the most generous, responsible, sweet-natured woman he had ever known. He would do everything in his power to please her. And he knew, beyond all doubt, that without her he would never be happy.

He set his candle on a small table, then took hers from her unresisting fingers and set it beside his. Before he could say anything, Cicely came into his arms. She closed her eyes and lifted her face. It seemed she thought he'd lured her into the parlor for kisses. Griffin grinned. Who was he to disappoint his future wife?

She tasted of malty ale, pepper, and rosemary. As he immersed himself in the rocketing excitement of feeling her against him, he knew no other woman could ever stir him this way. Her innocence was intoxicating. Her innate sweetness drew him to her more surely than flowers drew bees.

He moved his mouth to her slender neck, nibbling, nipping lightly, teasing with the tip of his tongue until she moaned softly. God in heaven, had there ever been a more dulcet sound?

She reached up and slipped loose the ribbon that held his queue, sending his hair tumbling free. Then she threaded her widespread fingers through the mass.

Red desire licked through him. Griffin captured her mouth and took it in a driving, carnal kiss. She clung to him. He filled his hand with her breast, stroking and kneading it through her clothing until he felt her shudder. Gradually, her hips took on the ancient rhythm. He cupped her buttock with his other hand, rubbing her against him, blind with primitive need.

He was reaching for the buttons of her form-fitting waistcoat when he caught a glimpse of them in the looking glass on the wall. What he saw stunned his mind into sanity.

This was not right. She was essentially a virgin. She deserved better than this. She deserved to be wooed. Gently. And when the courtship had reached the right moment, it should be her husband who initiated her into the pleasures of lovemaking.

Dragging in a long, steadying breath, he struggled to bring his desire under control. When she looked at him with her passion-hooded eyes, her parted lips moist and swollen from his kisses, Griffin almost abandoned his struggle. Another glance into the mirror renewed it.

"I have something important to discuss with you," he said, "and being so close to you has the power to befuddle my brain." He gave her one last, painfully brief kiss and moved back a few inches from her, though he did not release her.

She blinked. "Something to discuss?" She blinked again.

He saw the moment when she seemed to regain her focus.

"Yes?" she prompted, as if to let him know she was ready to cope with something that required her undivided attention.

He gazed into her golden, brandy brown eyes, imagining the years ahead of them. They would make love. Eventually, raise a family. Together they would build a future. "Will you be my wife?"

*   *   *

Cicely stared at him as the blood drained from her face. "Wife?"

Griffin nodded, a soft smile curving his lips. "I'm asking you to marry me."

A tight knot of despair twisted in her chest. She backed out of his arms. "I-I'm honored," she stammered, finding it difficult to draw enough breath. "But I can't. I can't marry you."

Griffin turned pale. "May I know why?" he asked. His words were evenly and precisely spoken.

Why? Why couldn't she have married Griffin instead of Edmund? Griffin, who made her heart soar with a single glance? Teasing, hardworking, passionate Griffin? He would not have abandoned her, humiliated her. At least, she wanted to believe he would not.

But she could not take the risk.

She knew she could not survive another resentful husband. And there was nothing to protect a woman, no guarantee that even the most ardent lover, over some trifle, might not turn sullen and brutal. A husband wielded so much power over his wife. So very much power.

As a widow she could go where she wanted, do what she chose. Her money was at only her disposal.

For the first time in her life, precious freedom was finally hers.

She could not lose it to any man.

Over these past months, Griffin Tyrrell had quietly taken possession of her heart. Were he to own her body, as well, he would have greater possession of her than Edmund ever had.

Her hands clutched distractedly at her waist. "I cannot think a gentleman would press a lady for a reason."

Anger flashed in his eyes. "Gentleman be damned. I wish to know. You may be a lady, Cicely, but more than that, you are a woman. A warm, loving woman who has been denied a proper husband. I'm not Edmund, surely you can see the difference! I would . . . cherish you."

Tears burned at the backs of her eyes as Cicely struggled for composure. "Oh, Griffin, do you think I don't know you're nothing like Edmund? You've been more considerate and husbandlike to me in two months than he was in six long years."

"Then why?" he demanded. "Why do you refuse me?" He spread his hands before him, unconsciously revealing the calluses from his labors to improve Cranwick. "*I wish to make you my wife.*" When she did not answer, he dropped his hands to his sides. "A more honorable estate than that I cannot offer you." When still she did not respond, he walked heavily to the door.

A sob welled up, threatening to break in her throat. "'Tis not your rank, or lack of it. Can't you understand? *I am afraid!*"

His hand froze on the doorknob. He turned back to her. "Of *me*?"

She shook her head. "Of your power. Of every husband's power over his wife. It is complete. Godlike. A woman's well-being, her very life, hangs on his goodwill. He may kiss her or beat her, indulge or abandon her as he chooses."

"Woman is the heart of life," he said. "'Tis a husband's holy duty to protect her, to keep her safe—"

Her crack of bitter laughter pierced the room. "As my father protected my mother? God save me from such safety! She bore his bruises even into prison, where she died. No doubt she welcomed death by then. His outrageous gambling had us all daily dodging creditors, but when he began to rub her nose in his dirty little affairs with the worst of trollops, her heart finally broke. She took to the card table and drove us further into debt—and bore the consequences of my father's temper. One night there was an argument among the players at her table, and she was accused of stealing. My father allowed her to be taken to prison. Only for a little while, he said, to teach her a lesson. He never even questioned if she'd been falsely accused." Years of anger at her father bled poison into her words. "How *well* he protected her. The fever that finally took my mother was not the true killer. My father should have been hanged for murder were his victim not merely his wife."

She dashed infuriating tears from her eyes with the back of her hand. "And what protection did I receive from my own dear husband? He brought me to this place and deserted me. He shorted my allowance established in the marriage agreement, providing only enough for my food and sometimes cloth to replace a worn-out gown. There was no escape, for I wasn't even allowed a horse. Oh, he had new furnishings sent, but that was likely more for his own occasional comfort than mine. Griffin, I was a prisoner for *years*. At his death I gained my liberty. For the first time in my life, I am free. Now you ask me to give myself over to your dominion."

Griffin crossed the room to her in a few swift strides. "I'm not your father, Cicely," he told her, his deep voice low and intense. "Nor am I the bastard who left you here by yourself. But you're damning me for their crimes. I've never lifted my hand to a woman, nor did I take a wife when I thought I couldn't protect her. How many soldiers left families behind here in England when they went off to fight in America? I left no one, for I knew I didn't have the power to keep her safe when I was so far away." The fierce light in his eyes softened. He lifted his hand and stroked the backs of his fingers along her cheekbone. "'Tis a hard thing to bear, knowing you have no one waiting for you, no one to miss you or care should you die."

She wanted to turn her face into his hand, to move into the embrace she knew he would offer, but the uncertainty and fear of choosing unwisely kept her still. Oh, how well she knew that lonely feeling. It started as a small, wistful yearning, but over the years it grew, consuming confidence and courage, until only an empty shell was left where once a soul had thrived.

Their eyes met. How beautiful his were, she thought, torn with longing. As silver as the moon, framed by the night of his lashes. His beautiful eyes that would never look at her this way again.

13

Griffin sat sprawled in the wing-back chair in his room, staring numbly into the empty fireplace. The glow of a single candle illuminated the other side of his chamber, leaving him to brood in the dark.

She'd wanted to believe in him, in the truth of what he told her, he'd seen it there, in her eyes. But the caution bred by her wretched experience had pulled her back.

Anger at her father, at Edmund Honeysett, roiled in his stomach. Damn them! Damn them both to hell. What kind of animals were they to misuse their women so? But he knew. Only men could be so cruel.

Griffin sighed heavily as he leaned his forearms across his knees, his hands clenched. As spiteful and mean-spirited as his own father's first wife had been, Griffin had never heard of Vincent Tyrrell's bullying her, and certainly never striking her, though she had done her best to provoke him. Griffin had never heard of his father's being so much as rude to the viper, much less abusive. With Griffin's own mother there'd been love words and laughter. On the rare occasions where there had been disagreements, they had been so passionately shouted that the entire household had hung breathlessly on every word. And afterward, when the inevitable quiet ensued, champagne had always been ordered to be left outside the closed doors of the master's bedchamber. The following morning his father's face would be wreathed in a smile, and his mother would blush and glow by turns. There had been no neglect in his father's house. No brutality or humiliation. His mother had been queen of his father's heart, and she had taken excellent care of it until the day they had died.

That was what he wanted with Cicely. It was what he offered her.

That's what she wanted, too; he would swear to it. Why else would it have been so grievous for her to reject his proposal of marriage?

He considered the matter for a moment. If she had been held prisoner at Cranwick for so long, perhaps she wished, as she said, to see the world and seek adventure. He had no doubt she would find adventure right here in Sussex, and that in plenty. What other woman did he know who had fobbed off a haunted manor on some unsuspecting codspate, been hauled down a public dock slung over a strange man's shoulder and kidnapped to return to the scene of her crime? Who else communed daily with a vile-natured Scottish specter? Or rode off to a dark forest to discuss putting that very specter to rest with an all-knowing blind hermit? No, if it was adventure she longed for, she need look no farther than Cranwick. Griffin frowned, puzzled. Why was she so set on the Continent? What was there that she could not find in England? Perhaps the answer held a key that would help him to persuade her to change her mind.

He surged up out of the chair. Persuade her he would! He paced to the draped tester bed, then back to the chair. He would *show* her she could trust in him. He'd convince her to believe he'd never allow harm to come to her.

This time, he would not fail to safeguard the one who looked to him for protection.

Griffin sat on the edge of the high bed and jerked off his boots. He pulled off his waistcoat and stripped off his stockings, defiantly tossing them across the back of the chair, when usually he took care immediately to put everything in its place. His breeches and shirt followed. Then he climbed naked into the bed. For too many years, necessity had forced him to sleep fully clothed in his uniform, his rifle close at hand.

Now all he wanted was to sleep with Cicely close at hand, so he might touch her in the darkest hour of the night to assure himself that she was real.

That she was his.

And that she loved him.

"The black lugger comes in a fortnight," Tom told Cicely and Kitty in a low voice as soon as he stepped into his cottage and closed the door behind him.

A stone suddenly dropped into the bottom of Cicely's stomach.

"Are you still willing ter take Kitty's place, Lady Cicely?" he asked, every line of his tanned face taut.

Cicely nodded, shooting a glance at Kitty, who sat on the edge of the bed, looking miserable and pressing her hand to the low small of her back.

As Cicely watched, Kitty's eyes abruptly widened. "Tom," Kitty said tightly, "'tis time for you ter fetch the midwife."

Tom leaped to his feet and crossed the small room in three quick steps. "Are you sure, love? Are you . . . did it . . . has there been water?" he babbled, taking her hand between his.

"Yes, a little while ago, when I went ter the privy. Now, please don't fret so. Just *go!*"

"Mrs. Kimball is with Barbara Rawle, at Timsbley Hall," Cicely said, trying to quell her rising panic. She'd never been present at a birthing, though her mother had borne two girls after Cicely.

"I'll drag her here by force, needs be!" Tom shouted, his expression a cross between militant determination and wild anxiety.

"You stay with Kitty. I'll get Dame Ingate."

"Dame Ingate!" Tom protested. "She's as old as the earth!"

"And she's had sixteen children, who all survived. She'll know what to do."

"No!" Kitty exclaimed. "I don't want Tom ter see me so. 'Twill distress him." Her face contorted and her body tightened. She tried hard not to cry out, but could not stay the pained moan that escaped her.

Seeing the look of agony on Tom's face, Cicely quickly pushed him out the door. "Go!" she ordered. "Dame Ingate will know what to do."

She didn't have to say more. Tom broke into a full run, heading toward the dame's house. Wiping her sweating palms on her apron, Cicely plastered a reassuring smile on her face for Kitty's sake.

"Come," she said. "Let's make you as comfortable as we can while Tom runs off to do your bidding."

"I need to walk," Kitty said, accepting Cicely's help to get to her feet. "It's better when I walk. Mrs. Kimball told me to walk when the labor pains started."

"Well, I expect she knows best." Cicely offered Kitty

her hand, and the young woman grasped it like a life-line.

Cicely started them walking around the interior of the small cottage, but Kitty insisted they go out to walk around the house on the flower-lined path. "I'll be anchored in the house soon enough," Kitty explained. "For now, I'd like to spend a little time—" Her face contorted, and she squeezed Cicely's hand so tightly, Cicely thought she heard bones snap.

"How long have you been having pains before the one that set us all in such a fright?" Cicely asked when Kitty's pain eased.

Kitty waved a hand. "A while. Mrs. Kimball said not to worry until they were close together."

"Oh, she did?" Cicely thought Mrs. Kimball sounded like an idiot.

Kitty smiled. "No need to worry, Cicely. I helped my mother birth my two brothers."

"Well, then, I suppose there's no need for me to be concerned." A pathetic lie if ever she'd heard one.

"Still," Kitty went on, "'twas an excellent idea ter send Tom for Dame Ingate. She'll know what's what, should a need arise."

"She'll likely bring one of her daughters along to actually . . . er . . . handle things. I hold Dame Ingate in high esteem. She's an intelligent female and has raised a family of intelligent, admirable children."

Their shoes crunched on the white oyster shells as they began their third slow turn around the outside of the house.

"Do you know, ter this day," Kitty said breathlessly, "she places flowers on the graves of her husbands on the anniversaries of their marriages. Love matches, all of them, and the first she defied her father ter have. The old man cast her out without a farthing and wouldn't speak ter her for years." Another pain seized Kitty and they stopped until it passed. Cicely looked around, impatient for Tom to return with Dame Ingate, fearing that Kitty might have the babe here on the sun-bleached path.

"Was it worth the sacrifice, this first love match of hers?" Cicely asked, trying to distract Kitty's attention from her growing discomfort.

Kitty nodded. "She believes so." They walked a little farther, Kitty leaning on Cicely's arm. "Often I've felt pity for rich folk, a-marrying strangers as they do, to bring their families more land and more guineas." She managed a wan smile. "When you have nothing, all you can offer is your heart."

A loud crunching of oyster shell heralded a breath-less Tom. "She's coming! Bringing her daughter along to help."

Kitty sagged against Cicely. "Please, help me ter bed."

Tom swept his wife into his arms and strode into the cottage, Cicely close behind. A few minutes later, Dame Ingate and her daughter, Lucy Name, arrived and shooed Tom out of the way. Then Mrs. Name examined the progress of the babe. "Dear me," she said with a smile. "Your babe is nearly here."

A labor pain seized Kitty, sending her arching almost off the bed.

Lucy Name turned to Tom. "Out." Looking at Cicely, she said, "Please take Tom outside, Lady Cicely, and stay with him."

Tom's face took on a mulish expression. "I'll not leave her."

"Oh, yes you will, my fine fellow," Mrs. Name returned, dwarfed by his greater size. "You'll wait out-side, because if you don't, Kitty will try ter put on a brave face, and right now what she needs ter do will hurt. She can't be a-worrying over you, too."

Tom went to Kitty and gently kissed her sweaty cheek. "I'll be right outside, love. I won't leave you."

She gave him a grateful smile and squeezed his hand. Then her face contorted, and she screamed.

The look of distressed horror on Tom's face was enough to prompt Cicely to grab his sleeve and tug him out the door. She pulled threepence from her pocket and gave it to a passing boy, with instructions to bring them two pints of ale and some beef broth. As the lad scampered off in the direction of Mrs. Fullard's ale-house, Tom paced. Back and forth in front of the house, tense and impatient. Each time Kitty screamed his face clouded with fear and guilt. Cicely tried to think of something to distract him, to distract them both, but her few attempts at conversation went unheeded.

Finally, the boy returned with the ale and the broth. Cicely paid him more than the errand was worth to reward his honesty and felt herself rewarded by his youthful grin.

She took the broth inside the cottage, letting Dame Ingate know that there was something fortifying for Kitty when she was able to eat. From the tin pail full of foamy brew, she poured four cups and took two back outside with her. She handed one to Tom, who immediately took a long draught.

"'Tis my fault," he mourned. "My greedy, lustful fault that my sweet Kitty suffers." He took another swig. "She could have had any man in Alwyn. *Any* man. But no, she settled on me. And look what it's got her." He fixed a self-recriminating gaze on Cicely, as if inviting her to agree with him.

"Likely it's got her a fine son or daughter," she said, and took a swallow of ale.

He brightened. "Do you think so?"

Cicely almost laughed, but managed to choke it back. The man was consumed with worry for his wife. She would not make light of that. "Yes, Tom," she said gently, seeing the rough-edged young man in a different light for the first time. "I do."

He plowed his big hand through his hair, leaving spikes of it sticking up. "I wish it were over with."

"We all do."

"Oh, my poor Kitty. If only she comes out of this alive, I'll never touch her again! I swear it!"

At another shriek from inside, Cicely downed the remainder of her ale in a single gulp. Was that what she wanted for herself? Months of discomfort and the final agony. Perhaps death? No, no, she thought shakily. She'd been fortunate Edmund had abhorred her, and she'd not even known it until now.

"What did your father do when your mother had her babies, Tom?" Cicely asked.

"This. Just what I'm doing here. He paced outside. Except the one time, when she had my youngest brother. There was a gale a-blowing then. My da sent the rest of us ter safety inland, and he stayed with Ma. He delivered Pat, he did."

Her father had gone off to play cards and drink with his cronies, Cicely thought bitterly, whenever her mother had been brought to childbed. When he'd returned, the following day, he'd lectured her mother for not bearing him a son.

As she watched Tom's journey back and forth across the small garden, first one way, then the other, she tried to imagine what Griffin would do. As she sat there on the weathered wooden bench, the sun warm on her back, the empty earthenware mug resting between her hands in her lap, she was filled with the oddly certain knowledge that Griffin would not go off to game and drink. Like Tom and Tom's father, Griffin would remain close by his wife.

With a small unhappy noise in her throat, Cicely thumped the cup onto the bench and launched herself to her feet, taking up the brisk, steady steps. She would not think of Griffin, of what she might have with him. She would not.

A thin, reedy squall came from inside the cottage, and both Tom and Cicely stopped in their tracks to stare in that direction. Minutes later, Dame Ingate appeared at the door, her wrinkled face wreathed in smiles.

"You've a fine, healthy daughter, Thomas Sparke," she said.

"Kitty," he croaked. "What of my wife?"

"She'll be having many more of your babes."

With an exclamation of relief, Tom ran into his house. Cicely followed more slowly, hesitant to intrude on the couple at such a moment, yet unable to resist the pull of seeing the new baby.

She stood just inside the cottage door and watched Tom and a pale Kitty as they reunited after the worry and pain of their daughter's birth.

Tom knelt by the side of the bed and tenderly kissed Kitty's damp forehead. Their eyes and smiles were for only each other. A few minutes later, Lucy Name presented the newborn to her parents. Tom examined his daughter's fingers and toes, his face glowing with awe.

Quietly, Cicely withdrew. She felt relieved that Kitty had come through her ordeal well, and that the child was in good health, but clearly the new family needed time alone. She picked up her hat and reticule and left the cottage. Before she made it to the lane, Tom caught up with her.

"Will you be coming back to help, you know, in a fortnight?" he asked. He rubbed his palm up and down the side of his breeches.

"Yes. What time shall I meet you?"

They agreed upon a time and meeting place, then Tom returned to the cottage, and Cicely headed toward the livery stables. The more she'd thought about it, the less she wanted to become involved in smuggling, but she didn't see how she could back out. Now, more than ever, Tom and Kitty needed money.

As she clucked to Octavia, and the mare moved out into the primarily pedestrian traffic of the village street, a small voice from the back of her mind told Cicely that here was the adventure she always talked about. Sneaking out to Maresmouth Cove at midnight. Hauling untaxed brandy and tea from the beach to the village to be stashed until smugglers came from inland to cart the stuff away to their buyers. There was danger aplenty, what with this official drive to collect every penny due the Crown. Why, the dragoons were only miles down the coast. And smugglers, if caught, the voice reminded her, could be transported.

Ruthlessly, Cicely crushed that derisive voice of her conscience. She was going to the cove in a fortnight, and that was that. She would keep her promise.

At dinner that evening, Griffin proved to be an excellent companion. Elegant in his dark attire, he entertained her with amusing stories of life in the army. Not once did he make reference to what had passed between them the night before. At first, Cicely eased out a sigh of relief, but by the time they withdrew into the parlor a perverse sense of annoyance nagged at her.

He went to the liquor cabinet and poured their drinks.

Eyeing him, she told herself one would never know this man had proposed marriage to her. Ha! Anyone could see how brokenhearted the poor fellow was by her refusal.

Griffin handed Cicely her drink.

"Hock again?" she said as she took it from him. "Am I so predictable, sir?"

He raised his eyebrows in mild surprise. "I do apologize. 'Tis only what you have asked for every other evening. What would you prefer?"

Feeling petty for her waspishness, she demurred. "No, hock will do, thank you."

He bowed slightly from the waist. "Next time I shall inquire before I pour."

She opened her fan. "It would be appreciated." She strolled across the room, waving the ivory and silk blade back and forth in a steel-wristed measure. Well, she could certainly see that his enthusiasm for matrimony had vanished as quickly as Alasdair avoiding a question. Oh, he was fair swooning with his disappointment.

When Griffin was silent for more than a few minutes, she very casually turned to see why, and found him enthroned in the usual chair, the right leg of his breeches pulled up and his stocking rolled down. He gazed at her in question.

"But where are the towels and the oil this evening?" he asked. "Surely you have not forgotten my massage?"

Her eyes widened with indignation. The audacity of the man! Had he no delicacy of feeling? Could he not see how her refusal of his proposal had been a painful knife in her heart? She studied his beautiful upturned face, trying to deduce his thoughts. No, of course he didn't. Cicely snapped her fan closed. Wasn't that just like a man?

She fixed him with an icy stare. "I did not notice you limping."

He smiled and she felt herself softening. Annoyed, she squashed her natural response to him. There would be none of *that*, not with this fickle creature.

"You didn't notice me limping because your ministrations have improved the condition of my leg," he said. "You have the healing touch, and I fear that if you neglect me, all your tender care will be undone."

He took her hand and she stiffened, trying to harden herself against the sweet enticement of his touch. Gently, he tugged her closer to him. It was impossible to ignore the warm strength of his palm and long, tapered fingers. Despite her will, the beat of her heart hastened.

"Please?" The deep, sensuous sound of that single word vibrated through the silence of the candlelit parlor.

"Let—" Her voice cracked. She cleared her throat. "Let Digby do it."

He pulled her a little closer. "If you never thought him capable before, why can he manage tonight?"

She tried to ease her hand from his, but his clasp proved unyielding. "'Tis time he learned," she informed him. "After all, soon I shall be gone."

He drew her the rest of the way, and she looked down at his exposed leg. As always, the sight of his ridged scars pierced her with the desire to soothe and comfort him. Sternly, she looked away.

"Come," he coaxed softly. "Digby's taken Hannah to Alwyn to visit her parents, despite a stream of halfhearted objections, I might add. Will you tend me one more time?"

One more time of touching him, of feeling his hard muscles and supple skin beneath her hands. One last time . . .

The thought rose up to tighten in her throat. "Very well," she murmured. No sooner had he loosened his fingers around hers than she fled the parlor.

She lingered in the stillroom, trying to settle her rioting emotions. How long could she bear this siege on her heart? she wondered desperately. She knew she couldn't survive such a storm every night for long. Yet she wouldn't consider leaving before she saw Alasdair to his rest. She might be his only hope for peace.

Leaning straight-armed against the old pine worktable, Cicely tried to fathom the reason behind her confusion and hurt.

She had been right to tell Griffin no. She saw no other choice she could have made. She wanted her freedom. She longed to see the sights that lay beyond the water of the Channel. How often had she climbed to the roof of the abbey and seen that gray-blue water from the banqueting tower? It had beckoned to her, bitterly reminding her of her prisoner status.

Taking her time, she assembled the oil and towels. As a last thought, she donned a long apron with a high bib that concealed what the low cut of her gown did not. Finally, she knew she must return or risk looking foolish, or worse—cowardly.

"I wondered what had happened to you," Griffin said when she entered the parlor. "I was about to go searching."

She did not look at him. Without answering, she knelt and poured some of the aromatic, herb-infused oil into her palm. Her annoyance with him gradually settled, distilling into something quieter, deeper, something that felt less like anger and more like a wound.

Her fingers kneaded his flesh. Her eyes lowered to his thigh, she worked in silence for several minutes.

"Tell me of these sights you wish to see," he said.

She kept her gaze on his leg. "What is there to tell? You've seen it all."

"Perhaps not all."

"More, much more than I."

"Won't you tell me?"

She shrugged. "Stor fjord. The Acropolis."

"The Acropolis is under Turkish rule. I wouldn't advise you travel there. What else?"

Why was he doing this? Couldn't he just be silent and let her finish this massage without his show of false interest? "The Pont du Gard," she said dully. "The Maison Carrée."

"At Nîmes. Yes. Go on."

"Florence. I wish to see Florence," she said more forcefully, determined to have done with this mockery.

Griffin's fingers on her hands caused her to pause and finally to look at him.

His hard-planed face wore an unreadable expression, but the fine scar that extended from the hairline at his temple to the edge of his high, elegant cheekbone was a pale filigree against his sun-gilded skin. "I will show you Florence."

She rose slowly to her feet, her emotions churning into a confusing gale.

"I will take you to Nîmes."

She backed away a few steps. "Please, don't do this."

He stood. "Don't do what, Cicely? Offer you the things you say you want?"

They stood apart, their gazes locked.

Her heart hammered. It was madness to stand here with him, when she couldn't even remember the reasons she had given for refusing to marry him. Her mind sought for them with the agility of a stunned crab scrabbling over shale.

"Good-night, Griffin. I think it best that we see as little of each other as possible from now on." She whirled around and walked quickly from the parlor, fumbling the door closed behind her. Then she hiked her skirts and ran to her bedchamber, where she closed the door and collapsed back against it, her breath coming in sobs.

Had the man no pity? Why did he toy with her when he'd made it perfectly plain how little she affected him? It was cruel, this cat-and-mouse game he played. She hated him. *Hated* him.

Gradually, her breathing calmed and she turned her gaze up to the ceiling without really seeing it. No. She knew that wasn't true. She didn't hate him. The corners of her mouth trembled. God help her.

She loved Griffin.

Griffin drew the wagon up in front of the modest, lime-washed cottage to which Uriah Coppard had given him directions. Griffin's eye did not miss the flowers that lined the neat path to the door, nor the beds of daisies under the front window. The place was in good repair. It spoke well of its inhabitants.

Before Griffin's feet hit the ground, a tall, big-boned young man came out of the house. Like so many others in the village, he appeared underfed. His shirt, breeches, and stockings hung loosely on him.

"I'm Griffin Tyrrell, the new owner of Cranwick Abbey," Griffin said, offering his hand. The younger fellow took it in a firm, manly grip. "You must be Tom Sparke."

"I am, sir."

"Congratulations on the birth of your daughter."

"Thank you, Mr. Tyrrell." Sparke's face altered from

caution to an expression of a man worn down with worry. "They had a hard night."

Cicely had avoided Griffin for the past day, since his offer to take her to the Continent, but Hannah had told him that the Sparkes' child could not tolerate mother's milk and no wet nurse was available to them.

"I'm sorry to hear that," he said. "But I think I may be able to help." He went around to the back of the wagon and removed the backboard.

The goat bleated at him and came to investigate.

Griffin caught the brown-and-white nanny up in his arms and set her on the ground, keeping her tether rope in his hand. "I've been told that your daughter is having trouble with mother's milk. When I was in America, I learned that sometimes a babe can keep down the milk of a nanny even when it cannot tolerate mother's milk." He studied the coarse hair on the top of the nanny's head and scratched the spot. Her ears flickered with pleasure. He was loath to part with the creature so soon after acquiring her, but to this man's child, the nanny could mean the difference between life and slow death.

Sparke stared at the goat. "I have no way to pay you for the beast."

"I can offer you work at Cranwick," Griffin said. "I'll pay fair wages, and, to tell the truth, I could use your help."

Sparke looked off in the direction of Cranwick and frowned.

Griffin refused to kick a man when he was down. "The goat is not yours. Her milk is. When your babe is weaned, bring the goat back to me. Until then, I'll provide for her food if you'll see to her shelter and water."

Sparke looked uncertain. Griffin could see the younger man desperately wanted to accept the offer, yet it went against his grain to accept charity.

Griffin handed Sparke the tether. He slid the backboard into place and walked around to climb up onto the seat. He reached for the reins.

"Why are you doing this?" Sparke asked.

Threading the leather straps through his fingers, Griffin regarded Sparke levelly. "Because we're neighbors now, and you need my help."

He flicked the reins and called to Octavia and Digby's Dobbin. Shell and stones crunching under the iron-rimmed wheels. He guided the horses toward Cranwick, where enough work for twenty men awaited him.

"I'll be back as soon as I can," Griffin said as he stepped his left foot into Apollo's stirrup and mounted. He adjusted the reins through his fingers. "Until then, Digby, your charge is to keep the ladies safe and sound."

Digby's chest visibly grew. "That I will, Cap'n."

Griffin's eyes met Cicely's. She didn't want him to go, not even to London for a short business stay. It was too far away. The roads were filled with highwaymen. Her objections and worries remained unspoken. She could have no claim on him.

Without saying a word, without breaking their joined gazes, he touched the fingertips of one hand to the brim of his leather three-cornered hat. Then, with a click of his tongue and a press of his thighs, he turned the stallion away to canter down the drive. Cicely swallowed back the tears that clogged her throat as she watched horse and rider until they turned onto the road and out of her sight.

The remaining party broke up to go to their separate tasks. She knew she should go to hers as well, but she felt too scattered, too edgy. She knew of only one thing that might help to soothe her.

She hurried to her bedchamber and from a locked drawer in the bottom of her wardrobe she withdrew a shallow, oblong box, and a large envelope. Quickly she donned her straw milkmaid's hat, tying it under her chin for driving in the chaise. Then she grabbed her reticule, her gloves, the box, and the envelope.

Three hours later, she sat with Kitty and baby Jane in a meadow beyond the Sparkes' cottage. Though Kitty was slow to regain her strength, Janie had recovered her health and weight since starting on the milk from Griffin's goat. Cicely fussed with her crayon, trying not to wonder how many others of the gentry would have parted with a prized animal to help a fisherman's babe.

She drew an unsteady breath and told herself light was so important, unwilling to think more about Griffin and her decision. Likely the light for this portrait would be better at Stor fjord.

"How much longer?" Kitty asked. "Janie is a-squirming."

"Janie is always squirming," Cicely murmured, frowning at the large sheet of rough-textured paper in front of her. It bore the partially finished likenesses of her subjects. From the shallow, oblong box, she selected an ocher pastel crayon and stroked on a trail of color.

"True, but when she gets like this it usually means she's hungry. If I don't feed her now, she'll set ter wailing."

Cicely looked up and managed a smile. "Well, we don't want that, do we?" She put aside her paper and pastel, then reached for Janie, wrinkling her nose at the infant. Kitty handed her daughter over.

Such a precious little girl, Cicely thought, her heart expanding as she studied the cap of soft blond hair, bright, inquisitive blue eyes, and rosebud mouth. Worth any amount of pain. She savored the warm weight in her arms, and held out a finger for Janie to grasp with tiny, perfect fingers. Sharp yearning pierced Cicely.

Kitty took up the pottery baby feeder, walked over to where she'd tethered the brown-and-white goat. In a matter of minutes she'd filled the feeder. From her apron pocket she pulled a bit of clean rag, which she stuffed in the end of the feeder's spout.

"I don't know what we would have done if your Captain Tyrrell hadn't brought us this goat." She settled Janie back in her arms, and placed the rag-plugged spout of the feeder at Janie's lips. Immediately the infant began suckling and Kitty watched her with adoring eyes. "We might have lost her."

Cicely busied herself arranging pastel crayons in their box. "He's not *my* Captain Tyrrell, Kitty."

The faint buzzing of insects in the waving grass made a lulling song.

"Well, he ought ter be. He'd make a good match for you, if you want my opinion."

"I'm not looking for a match."

Kitty adjusted her child's position in her lap without Janie ever breaking contact with the spout. "You still have it in your head ter go off travelin', don't you?"

Cicely nodded. Oddly, what she'd lived for these past six years seemed less exciting now, the glow of far-off places had somehow dimmed.

"I know Mr. Honeysett was a mean-spirited man, though 'tisn't right ter speak ill o' the dead. We both know there are many men of his kind in this world. But I don't think Captain Tyrrell is like that. And I'm not just saying that because he brought us the goat and like as not saved our Janie's life."

One corner of Cicely's lips curved up. "No. Of course not." As if everyone in Alwyn didn't know that Kitty thought Griffin deserving of a knighthood.

"'Tis only that I dislike seeing you without someone of your own. Have you not been lonely these past couple of months?"

"No." She didn't want to hear this, but something in her listened to Kitty.

"You were lonely before, though."

"Yes, and I was married."

Kitty softly stroked her baby's fine hair. "Ter a man who was never here. Captain Tyrrell is here. He plans ter stay here, he said as much ter Tom."

"How nice for him."

Kitty reached out and lightly clasped Cicely's wrist. "Though you were like a prisoner there, I don't think you hate Cranwick."

Cicely considered for a moment. In her mind's eye she saw the lush serenity of Cranwick now. Always it had been lovely, but under Griffin's hand it thrived. The tenants had always been kind to her, despite her husband's marked absence. "No. I don't hate it."

"Then why would you not wish ter be Captain Tyrrell's wife? No insult to my own Tom, but the captain is the handsomest man I have ever seen in my life. He's like a prince from a fairy tale."

"A warrior prince, clad in silver mail, riding a black, fire-breathing stallion," Cicely said bemusedly.

"Yes. A warrior prince. 'Tis him exactly."

"But now he's a farmer."

Kitty smiled mischievously. "Mayhap he only wants us to believe that."

"He is quite convincing." Down to the dirty, torn, sweat-stained clothing Hannah washed, and she, Cicely, daughter of a proud and ancient line, mended. She smiled. Not only mended, but took a certain satisfaction in it.

Kitty's smile faded and she grew serious again. "I feel it in my heart. He is the one for you."

The muscles in Cicely's throat tightened, and she plucked one blade of grass after another. "I want my freedom."

Setting the feeder on the old quilt spread beneath them, Kitty tossed a rag on her shoulder, then hefted Janie up and began patting her back. "Seems ter me, there must be many sorts of freedom. After all, I feel free, and I'm a wed woman. I trust Tom. We need each other, you see? Only together we're happy. Apart . . . well, life wouldn't be worth the living."

"I envy you your happiness," Cicely said. "It seems so complete."

Kitty laughed, and the baby burped. "There's my good girl," Kitty crooned as she carefully wiped Janie's drooly mouth. She placed the infant on its stomach on the coverlet in front of her and lightly rubbed the soft bare back. "We have our moments, do Tom and I." She shrugged. "'Tis natural. Only angels never argue, and we're not angels, I'll tell you that." Her smile returned. "Ah, but making up after a tiff . . ." She gave an exaggerated sigh and fluttered her eyelashes.

Cicely chuckled at Kitty's foolery.

"When we go ter bed hungry of a night or the king's men threaten," Kitty said quietly, "Tom and I have each other."

With Janie asleep, Cicely could make no progress in her portrait, so she and Kitty agreed to get together in a few days.

All the way back to Cranwick, Kitty's words echoed through Cicely's mind.

I feel it in my heart. He is the one for you.

*   *   *

The liveried majordomo stepped silently into the elegantly furnished room where Griffin waited. "His Grace will see you now," he said. "This way, if you please."

The servant led Griffin through the exquisite London house. At last he opened the paneled door to reveal a room lined with cases of leather-bound books. In the center of the room, seated at a heavily carved walnut table, was seventy-year-old Thomas Holles Pelham, duke of Newcastle. Now a man of failing health, he had worked all his adult life to advance the interests of the Whig party. He had been lord-lieutenant of Middlesex and Nottingham, then secretary of state, a position he'd held for thirty years before twice becoming prime minister. He was one of the greatest landowners in the country, and in Sussex his power was undisputed.

As Griffin was shown into the room, the duke rose and came around the table to greet him. "Lord Griffin, you were just a boy when last I saw you." The old man offered his hand.

Griffin clasped it in a firm handshake. "Your Grace has an excellent memory."

Newcastle waved Griffin to a cozy sitting area. The duke eased himself down into an armchair and gestured Griffin to take the one next to it.

Eyeing Griffin's somber-colored, and, for this rarified strata of society, plain clothing, Newcastle said bluntly, "What brings you here?"

Griffin trod an unknown path. This man knew him only by long association with Griffin's father, and had seen Griffin only once, long ago. It was a dangerous gamble, but one Griffin knew he must take.

"I have come to ask a favor of you, my lord," he said quietly.

Newcastle sighed and turned his head to look out the tall window. "I think you should understand, I am no friend to your brother."

"Which is the reason I have come to you."

Turning his head back, the duke studied Griffin for a long moment. "I had heard there was no love between you."

Griffin made no reply.

Newcastle chuckled. "Suppose that description fits many your brother has met." His smile vanished. "Including the poor female who was his mistress. A bit of beastly business, that."

Within an hour of arriving in London, Griffin had heard of the pregnant girl who'd taken her own life after being publicly cast off by her paramour—Randolph Tyrrell.

"The bishop of Durham has told me that you're quite mad. In fact, he's told several peers of your unfortunate dementia."

"The bishop was convinced of my madness by a generous contribution of land from Randolph."

"There are those willing to believe what the bishop says."

Griffin smiled aridly. "There are those who don't wish to question what they're told if it means making an effort. And they may be satisfied with the present balance of power."

Newcastle nodded thoughtfully. "Quite true." He continued in a brisker manner. "Perhaps you'd like to tell me the purpose of your call here."

"The matter about which I've come to speak with Your Grace concerns Sussex." The duke's family, the Pelhams, had been settled in Sussex since the reign of Edward I.

The elderly duke lifted an eyebrow. "I suppose you think that shall get my interest."

"Yes, Your Grace."

"Well, you're right. Tell me of this request."

Griffin explained the village's situation. "Their hunger worsens daily," he finished.

The duke rubbed his chin. "Hmm. You're quite eloquent, young man. Mayhap you have a place in government."

Griffin smiled. "I've already served the government from the back end of a sword and a pistol. Now I believe I can best serve my country by helping to keep peace in my adopted county."

"Ah, yes. Sussex. A more beautiful place in England I'm sure I don't know. But you say the people of Alwyn and many of the surrounding farms are starving?"

"Yes, Your Grace. And the king's dragoons are raiding down the coast. Alwyn is suffering enough. They're starving. Must they also endure soldiers overturning everything in their homes and shops? A few miles down the road, a woman was assaulted by a soldier in his cups."

Newcastle scowled. "A fortune in taxes is lost each year to uncustomed goods smuggled into Britain, Lord Griffin. 'Tis intolerable. The treasury must have its taxes. If people want their luxuries, they must pay."

Griffin rubbed the side of his thumb back and forth over the nubbed surface of his embroidered coat as he carefully chose his words. "These fishermen and farmers have no luxuries. In the best of times, they consider themselves fortunate if they are able to feed their families and keep them warm and dry in the winter. In the worst of times, they may—or may not—work as laborers for the occasional smuggler. If you wish to find who buys uncustomed goods, look in the houses of the gentry and prosperous merchants. They can appreciate quality, yet value a bargain."

Were the Pelhams above reproach? Griffin doubted it. French brandy and good tea at reduced prices were sore temptations to all who'd become accustomed to such indulgence. The easy availability of the goods along the coast would keep the cellars and tea chests of the wealthy stocked. He turned a bland look on Newcastle. "But we both know the great families of Sussex would not think of trading with smugglers to save a few guineas."

Newcastle fixed a sharp gaze on Griffin. After the span of a few heavy heartbeats, a slow smile spread across the old gentleman's face. "I see a lot of your father in you, my boy, bless me if I don't. Bold as a five-pence doxie, he was. Nothing like Randolph. Mind, I dislike speaking ill of the dead, but Lady Tyrrell—the first one—was a poisonous female. She seems to have taught him well."

"I have not spoken with Randolph for years, Your Grace."

"So I've heard."

Griffin arched an eyebrow. "Now why would the duke of Newcastle be interested in the affairs of a lowly second son?" The old bitterness left an acid taste in his mouth.

Newcastle slanted Griffin a sly, knowing look. "There's an Arab saying: 'The enemy of my enemy is my friend.' Do you know it?"

"A wise adage."

From beneath wrinkled, hooded eyelids, the duke studied Griffin. "Yes. Yes, it is." He levered himself out of his chair. Griffin also stood, comprehending the dismissal.

The duke sighed. "That new justice of the peace in Sussex is too zealous for his own good. Doesn't understand the concept of service to society. Well, I wouldn't worry, were I you," Newcastle said, seeing Griffin to the door of the library and opening it. "Anything can happen. Who knows? The dragoons may just give up and go home."

"One prays that it is so, Your Grace."

"Good day, Lord Griffin. Perhaps we'll chat again some time."

Griffin smiled. "Your servant, sir."

As if he responded to his master's thoughts, the majordomo appeared to lead Griffin back through the house to the front door.

The meeting had gone as well as could be expected, Griffin thought as he walked out to the street to hail a hackney carriage. Now he must wait to see if his visit bore fruit. Perhaps he'd at least managed to spare the people of the parish an unwanted visit by dragoons. For those who *were* working with the smugglers, such a visit would have meant transportation.

And it never hurt to have a powerful ally.

The black lugger, almost invisible in the light of the quarter moon, was anchored some distance from the shale beach where the villagers had gathered. Behind them soared steep cliffs of sandstone rock that, in the light of day, glowed honey gold. The boats that had been rowed out from the lugger had been pulled up onto the shale, where the uncustomed goods had been neatly stacked. A line of villagers extended up the beach. Here and there a hooded lantern cast a flickering ray of light.

Cicely stood in line behind Tom, who towered above her. She'd worn her oldest, most faded work clothes. At the Sparkes' cottage, still-weak Kitty had directed Cicely to remove her round-eared cap and wrap Kitty's shawl over her hair and about her neck and shoulders, so that she'd look a proper fisherman's woman. As an added precaution against her being recognized or having her good looks attract unwanted attention, Tom had applied foul-tasting bootblack, making it appear as if her two front teeth were missing.

A burly man wearing dark clothing checked off on a list each article taken and wrote down the name of the individual who'd taken it. When their turns came, Tom hefted four half-ankers of spirits. The slightly flattened casks, each containing a little over four gallons, were paired together with rope, allowing him to drape them over his shoulders so that two casks rode against his chest and two against his back. After Tom gave the smuggler a false name for Cicely, claiming her as his cousin Fanny from Selsey, she was given a bale wrapped in oilskin. The smell of tea leaves testified as to the contents. She struggled to lift the parcel, finding it bulky and awkward.

The big clerk took it from her and set it on top of her head. Quickly he showed her how to balance it with her hands. "The women in the West Indies carry their burdens in such a fashion," he explained.

Knowing how much Kitty and Tom depended on the shillings she would earn for her night's work, she didn't want the smuggler to think she couldn't cope with the bale. She gave him a nervous smile, then remembered the blacked-out teeth and quickly pressed her lips closed.

She and Tom made their way back up the beach. At the foot of the cliffs Tom took her elbow.

"This part is a bit tricky if you've never carried anything up this path," he told her in a low voice. "I've been up and down it most the days of my life, a-carrying fish or gear. You'll do fine, Lady Cicely. I'll just hold your arm ter help you keep your balance."

Seeing his face creased with worry, she smiled reassuringly up at him. "I've taken this path before, Tom. It's plenty wide for me to manage this weight."

He gave her a grin. "A right rose you look tonight, Fanny."

"Flatterer."

His big hand at her elbow, she walked ahead of Tom. It did not take her a minute to realize that the bale she carried was wider than the path. In order to avoid catching the square package on the cliff face, she had to walk closer to the outward edge of the path. Immediately she slowed her steps.

"You've got ter move more quickly," Tom cautioned her from behind. "They'll not tolerate anyone holding up the line. Every minute of delay could mean discovery."

She trod faster, her eyes glued to the steep path, trying not to notice the way the beach fell farther and farther below her. Her heart galloped.

Halfway up the cliff she discovered only air where her left foot would have gone had her gaze not been so tightly affixed to the ground. She took a panicked step back, colliding with Tom. She heard someone bite off an oath behind him. Tom's fingers squeezed encouragingly on her arm, but he made no attempt to force her to go on.

I can do this. She saw that a small cliff fall had gouged a bite out of the track. Even so, fishermen negotiated this route every day, she told herself. If she didn't move now, the smugglers might grow nervous.

She curled her fingers more tightly around the twine binding on the parcel she balanced. Taking a deep breath, she stretched her legs and stepped over the cavity in the path.

Cicely heard Tom's sigh of relief, but could do no more than allow it to register in her mind, so focused was her attention on the track she climbed. Where there was one gouge, there could be more.

Finally, after what seemed like hours, she stepped onto the top of the cliff. "Go stash your bale in the bell tower," Tom told her. "I'll meet you back here in a few minutes for the next load."

Her stomach clenched. "We must climb that path again?" She did not see how he had so easily carted his greater burden up that incline without fear.

He nodded. "But don't you fret, Lady Cicely. You a-carried the bale up the side of that cliff as good as any goat."

"High praise indeed."

Tom gave her a nod and left.

Cicely battled the bale all the way up the narrow stairs to the church belfry, where she found others had already stored similar packages. She stood a minute, looking around as she caught her breath.

When the stone church had been renovated at the end of the last century, this tower, with its single bronze bell, had been added. She studied the bell's dark shape. It was three times her height and almost as wide at the bottom. Only the vicar or the sexton were permitted to pull the heavy rope dangling to the ground floor. Once set into ponderous motion, the bell clanged its message out across the countryside, calling to worship, alerting all to an emergency, or acknowledging a death.

The tall windows of the belfry were open tonight, to allow in the faint, slanting rays of moonlight, but after the last parcel was deposited, she knew the shutters would be closed and that they would remain so until the uncustomed goods were removed by the inland contingent of the smuggling gang. On that night, the people of Alwyn and the surrounding farms would stay in their houses with their windows covered until morning.

Adjusting Kitty's shawl around her head, Cicely trudged down the steep stairs, ready to carry her next burden.

She made two more heart-pounding trips. Both times she was given a bale, likely because she could not carry the "tubs" that most of the men hefted.

Now, as she tucked the last of her parcels into place in a corner of the belfry, she rubbed the back of her neck. This was a night she never wished to repeat.

She heard a noise behind her and straightened, moving aside for the next human mule to place her bale on the pile. But no one came forward to stack an oilskin-wrapped bundle.

An odd prickling ran down her nape, a warning of trouble. Cicely whirled around to confront the intruder.

There, next to the trapdoor, stood Griffin.

14

In the dim light of the quarter moon, Cicely saw he wore no coat or waistcoat. Clearly he'd left the house in a hurry, for he had on only his white lawn shirt, his black breeches, and boots. Stray tendrils of hair had escaped his queue.

His face was a thunderhead. All that was wanting were bolts of lightning shooting from his eyes. Even when he'd hauled her off the dock in Portsmouth and deposited her in the carriage she had not seen him looking so furious.

"Hello, Griffin." She tried to sound casual, as if they frequently met in the church bell tower in the dark, early hours of the morning. Instead, her voice came out as high-pitched and uncertain as a child who's been caught doing something she knows she should not.

"I don't need to ask what you're doing here," he said, his voice unnaturally calm with leashed fury. His eyes glinted in the moonlight.

Mustering her courage, she lifted her chin. "No, but I might ask why *you're* here."

His eyes narrowed as he peered at her through the faint light. "What the hell happened to your teeth?"

Quickly she rubbed at the boot blacking. Catching herself, she whipped her smeared hands down from her mouth. "'Twas a precaution," she informed him imperiously.

"It was the only one you took." He moved toward her, his steps as measured as his words. "I came here because I arrived back from London to find you gone. I searched every nook and cranny on the manor. I even went up on the roof of the abbey. I gave Alasdair the perfect opportunity to eliminate me, do you understand? One strong breeze, and he wouldn't have had to worry about me anymore. But he was off playing with the puppy, no doubt, and missed his chance. The chance *I* gave him because I was searching for *you*."

"I didn't ask you to," she pointed out reasonably, easing back a step for every one he took forward.

"No. You didn't. I took it entirely upon myself. But I was worried, you see." His voice rose. "I was unhappy that I had distressed you, then left you, so as soon as I arrived home this evening I went to your room to apologize. Ha!"

Gradually they circled the bell.

"Well, you *did* distress me," she insisted. "You distressed me excessively."

"So of course you ran off to Alwyn to help smuggle tea." But for that dangerous growl underlying his words, they would have taken the quality of pleasant conversation. "I don't know why that did not occur to me."

They began their second lap around the bell.

"I promised to help someone," she informed him

haughtily, thinking her hauteur might have made more of an impression were she not backing away from him.

"Of course. Risking your pretty little neck for people who would never help *you*. In the years you struggled to keep Cranwick from falling into ruin, how many of them came to your aid? I'll wager not above four. And they bloody well weren't risking their lives as you do for them!" he shouted.

Out of the corner of her eye, she saw through the open window that a crowd of villagers had gathered below, but she could give the matter no thought with Griffin advancing on her. She'd never seen him so angry.

"They thought they were. The men feared for their—" her voice died. Spoken aloud, their reason would sound even more outrageous.

"Speak up," he ordered.

"Their manhoods," she muttered.

He stopped and stared at her. "Their *what?*"

She cleared her throat. "Their manhoods," she said more loudly. She halted.

He laughed, but the sound held a wild edge to it. "For the love of God! Cranston had fourteen children. His son after him had five. There has been no owner to live there since then. Until now."

"I know that," she snapped, embarrassed for the villagers.

"So they turn down honest work." Disgust saturated his voice. "They let their families go hungry."

"They're afraid," she repeated lamely.

"Well, they should be!" he roared. "They risk not only their own necks, but those of their wives and children doing this. I'll not have any man risking yours!"

Her temper ignited. "*You'll* not have? Who are you to dictate whom I see and what I do?"

He moved so quickly she was in his grasp before she

knew it. His hands closed around her upper arms. In the faint moonlight his eyes were disks of black rimmed with woodsmoke gray. He brought his hard-planed face close to hers. "I am the man who loves you!"

Cicely stared at him, stunned. There beneath the seething mantle of Griffin's anger, she glimpsed . . . fear. Realization crashed over her like a breaking wave. He was afraid for her.

He did love her.

The man who'd fought battles in America and Cuba and twice been badly wounded, who refused to be driven from his new home by a ghost others held in terror, the man who stubbornly worked from dawn until dark—that man was afraid for her.

She could not recall ever having been so important to anyone before.

As she stood there in the open belfry gazing at him, his love became real to her. For the first time, she was not afraid to accept its existence.

Hoping she wasn't in a dream, she stroked her fingertips along his firm jaw. It was rough and shadowed with a day's growth of beard. His skin was warm and undeniable.

He pulled her to him, and crushed his lips to hers. Her breath stopped in her throat. The belfry whirled around her. She curled her fingers into the cloth of his shirt and answered his fierce demand with her own.

When he finally lifted his head, a loud cheer went up. Feeling slightly dizzy, Cicely was startled to see a large crowd gathered in the churchyard below.

"The whole town is down there!" she whispered.

"We're going home," Griffin growled, taking her hand and briskly descending the stairs. She raced to keep up with him.

When they entered the churchyard she did not miss

the wide grins and good-natured joking, but Griffin did not stop until Tom stepped into his path. The two men were of a height, but while Griffin was long-muscled and lean, Tom was bulky with brawn.

Tom scowled at Griffin. "What call do you think you have ter—"

Griffin's fist shot out and connected with Tom's jaw. The burly fisherman reeled backward, stumbled over a stone sundial, and sat down abruptly in the grass.

Griffin shook his abused hand and thrust it under his other arm, holding it against his side. Tom rubbed his jaw and glared up at his assailant.

Griffin glared back at him. "That's for putting Lady Cicely at risk, Sparke," he said tightly. "If you're so worried about your damned cock that you'll let your family starve, that's your affair. But never again seek to remedy your lack of courage by taking advantage of my lady's tender heart." And with that, Griffin stalked to his horse. With a creak of leather, he swung up into the saddle. He reached down and offered Cicely a hand up. Still dazed by the realization that the man she loved cared for her more than his own safety, she did not hesitate to take it. Placing her left foot on his, which rested in the stirrup, she mounted behind him. Tentatively, she placed her arms around his waist. Beneath them, she felt tension thrum through his taut muscles.

Gathering up the reins, Griffin nudged Apollo with his heels, and the stallion headed toward home.

No sooner had they passed the gate into Cranwick, than Alasdair appeared. He floated next to Cicely, his hair and plaid moving in the agitated breeze that surrounded him.

"Foolish female!" he cried. "Don't ye know how dan-

gerous it is to go slippin' away at night? Rogues abound
everywhere! Robbers! Assassins! 'Tis no a safe place
outside these gates for a pretty lass to go out by herself.
I told ye, did I no?" He moved up to Griffin. "I told her
when she sneaked off, the saucy wench! *I* saw her.
Where were ye? Sleepin', I've no doubt. Och, a fine
protector ye are! God's blood, an army could ha'
marched in here and made off with her, and ye'd have
snored on." Alasdair moved back to Cicely and his fair
eyebrows climbed up. "What's wrong with yer teeth?"

Cicely tried to rub it off with her thumb, managing
to smear more of the blacking on her already-grubby
hand. "There are no rogues or bandits on the roads
around here," she told him peevishly.

"No, just smugglers," Griffin said flatly. "Men who'd
as soon violate you and cut your throat as take a chance
that you might slip and tip off a customs man."

Alasdair gasped. "Smugglers? Christ, ye've lost yer
mind to be doin' business with *them*. And wouldn't
they love to get their wicked hands on the likes of a
sweet lass such as ye?"

The thought sent a chill through Cicely. She'd never
had dealings with smugglers before. When all was said
and done, they might bring money to this area, but they
were still criminals with much at stake. What might
they not do to protect themselves from discovery?

"All I did was carry three bales of tea from the beach
to the church bell tower," she said.

Griffin fixed her with a stern look over his shoulder.
"You were on that cliff path? Carrying a bale of tea?
Damn it, woman! You should never go on that path.
'Tis steep and too bloody narrow."

"How would you know?" she snapped. "You never
leave this manor."

He lifted a warning eyebrow and turned around to

settle back in the saddle. "Do not presume to think you know everything, madam."

Alasdair floated forward to Griffin. "She never did this before ye came here. A good lass, she was, usin' superior sense." He pointed a translucent finger at Griffin. "I'm layin' the blame at yer feet. Belike ye've driven her mad. Aye, that's it! Ye've driven her quite mad. 'Twas inevitable, methinks, what with ye bein' forever underfoot. Ye invaded her house, and look what's come of it."

Griffin gritted his teeth, wishing he could throttle this vaporous gadfly. "*I've* driven her mad? I'm not the one who turns into a goblin whenever anyone other than Cicely comes to Cranwick. She's worked herself near to death because you've terrified everyone until they won't set foot on this manor."

"Cowards," Alasdair sniffed. "Cowards one and all. Can't take a bit of fun, and that's a fact."

Griffin swore and nudged Apollo to greater speed. To his surprise, Alasdair did not follow.

In the dower house stables, Griffin pulled Cicely down off the stallion's back and set her on the ground. "Go to bed," he told her. He needed to work off the anger that burned in him.

Her lips parted, as if she wanted to say something. Then they closed and pressed firmly together. She spun on her heel and marched out of the stables.

Twenty minutes later, Griffin closed the stable doors and stalked into the house.

The kitchen was dark save for the low-burning fire in the fireplace. Fumbling around, he found the supply of candles, and lighted one from a slip of wood ignited by the kitchen fire.

He made his way through the dark house. When he

saw the sheet of light beneath Cicely's door, his hand went to the knob. He paused. No. It was too dangerous. He could not vouch for his actions now. His temper was still too high, his fear for Cicely too acute. Tomorrow he would be more rational.

He continued down the hall to his chamber. As he stripped off his clothes, a glance at the clock on the desk told him it would be dawn in a few hours.

Slipping naked into bed, he lay there for several minutes, the sheets cool against his skin. His mind seethed, skipping from one memory of this evening to another.

Finally he threw back the covers. He pulled his claret brocade dressing gown from its peg in the wardrobe and shrugged it on. Silently, he paced on bare feet to the window and impatiently shoved aside a drapery to reveal a black, starry sky. He swore vehemently, his voice low and strained.

She could have been hurt. His fingers clenched on the heavy drapery, his stomach knotting at the thought of it.

And she'd been defiant, damn her tempting little hide! She was so bloody set on having her adventures, she refused to open her eyes to the danger. Well, she wasn't going to put him through another hell like the one he'd lived after he'd found her missing. By God, she had to face facts!

Griffin stormed out of his chamber, down the hall to Cicely's door. He flung it open.

She turned from her window as he stalked into the center of her room. He saw she'd washed. No sign of boot blacking remained. In the dimly lighted room, her face was as pale as ivory, and the mass of gleaming hair that fell to her waist captured glints of gold and copper from the candle that burned on her bedside table. The flowing, white lawn night shift endowed her with the ethereal air of a faery queen.

God, he thought. So slim and delicate. Yet she had survived so much. He remembered how, this night, he had combed the manor for her. Before the first hour of his search had passed, a dread had begun to build inside him. By the second hour that dread had grown into a gut-twisting fear that she'd fled him.

When he'd spied the activity on the beach and the lugger at anchor, and half an hour later, Kitty had confirmed his suspicions, his fear had turned to indignant wrath that she could be so foolish as to endanger her precious life.

Cicely walked toward him, hesitantly at first, her eyes searching his face. Then her bare feet moved more quickly, more surely, across the floor, carrying her straight into his arms.

His arms immediately closed around her in a desperate embrace. Cicely expelled a shaky breath of relief. So many fears had rushed through her as she had crossed the room to Griffin. What if he'd changed his mind? What if she wasn't who he imagined her to be? What if . . . what if . . . what if . . .

But as his beloved mouth rained kisses over her upturned face her apprehension dissolved. As his palms roamed restlessly up and down her back and his lips grew more ardent, another sort of tension slowly wound within her.

"I was mad with worry for you," he said against her temple, his low voice vibrating in his chest. "Smugglers are criminals, desperate men. Some have killed."

At the feel of his moist tongue tip on the outer curve of her ear, her breath fluttered in her throat. "I know."

"I would not have you harmed."

"I know."

His fingertips skimmed her jaw, and she turned her cheek into his palm.

He covered her lips with his, stroking her inner edges with his tongue. His arms tightened around her, and his tongue glided farther into her mouth until it found hers. The warmth of his skin, the heady, masculine scent of him fused with the stimulating fragrance of pine balsam soap, filling her nostrils, intoxicating her more thoroughly than any brandy the smugglers had ever pulled ashore.

Her hands moved to his chest, and discovered the part in his robe. Beneath her palms there was no longer the pattern of brocade, but the more complex texture of short, springy hair over smooth flesh. Startled, she stopped. Never had she touched a man's bare chest before.

He did not move.

Ancient curiosity prompted her to explore this inviting expanse. Slowly, her hands slipped beneath the edges of the brocade lapel, gliding over marvelously subtle contour. Warm flesh against her palms, cooler fabric against the backs of her hands. She encountered small pebbles that could only be his nipples. She felt him go taut.

She lifted her gaze to his.

He loosened the sash of his dressing gown. The lapels parted. With a subtle roll of his shoulders, the garment whispered down his body to the floor.

Cicely stared at him. Wide smooth shoulders, deep chest covered with an ink dark mat of short, crisp hair that narrowed over his hard, ridged abdomen. Her gaze followed the trail of dark hair to its end.

Her eyes widened.

"What is it, sweetheart?" he asked softly.

"'Tis so large!"

He chuckled deep in his throat as he gathered the

billowing folds of her night shift into his hands, and she detected a note of satisfaction. "You'll be glad for it."

"Edmund was never so . . . so . . . immense."

In the candlelight, Griffin bared his teeth in a savage smile. "I'll serve you better than Edmund." He slipped her night shift over her head and tossed it aside.

Nervous under his gleaming gaze, Cicely instinctively drew in on herself, trying to become smaller, less noticeable. He stopped her with his hands on her shoulders.

"Edmund never looked at me . . . never saw me . . . like this."

"I'll do many things Edmund never did." His eyes darkened to pools of midnight ringed with silver as his gaze moved over her like a private touch. Her pulse quickened.

He gathered her back into his arms. The feel of his bare skin against hers felt so right she burrowed closer. He burned against her, large and rigid and demanding.

With a curved forefinger, he tilted her head up and claimed her lips. She twined her arms around his neck. Slipping loose the ribbon that held his queue, she laced her fingers through the thick silk of his hair.

His kiss deepened. His splayed hands rode restlessly over her back. They moved down to palm her buttocks, holding her in place against him as he rotated his hips.

Sharp desire shot through her. She pressed her short fingernails into his scalp, and he did it again. And again. Her blood sang through her veins, feeding the deepening ache that throbbed in her.

He slid his hands slowly up her waist, her ribs, until his fingers touched the underside of her breasts. She shivered as sparks ran through her.

Lightly, ever so softly, he brushed his fingertips around and around one breast, gradually nearing the tip. Cicely's breathing hastened. Now a steady stream of sparks had spread to hum under her skin. She whimpered as sensation grew more intense.

Griffin swept her up into his arms and strode to her bed. Shouldering aside the damask hangings, he laid her down. He stretched out beside her and returned his attention to her breast. The slow, steady course of his fingertips wound that coil inside her tighter and tighter.

He dipped his head and took her nipple into his mouth. A gasp wrenched from her throat. He lightly raked the beaded tip with the edge of his teeth, and she clutched handfuls of coverlet at her sides. He swirled it with the tip of his tongue, and she arched up off the bed, strangling a cry for fear Hannah or Digby would hear and come running.

Then he tended her other breast, lavishing it with the same attention until her head thrashed from side to side on the pillows. She longed to beg him to stop, but feared that he would.

He sat up, regarding her from beneath hooded eyes. The drapery of his dark hair swayed as he straddled her hips, keeping his weight on his knees.

She lay there looking up at him, certain she could never see as breathtaking a sight as Griffin Tyrrell in full splendor. Beautiful. Tall. Powerful. He was a man to be reckoned with. He had awakened her, body and soul.

He took her hand and guided it to him, coaxing her hesitant fingers to close around him. "Don't be afraid," he said.

To her amazement, she encountered skin like satin. Beneath that satin was steel. Emboldened by his sudden stillness, her fingers moved upon him in discovery. Abruptly his hand clamped over her wrist to lift her hand away. Surprised at this sudden change, she looked up. For the first time she noticed the perspiration on his forehead and top lip. The muscles in his neck stood out.

She snatched her hand back, certain she had hurt him.

He smiled and brought her fingers to his lips. "'Tis only that I want you badly, Cicely. Your kiss inflames me. Your touch threatens to shatter my control."

"I-I'm sorry."

He smoothed his palm over the soft plane of her belly. "I'm not." With lips and teeth and tongue, he followed the path his hand had led. Thus he moved down her body, until he arrived at her Venus mound. He paused to blow a soft breath, causing the chestnut curls to part.

Suddenly self-conscious, she tried to rise, but he gently pressed her back down again.

His fingertip moved through the parted curls and into the most intimate part of her, tracing the outline of each fold until it reached its moist destination.

A delicate movement of that probe sent a spear of blinding pleasure through her. But he didn't stop with that single touch. With his clever fingers he sent her into a deluge of piercing, spiraling sensation that grew increasingly tighter, more intense, driving out awareness of anything but that one bright point and the storm of physical joy. Then an odd tickle whispered down her spine, and all at once everything exploded in a golden burst. It surprised a sharp cry from her as she bowed up off the bed.

As the storm finally ebbed and a relaxed glow spread through her limbs, she heard his deep-chested rumble of satisfaction.

His lips grew more demanding, drawing her out of her contented cocoon. His knee nudged her thighs apart, and he lowered himself over her.

His lips grew more ardent, heating her blood. She clenched her fingers in his hair, returning the hungry, open-mouthed kiss with a fierce passion that matched his own.

He entered her in a single, slow stroke that left her feeling stretched and invaded. This was nothing at all like what she'd experienced before! A moment of panic seized her.

He stroked her cheek. "Sweetheart," he soothed. "Sweetheart, calm yourself. Tell me, am I hurting you?"

She stared up at him, her eyes wide. "No."

"Good." He brushed his lips softly against her forehead. "'Tis only that you're unused to a man. Your body will accustom itself to me. Be still a moment, and you'll see I speak the truth."

She did as he asked, and gradually the tightness grew less alarming. She released a shaky breath, feeling foolish. "It wasn't like this with—" She caught herself as she realized how ridiculous she was even to utter Edmund's name in the presence of this man who had taught her so many new things about her body.

"Edmund is in the past," he said. "You're with me now, Cicely. Things will be different. Have I not proved that? Trust me."

He moved his hips, slowly withdrawing almost completely. An unexpected sense of loss washed through her, sending a protest to her lips.

He thrust back into her, invading her with erotic pleasure. "Trust me," he whispered.

Again and again he entered her, until her body mysteriously accepted the union as natural. Exciting. Essential. The world consisted only of Griffin, his tense face and straining shoulders, of the exquisite, golden-sparked friction, the familiar coiling inside her.

But this time he was with her, murmuring sweet, assuring words, stroking her with his strong hands. This time they were joined, body and heart.

This time she was no longer alone.

Her release crashed around her, and the cry she

voiced was an exaltation that echoed within her like the ringing of a thousand silver bells on a clear spring day.

In the next moment, Griffin's body stiffened, and he reared up on the columns of his arms. His damp face tightened. He threw his head back, his hair splaying out in an arc of night-shadow, his throat working to extinguish his shout.

Slowly, his taut muscles eased. He rolled to his back and tucked Cicely close to his side. She wrapped her arms around him. As their breathing gradually eased, she thought of what had taken place.

Griffin's love had elevated a basic animal act to something higher, something . . . holy . . . a communion so perfect and profound she instinctively knew few ever achieved it.

His tender patience with her fears, placing her needs before his . . . no one had ever before done these things.

Before Griffin, no one had cared. Her gaze swept over his still face.

Before Griffin, she had not cared enough.

He turned his head. A slice of gray dawn crept through the window curtains to slant across his face, illuminating one high cheekbone lapped by a scar, a straight nose with almost imperceptibly flaring nostrils, and solemn, sensual lips.

"Marry me," he said softly.

He'd shown her what it was not to be alone. Not to be filled with haunting emptiness. His touch had gone beyond her sensitive flesh, past sinew and bone to the sanctum of her soul.

She met his silver-gray gaze. "Yes."

He looked at her a moment, then his mouth curved in a tender smile. He pressed a kiss to her temple, and settled her a little closer to him. She felt him release a long breath.

"I have . . . a question," she said hesitantly, after a few minutes.

He turned his head toward her and lifted his eyebrows in inquiry.

"I know you tire of the comparisons with Edmund," she continued, "even though they have been favorable to you."

"Cicely—"

"I know men are different from one another, but . . . Edmund—" She broke off, finding it mortifying to confess that her husband had avoided touching her, had, in fact, refused to after the first time. But she wanted Griffin to know, in case he worried that she was barren. She tried again. "Edmund—"

"Did not like women," Griffin said.

"Well, he did not like *me*," Cicely admitted, unable to look Griffin in the eye. "Mayhap there was another woman he preferred."

"He preferred his valet."

Cicely frowned down at Griffin's ribs, confused. "His valet?"

With his fingertips at her chin, he gently coaxed her head up until she faced him. "Sweetheart, Edmund preferred other men to women. His valet was his lover. You never could be."

"But . . . he did come to me once."

Griffin's mouth hardened into a forbidding line, but he said nothing.

"He was rough and hurried. It hurt. He left me weeping." She swallowed against the painful memory. "I thought . . . I thought 'twas something I had done wrong. All those years—" Grief over lost years, rage against such betrayal rose up to knot in her chest. "I thought it was *me!*"

She sat up, unable to remain still. She scrambled from the bed to stand in the farthest part of the chamber. The wall pressed against her naked back. She rammed the fingers of both hands through her hair, covering her face with her palms, wanting to blot out the realization as easily as she could the light. A ragged sob tore up out of her chest.

Warm, strong hands slipped around Cicely, drawing her into the safe haven of Griffin's arms.

She clung to him, laying her cheek against his chest. "I was sold," she wept bitterly. "Sold to a man who despised me, who would never even give me children." Red fury boiled up. "I hate them! My father . . . Edmund . . . his father . . . I hate them all!"

He stroked her hair. "They're bastards, right enough. No one could deny that. But perhaps none knew."

"Or cared. Neither my father nor Edmund's bothered to answer my letters, even when I wrote that Edmund had shorted my allowance."

"You're free of them now, my heart. And their conniving was for naught. Edward died without leaving an heir, and you are no longer under their thumbs."

A hiccup interrupted her sigh. "My father still has my two sisters to use as bargaining chips."

"Have you heard from them since you were married to Edmund?"

She shook her head. "No." It had hurt her until she realized that her two younger sisters had likely been kept from corresponding with her.

He brushed a kiss on her temple. "We'll see what we can do."

Hope surged in her. She lifted her head.

"I cannot promise them fat dowries," he cautioned her, "but I'll not let them go to husbands in their shifts."

She drank in the dawn-illuminated sight of him, recommitting every detail of his face to memory. Oh, but she had made the right choice, she thought. He was not a wealthy man, yet, for her sake, he was willing to take on the burden of providing for two marriage-aged females.

Cicely smoothed her fingertips over one soot black eyebrow, unable to speak all that was in her heart.

His silvery gaze moved over her upturned face. One corner of his mouth moved slightly upward. He took her hand and brought it to his lips.

"I love you," she whispered unevenly.

"As I love you." The rich baritone of his softly spoken words vibrated in his chest, traveling into hers through their embrace.

They stood together a little longer, just holding each other, refusing to allow the world to intrude on the magic of their discovery.

Finally, with a sigh, Griffin released her. "I must return to my room," he said, bending to retrieve his dressing gown. "Else I am certain to be discovered coming from your chamber by Hannah or Digby."

She quickly pulled on her night shift and then saw him to the door, where they shared a lingering kiss.

"I'll get a license," he said.

"Please do," she urged breathlessly.

As he was turning to go, they heard whispers from around the corner at the end of the hall. A woman's giggle was quickly silenced.

Griffin and Cicely looked at each other. Griffin strode down the corridor, Cicely hurrying at his heels. When they came to the corner, Cicely's eyes widened.

Standing outside the door to Hannah's bedchamber were Hannah and Digby in a disheveled state. Bits of straw clung to both their mussed hair and misbuttoned garments.

They were locked in an embrace.

15

As dusk deepened, Griffin hammered the last nail for the day in the new door for the cow byre. He gathered his carpentry tools and started off toward the dower house. How Cicely had managed the manor as well as she had with such few resources continued to amaze him.

He looked around for Honeysett. The puppy had followed him around today, snuffling, scratching, and frolicking underfoot. Every so often Griffin would feel as if he were under observation and look down to find the mongrel pup sitting near his ankles, solemnly watching him work. At noon, Griffin had shared the lunch Cicely had wrapped in a cloth.

Griffin saw the pup trotting up ahead of him, and a deep contentment settled over him. For the first time in twelve years he had a place in the world. Oh, 'twas nothing lordly, but it was better, much better, than he'd once thought to have. Once he had not expected to live beyond the year, and, later, past the moment. Now, he had Cicely and a future. He smiled as he walked, keeping a casual eye on the pup.

This morning he and Digby had ridden into Alwyn so that Digby could call on Hannah's father to ask for her hand. Mark Boulden had finally given his permission. Afterward, Griffin had procured two licenses. The wedding dates had been chosen and the arrangements set into motion. Griffin grinned. Soon Cicely would be his wife.

Now as he and Honeysett passed the front of the abbey, the door slowly swung open. With a cheerful flurry of barking, the puppy scampered into the house.

It had been a while since Griffin had entered the abbey. Now, keeping an eye on the puppy, he followed. He had in mind to search the rooms for the master's chamber, which he and Cicely would eventually make theirs.

Honeysett had a difficult time climbing the steps of the great staircase, so Griffin picked him up and carried him to the top landing. Promptly, the puppy took off toward Alasdair's wing.

The front door of the abbey opening could have been none other than an invitation to Honeysett—not surprising considering how much time the ghost and the pup spent together. Unlike other animals, Honeysett had never been afraid of Alasdair, and a bond had immediately sprung up between pup and ghost. Still, Griffin hesitated to allow Cicely's foundling to run off into the neglected part of the abbey unless he was certain at least someone—or something, in the ghost's case—was watching over him.

Griffin called Alasdair's name as he followed the puppy into the cobweb-hung corridor. A cool breeze teased at the gray draperies of web, causing them to shiver. Griffin scowled. "Alasdair!" he called again, nervous impatience colliding with an edge of temper.

Another door opened, this one at the end of the hall. Hinges long unoiled screeched an eerie song.

The puppy bounded off in that direction and disappeared into the room. Griffin broke into a run and pursued him, his boots thundering on the wood plank floor, sending up a haze of dust. Just as he arrived at the chamber, the door slammed shut.

Griffin swore vilely under his breath as he tried to open it, only to find the thing refused to budge. "Only the other day," he said loudly, "Mr. Joyes told me he'd learned how to perform an exorcism. I do believe he's eager to test his mastery of the ritual, and I certainly have no qualms about—"

The door opened.

Griffin smiled nastily, but before he could enter, an icy wind blew through the corridor. A prickling down his back sent Griffin whirling around to see what stood behind him.

A death's-head the size of a tenant's cottage leered down at him. "BEGONE!" it rumbled.

Furious with his own nervousness, embarrassed at being reminded how he'd run at his first encounter with Alasdair, Griffin turned back to the room and stalked inside, ready to scoop up Honeysett and head for the dower house.

Until he saw what hung in the chamber.

Every wall was covered with pastel drawings. Griffin stared around him. Bare of all furniture save a few small tables on which burned myriad candles, the place had the feeling of a shrine. Twinkling pinpoint lights expanded into golden luminescence that revealed scenes of domestic camaraderie among families he recognized as being from the village, landscapes he'd seen here on the manor, and portraits of men, women, and children, some of whom he could name, others he could not. Even Alasdair's likeness had been captured on the rough-textured paper in colored chalk. The artist had a discerning eye for detail and a talented hand. Oh, compared to the paintings his father had collected, there was a certain unschooled element about these drawings, but perhaps the artist had received no training.

He walked over to the portrait of Alasdair to study it more closely.

"Ye canna see through me in the picture."

Griffin glanced over his shoulder to see Alasdair standing just inside the doorway.

"'Twas a kindness on the artist's part," Alasdair said. In the pale, ghostly eyes that gazed upon the drawings, Griffin detected the softness that came of deep affection. A faint breeze wafted through the room, causing the papers to sway and wave.

"The artist is very talented," Griffin said. "The people and places are clearly recognizable, and there is a certain . . . style."

Alasdair nodded, but he never took his gaze from the drawings.

Unlike everything else in this wing of the manor house, these were not old. There were only two portraits missing here. His own, and that of Cicely. He didn't expect to see any drawing of him in a collection belonging to Alasdair, but if there was one of Cicely, it would certainly have been here.

As if by sixth sense, Griffin knew the name of the artist. "Cicely made these, didn't she?"

Tendrils of Alasdair's pale hair floated on the ever-cooler breeze that came out of nowhere to swirl inside the room. "Aye. He laughed at her about her drawin'. The slimy bastard was cruel about it."

"Edmund."

"Edmund, right enough. But he wouldna come here, ye see? Coward that he was, he'd no step a foot into this wing. So her drawin's were safe from him, and when he dinna see them, he let her be."

Griffin frowned. "And why, might I ask, didn't you attempt to drive *him* off?" he asked indignantly. "You've certainly done your best to get rid of *me*."

Alasdair shrugged. "He was so pitiful an excuse for a man, he wasna worth any effort at all. And he was Cicely's rightful husband. She tried to be a good wife, and no mistake, for all that he was a buggerin' swine. Even to tryin' to seduce him into performin' his husbandly duty." Alasdair looked away. His jaw clamped tight for a moment.

"She *told* you this?" Griffin asked incredulously.

"Nay, o' course not! She's much too delicate to broach such a subject. I saw her actin' so agreeable with him as they dined, pourin' his wine with her own hand. Speakin' to him of children. Seems he remembered his duty to his family, if no to his wife." Alasdair's lips curved in an evil smile. "He'd been unsuccessful gettin' an heir off his valet." The smile vanished. "He went to her chamber that night."

Griffin bent down to scoop the puppy into his hands. He did not like thinking of Cicely being touched by any man but him.

He also objected to Alasdair's possessiveness toward her. But he knew firsthand how impossible it was not to love Cicely, and he had known her less than three months. Alasdair had had Cicely all to himself for six years. How painful it must be to love a woman, to have her with you daily, all the while knowing you can never be her husband or lover, but only a companion.

Untouched, untouching, yet filled with the need. Perhaps that was Alasdair's real punishment.

A pink wet tongue made several swipes across the back of Griffin's hand. His fingers stroked Honeysett's smooth coat. His gaze met Alasdair's eerie translucent one. "Cicely and I are to wed," he said quietly. It didn't seem right not to inform the spectral Scot himself.

"She told me."

Griffin nodded. How like her to consider her friend's feelings.

The breeze in the room strengthened, growing rapidly to a howl. The temperature plummeted. Alasdair grinned gleefully as he levitated. With a swirl of his fingers, hail pelted Griffin with stinging blows.

Clutching the puppy in his arms, Griffin strode out of the room, but the hail and wind followed him. Deep laughter echoed throughout the house.

"Ye'll no be her first husband, *Sasannach*," came Alasdair's voice rolling through the rooms. "And I'll do my best to see ye're no her last!"

The front door slammed shut behind Griffin, who caught up the tools he'd propped against the outside wall and stalked toward the dower house, swearing. Despite the hail, he was completely dry. Another cursed trick by a bloody cursed trickster.

Honeysett fidgeted in the crook of Griffin's arm, making it clear he wanted down. As soon as Griffin complied, the small mongrel streaked back toward the abbey. The front door opened a crack, through which the puppy disappeared. The door closed again.

Griffin sighed. He'd taken Cicely from the ghost. He'd not try to deny him the pup's company as well.

Even ghosts, it seemed, grew lonely.

Bright and early the following morning Griffin decided that it was time to improve the first impression a visitor

or passerby collected of Cranwick. He filled a bucket
with water, took up a brush with stiff bristles, and
headed toward the lichen-covered stone pillars on
either side of the entrance drive. He viewed the tall
weeds with a critical eye.

"One would think the place abandoned," he muttered, pulling out the unwanted growth by the roots.
He'd have to get out here later with a scythe. Dipping
his brush in the water, he wet the surface of the stone
pillars. Then he touched the brush to the sandy ground
and went to work scrubbing the lichen off the columns.
They reminded him of Alasdair's headstone. That thought
drove him to scrub harder.

He paused after a while and wiped his brow with his
arm. It was then that he saw Tom Sparke walking down
the road toward him.

Griffin watched him a minute, unsmiling. Sparke's
pace slowed perceptibly as he approached.

Without a word, Griffin turned back to scouring the
entrance pillar. A few minutes later, he heard the
crunch of footsteps on the dirt road. Abruptly they
stopped. A long moment of silence passed before
Griffin finally turned from his work.

Sparke stood bareheaded on the edge of the road.
He fingered the brim of the hat he held. "Congratulations on your coming marriage."

"Thank you." Sparke hadn't walked all the way to
Cranwick to congratulate him, Griffin was certain. So
he waited.

Finally Sparke spoke again. "I'd have a word with
you, Captain Tyrrell."

Griffin gave him a short nod. "Say your piece."

Sparke was silent a moment, and from the corner of
his eye, Griffin saw the younger man's jaw muscles
bunch. "You were right about Lady Cicely. 'Twere a

stupid thing ter do, acceptin' her offer. Women are just too tenderhearted for their own good. They don't think. I know that. They walk inter trouble a-trying ter help the folk what's dear ter them. Like angels without wings, they are."

Griffin studied Sparke. Mayhap the fellow was not beyond decency after all. At least the lad appeared to be trying to make amends. Apologies for unconscionable acts were never easy. Griffin decided only an oaf would choose to rub Sparke's nose in his blunder. Tempting as that prospect was, Griffin chose to give him another chance, but not without first making his own position unquestionably clear.

"Because they don't have wings, they need our protection," he said. "As men, we have a responsibility for their safety."

"I do know that, sir." Sparke's gaze dropped down to the hat with which he fidgeted.

There was something else on Sparke's mind, that was obvious. Griffin let him take his time.

"I was desperate-like, that's the only reason I agreed ter let Lady Cicely help me. I knew better, even then. But my wife was hungry, and she was carrying our babe. Still, that didn't make what I did right. An' after that night, you know, when the black lugger came, I got ter thinking. Fear is what made me agree ter have Lady Cicely carry illegal goods. My fear made me do something I didn't like. Something that made me . . . not like myself anymore. If I've got ter be afraid, I'd at least want ter get some of my self-respect back. Farmwork don't pay as good as what the smugglers give for a-carrying, but 'tis safer. I've got a wife and daughter ter think of now. You said you had work for me."

Griffin studied Tom. He was young and strong, and despite his ridiculous belief that Alasdair gave a damn about anyone else's manhood, he'd shown up. And he, Griffin Nelvington Tyrrell, master of one long-neglected manor, was in desperate need of help.

"I do," he said. "Are you ready to start now?"

Under his sun-darkened skin, Tom turned a little pale as he shot a panicked look down the drive, which ended at the abbey. "I am, sir."

"John Longley says he cannot remember Alasdair ever hurting anyone. Lady Cicely has read every reference to him she can find in the abbey's library, and she's found no mention of anyone suffering other than cold or fright." Or pained ears, Griffin amended as he remembered Alasdair's shrieking that first night he'd tried to stay in the manor house. Of course, there had been none of that particular trick since Griffin had threatened to allow Mr. Joyes a chance to perform an exorcism.

"I'm glad ter hear it, sir," Tom said as Griffin led him onto the manor, in the direction of the outbuilding where the tools were kept.

Approximately fifty feet onto the property, Griffin heard a familiar *pop* and turned to find Alasdair in his favorite guise as an enormous death's-head.

Tom went pale as he stared at the thing. Then his eyes rolled back, and he went down, crashing onto the ground like a felled tree.

"I dinna even have a chance to speak," the death's-head complained. With another discharge of air, Alasdair appeared in his kilted form. Fists propped on his hips, he surveyed the still figure of Tom Sparke. He grinned. "Och, I must be gettin' better. This one swooned with just a look at me."

"It takes so little to make you happy," Griffin observed sourly, as he knelt to check Tom's breathing.

"A man takes what amusement he can. After two

hundred years, there's little that amuses him. Save for terrifyin' *Sasannaich.*"

"So I see," Griffin said. Sparke appeared to be all right. He'd merely swooned, as Alasdair had said.

Griffin rose to his feet. "Well, this is one fellow with whom you've likely succeeded." He was tempted to swing a punch at Alasdair, but he knew he'd never have the pleasure of feeling his fist connect with the damn Scotsman's jaw—or anything else on the ghost. "What's Tom Sparke ever done to you?" he asked, feeling suddenly weary.

Alasdair scowled. His ever-present cool breeze swirled more quickly around him, stirring his hair and the folds of his plaid. "He'd ha' turned me over to yer queen's men as quick as lookin' at me."

"We haven't had a queen for almost two centuries, and England and Scotland are now part of the same kingdom."

"I knew that," Alasdair said loftily, drawing himself up. "Sweet Cicely told me. Mayhap I forgot for the moment."

"See here, Alasdair—" Griffin broke off what he was going to say. Alasdair's use of such informal terms when he spoke of Cicely rankled, but he'd be foolish to let the ghost know that it bothered him. Griffin decided on a different tack. "This fellow came here to work. The manor is falling to ruins. One or two people cannot perform all the labor required."

"That's *yer* problem," Alasdair informed him. "I dinna like a herd o' strangers on my land."

"*My* land, and you'd best remember that. One more incident like this one, and I'll have Mr. Joyes out here quick as you can blink an eye. Do you understand me?"

Alasdair grinned. "Nay, ye'll not."

"And what," Griffin asked with deadly softness, "makes you say that?"

Floating up, Alasdair assumed the position of sitting cross-legged, his forearms resting against his knees. "Because ye've feelin's for Cicely, and she canna bear the thought of what exorcism would do to me. Nor can I, so I'll no press the matter with ye. But I'll no just stand by and allow an army of intruders to come stampedin' onto Cranwick, so there ye have it."

It took every ounce of willpower for Griffin to maintain a calm stance in the face of such a pronouncement. "I'd not wager too heavily on your theory, were I you," he said with restraint that amazed even him. "But if you're so inclined, you might remember that she sees me toiling day after day to improve an estate that one day *her* children will inherit. On the other hand, she will know that you are willfully trying to destroy it."

Alasdair glowered back at him, but did not immediately reply. The agitation of the breezes surrounding him increased. "Be damned to ye!" he snapped. With a sharp *pop*, he vanished.

A soft groan cut through Griffin's frustration to catch his attention.

Sparke struggled to sit up. Blearily, he peered around. "I thought I saw—" his eyes widened, and he bolted to his feet so fast, Griffin had to steady him before he went down again. "The demon! I saw the demon! I saw— What *was* that thing?"

"It was just Alasdair trying to scare you off."

Sparke ran his shaking broad palm across his face. "Alasdair? Not much of a name for a demon, is it?"

Griffin chuckled despite his concerns. "Somewhat less impressive than Beelzebub, I admit. But then, Alasdair isn't a demon. Merely an unsociable ghost."

"Is there a difference?"

Griffin took heart that Tom wasn't already making his way down the drive toward the road. "I don't believe Alasdair is truly evil. Just temperamental and a bit selfish." And very lonely.

"Well, I don't feel any different," Sparke said, rolling his eyes up as if taking mental inventory. "Mayhap Lady Cicely was right about the curse."

"Do you still want to work at Cranwick?"

Spark hesitated, then slowly nodded. "I do. I'll not have my Janie a-growing up knowing her da is a tubman for smugglers."

The knot of desperation in Griffin's gut eased. "You likely haven't seen the last of Alasdair," he warned.

The big fisherman shrugged. "If he's no more wicked than he was this time, I'll manage." He smiled sheepishly. "I'd hold it as a favor were you not ter speak ter anyone of me swooning."

Griffin grinned. "Agreed."

Feeling as if some of the weight on his shoulders was lifting, Griffin led Tom in the direction of the toolshed, explaining what he needed done.

Cicely sang a sprightly song of true love blossoming in May as she vigorously applied furniture polish to the top of the console table in the entry hall of the manor house. Griffin had kissed her tenderly this morning, as he had every morning since she'd agreed to marry him, and they'd set the wedding date eight days ago.

It was that same morning that Hannah had moved back in with her parents until she and Digby wed, which was planned for the week after Cicely and Griffin spoke their vows. So every morning Hannah walked from her parents' cottage to Cranwick, and every evening Digby saw her home. Hannah's move back into her parents' home had been her father's idea. To reduce temptation, he said. Cicely chuckled to herself. Anyone could see it didn't reduce temptation at all, only opportunity.

Cicely smiled as she continued to polish the furniture. For this past week, since Griffin had walked into her moonlit chamber, she had been happier than she'd ever been in her life. She savored the sweet morning kisses from Griffin as he came into the kitchen for breakfast, and his heated, meaningful glances when no one else was looking. She felt as if she were being courted across the back fence, and behind Digby's newly self-righteous back.

She laughed aloud for the sheer joy of it, and listened as the merry sound echoed through the abbey. Why, she'd even found herself giggling like a lovesick milkmaid these days. Her parents would have been appalled at such silly behavior, but she had a feeling Griffin's mother and father would have understood.

Pop! "Must ye make all this infernal racket?" Alasdair demanded peevishly. "'Tis enough to disturb the dead!"

She tried to hold back the laughter that bubbled up in her throat, she really did, but it escaped anyway. "I do apologize, Alasdair," she said hastily when he glared at her. "It's just— Never mind." Except for the irrepressible twitching at the corners of her mouth, she managed an appropriately solemn expression. The jest really wasn't even funny, when one considered the spirit's unhappy plight.

Alasdair turned away and looked out the leaded window at gangly seventeen-year-old Benjamin Smith herding a handful of sheep out to the lawn in front of the manor. From where she stood, Cicely saw Alasdair's throat work, and her amusement faded.

"Alasdair?"

Briskly, he strode away from her. "Isn't it enough that ye've ruined my reputation with the villagers and now they dinna hesitate to come and go as they wish without so much as a 'by-yer-leave'?" he demanded.

She caught the low edge in his voice and stared at him. "It isn't as if you've really been trying to chase them away," she said.

He walked back and stopped in front of her, but his gaze did not meet hers. Instead, he scowled down at his long-fingered hands. "Was yer life so terrible, then, here, alone with me?"

His question caught her off guard, but she didn't miss the intense undertone concealed beneath casually spoken words. How could she make him see that he was important to her? Important . . . but impossible to love as she loved Griffin.

"Life here has been hard," she said slowly, not wanting to injure this spirit for which she'd come to care so deeply. "When I arrived here, I was only fifteen, newly wed and abandoned. You had the power to make my life a hell. But you didn't. Instead, you chose to share your precious domain with me, an intruder. You made me feel as if I might matter to someone. And, oh, Alasdair, I needed that. I needed that badly." She stretched out her hand to him, then remembered it would pass through his form. She curled her fingers closed and withdrew her hand. "'Twas you, and you alone, who kept me sane. You gave me courage. You saved me from despair."

Denied the ability to touch him, Cicely tried to reach out to him through her gaze. The pain she found in his ghostly eyes pierced her with the force of a driven lance, vibrating through her chest with anguish. She pressed her lips together and blindly turned toward the door.

"Wait."

The single, whispered word stopped her short. She squeezed her eyes closed. What could she do? What could she say to ease the misery? To make his hurt go away?

The cool air that eternally surrounded him brushed against her back with the softness of a sigh, and she knew he stood close. "I always knew our time couldna last forever. And I knew I couldna ever be a real man to ye. But . . . the make-believe was verra sweet while it lasted."

Her heart clenched against the wistfulness she heard in his voice. "Alasdair—"

"Nay, Cicely. I know. Griffin's right. Ye are tender-hearted. But yer no lackin' for courage. Ye never have been. I gave ye nothin' but my company and my love. The courage was always yers. As for despair . . . well, I dinna think it's in ye to ever give up. Hidden deep within ye, there's fire-forged steel. 'Tis only yer inno-cence that conceals it from the eye, but it's there, and no mistake."

She drew an uneven breath. If only Alasdair did not hurt. If only he could be at peace. But she had thus far failed him even in that.

"Dinna worrit for me, lass." His softly spoken words passed her ear like a night breeze through the elms. "I'll be here if ye have need."

"I'll always need you, Alasdair," she said chokingly. "You have a place in my heart."

"'Tis good to know someone will think of me fondly." She heard the sad smile in his voice. "But it is to yer Griffin that ye should turn now. Still, I'll be here. Where else can I go?" And when the warmth of the morning returned to heat her, she knew Alasdair had faded back into that place where damned hearts and souls dwelled.

She hurried from the abbey and went to her sanctu-ary in the woods, where she sat a while, trying to collect herself. Finally, she crept out of her secret place among the trunks of the poplars and hastened to the dower house to check on the progress of the noon meal and dinner.

Griffin had hired short, wiry Henry Diplock as cook, because the fellow had claimed to be good at it. Griffin knew Cicely needed help and had hired him. Henry, however, had lost his left hand in a fishing accident, and Cicely wasn't entirely convinced the hook Henry now wore on the stump of his wrist could compensate well enough to meet the rigors and demands of being a full-time cook.

When she arrived in the kitchen, the yeasty aroma of rising dough and the smell of simmering chicken made her mouth water.

She discovered Henry had donned a long, white apron which covered the front of his simple shirt, waistcoat, and breeches. Below the hem of the apron she saw his dun-colored stockings had been carefully darned and his shoes blacked. His dark blond hair was pulled back in a stubby queue.

It was clear to her that Henry was in complete control of the kitchen, and, for the first time since the accident two years ago, he appeared to have found his place. On a corner shelf, covered by a linen towel, dough rose in an enormous bowl. In a pot on the fireplace stove, a chicken stewed. A fragrant berry tart rested on the table. As she watched, Henry deftly combined the ingredients that she knew went into the making of a white fricassee. Having a hook instead of a left hand didn't seem to slow him down.

"Are you worried, Lady Cicely?" he asked without pausing in his work. "Afraid this hook might give me some trouble here in the kitchen?"

Cicely's cheeks warmed. "I confess it concerned me a bit, but you look quite at home here."

Henry grinned. "My ma always said I cooked better than she ever did. Mayhap that's not entirely true, but I've always enjoyed working with food. I've got a friend what found employment as a cook in a gentleman's house up north a few miles. He's taught me a lot. Sends me receipts ter try. You know, nothin' so fancy as I couldn't find the ingredients, but nice dishes I believe you'll enjoy."

"I'm sure I will if this is any example of your work." She inhaled deeply. "Oh, it smells lovely."

He blushed with pleasure. "Thank you, m'lady."

"I look forward to luncheon, Henry," she assured him as she swept from the kitchen. Another wise choice by Griffin, she acceded.

The thought of him brought back her earlier blissful glow, and she smiled. Where was he now on the manor? What important task did he perform? She found herself counting the minutes until the noon meal, when he'd return to the dower house.

Hannah bustled past Cicely, her arms loaded with bed linens to be aired out. "Dreamin' of the captain, I see," she teased.

Cicely laughed. "And do you never think of Digby?"

"Of course! I think of his pretty brown eyes and sigh. Then I remember . . . well, *other* things, and my knees go all watery-like."

Cicely remembered other things, too. Each night she lay alone in her bed and longed for Griffin to come to her. But he was trying to restrain himself during the two weeks that separated them from a marital bed. Her only consolation was knowing that he wanted her as much as she wanted him. His body revealed his eagerness every time they stole a kiss or exchanged long, lingering glances across a room.

It didn't help that Digby had appointed himself

chaperon to Griffin and Cicely. Misery loved company, it seemed, for Digby was miserable without Hannah. Had he not been so bent on seeing that his master and mistress did not enjoy themselves either, she might have found his pining a great deal more endearing.

Finally, she could no longer put off returning to work in the abbey. She gathered up her rags, furniture polish, and broom, then walked back to the manor house.

If Alasdair was present, he did not make himself known to her. Likely he was off floating about the property. Or up in the banqueting tower. She tried not to think of him yet, for the pain she'd read in his eyes still cut deep.

With a heavy sigh, she set about cleaning. With soft cloths she applied furniture polish, the honeyed scent of wax and the sharp smell of turpentine filling the parlor. She amused herself by singing as she worked.

"Hark! A songbird has found its way into the abbey," a familiar voice announced.

Cicely's heart leaped. "Griffin!"

Laughing, he pulled her into his arms. "I thought I'd never shake off our watchdog," he said, nuzzling her ear. "Begads, the man is determined to spoil our play."

She dropped her cloth and threaded her fingers through his hair, expectantly lifting her face toward his. Griffin obliged her with no hesitation, capturing her lips with his and parting them in a hungry kiss that sent flutters into her stomach, and a slow, steady burn in her blood.

When Griffin finally lifted his head, he gave her a sultry smile. "My kitten is turning into a tigress," he said, his hands restlessly moving over her back.

"And what do you think of the transformation?" she asked, her voice more breathless purr than tone.

"I like it," he said. He ran his fingertips along the side of her neck. "Very much."

Just as their lips brushed again, a heavy knock sounded at the front door.

Griffin scowled. "I suppose that's Digby."

"Why would he knock?"

"To disturb us," Griffin grumbled.

He released her and strode out of the room, Cicely following close on his heels. His boots rang on the stone-paved entry hall. He flung open the door.

A shuttered nonexpression slammed down over his face.

Alarmed by the sudden change in Griffin, Cicely cautiously looked to see who had knocked.

A man in his early forties, who stood only slightly shorter than Griffin, waited at the threshold. He wore a brown bagwig of the best quality beneath his plumed, black three-cornered hat. Dark eyebrows curved over green eyes, and a straight thin nose ended in pinched-looking nostrils. The painted full lips of his wide mouth suggested an avid sensuality.

Elaborate silver braid trimmed the deep cuffs of his blue coat. Silver embroidered vines edged his scarlet satin waistcoat. His clocked gray silk stockings were finely woven, and the silver buckles on his shoes were studded with diamonds.

"Hello, Brother." The stranger's lips curved up slightly, but the smile did not reach his eyes. He favored Cicely with a brief, cursory glance.

This lordly fellow was Griffin's brother?

"Hello, Randolph." There was no welcome in Griffin's words.

"Well, aren't you going to invite me into your"— Randolph's gaze swept the area and clearly found it lacking—"house?"

Griffin hesitated, then stepped back. Randolph strode in with the confidence of a king entering a vassal's hut. As he looked around, he thrust his hat, gloves, and crop at Cicely, who automatically accepted them rather than let them drop to the floor.

"A bit old-fashioned for my tastes, little brother," Randolph announced. "But certainly better than I expected *you* would ever obtain."

"But then, you never expected to find me alive."

Randolph smiled, but, as before, it never reached his eyes. "True. Quite true. My sources had informed me you'd been killed in that little forest skirmish."

"How disappointing for you," Griffin said.

Randolph sighed. "One must learn to live with one's trivial reversals. Still, there will be other chances."

Cicely could scarcely believe her ears. Had Randolph tried to have Griffin murdered?

When he noticed Cicely still standing there, holding his possessions, Randolph clacked his tongue in disapproval. "Griffin, your manners are as deficient as ever. You haven't introduced me to this ravishing creature."

Cicely stiffened under his brazen perusal. She lifted her chin and regarded the rude fellow down her nose. "And you are . . . ?"

Randolph laughed delightedly. "Ah, the puss has claws." He accorded her a courtly bow. "Randolph Tyrrell, duke of Marwood. Your humble servant, madam."

She doubted that. But—Griffin's brother was a *duke?* Before she could reply, Griffin spoke up.

"She is Lady Cicely Honeysett, the former owner of Cranwick. She is here today only to recover a few items she left behind. Tomorrow she leaves for France."

Something in his unreadable expression, in his voice, kept her from showing her surprise at his lie. Instead, she decided to play along until he could explain.

"I fear my orders to the servants must not have been as precise as I might have wished," she said. "They neglected to pack several of my possessions, thinking they were to remain with the house."

"I am devastated that I could not have met you sooner, Lady Cicely. You see, I am the new owner of Blekton and have only arrived today." He turned a cool smile on Griffin. "When I discovered that my dear little brother lived in Sussex, why, nothing would do but that I purchase the manor bordering his."

Cicely suppressed a shiver. Something about Randolph . . . This man was maleficence in comely guise, and he meant no good toward Griffin.

She forced her lips into an upward curve. "How nice for you," she said, handing Randolph back his accessories. "It grieves me that I must request a delay in your brotherly reunion, Lord Marwood, but, truly, I am pressed to meet my schedule. Ordinarily, I would not make so bold as to interfere in such a touching scene, but I am depending on Lord Griffin to locate a trunk of my books." She gave Griffin an apologetic look. "You *did* promise your help, sir, and now I have no time to spare before I retrieve what is mine and convey it to the ship. I vow that captain will not wait for me again." On Randolph she turned the most flustered-female expression she could muster, batting her eyelashes shamelessly. "Oh, pray, do understand, Lord Marwood!"

He bowed over her hand. "Of course, Lady Cicely." His gaze slid toward his brother. "I have all the time in the world."

After she walked with him to the door, she watched him accept his horse from the stable lad—a new member of the staff, the son of a farmer whose crops had been demolished by the blight. The boy was clever and had learned quickly that animals were never to be brought too close to the manor house because of Alasdair.

Apparently the duke disliked taking the several extra steps it required to get to his horse, and he took the boy to task. Quickly, Cicely rushed out, interposing herself between the peer's annoyance and the innocent lad.

"I ask your indulgence, Lord Marwood. The boy was merely following orders. Horses mislike coming too close to the abbey, so he was asked to keep them at a certain distance."

Lord Marwood lifted an imperious eyebrow. "Oh? And why is that?"

"A ghost."

"A ghost? Ridiculous! Tell me that *you* don't believe such drivel." His gelding sidestepped nervously.

"I do not pretend to have answers for everything, sir."

Despite his firm hand on its reins, Marwood's horse danced around, snorting, its eyes wide. "Good day to you, Lady Cicely," he said briskly, clearly impatient with his frightened animal.

"And to you, sir."

She watched the duke wheel his gelding around and canter down the drive, to disappear finally around the corner of the stone pillar entry. When he was out of sight, she ruffled the boy's hair, then returned to the house to question Griffin.

But he gave her no opportunity to ask anything. "I've work to do," he muttered, and strode from the house.

Cicely knew something was terribly wrong. It was a foreboding that twisted deep in her gut. Just as certainly, she sensed Griffin needed time alone.

Uneasily she watched him move farther and farther away from her.

*　　　*　　　*

By dusk Griffin had not returned.

After having restlessly prowled the dower house for an hour, trying to concentrate on her work, Cicely gave up and hastened to the abbey. As she closed the front door behind her, flames came to life on candles throughout the manor house.

"Thank you, Alasdair," she said softly, relieved that he did not feel inclined to sever their friendship.

With the familiar burst of air, he appeared beside her. High-pitched puppy barks sounded from upstairs. A minute later, Honeysett scampered down the dark wood stairs, to sit smiling, tongue lolling, at Alasdair's buskin-clad feet.

"He's quite fond of you," she said. "We scarcely ever see him. He spends all his time with you. Is he eating as he should?"

"Aye. Eatin' and drinkin', spillin' his water everywhere. Breakin' him to the house is a rare treat," Alasdair said sourly, but then he went and ruined his facade by smiling down at the eager puppy.

"I'm worried, Alasdair."

"I know, lass. The great coof has no returned, has he?"

She headed toward the staircase that led to the banqueting tower and Alasdair strode beside her, with Honeysett trotting at his feet. "His brother came here this morning," she said. "What an awful man! And it's clear that he and Griffin do not get on. In fact, I've never seen Griffin so . . . so . . . *remote*." She worried her bottom lip as they climbed the wooden stairs, only her footfalls and those of the puppy making any sound.

"His brother, did ye say? I've n'er heard him speak

of a brother, so I suppose I dinna think of him havin' one."

Griffin had always seemed so self-sufficient, so self-contained, that until that afternoon among the castle ruins, she, too, had not thought of him having brothers or sisters. When she'd asked him, he'd denied having any.

Cicely recalled his reaction when he'd opened the door to find Randolph standing there. She'd sensed in him an instant coiled tension, a sharp watchfulness that she'd have associated with a hunted animal faced with a baying pack of hounds more than a reunion of brothers.

"I've got to find him," she said. "Something is vastly wrong."

When they reached the top of the stairs, she scooped Honeysett into her arms and carefully negotiated the way to the tower. Alasdair chose to float.

Dusk was settling over the land, streaking the sky with red and bronze and purple. Cicely moved from window to window in the tower, anxiously scanning the landscape for Griffin.

"There, lass." Alasdair raised his arm to point the way.

Sure enough, there in the distance, at an hour when everyone else had gone to their homes, a solitary figure labored.

Honeysett still in her arms, Cicely hurried out of the tower and back across the roof, then all but flew down the steps. Setting the puppy on the floor, she took a lantern from the pantry in the kitchen, paused to light it, and then raced out of the house, heading in Griffin's direction.

The puppy stretched his short legs to keep up, and Alasdair jogged easily beside her, offering no comment.

The sun sank low, stealing the light. Weeds and

grass dragged at her stockings, at the hem of her skirt. The lappets of her cap slapped softly against her jaw. A painful stitch snagged in her side, stabbing her with each breath as she ran.

Griffin stabbed his shovel into the earth with savage violence, tearing away dark clumps of soil with a ragged grunt, then sending them sailing through the air to a growing heap. The irrigation ditch had grown greatly in length since she'd seen it yesterday afternoon.

His shirtsleeves had been rolled up onto his forearms. Smears of dirt marked his garments and skin. Locks of hair had escaped his queue, and the sheen of sweat glistened on his smudged face. But it was his expression of mingled despair and rage that brought Cicely to a halt.

She turned to look at Alasdair, who gave her a single nod. Silently, he walked away, in the direction from which they'd come. Honeysett trailed slowly behind him.

Griffin kept working. It frightened her a little, the way he slammed the blade of that shovel into the ground again and again. She hesitated a moment, studying him. Apprehension grew in her as she watched him.

She moved closer to him, allowing the lantern to encompass him with its soft light. "Griffin."

He kept digging as if he hadn't heard her. With each blow of his shovel she heard a guttural sound in his throat that hovered between growl and moan.

Cicely stepped closer. "Griffin?"

"Go back to the house."

She knelt on the ground, bringing her nearly face-to-face with Griffin, who stood in the ditch. She set the lantern down and buried her trembling hands in the folds of her apron. "I'll not leave you."

Abruptly he stopped, the shovel embedded in the earth. He turned his shoulder to her. "Yes, you will."

Concerned that he worried she might leave him forever, she shook her head. "No, Griffin. Never."

His face gilded half-silver by the moon, half-gold by the light of the lantern, left Cicely breathless. Yet it was something else, something that reached her from within his heart that had truly captured her and made her his.

His winged eyebrows drew down in a scowl as he gazed into the distance. "Yes, you will. You must."

Impatient and worried over the distance he seemed determined to set between them, Cicely scrambled down into the ditch with him. She came around to stand in front of him. "I say I'll not go anywhere. Anywhere without you, that is."

He glared down at her. "'Tis no longer safe for you here."

"Why?"

Griffin did not answer her immediately. At his sides, his hands curled open, then clenched into fists. "Because he knows I'm alive now. And he knows where I am."

"Him. Your brother?"

His lips drew back, baring strong white teeth, stark against the dark of his smudged face. "My brother." He spit the words like the foulest curse.

She moved closer to him, searching his face for some clue. "Tell me, Griffin," she whispered.

He raked his fingers through his hair, tearing more locks from their confinement. He looked at her a minute, then expelled a ragged breath. "I'd thought that it was over, that he'd called an end to his . . . hunt. It seems I was wrong."

Grasping his arm, she demanded, "What hunt? What power does he have over you, Griffin?"

"Power?" Griffin laughed. The harsh, humorless sound rose and faded on the cool autumn air. "He's a duke! His power extends throughout the kingdom. And he would like nothing better than to see me dead."

Cicely gasped. "How do you know this?"

"You mean besides his telling me? Besides a hunting 'accident'? Besides assassins in the dark? When the bullet from his hunting rifle failed to do more than graze my face, and his assassins and highwaymen did not manage to murder me, he moved to more subtle machinations. No one near me is safe."

"Did he tell you that as well?"

"No." His mouth tightened, and he looked away.

She wanted to hold him, to comfort him, but she doubted he'd accept it at this moment.

Cicely defied the risk of his rejection, and slipped her arms around him. He stiffened, and for a moment she feared he would push her away. Then he fiercely clutched her to him.

"Why is your brother trying to kill you?" she asked.

Griffin held her a minute, his cheek warm against the crown of her head. "Because he isn't my brother. And he isn't the real duke of Marwood."

Stunned into momentary silence, she struggled to allow the import of his outrageous statement to sink in. "Then who," she asked, "is the real duke of Marwood?"

"I am."

She drew away to look at him, hoping to discover this was naught but a strange jest. Instead she found his face composed. "You are the duke?"

"My father's first marriage was to a woman who resented him. She felt she'd married beneath her station. His family wasn't as old or wealthy as hers. A circumstance she never allowed him to forget."

Cicely sighed. "It seems some parents choose poorly when it comes to their children's mates."

"So it does," he agreed.

She raised her head. "Was she your mother?"

Griffin kissed her forehead. "No."

She laid her cheek back on his chest and he continued.

"I suppose it wasn't too surprising that my father looked elsewhere for affection. He fell in love with an opera dancer and took her as his mistress. Out of love for him," he went on, "she bore the insults and indignities the duchess heaped on her. My aunt told me that my father grew increasingly angry at his wife's vindictiveness. She'd made it clear she didn't want him, yet she didn't want any other woman to have him. He brought his mistress to live on his country property, in a house of her own."

Griffin rubbed his thumb back and forth over her arm. Cicely felt the faint scratch of grit and knew his thoughts were far away. "The duchess conceived," he said. "The servants told him later that she was anxious to bear the duke a son. She felt threatened by the great affection he bore his mistress. When his wife presented him with a son—Randolph—my father was delighted. At last he had an heir. Of course, a man dare not risk all on one child, but while the duchess conceived many times after that, she miscarried or the children were stillborn. When Randolph was twelve, she died of an inflammation of the lungs."

Under her cheek, Cicely felt the solid warmth of Griffin's body through his shirt. Even though she had evidently been unkind to her husband, Cicely couldn't help but feel a little sorry for the unhappy duchess.

"My father promptly married my mother. A year later, I was born."

"Where was Randolph?"

"With us. My father wished to prepare him to fulfill his station in life. A duke has many responsibilities. My father also made provisions for me. A trust fund. Land. I was to lead the comfortable life of a gentleman."

Cicely's gaze took in the shovel and the ditch in which they stood. "What happened?"

He was silent a moment. "My father and I went searching for a medal he'd been given as a boy. I was eighteen, home on a visit from Oxford. We looked everywhere for that thing, going into places even he had never been. It was in a room beneath the house that we found her."

"Her?"

"Randolph's real mother."

Cicely lifted her head and studied his still face. "His real mother was kept in a dungeon? Who was she?"

"It was as close to a dungeon as one could get in a country house that was only fifty years old, even one as enormous as Ashton. No one went to that area anymore; it was used for storage. She told us the only people she'd seen in years were her son, Randolph, and the maid that brought her meals and fresh clothes. I remember the room was made up rather comfortably, but for the gloom. No windows, only candlelight." He drew a long breath and let it out. "I think she teetered on the edge of madness. Who wouldn't after spending thirty-one years in such confinement?"

"But why was she there? And how had Randolph come to be duke?"

"She told us that she was Randolph's mother, Lucy Larkin. That the duchess had delivered a stillborn son that stormy night so long ago. In her desperation, she took Lucy's newborn, illegitimate son. The babe was passed off as the heir, and contrary to the agreement she'd struck with the duchess, Lucy was immediately confined in the room where we found her." Raven black eyebrows drew down. "She talked on and on about her son, who still slipped down to see her occasionally, and several times she mentioned the maid whom she believed to be the only other person to know of her existence. The poor woman wept when we brought her out of her prison. She was terrified Randolph would discover she'd left her cell and be angry with her. Daylight hurt her eyes."

Any sympathy Cicely might have had for the duchess vanished. Her dislike of Randolph grew. What kind of man kept his own mother secretly imprisoned? But the answer was evident: the kind of man who enjoyed being a duke.

"How did Randolph find out about his real mother? It strikes me that the duchess was too desperate to provide an heir for her to say anything."

"And so she was . . . until she fell ill. Suddenly her mortality was upon her. Fearing for her soul, she made a deathbed confession to her chaplain, not realizing that Randolph had refused to be parted from her and so had concealed himself behind some draperies. He overheard everything. After the duchess died, he ventured into the basement, where what she'd said was confirmed. He discovered the woman who bore him.

"Father and I confronted Randolph with the evidence of the crime, and he denied it. Face-to-face with the trembling little maid and poor Lucy, he laughed at us, and denied the whole thing. My father discovered the chaplain had died shortly after the duchess. A heavy stone statue of one of the apostles toppled over and crushed him when he was at his prayers." From Griffin's tone, Cicely knew he didn't believe the statue had fallen over on its own.

"The day after our confrontation, the maid who'd brought Lucy her meals vanished without a trace. Randolph claimed that she'd probably run away from our foul accusations."

Hair prickled on the back of Cicely's neck.

"I had to return to Oxford, but I received a letter from my father saying Lucy had been found dead in her room. Father believed it was murder. The doctor disagreed. So my parents left for London to speak privately with an authority on poisons. They were killed in a carriage accident on the way."

"Another accident?"

Griffin gave a short sharp bark of humorless laughter. "Not likely. They were struck by a runaway coach drawn by panicked horses. An empty runaway coach. On a lonely stretch of road."

It sounded too coincidental, Cicely thought. If Griffin were eighteen at the time, Randolph would have been thirty-one—old enough and with sufficient experience in the world to find the resources for such murder. "What happened then?" she asked.

"While I was still stunned with grief in Oxford, Randolph moved quickly. He managed to overturn my trust and the bequest of land to me, claiming my father had not been in his right mind. Miraculously, he produced three so-called witnesses of my father's dementia. His trickery worked, and I was made Randolph's destitute ward."

From her brief encounter with Randolph, Cicely knew she'd never, ever wish to be in that man's power. She held Griffin a little closer. "What did you do?"

"At first I tried to have Randolph arrested, but that only made me a laughingstock. The more people I tried to tell what was happening, the greater risk I took of being thrown in Bedlam. Randolph was simply too well covered to be overturned by a green lad shouting wolf. But I was the only one left who knew his damning secret. Rather than fall victim to one of Randolph's 'accidents,' or spend the rest of my life locked away in a madhouse, I ran. I thought I could hide in the army. My aunt and uncle secretly conspired with me to obtain a commission for me in one of the less prestigious regiments bound for India. But there was no escaping Randolph. He arranged for the regiment to be sent to the heaviest fighting in America."

"Where you and your cousin were ambushed by French and Indians."

"And I was shot by an Englishman. I turned to find him taking aim. I was a clear target. I'd been wounded, and I could no more elude him than fly. 'I've been told to tell you that Lucy's boy says adieu,' he said. You know the rest."

"You thought you'd gotten a bargain in Cranwick," she said, guilt washing through her.

"Perhaps it will be a bargain still, when Alasdair is put to rest."

She lifted her head. "And what of me?" she asked, trying to lighten his mood with a little teasing. "Do you not consider a wife and a manor for the price of one a bargain?"

He cradled her face between his palms, and set his mouth to hers. Readily, she parted her lips, and his soft sigh breathed into her.

Griffin's kiss possessed a haunting tenderness. The gentle touch of his firm, warm lips. The moist whisper of his tongue across hers. The way he held her as if she were rare and precious. All were filled with an almost-tangible yearning.

Then he set her away from him. "You cannot be my wife, Cicely."

Her eyes widened. "What?"

Griffin wrapped his hand around the long handle of the shovel, and looked down at it. He seemed so remote that he might have been back in that New World forest and been closer to her than he was now. Drawing in a long breath, he straightened. He faced her, unsmiling. "I'm not going to marry you."

Cicely felt as if she'd been struck. She stepped back under the blow of his words. "A jest?" she asked, her voice humiliatingly uneven.

He shook his head. "Pack your things and go to France."

She swallowed hard. It took all she had to counter him. "No. I won't."

Moonlight slanted down across his face, sliding silver over his eyes and the tops of his cheekbones, the blade of his nose, and the curve of his top lip. His gaze was implacable.

"Yes," he said. "You will."

She stood rooted where she was as he jerked the shovel from the ground and leaped out of the ditch. Numbly she watched him stride away, until he was gone, swallowed up by the dark.

16

The following morning Cicely and Griffin passed each other in the kitchen without a word. With miserable satisfaction she noticed the dark circles under his eyes. It took willpower stiffened by pride to keep her gaze from following him, but when he paused next to her, even pride failed. She looked up to find him staring at her.

His lips parted, as if he wanted to say something, and breathlessly she waited.

His mouth closed firmly. He turned and walked out the door.

Her heart clenched with pain. She rushed from the kitchen and made her way to her chamber. Doubtless he'd gone back to work on that cursed ditch, she thought savagely as she thumped her door closed behind her.

I'm not going to marry you. Pack your things and go to France.

The words that had echoed in her mind all last night

returned, bringing fresh tears to her eyes. Furious, she
dashed them away with the backs of her hands, then
took several long breaths. She would not weep, she
decided. The spark of determination flickered in her,
then took hold. Weeping clouded reason.

She had lived in the same house as Griffin Tyrrell for
almost three months. She'd taken her meals with him,
massaged his leg, shared his company in a thousand different moments. She might not have known that his
father had been a duke, but she did know that this cava-
lier treatment of their engagement—short though it
might be—was not typical of Griffin. He simply did not
take such matters lightly.

Quickly she went to the washstand and poured water
into the basin, as she considered her course of action.
After bathing her face with the chill water, she swirled
on her cloak and hurried out of her chamber. She
needed time to think. She could consider the situation
on the way to Alwyn, where she planned to take food to
the unfortunate.

Not a quarter of an hour later, Octavia trotted down
the road to the village. Seated in the chaise, its top
pulled up against the early cool weather, Cicely reflected
that it was a relief having sufficient help at the manor.
After Tom had ventured to work at Cranwick—and suffered no obvious ill effects—Israel Oldreave had come
seeking employment, then seventeen-year-old Benjamin
Smith, the lad who had gone to retrieve Hannah and
the luggage back from Portsmouth. Shortly after that,
Henry Diplock and the others had shown up. Finally,
Griffin had enough help to make the improvements
he wanted to Cranwick and to properly maintain the
manor.

Now as the chaise rattled down the country lane,
Cicely turned her attention to the matter of Griffin.

He was protecting her.

It didn't take much reasoning to determine why. Just as it didn't take much imagination to enumerate the ways in which a man like Randolph might extract his revenge. Ways which would be decidedly unpleasant for her.

Very well. She understood *why* Griffin was trying to protect her. Now she must make him realize that despite the possible danger to her, nothing—*nothing*—could devastate her more than losing him.

Cicely guided Octavia into the yard of the livery stables. With a wan smile, she accepted Mr. Wilshaw's hand down. The smells of horse, freshly turned hay, and leather polish intruded faintly on her preoccupation.

With new purpose, she settled the large basket of food on her arm. She must simply show Griffin that she was not about to be driven away. *She* was the mistress of her fate now, and no one else, no matter how well intentioned, was going to decide what was good for her and what was not. Only she would determine when to leave and when to stay.

As she swept down the wooden walkway, she felt the storm that had raged inside her since last night ease to a clear, resolute calm.

She had given her heart to Griffin. He would have to learn to live with it.

Three hours later she went to buy yeast from Mrs. Fullard's brewery, situated behind the sturdy widow's alehouse. Now that Cicely had help at Cranwick, bread could be made there instead of buying it from Mr. Ginger, the baker.

She was surprised when the towering Mrs. Fullard

herself answered the jangling bell above the kitchen door.

"I was a-hoping ter see you," Mrs. Fullard said in a low voice as she led the way across the yard to the brewery. Hens and ducks scurried out of her path.

Cicely hurried to keep up with the older woman. "I'm pleased to see you, too, Mrs. Fullard."

A grim smile broke over the brewery owner's handsome features as she removed an impressive ring of keys from her girdle and inserted one into the lock of the large shed that housed the village's source of yeast and ale. The strong malty odor of fermenting barley and hops engulfed them as she swung open the door. Mrs. Fullard lighted a candle in a holder just inside the entrance, then indicated that Cicely should follow her inside, closing the door after her. Cicely had never been inside the brewery, but Mrs. Fullard gave her no opportunity to look around.

"His lordship is in my alehouse," she said in a low voice. Without explanation, Cicely knew whom she meant. "He wasn't here long before I overheard him say ter another o' my customers that he'd been to call on the captain—*his brother.*" Mrs. Fullard looked to Cicely for confirmation.

"So he claims. I cannot say more at this time."

Mrs. Fullard's eyes widened, but she continued. "Well, seems his lordship thought you was a-leaving like, but one o' the men gone and spilt the porridge that you and the captain was engaged." Mrs. Fullard shook her head. "Oooh, the look on that duke's face! Well, he changed as fast as you can blink an eye, smiled he did, but not before the other fellows and me saw that he were sore angry. Not hurt, as you'd expect, but red-eyed angry. He's not a one I'd like ter cross, I don't mind tellin' you. I thought you should know."

"Thank you, Mrs. Fullard. I appreciate the information."

"Forewarned is forearmed I always say."

Cicely made a few more stops to check arrangements and supplies for her upcoming wedding party. At the draper's she discovered that the lace trim for the wedding day dress she was sewing had arrived. When she'd obtained all the items on her shopping list, she headed back toward the livery. As she neared the stables, she breathed a sigh of relief. She had managed to avoid an encounter with Randolph.

"Well, well, if it isn't Lady Cicely," a familiar voice drawled.

Her stomach clenched.

Only years of drilling in manners and deportment allowed her to turn to face Randolph with an appearance of calm, but even as she did, a shiver of revulsion rolled down her back.

"Good morning, Your Grace," she said, giving him a brief nod of acknowledgment. She continued walking when what she really wanted to do was pick up her skirts and run as fast as she could.

He fell in step with her, his longer legs making of her pace little more than a leisurely stroll. Today, instead of a crop, he carried a silver-headed, ebony walking stick. She eyed the potential weapon.

From beneath hooded eyes, Randolph slid her a glance. "Imagine my surprise at seeing you so far from a seaport."

She made no reply.

"Pray, what detained you from making your ship?" he inquired smoothly. "Were you unable to locate your . . . books?"

"I know where my books are, thank you."

"Ah." He looked down the walkway, ignoring Mrs.

Kimball and her daughter as they passed. "Then could it be," he said without looking at her, "that you never intended to sail to France?" He turned and locked gazes with her. "That you are, in fact, my dear brother's intended?"

Since anyone in Alwyn could confirm their engagement, Cicely saw no advantage in lying to him. "We both know that I am, sir. Please make your point." Now was not the time to protest his use of the word "brother."

He frowned. "Why did Griffin tell me you were the former owner of Cranwick—"

"I am."

"Well, that, at least, is true. But you were not there to recover books, were you? 'Twas an unkind lie. I am . . . wounded."

Cicely shot a glance at him from the corner of her eye. "You don't look wounded in the least, Your Grace. You look annoyed."

Randolph smiled thinly. "You are a saucy thing. I see why Griffin fancies you."

She wondered how anyone could ever have thought Randolph and Griffin were brothers. They were essentially as different as fresh springwater and rancid oil, she thought. Griffin was bold and affectionate. *This* man slithered around and never even truly smiled.

"Does he speak of me?" Randolph asked.

"No, Your Grace."

Randolph lifted his cane and waggled the top, as he might his finger. "Tut, tut, my dear. Cannot you dispense with formality and call me Randolph? After all, we are soon to be family."

A hideous thought. Cicely swallowed.

"Now, you must relate all that dear Griffin has said of me."

"He has said nothing. Other than that he had a brother," she added, hoping to allay possible suspicions.

Randolph's smile slowly widened. "No matter. I own there is no love lost between us."

"How sad."

"Yes. Isn't it? I hold Griffin entirely responsible."

"Why is that?"

"He has spread the vicious lie that I am not the son of the late Vincent Tyrrell, my own dear father. At first I was cut to the bone, my dear, to the very bone. I couldn't imagine why Griffin hated me so." Randolph examined the stitching on the back of his kid glove. "But I was wrong. He doesn't hate me at all. He actually *believes* he is the true duke of Marwood, that I am naught but an impostor. How I grieved when I realized that. So young for the dementia to have struck." He raised his eyebrows in question. "You knew, of course, that our father was afflicted by the cursed malady, did you not?" She shook her head. "Well, 'tis so. And many's the time I've been tempted to have Griffin removed to Bethlehem hospital."

Cicely's breath stuck in her throat. *Bedlam.*

"I believe there are more savory lunatic asylums, though, don't you? Mayhap it would be a greater kindness to keep him chained in a room at Ashton. After all, there is the family name to consider, and he certainly has done it no good by speaking to my fellow peers, accusing me of having murdered my own mother. Now I ask you—my own mother?" Randolph sighed heavily. "Of course, to hear him tell it, my mother was little more than a common slut, and I a nameless bastard. Poor Griffin. Poor deluded soul. Everyone knows my mother was the duchess of Marwood, who died of a fever when I was twelve."

How convincingly Randolph had captured the manner of an injured sophisticate. If Cicely had not known Griffin, even she might have believed him. But she did know Griffin. Not for a second could anyone convince her that he suffered from dementia.

A feral light flickered and glowed in Randolph's eyes as he leaned close to her. "You must cry off at once from your engagement, my dear. Marrying my brother is folly. Not even the love of a good woman can save him now."

The underlying threat did not escape her.

He paused to study a display in a shop window. She numbly nodded to Mr. and Mrs. Joyes, who gave her a pleasant greeting as they passed. As she plastered on a smile for them, she prayed they wouldn't stop to chat. They continued on their way, ignored by the duke.

"I cannot cry off, Lord Marwood," she said. "I have an affection for Griffin." How insipid that sounded next to what she felt—passion as strong as the tides.

He regarded her down his nose. "You, madam, are a fool."

She met his gaze squarely. "One of us is, sir." Randolph was not a man who would respect, indeed, likely even comprehend such feelings as love and loyalty. She suspected the closest he could come to such emotions was dark obsession.

At the livery stable, a nod from Cicely sent Mr. Wilshaw to retrieve Octavia and the chaise.

"You may be putting yourself in danger from a lunatic," Randolph warned, his voice pitched for her ears only.

She pointedly studied his face. "I am aware of that."

He scowled. "So be it."

Mr. Wilshaw led Octavia out of the stables, her shod hooves ringing against the cobbles. Behind her, the wheels of the chaise rattled.

Randolph surveyed the shiny, patched little carriage. "Is this the best my brother can do for you?" he asked.

His disdain infuriated her. Before Griffin, she'd had no transportation of any kind. He'd given her Octavia, then dug the chaise out of the back of the stables. He'd checked the conveyance for soundness, patched the cracks and holes in the leather seat, and buffed its dimmed lacquered finish to a gloss. The chaise could not have been more precious to Cicely were it made of solid gold.

"Good day to you, sir," she said coldly. She brushed by him, ascended the metal step, and climbed into the chaise unassisted.

She flicked the reins, forcing Randolph to jump back out of the way or be run over by Octavia, who trotted smartly out into the traffic on the street.

All the way back to Cranwick, the true magnitude of the situation loomed before her like the black clouds of a storm on the horizon. Randolph would try to have Griffin killed or—perhaps worse—chained to a wall in some room in Ashton, Griffin's ancestral home. There he would be at Randolph's mercy.

This time Griffin would have to fight back or he'd surely lose his life.

She knew he feared for her safety. Anyone could understand how the memory of his cousin's death haunted him. But no battles of international scope raged in this little corner of Sussex, nor was she some green youth unable to accept the immediacy of death.

Whether or not he was willing to admit it, Griffin

Tyrrell needed an ally, and, as things looked this moment, she was the only one offering.

When she arrived back at Cranwick, she turned Octavia over to the boy who hurried around from the stables, then went in search of Griffin. She found him showing Tom how he wanted a fence mended.

Griffin finished giving his instructions and walked over to where she stood. His face wore a guarded expression.

"What are you doing out here?" he asked gruffly.

"I have just returned from Alwyn," she said, first hurt, then annoyed at his attitude. "Randolph learned that we're engaged."

"How?"

Exasperated, she replied, "Everyone in the parish knows. It was bound to slip out sooner or later."

"I hope you corrected that erroneous information."

"What erroneous information?"

Griffin frowned. "That we're engaged."

"We are."

"No," he said. "We *were*."

"Are," she insisted.

"I told you, there will be no wedding."

She lifted her chin. "Randolph tried to persuade me to cry off."

Griffin regarded her from beneath thick black lashes. "And what was your response?"

"I told him no, of course. And he called me a fool."

Griffin made no effort to dispute Randolph's accusation, but merely arched an eyebrow.

She glared at him, frustrated with his stubbornness. "I am not a fool!" she objected heatedly. "But *you* certainly are behaving like one."

"Haven't you heard?" he threw over his shoulder as he turned and strode away. "I'm a lunatic."

*   *   *

That was precisely the name Cicely called him that evening, when he moved his belongings out of the dower house, into the stables behind the abbey.

From experience, Cicely knew Digby wouldn't be back for another two hours, delaying his parting from Hannah until Mr. Boulden chased him off. Everyone else had returned to their homes for the night.

"There is no need for you to move to the stables," she insisted, hands on her hips, as he loaded his trunk onto the farm wagon. "This is absurd!"

She might as well not have spoken at all, for the attention he paid her. Without a single word of response, he climbed up onto the seat of the wagon.

"If you must do this, move into the dower house stables," she persisted, frustrated that he refused to even argue with her. "At least that one has a room with a bed."

"You'll be safer here without me. Randolph won't send assassins in the night to you. That would lack drama and excitement—not his style." He clucked to Dobbin and the wagon began to roll.

"Coward!" she shouted, casting all dignity to the wind. "You're nothing but a . . . a . . . *coward!*" Furious that she couldn't think of a more despicable word to call him, she kicked at the ground and felt a twinge of satisfaction when a pebble launched in the wagon's direction.

She'd cajoled and shouted and all but thrown a tantrum in her attempt to persuade him to listen to reason. There was no need for him to move out of the dower house. No need for him to cry off their wedding. And certainly no need for him to refuse her offers of help.

As she stood there in the deepening twilight, watching him until he disappeared from sight around the corner of the abbey, her anger drained out of her, leaving behind only the choking ache in her heart.

He never looked back.

Griffin awoke after a sleepless night to find Digby squatting on his heels in the straw, watching him.

"The deuce take it, man," he grumbled, rolling over onto his other side and closing his scratchy eyes again. "Leave me in peace."

"Begging your pardon, Cap'n, but Lady Cicely sent me out to fetch you."

Instantly, Griffin bolted to his feet. "What's wrong? Where is she?" he demanded, grabbing Digby by the shoulders. "Speak, will you?"

"I'm tryin', sir. Nothing's the matter. 'Tis only that you're to visit the hermit today."

Griffin blinked uncomprehendingly. "Hermit?"

Digby smirked. "Had a bad night, did you?"

"You needn't look so pleased." Wearily, Griffin rubbed the back of his stiff neck. "Now, what's this about the hermit?"

"Her ladyship says you're goin' to see the hermit again. It's time, she says. She thought you'd want to freshen up an' have a bite to eat before leaving."

Griffin searched his brain for any recollection of the moon's phase last night, but all he could remember was the knot in his gut as he'd packed and departed the dower house.

Cicely had tried to persuade him to stay, and nearly managed. He found it difficult to deny her anything. But this had been for her own good. Had she left when he'd told her to, she'd have been safe, but he couldn't throw her out on her own. The world was too cold and savage a place for a woman of such gentle innocence. He had no doubt it would devour Cicely in a trice. She had no other, more advantageous, protector, so it seemed she must take her chances with Griffin. The best he could do for her was to place as much distance as he could between them. But each step he moved away from her struck away another piece of his soul.

Randolph wanted him dead, or worse, in a lunatic asylum. Cicely wanted him with her. Although experience had warned her against marriage, she wished to wed him. And he wanted her. God, how he wanted her. In his house. In his bed. For the rest of their lives.

Truth to tell, the phase of the moon hadn't interested him last night as he'd driven away from her, the angry cry of *coward* ringing in his ears.

"Tell Lady Cicely I'll be in to breakfast presently."

Without further comment Digby left, and, by the gray light of dawn, Griffin drew a bucket of water from the well. In the stables, bits of straw showered from his clothing and hair as he stripped down. After his ablutions he dressed in a clean suit of clothes. He caught himself smiling when he noticed the minuscule darned spot in one of his stockings. Cicely's fine stitches had ensured the mended place would not draw attention. As he finished dressing, Griffin wondered why the mending of a man's stocking seemed as intimate as a sigh of pleasure in the night.

In the kitchen, he discovered everyone but Cicely had already broken his fast and fled. Even Henry seemed strangely absent.

The two of them ate in silence for most of their simple meal of porridge, toast, and cheese.

"Suppose I have conceived?" Cicely asked.

Griffin choked on a swallow of tea.

She frowned. "I said—"

"I heard what you said. Christ, Cicely, how could I not? Are you saying—"

"No. That is, I don't know. But suppose I have?" she asked, her chestnut eyebrows arching high in question. "What then?"

He picked up his cup again. "I suppose we will have no choice but to wed." As soon as the words were out of his mouth, he sensed they were not the right ones.

Her eyes widened. "Oh! Thank you very much!"

He set his cup down untouched. "No. Wait. I didn't mean it like it sounds—"

"I think you've made your sentiments quite clear," she said stiffly.

"What I meant was—"

She stood abruptly, throwing her twisted, wadded napkin down on the table. "It appears *I* am the only lunatic here." Her head high, she swept out of the kitchen, scooping up a large covered basket on her way. The door slammed behind her.

"Damn it all," Griffin muttered. Soaring to his feet, he stalked after her.

Outside in the stable yard, she was fumbling with the buckle of a saddle strap she'd threaded through the handle of the luncheon basket. Octavia turned large brown eyes on Cicely. Sympathetically the mare nudged her mistress with her nose, knocking Cicely's hat askew.

Damn, but he'd managed her simple question badly. Gently, Griffin took over the strap from her.

"Cicely," he began.

She interrupted him briskly. "I think we should say no more on the subject."

His mouth tightened with frustration and self-censure as he finished securing the basket. Doubtless anything else he could say would only worsen the matter. Still, he hated to see her this way, so stiff with hurt she could not bear to look at him.

He was responsible for her misery. He knew that. He also knew he must not only give up this woman whom he loved more than his own life but also, for her own safety, drive her away from him as quickly as possible. The knowledge tore at his insides until sometimes he wanted to gasp from the pain.

They rode together, each sealed away from the other by anger, anguish, and guilt. Time dragged by as it had not the first time they had made the trip to the hermit. As noon arrived, they came to the castle ruins.

"Do you wish to stop to eat?" he asked.

As Cicely regarded the ruins, her eyes glistened moistly. She shook her head. "Not here."

Griffin accepted her decision without a word, and they rode on.

Sometime later they stopped on the side of the road and consumed the packed meal. It was a perfect autumn day. The sky was bright, and the air possessed a delicious crispness. The leaves of the Weald forest gathered colors. For all the pleasure Griffin took from his surroundings, the blue sky might well have been black with storm clouds and the trees leafless.

Cicely stiffened when he helped her up into the saddle. Their gazes met for the first time since that morning, and Griffin felt as if she must be looking on his raw and bleeding soul.

"I'm not going to leave you," she said quietly.

A part of him rejoiced, and reluctantly he tried to crush it. He looked up into her solemn face and ached to take her into his arms. He felt battered from offering her so much hurt, yet he must try one more time to drive her away.

"There is nothing for you," he said. "No reason for you to stay."

She blanched, but she did not flinch. Her gaze did not waver from his. "Yes," she replied. "There is."

He felt her gaze on him as he turned away to mount Apollo, and he was careful not to look her way. His eyes trained on the road, he nudged the stallion with his bootheels, and they resumed their silent journey.

Dunstan was waiting for them on his front porch when they arrived at his cottage. A carved tray with a stone jar and three horn cups sat on the stool next to him.

As they dismounted, he rose to greet them. "Welcome, my friends," he called. Then as Cicely approached him and kissed him on the cheek, his smile faded. He skimmed his fingers over her face, light as dragonfly wings. "What have we here?" he asked, frowning. He took the hand Griffin offered him and shook it, but did not release him. Instead, the hermit's fingers traced his face as well.

Shaking his head, muttering to himself, Dunstan gestured them to the stools they'd occupied on their last call. "Cicely, my dear, will you pour?" he asked.

She did as he bade and when everyone had a cup of the fragrant apricot cordial, he turned his blind eyes toward the forest, but spoke to them.

"Magic," he said, "is a rare thing. It is granted to few. Those who discard it lose something more valuable than mere gold or jewels."

Griffin frowned into his cup. He hadn't ridden all this way to hear Dunstan babble on about magic. He looked up just in time to see Dunstan turn his face to him.

"It is worth fighting for," he said sternly.

Griffin felt his temper fraying. "What can you tell us about Alasdair?"

He had the uneasy feeling that Dunstan studied him for a long moment before the old man turned away, but that was foolishness. The man was blind.

Instead of answering Griffin's question, Dunstan turned toward Cicely. He held his hand out and she took it. "To some, magic is not quite so obvious as to others."

"Yes," she said. "I know."

Impatient with their mysterious gibberish, Griffin tossed back the rest of his cordial and rose to his feet. Restlessly he walked the length of the hermit's covered porch. When he reached the end, he turned back to walk the other way and found them both looking at him.

"What," he said tightly, "about Alasdair?"

Dunstan sighed. "The Green Lady placed a bane on him."

"So you said last time we were here."

"In order to end the bane and find his rest, Alasdair must perform an act of sacrificial kindness."

Griffin scowled. "Because this Green Lady got a bit wet when Alasdair wouldn't help her?"

"The storm was fierce. Because of Alasdair's selfishness she was forced to wade through the mud, in rain and wind, with the threat of being struck by lightning. And since I spoke with you last, I have discovered that she was heavy with child at the time."

Suddenly Alasdair's refusal to aid the woman took on a grimmer aspect. "Oh."

"I cannot comprehend why Alasdair did not assist her," Cicely said, a slight frown creasing her brow. "He is not a bad spirit, so surely he was not a bad man."

As little as Griffin liked Alasdair, even he could not

picture the Scot turning away a damsel in such distress.

"As to why he did not help her, you will have to ask him that," Dunstan said. Leaning heavily on his staff, he rose from the stool. "Now I have answered your question: Only Alasdair has the power to attain his peace." He patted Cicely's hand. "Do not forget what I have said about the other, more hidden, magic to be found at Cranwick." He turned his head slightly, and Griffin knew he was being included in the old man's admonition. "Do not squander it."

Slowly he made his way to the door of his cottage. It seemed their short stay had exhausted him. "Safe journey to you both," he said, then hobbled over the threshold and vanished from their sight.

It was late when they arrived back at Cranwick. Henry had left them mutton, thick slices of bread and several small, dried apples for their dinner, which they ate by the light of a single candle.

"I'll tell Alasdair," Cicely said after she'd swallowed the last bite of her meal. She doubted the solution to the bane would make him happy.

Griffin nodded. "It will be easier for him. I doubt he'd like the news coming from me."

The candle's soft illumination cast a golden glow across Griffin's forehead, the bridge of his nose, and the tops of his high cheekbones. Shadows pooled around his eyes. His wide, sensual mouth rested in a neutral curve.

How she longed to see him smile again. Randolph's appearance had stripped away all the laughter that had livened the manor. It had changed Griffin from her teasing lover to this brooding man. She wanted her own loving Griffin back, but she couldn't seem to reach him. The thought depressed her even further.

"Tell Alasdair tomorrow," Griffin said. "It's too late for you to try to face that tonight."

She nodded wearily. Tomorrow perhaps she could find softer words to break the news to Alasdair. "Are you returning to the stables?" she asked.

"Yes." The single, clipped word did not invite comment.

Rising to her feet, she allowed herself the luxury of trailing her gaze over his shadowed face, hungrily drinking in the wondrously familiar details of black, winged eyebrows, glinting silver eyes, firm, sculpted lips. Then she turned and walked from the kitchen, praying with every step that he would stop her. She wanted so badly for him to reclaim her that the yearning burned in her belly and clutched in her throat.

Griffin held his silence, and she forced herself to leave the room, to make her way to her chamber, where she would spend another sleepless light.

For hours, she lay awake, trying to find a way out of the situation for Griffin, but always the answer remained the same: Like Alasdair, Griffin alone held the power to change his plight.

Finally she fell into a fitful slumber only to be wakened by Hannah well after dawn. Lacking an appetite, Cicely dressed and went directly to the abbey, Honeysett trotting beside her.

"Alasdair," she called, standing in the entry hall.

He materialized in front of her. "At yer service, sweet Cicely." He peered into her face. "Och, and don't ye look as if ye've no slept a wink? Poor wee lassie." He propped his fists on his slim, plaid-draped hips. "'Tis that *Sasannach* who's done this to ye, is it no? Nay, dinna try to defend him. He's no worth a minute of yer worry. The low cur! I should have known he'd no be good for ye—"

"I spoke with Dunstan."

Alasdair fell silent.

Cicely searched for the right words. Finally she decided none could take the sting from what she must say. "In order to end the bane the Green Lady placed on you, you must perform an act of sacrificial kindness."

His eyes widened. "Sacrificial kindness, is it?"

Chewing her lower lip, Cicely nodded.

"That witch! As if she'd e'er performed a kind deed in her wicked faery life!" The ever-present breeze that surrounded Alasdair grew chill. His hair and clothing stirred more rapidly as the current grew more agitated. He stormed across the entry hall, into the drawing room. "I was hidin' from Elizabeth's soldiers, who were huntin' me for a Jacobite spy. I'd just lost the love o' my life, the woman who'd given me shelter and more, she'd given me her heart. I was mad with grief! How was I to know—"

"Were you?" Cicely asked.

"Was I what?"

"A spy."

"Of course I was a spy! I even donned those ridiculous puffy breeches the *Sasannaich* pranced about in to disguise myself. Dinna ask me how I came to be wearin' my own fine plaid after I . . . well, returned. Perhaps that damnable faery took a wee bit o' pity on me."

"And you loved the woman who owned Cranwick? Alasdair, you've never told me any of this, and I've asked many times."

He gave her a mulish look. "I dinna always remember."

She raised an eyebrow. "Is that so?"

"Aye, that's so! A man canna always remember what happened two hundred years ago! Memories come and go," he added sullenly.

"What was her name? How did you meet her?"

Alasdair wandered out of the entry hall, and she followed. "Her name was Mary Bowers," he said, his voice taking on a faraway quality. "Och, she was a bonny lass. Hair the color of fresh butter and eyes the blue of summer sky. So sweet and gentle, she was." He led them into the drawing room, where light flooded through a myriad of small, thick panes of glass in the leaded windows. As usual, he stayed back from the rays of sunlight, which would shine right through him. "She found me hidin' on the edge of her property. I was wounded and starvin'. Just outside London, I'd been ambushed by soldiers. One got me in the shoulder with his sword. I'd managed to win free and stolen a horse from a nearby farm. I dinna know my way about this bloody country, so I'd headed south, hopin' to board a ship for France. Had Mary not found me and taken me in, I'd likely have died."

"I'm surprised she didn't turn you over to the authorities."

Alasdair's handsome face lit with a soft smile. "So, I think, was she. But she was a tenderhearted thing. And lonely. A widow, whose husband had died at sea a few days after they'd wed."

"How long were you together? In the house, I mean."

"Long enough for us to come to love each other. We even made plans. I'd sail to France, where she would join me. We'd wed and buy a wee farm, where we'd raise a family."

Fascinated with this unknown side of Alasdair, she absently sat on the edge of a chair. "What happened?"

He looked away and shrugged. "A small cut on her hand went bad. She wouldna allow the surgeon to remove the hand, and . . . she died."

Sympathy for two lonely hearts expanded in Cicely. "Oh, Alasdair. I'm so sorry."

"She'd told everyone I was her cousin from Edinburgh come to visit her, so I was allowed to make arrangements. 'Twas the only time I left the manor, as the hunt for me was still ragin'. The people of the village mistrusted me for a foreigner and, worse, a Scot. I dinna think they believed I was no a spy. They tolerated me long enough to attend her funeral, for she was well liked, for all that she was shy. I had her buried in the churchyard . . . next to her husband." His throat worked a moment. Finally he continued, still not looking at Cicely. "On one of her trips to Alwyn, she'd changed her will. I was to inherit everything, includin' Cranwick. I dinna know it until the lawyer called on me, shortly after the funeral. 'Twas that night that the Green Lady knocked on my door."

He clenched his fists, flung back his head, and sent forth a low moan that rose to a heart-wrenching wail. It echoed through the house, as his face spasmed with grief and rage. Furniture began to fly. Figurines leaped off the mantel to shatter on the floor. Icy wind shrieked through the abbey, tearing at Cicely's clothes and hair.

"Alasdair!" she cried, dodging a small table that whirled past. "Alasdair, stop it! Please! Calm yourself!"

Honeysett set up a forlorn howl. Afraid he might be crushed in the chaos, Cicely snatched him up. Clasping him to her, she raced out of the house to discover Alasdair's mournful wail could be heard over the manor. Workers had stopped their labors to stare in the direction of the abbey. A cool breeze whispered in the treetops.

Distractedly, she noticed a man running toward her. As he drew closer, she saw it was Griffin. He arrived wild-eyed and out of breath.

"Are you all right?" he panted, frantically inspecting her for injury. "Speak to me! Tell me you've not been harmed!"

Surprised at his anxious concern, she obeyed. "I've not been harmed. Griffin, truly, I am well. 'Tis Alasdair."

His long-fingered hands firmly on her shoulders, he dragged her to him and breathed a sigh of relief. "Thank God you're safe."

He held her like that for several moments, and, with her one free arm, she clung to him. She'd been right! He loved her still!

Finally, Honeysett wormed his way up from Cicely's grasp to lick at their faces. Griffin released Cicely and stepped back. Wiping the wet trail off his cheek with the back of his hand, his expression shuttered away any emotion from his face.

"I would have told Alasdair myself, had I thought he might injure you," he said.

Disappointed at his retreat, Cicely took heart in her discovery—he still loved her. Now she had something to work with. "What I told him seemed to bring back memories for him. Painful memories. The night the Green Lady came to his door he was mourning the death of a woman he loved. Also, he was still being hunted by soldiers as a spy and the villagers were not friendly toward him. He was insane with grief and disoriented. Under the circumstances, I think I, too, would have refused to open the door."

"He didn't know she was with child?"

Cicely shook her head. "He didn't even know it was

a female at the door. He thought the soldiers had caught up with him."

Griffin looked back at the now-quiet manor house. A puff of breeze wafted on the air, then all was still.

"It doesn't seem quite fair, does it?" he asked.

"No."

Griffin rubbed the back of his neck. "I can't believe I'm standing here, casually discussing faeries."

Cicely smiled. "Not everyone can, you know."

"What?"

"Casually discuss faeries. Most never have the experience with them that you do."

"I have no experience with faeries. My experience is with a ghost."

Honeysett wriggled impatiently in her arms, and Cicely set him on the ground. "And everyone knows how much more real ghosts are than faeries."

Griffin made a disparaging noise in his throat as he turned and began his walk back to where he'd been when Alasdair had begun wailing.

Cicely watched him for a few moments. His limp had returned. He hadn't been massaging his leg.

"Come along, Honeysett," Cicely said, depressed.

She started toward the dower house, but turned her head in time to see the puppy streaking off in pursuit of a hare, in the direction of the abbey. All too clearly she remembered the last hare he'd chased. It had almost gotten him trampled.

Muttering about easily distracted males, she hoisted her skirts and took off after him. Ahead of her, she saw first the hare, then the puppy disappear through the open kitchen door.

What was the door doing open? she wondered, until she saw that some of the windows were open as well. Well, furniture had been set dancing, why not doors and windows? She dreaded the condition in which she'd find the house.

Cautiously, she entered the kitchen to find chairs and utensils scattered over the flagstone floor. She stepped over the shattered bits of an earthenware platter and hurried out of the room. As she moved from room to room, her hope that the rest of the house was not also a shambles dwindled. "Oh, Alasdair," she murmured.

As she passed back through the arches that led to the pantry and the kitchen and the scullery, she heard a noise. Pausing outside the open door that led into the cellar—originally a secret room for storing smuggled goods—she heard the small growl again. In the pantry she located a candle. She fumbled with the steel and flint from the small box she carried in her apron pocket.

Finally, she succeeded in lighting the wick, and, lifting the candle, she went down the wood stairs into the cellar, which was now used solely for storage. There was seldom need to come down here. Skeleton cases of shelves had been constructed years ago to hold crates and boxes and trunks. Chairs, cabinets, and bedsteads covered with holland cloth populated the far side of the underground chamber. Cobwebs hung from the corners of the ceiling, and a layer of fine dust lay everywhere.

The candle's light fell on the small form of Honeysett, his tail wagging as he growled at the terrified hare huddled behind a case of shelves. Only an ornate birdcage stood between dog and rabbit.

"Shame, Honeysett," Cicely scolded mildly. "Look how frightened this poor creature is." As she secured the struggling puppy in one arm, she raised the birdcage with the other. In a streak of brown, the hare bolted for freedom. But Cicely lost interest in it as she saw what lay hidden behind the shelfcase.

There, in the wall, cloaked with cobwebs, was a door.

17

Griffin rough-handled the shelf case aside, then examined the old door, running his hands along the crude frame, sweeping away cobwebs. He lifted away the strip of timber that barred the door against being opened from outside.

"Where do you think it leads?" Cicely asked.

He shook his head. His ink black queue swept back and forth between his shoulders. "I've no idea." His teeth flashed a grin, pale in the gloom of the cellar. "But we're going to find out. Bring the candle closer."

She stepped forward to squeeze between Griffin and the displaced case of shelves. Her shoulder brushed his, and even through the layers of their sleeves, she felt the sparkling shock of that contact. Griffin tightened and drew away.

Disappointed, she lifted the candlestick, pretending nothing had happened. Light fell on the old latch. Griffin set his hand to it and pulled. The door resisted. Then, with a shriek of long-neglected hinges, it opened. Griffin and Cicely looked into dark so dense it appeared solid. He took the candlestick from her and stepped over the threshold.

Light fell on roughly cut rock, which, as Griffin advanced, expanded into a tunnel.

"Stay here," he said, then ducked his head and entered the passageway.

Cicely made no response, then followed him.

The heavy smell of earth crowded in on her. She stumbled over a wooden crate that had been set end-up to serve as a makeshift table. On it, a few candles had been allowed to burn down into pools of wax. Griffin paused to study it a moment. He ran his forefinger across the waxen circles, then examined his fingertip. He frowned. Without offering a clue to what he was thinking, he walked on. Grit and pebbles crunched beneath his boots.

He stopped suddenly, and Cicely ran into his back. He cast her a disapproving look. "I told you to stay in the cellar."

She smiled brightly. "Yes, you did."

He made a disgusted sound in his throat, but instead of insisting she remain behind, as she expected, he said, "Just stay close to me."

The height of the ceiling required that Griffin walk slightly stooped. His shoulders seemed to span the passage's width, blocking out much of the light. They walked in silence, save for the echoes of their footfalls. After moving through the thick dark of the tunnel for what seemed an eternity, they found it opened onto a large chamber.

No man had shaped this place. The fantastic spires and columns of stone could only have come from nature.

"I had no idea this was here," she said. Her softly

spoken words careened from hard walls in a sibilant stream of whispers.

Griffin pointed to a rough semicircle of light across the cave. "I'll wager this opens onto the beach."

"A smuggler's storehouse?" she ventured.

"What better place than this?"

As they crossed the cavern, Cicely spied another man-made passageway. She drew Griffin's attention to it.

Carefully they made their way across the floor of the cave, following a path that had been worn over years. Brackets for torches had been anchored in the walls, the stone around them blackened from smoke. They saw several more upended crates with candle stubs. At each one, Griffin paused to conduct his private inspection.

"There's room here to store the cargo of three black luggers," she said, then heard her words repeated eerily as her low voice echoed through the cavern.

Cicely touched Griffin's shoulder to get his attention. "Look, another passageway."

He extended his hand to help her climb the slope to the other tunnel. "It would seem the smugglers who use Maresmouth Cove now know nothing of this place. Why take the risk of hiding goods about the village when this cave would serve them better? They could conduct their business more secretly, and it would be easy to defend."

They followed the second tunnel without speaking. She fretted as she calculated distance and direction.

Like the passageway from Cranwick, this one kept to a straight course. And like that Cranwick passageway, it ended in a door. They also found yet another of the wooden crates. Once again, Griffin touched his finger to each of the pools of wax. She studied his expression, trying to fathom what was going on in his mind, but his shuttered features gave nothing away.

He leaned down, and in her ear, asked, "Have you an idea where this door leads?"

She chewed her lip. "I believe we should be below Blekton." As soon as she named that manor aloud, a chill shivered down her back.

This place was not inconsistent with what she knew of the two manors' histories. Once the two families had been related, and smuggling had always prospered on this coast. Mayhap the families who had owned Blekton and Cranwick had taken advantage of this cave and their remote location to fatten their coffers. It wouldn't be so unusual. What was unusual was that, of all the estates in Sussex, one or two even close to Cranwick, Randolph had chosen Blekton. With the resources at his command, she failed to believe that snake didn't know about the tunnels and the connecting cave. What was he up to?

Absently, she took one of the candles from her pocket, where she'd placed three before going to find Griffin. They had been her precaution against being left behind if he'd insisted on exploring without her. Now she handed the candle to Griffin to light from the stub he carried. He did so, but retained the remaining bit in his hand. Then he moved to the door and carefully tried to open it. It remained firmly closed.

He inspected the door itself, its frame, and the area around that. Then he turned and led the way back down the tunnel. When he came to the cave, instead of following the path to the opposite side and the passageway to Cranwick, he headed toward the scrap of light they'd seen earlier.

As Griffin had predicted, the mouth of the cave exited the cliff above the beach. Someone had thought to disguise the hole with a thin slab of rock, which Griffin moved aside.

"Likely a rope ladder was used to bring everything up," Griffin explained as they knelt and peered over the stone lip to the hissing surf covering the small shale beach twenty feet below.

Cicely eyed the circumference of the entrance. "'Tis somewhat small." Crouching so close to Griffin made it impossible to concentrate on smugglers. She took a breath and turned her head to hear Griffin's response. Instead, she found him gazing hungrily at her. Her heart leaped into a clattering gallop.

"Yes," he said gruffly, his silver eyes roving her face with the eager need of a parched man finding an oasis. "It would be dangerous." He lifted his hand, and her breath stopped. Touch me, she wanted to cry. Touch me. Kiss me. I'm yours. . . .

Abruptly, he dropped his hand and looked away. "We should get back to the abbey."

She swallowed hard, then nodded.

The return trek to the small timber door into Cranwick Abbey's cellar seemed to take hours longer than the journey out. Few words were spoken between them, and then only out of necessity. Although little had been said on their foray out, now the lack of conversation seemed oppressive. Cicely released a breath of relief when she finally sidled through the opening into the abbey.

Griffin did not follow immediately. When she turned to see what kept him, he stood frowning at the crate and its candle stubs.

Curiosity finally overcame Cicely. "What fascinates you about those crates and candles?"

He led the way out of the cellar, where Honeysett danced around their feet in joyful greeting. Cicely scooped

the puppy into her arms and stroked the satin fur on his
bobbing head.

"There was dust on all but two of the candles I
found."

She dodged Honeysett's pink tongue aimed at her
chin. "Which two?"

"There was none on one of the candles at Blekton's
door."

Her eyes widened. "Oh?"

"Nor was there dust on the one outside this door."

A mist of dread spread through her. She tried to deny
her fear. "But they could have been put there weeks ago,
perhaps even months. Compared to the years of accu-
mulated dust on the others, a month's worth would
seem as nothing."

"There was no dust, Cicely. And when we first set
out, the wax I found at Cranwick's door was still warm."

Griffin woke to a rough shove. Instantly he slipped his
primed pistol from its place beneath the rolled blanket
he used as a pillow. He spun to one side and jumped to
his feet.

Facing him was a wiry man in his late middle years, his
gray hair pulled back into a short queue. He held a shovel
in his work-roughened hands as if he knew how to use it.

"Here now," he snapped. "Who are you ter be a-
sleepin' in Lady Cicely's stable, an' her nowhere ter be
found? What have you done with her?"

"It seems to me you're in no position to ask questions," Griffin said.

The older man eyed the pistol. "What have you
done with Lady Cicely?" he demanded. His hands
shifted on the shovel's handle, as if he considered
rushing Griffin.

"I've done nothing with Lady Cicely," Griffin said pleasantly. "May I ask your interest in her?"

"'Tis naught to you. Everyone's heard how the bastard who bought Cranwick dragged her back from Portsmouth over the matter of the demon. She's a good girl, and she'd make her best effort to comply. Yet the demon remains. Now, where is she?"

"Allow me to introduce myself," Griffin said cordially. "I am Griffin Tyrrell, the bastard who purchased Cranwick."

"Sleepin' in the barn? Not likely, I'd say."

Griffin shrugged. "Believe what you will. I didn't catch your name."

"Will. Will Allcorn."

The name rang a bell in Griffin's memory. "Allcorn. Yes, I recall Lady Cicely speaking of you."

Allcorn regarded Griffin suspiciously.

"But I thought you'd moved to Cinderlea. Weren't you working your cousin's smith after he was transported?"

"Yes. For his wife and children. They're waiting for me outside. I've come with a message for Lady Cicely," Allcorn insisted. "An *urgent* message. Will you, or will you not take me to her? Time is short, Mr. Tyrrell!"

"Very well." Griffin swept his arm out. "After you."

Outside in a wagon every bit as old as the one belonging to Griffin, sat a woman of about thirty years of age. Against her huddled two sleeping children, a boy and a girl, who looked to be about ten and five, respectively.

Allcorn swung up onto the seat and took up the reins.

Griffin hoisted himself onto the back of the wagon bed. "To the dower house."

Digby must have heard the sound of the horses'

hooves plodding on the ground, or the rumble of wheels, because he came out of his room in the dower house stable to meet them. This would be his last night there, for tomorrow, after their wedding, he and Hannah would begin their new life together in the cottage Griffin had offered them on Cranwick.

Griffin and Digby each took a heavy-eyed child, and Allcorn helped the woman down from the wagon. The front door of the house opened, and Cicely hurried out, wrapped in her dressing gown, mules flipping against the soles of her feet.

"Will!" she exclaimed and rushed to embrace him. "Oh, 'tis good to see you!"

In the light of the lantern she carried, Griffin saw the open joy of her expression, and the answering smile on Allcorn's weathered face.

"Mr. Allcorn has come with an urgent message for you," Griffin said, and for the first time, he noticed the bundles of clothing and possessions in the back of the wagon.

At Cicely's questioning look, Will Allcorn nodded. "Soldiers are in Cinderlea. They're awaiting word from Lord Marwood to march into Alwyn."

Cicely looked toward Griffin with shock-widened eyes.

"To search for uncustomed goods?" Griffin asked.

"Yes. The soldier I plied with drink told me everyone expected they'd be marching soon."

"Dear God," Cicely breathed.

"The smithy was to be confiscated on account of Matt's helping the smugglers. I'd hoped"—Allcorn straightened—"I'd hoped you'd have a place for his wife, Madge, and their little ones. Madge is a right fair seamstress, she is. Me, I'll earn my way, as I always have."

Cicely hugged him again. "Well, of course we have a place for you, for all of you!"

"Cicely," Griffin said, "why don't you settle Mr. Allcorn and his family in the dower house tonight? Tomorrow, after the wedding, we can inspect the Harrow cottage out near the west boundary and see if it might be suitable. Digby, come with me."

"Right you are, Cap'n," Digby agreed quickly.

Allcorn spoke up. "If you're going ter a-warn the village, I can help. They all know me."

Griffin liked Allcorn better by the minute, even if the other man did think the owner of Cranwick was a bully and a bastard. "Can you ride?"

"I can hang on ter a horse, if that's what you mean."

"Good enough."

Within five minutes, Octavia had been saddled, and Allcorn hoisted aboard. In ten minutes more, Griffin and Digby had saddled Apollo and Dobbin and the three men were hurtling down the drive toward the road.

Anger filled Griffin as he rode through the chill autumn night. Randolph had begun this latest, and possibly last, battle with his usual tactics: aiming at those around Griffin. The innocent. But the next volley would be aimed at Griffin himself. The impostor's handwriting might as well have been scrawled on the walls of the tunnel that led straight to Cranwick's cellar. Smuggling, it seemed, would be his crime of choice. Likely he planned for Griffin to die while caged in one of the prison hulks, convicted of trafficking in uncustomed goods.

Because only Griffin's death could free Randolph from forever having to look over his shoulder.

Then, like some terrible cuckoo, Randolph, with not one drop of Tyrrell blood flowing through his veins, would wed and raise his children to inherit what Griffin's family had, for centuries, labored and fought to build and protect. No one would realize that none of them were Tyrrells. Perhaps, eventually, even they would not know.

A clever, ruthless scheme.

But Griffin had plans of his own.

The following morning, Digby and Hannah were wed in the old Norman church. Afterward a breakfast was held at Cranwick for the wedding party and their guests. Because the dower house wasn't large enough to hold everyone, three long tables were set up outside. Yellow tablecloths fluttered in the breeze and a bright autumn sun lighted the sky.

Despite their perfectly executed plans for the gathering, the festive spirit was missing. Apprehension and fatigue kept conversation sparse and low. Even Alasdair made no real attempt to frighten anyone, though Nan Boulden swooned as usual. He merely strode through diners making sarcastic remarks and vanished. Finally, after the guests dragged home, Griffin and Cicely saw the bride and groom to their new address.

Afterward, Griffin and Will drove the wagon out to the Harrow cottage, which had stood empty for the past three months, since old Mr. Harrow had given up farming and gone to live with his daughter's family in Hastings. The two men deemed the house sturdy enough, then Cicely helped Madge with the fractious children when their few possessions were taken to the tenant's cottage.

Cicely bounced Madge's five-year-old daughter on her knees, and the child laughed with delight. The sound filled the kitchen with notes of sunshine. "What really happened to the smithy?" she asked the other woman.

Madge, a tall, muscular woman with a prematurely lined face and sandy-colored hair, stopped refolding the clothes unrolled from a bundle. "A man come to our door last night. Said the smithy was going ter be confiscated, 'cause Matt aided smugglers. Said he'd buy it from us right then and there, so's we'd at least get something for our trouble. Didn't want to pay but a pittance for the place. 'Tis a good smithy, Lady Cicely. Matt worked hard to make it so. Well, Will got suspicious. I didn't like the fellow none too well, either. Maybe the man had seen Will chatting with that soldier, we thought. Maybe his business had nothing to do with the smithy at all."

Madge shrugged. "We told him we needed ter think on the matter some, and that we'd give him an answer the next morning, though how, I don't know, since we'd never seen him afore. Cinderlea is a small town, and strangers stand out like a cow in a field. He didn't give us any address. Just said we'd be sorry for taking our time. Why, the door hadn't closed behind him, then we were packed up and on the road here to a-warn you." She needlessly smoothed a child's shirt. "Will seemed to think we'd be safer with you." She looked up, searching Cicely's face with worried eyes.

"From what you say, I must agree with Will." Cicely smiled, despite her own apprehension. "And certainly you are welcome."

The move to the cottage was accomplished in little time. The place had been kept in good repair, though birds and a family of mice had made nests in the chimney and in the cupboard. Griffin went back to the dower house to attend to some important correspondence he claimed needed immediate attention, and

Cicely stayed to help Madge and Will finish putting the house in order. She wanted to help them, but she also welcomed the activity to divert her from the strain of waiting to hear if the dragoons had ridden into Alwyn.

A fever of anxiety infected everyone at Cranwick. Will said little. Madge dropped a cup that shattered on the floor, and Cicely noticed her hands were shaking. The woman had been through too much. She'd lost her husband to transportation, and now she'd been uprooted and hurried through the night to a strange place where danger hovered over everyone's heads.

Cicely took the broom out of Madge's hands and set it aside. "You need to rest."

"I can work," Madge insisted.

"There is little more to do, and rest is what you need," Cicely insisted firmly. "Else you'll be no good to yourself or your children. Now the beds are made up." She led Madge to hers. "Have a bit of a lie-down. I'll see the children get a nap, too."

"But—"

"Tonight you can all join us for dinner at the dower house."

With a weary smile, Madge laid her head on the pillow and closed her eyes. Minutes later, Cicely heard her even, slumberous breathing.

In the common room, Cicely told the children a story and sat with them until they fell asleep. Then she went outside to find Will.

"I could no more sleep than fly," he told her flatly when she tried to coax him to rest.

"Come down off the roof, if you please," she said. "I cannot persuade you when I must squint up."

Will laughed. "What you really mean is that you can't wrap me around your little finger."

She gave it one last try. "You might fall off, Will. You're much too tired to be climbing around there. Do it when you're better rested."

"Winter won't wait for my rest, missy, and well you know it."

She heaved a sigh of frustration. "Well, there can't be many holes. Mr. Harrow took good care of the house, and you, yourself, checked it periodically."

"I did. Now I'm a-checking it again."

"And have you found anything?"

"No. But that don't mean I won't."

Perversely, his stubbornness made her smile. He'd been stubborn for as long as she'd known him. "Very well, then, be that way. Just promise me you'll rest as soon as you've taken care of any holes."

"I'm not one ter make promises I don't know I can keep."

"Impossible man! You know very well you can keep that promise. Griffin may later have need of your help, Will," she wheedled. "You will be useless to him if you're exhausted."

Will met her trumped-up innocent look with a narrow-eyed gaze. "I know what you're doing, missy."

"Is it working?" she inquired sweetly.

He huffed out a breath. "Yes. I'll rest after I finish with this roof, and only because you're right—the cap'n may soon need me."

As Cicely walked back inside the cottage, she hoped Will was wrong.

Griffin scrawled the salutation of his last letter, then began, "The enemy of my enemy is my friend." He went on to give details of all that had transpired lately. Then he sealed the letter, pressing into the glob of warm wax the signet his father had given him on his twelfth birth-day: the seal of the viscount of Kimsbury. Each of the six letters bore the same seal.

He entrusted this vital batch of letters to Tom, along with specific instructions on to whom they were to be delivered. Then he gave directions on where to find these men, along with a small purse of silver coins for expenses.

"As I've said, this may prove a dangerous mission," Griffin warned. "If you wish not to undertake it, you've but to say so. I understand your responsibilities as a father and husband. I'd deliver these myself, but I dare not leave."

"Pardon me, sir, if I'm talking out of turn, but this enemy—he's your brother, ain't he?"

Griffin hesitated, disliking the need to drag the innocent into his long-standing battle with Randolph. But Randolph, he knew, wouldn't hesitate to trample by-standers. Better they be warned and allowed to make their own decisions.

"He's not my brother." Griffin explained the bare, dry, deadly facts of his history. He knew he risked Tom's good opinion of him. Indeed, Tom and the others might choose to believe what everyone else had—all except Cicely: that Griffin Tyrrell was mad.

As he finished his brief synopsis of the events that had brought about the present situation, Tom scowled down at the letters in his hand.

"I'm sorry, sir," Tom said when Griffin had fallen silent. The young father's eyes remained on the sealed letters in his hand.

Disappointment sank like a stone in Griffin's stom-ach.

"I can't ride a horse, sir. That is ter say, I've never been on one."

Let the lad bow out with some grace, Griffin's conscience told him. This isn't his fight. "I understand."

Tom looked up, squaring his shoulders almost imperceptibly. "But I can drive a wagon. Mayhap Lady Cicely's chaise might be faster, if I'm not out o' line, Cap'n." His ears pinkened.

Relieved, Griffin nodded. "Can you handle a pistol?"

"I never have. But Mr. Ginger, the baker, can, I'll be bound. Or Mr. Coppard. He used ter go hunting."

"Do you think he'd be willing to go with you?"

"Don't know 'til I ask." Tom grinned. "But I know there were tubs of brandy and parcels of tea stored in their shops."

"Excellent."

"I do have a favor ter ask of you, Cap'n."

Griffin raised his eyebrows in query.

"Take care o' my Kitty and my Janie for me, will you?"

"Send them to me before you leave, Tom. They'll stay at Cranwick while you're gone. I swear to you, I'll do everything in my power to keep them safe."

"I know you'll protect them, Cap'n." He hesitated, then seemed to come to a decision. "And, Cap'n, I think you should know, the black lugger is coming back. They'll be anchoring in Maresmouth in three nights."

"My God, man, there'll be carnage if they do. Can you warn them off?"

Tom shook his head. "I don't know how ter contact them. Henry might, though."

As Griffin watched Tom stride out of the room and down the hall, he swore that this time he would not fail. The time for running was over.

This time, he must defeat Randolph.

*　　　*　　　*

Cicely cradled Madge's small daughter, who had crawled into her arms and fallen back asleep. If the child wished to be held, Cicely was more than willing to accommodate her. The cottage was quiet in this late afternoon. Even Will slept, snoring softly on the far side of the room.

She leaned her head back against the wall, and closed her eyes, enjoying the warmth and weight of the child in her arms. A fire crackled cheerfully in the fireplace. If only everything was as peaceful as it was in this room.

Suddenly she had the odd feeling she was being observed. She opened her eyes and looked around.

Griffin stood in the narrow doorway. His beautiful face wore an expression that was watchful and solemn and filled with yearning. As soon as he discovered she'd seen him, the shutters slammed down.

Too late, Cicely thought. *Much too late, my love.* In those brief seconds she'd glimpsed what lay behind all that careful distance he kept between them. She remained where she was a minute longer, studying him as she held the sweet, sleeping child.

A course of action that had been percolating through her brain since Griffin had taken it upon himself to save her from Randolph grew clearer than ever. Content that she had nothing left to lose, and a future with Griffin to gain, she determined that when the moon rose tonight, she would act.

Carefully she disentangled herself from the little girl, and quietly crossed the room, stepping outside to join Griffin.

"I've urgent mail to be delivered in London," Griffin said in a low voice, making no offer to tell her what was contained in the mail. "May I send Tom in your chaise?"

"Of course. What horse will he use?" It pleased her that Griffin had chosen to ask her, when it was within his power simply to take what he needed.

"Nutmeg, I think," he said, choosing the gelding named for its color. "He's younger and stronger than Octavia. Besides"—Griffin's mouth curled up in a half smile—"I'd not ask you to part with your mare as well as your chaise."

She ached to touch him, to encircle him with her arms and hold him close. She wanted to hear the familiar, reassuring beat of his heart.

"We would be wise to have Kitty and the babe stay at Cranwick while Tom is away," he continued.

"I'll give them my chamber in the dower house and move back into the abbey."

Griffin scowled. "What of Alasdair?"

"I see no reason he should object to my return."

"I imagine not."

She heard the edge in his voice. "I'm not in love with Alasdair, Griffin," she said, looking directly at him. Whether her words were issued as a challenge or reassurance, she couldn't say for certain.

"He would have had it otherwise, were it within his power."

"Doubtless were it within his power, his Mary wouldn't have died. They would have wed in France and lived to a ripe old age together and he wouldn't now roam the manor."

"Doubtless," Griffin murmured. Slowly, he reached out and stroked her cheek with his fingers. Not daring to breathe, she closed her eyes and covered his hand with hers, turning her face into the curve of callused strength to press a kiss to his palm.

His eyelids lowered, shielding what lay in his silvery eyes behind thick curling lashes. But there was nothing to conceal the motion of his throat as he swallowed heavily. Or the jump of the muscles in his angular jaw. A thrill of elation speared through her, reinforcing her decision.

He slipped his hand away from her and strode back to his horse. Swinging up into the saddle with the creak of leather, he glanced at her, then rode away. She watched him until he disappeared among the elms.

"So that's the way of it," Will said as he rose from his cot and joined her at the doorway.

She sighed, not bothering to deny her feelings for Griffin to her old friend. "I fear so." She smiled. "I love him, Will. And I plan to make him my husband."

18

Griffin lay stretched out on his blanket on the straw, his arms folded behind his head. After he'd bathed, he'd donned only a fresh pair of old breeches to sleep in. Here in the stables it was warm. The lantern hanging from its peg cast a soft amber glow over the stable box he slept in. To his left, Apollo and his mares dozed in their individual boxes. Outside, crickets sang.

Uriah Coppard had volunteered to accompany Tom, pointing out that he had no wife or young ones dependent upon him as did Mr. Ginger. Out of appreciation for Uriah's generosity, Mrs. Ginger had offered to run his butcher shop for him as best she could while he was away. A fiction regarding a Kentish cousin's wedding and an ailing aunt was concocted to cover their absence. Kitty, once again flush with health, and Janie now slept in the dower house, awaiting Tom's return.

Yesterday afternoon, when Griffin had been working on the books, Hannah had determinedly brought out a nearly completed ivory satin gown to show him. "The dress she'd planned ter be wed in," was all Hannah had said. As he'd stared wordlessly at the lovingly stitched garment, he knew that in his attempt to protect Cicely from Randolph, he had managed to shred not only his hopes and dreams, but hers as well. 'Twas for the best, he'd told himself. It was the only way he could think to keep her safe.

But last night something had happened to Griffin. When Will had brought news of the waiting soldiers, and it had become clear that, once again, Randolph's path of destruction would be wide, something inside Griffin had broken free.

Oddly, what he'd felt was not his usual rage and frustration. Instead, he'd experienced a quiet puissance. At first it had trickled into his consciousness, distracting him. Then, like water through a collapsing dam, it had claimed him in a roaring surge. And when it was done, he saw his course more clearly.

He could easily imagine how Randolph planned to use the cavern and tunnels that connected Blekton and Cranwick to deliver Griffin into the prison hulks and convenient death.

Soldiers, treachery, and death. Griffin smiled grimly. Really, Randolph was becoming quite predictable.

But before that impostor had the chance to execute his first move, Griffin planned to wed Cicely, if she'd still have him. Randolph already knew she was important to Griffin, so he would not fail to target her.

Under the circumstances Griffin was not an ideal champion for her. He was, however, better than no champion at all, which was what she had now. At least, if Griffin died, she would inherit Cranwick. Perhaps she could sell it again and finally be free.

*   *   *

Cicely looked out the window of her bedchamber to find the moon had risen nearly midpoint in the dark autumn sky. With a last glance in her looking glass, she smoothed her hand down her brocade-covered stomacher. *A woman of action, a woman of action,* she repeated to herself. She straightened her shoulders and swept out of her room. With only the rustle of her skirts, she hurried through the abbey and exited the kitchen, into the courtyard, relieved that Alasdair had not intercepted her.

Her breath faintly frosted the night air as she hurried toward the stables. Outside the closed building, she wriggled and adjusted her gown, tugging at her most daring wide décolletage until she was satisfied with the expanse of pale flesh revealed. Taking a deep experimental breath, she ascertained that her breasts all but burst from their constraint.

Her hand hesitated on the latch. *A woman of action.* Slowly, she swung the door open.

A lantern illuminated the far side of the stables, allowing the rest to be swallowed in shadow. She stepped inside and tried to close the large door quietly. To her consternation, a hinge creaked.

Griffin rose to his feet in an empty stable box.

His dark hair was loose, tumbling past his wide, smooth, naked shoulders. Cicely lowered her gaze to his deep chest, to the top of his bare ridged abdomen. Further details were blocked from vision by a wall of the box.

"I hope the view agrees with you," he said politely.

She walked toward him. Halfway across the floor she remembered to add more sway to her hips.

"What are you doing here, Cicely?" he asked before she could reach the closed box door.

"I think that should be obvious." Over the top of the stall she saw he wore a pair of breeches—and nothing else. A slow smile curved her lips. He'd made her task easier. She allowed her gaze to take in his long, lean, muscled legs, his narrow hips. Without seeing it, she knew how the tight curve of his backside would look in those snug breeches, and the memory made her swallow dryly.

"To ogle me?" he suggested helpfully.

She opened his stable box door. "Oh"—she closed it firmly behind her—"more than that." A downward glance revealed the swelling in the front of his breeches. "Much more." She stopped in front of him.

"You've let your hair down," he observed.

She tossed her head, knowing from all the practice in front of her looking glass that evening that the cloak of her shining hair would ripple down to her waist. "I remember how you liked my hair that night in the parlor, when I was on my knees in front of . . . the fire."

The night crowded in, isolating them in the lantern's glow from the rest of the world, from an uncertain future. There was only now. Only each other.

She took a step closer to him.

"Your feet are bare," he murmured.

She followed his gaze with hers, and on the way down, noticed his more prominent erection, now pressed firmly against the fall of his breeches. "Yes. They are." She slipped a toe lightly over his instep. "Yours are, too."

"So they are."

Softly, she traced a forefinger from between his collarbones to the top of his breeches. "Your chest is bare."

He moved the blunt tip of his much larger forefinger from the base of her throat downward, running softly, along the crevice between her breasts, causing her breath to quicken. It caught in her throat when he skimmed along the neckline of the gown. "So is yours."

"Mmm-hmm." With satisfaction, she noticed the pulse at the side of his neck beating more rapidly.

He spread his hand at the side of her ribs, drawing her closer with a whisper of pressure. He lowered his lashes, fixing his gaze on the tops of her breasts. "You never answered my question."

She threaded the fingers of one hand through the ink dark mass of his hair, enjoying the silken feel of it. "What question?"

"What . . . are you doing . . . here?" His voice held a faraway, distracted note.

Encouraged, Cicely moved a little closer to him. Her skirts brushed the front of his breeches and he sucked in an uneven breath.

Lifting her face toward his, she allowed her eyelids to lower and her lips to part. "I've come . . . "

His gaze never wavered from her face. "Yes?"

She could feel the intensity of his eyes. Nervously, she moistened her lips with the tip of her tongue. "I've come to . . . "

"Yes? Tell me." His words rumbled in his chest.

She stretched out her arm.

He lowered his head, slanting it to accommodate her lips.

She leaned to the right, reaching around him.

He missed her mouth, and his eyes opened in surprise.

She felt the handle of the basket she'd hung on the wall peg this afternoon when she'd hatched her plan. Organization was vital to a woman of action. How else could her actions be imbued with admirable grace and elegance?

Triumphantly, Cicely straightened, carrying the

basket with her. She barely glimpsed his disgruntled expression. In the next instant, it was gone, and she told herself she had imagined it. She whipped the cover off the basket to reveal a towel and a stone jar. "I've come to massage your leg." Again, she congratulated herself on her cunning plan. Massaging his leg had never failed to put Griffin in an amorous mood—an essential element in any successful seduction.

He arched a raven's wing eyebrow. "How fortunate the oil and towel happened to be so close at hand."

Cicely ducked her head, blushing hotly. Perhaps she had placed the basket a trifle too conveniently to appear fortuitous. She picked at a rough bit of willow woven into the basket. Was that so awful? No, she decided. And she would not let it deter her plan. Their future was at stake.

"Perhaps," she said, magnanimously ignoring his comment, "you would be so good as to unbutton your breeches."

His mouth curved in a wicked smile. "But of course." Before she realized what he was doing, his hands had gone to the front of his breeches, unfastened three buttons at the waist, and moved on to the fall.

"I meant the knee!"

His fingers hesitated. "Eh? But you said—"

"I know what I said," she insisted, her heart beating in a panicked dance. Oh, this had all seemed so much clearer, so very much easier when she'd considered it this afternoon. Now she found her courage slipping like a boot on rain-slick cobbles. *A woman of action*, she repeated to herself. She worried her lip between her teeth.

"Very well," he said. "My knee." He bent over and slipped the buttons through their holes. He straightened. "Now what would you have me do?"

It was difficult to think when Griffin stood so close to her, his naked chest filling her vision. When all she wanted to do was to rub her cheeks against that springy hair. Run her hands all over his marvelous body. Tear his breeches off and throw herself on him. Clamping down on the torrent of her desire, she dragged in a deep breath. "Please, sit down and roll up that leg of your breeches so that I may reach the . . . uh, area."

With lithe grace, he sat down on the blanket and complied. Cicely followed him down, setting the basket to one side, arranging her skirts around her to present the most attractive picture. Thank heavens she had decided against the hoop. Taking up the jar, she poured a small pool of golden oil into her palm. It rolled cool against her skin. She allowed it to glide between her hands, taking her time, allowing the aromatic lotion to warm. Then she leaned over and slipped her palms up his thigh.

He tensed. She drew her fingers down to mid-calf, spreading the fragrant oil over him. Finally she began to knead his thigh. Minutes passed, and the only sound in the stables was Griffin's sharp, shallow breathing.

Slowly he reached out and slipped the shoulders of her gown down her arms. She gasped when he lifted her breasts free of the layers of silk and linen.

"Your hands are cold," she protested halfheartedly, torn between pique at having her carefully laid plans altered and the thrill of his touch.

He brought his face close to hers, following with her as she leaned back. She bumped against the stable box wall. "I know how to warm them," he said, his words rumbling in his chest, redolent with promise.

"You have known all along." She pressed against the wooden wall. When he moved to kiss her, she flattened two palms against his solid chest. She needed to know.

"What changed your mind?" she asked. She tipped up her chin, "You *have* changed your mind, haven't you?"

Catching one of her hands, he lifted it to his mouth. Into her palm he placed a lingering kiss that made it difficult for her to breathe. "You've made me realize I can't live without you," he declared.

She brightened. "I have? I mean . . . excellent. Precisely what did I do to bring about this epiphany?"

Languidly, the tips of his fingers drifted down her breast, setting off sparks inside her, igniting a throbbing heat low in her body. Brushing almost, but not quite, to her nipple, his fingers began the circuit over again, disrupting her concentration. "Seeing you here, like this. So lovely. So very desirable. Your hair the color of ripe chestnuts. Your lips as sweet as summer berries."

When she tried to speak again, he cut her off with a kiss that seared her into willing silence. He slipped his arm behind her head and gently laid her down on the blanket. She framed his face with her hands and eagerly stroked his tongue with hers. His breathing became erratic, his kiss more demanding.

The hard proof of his arousal pressed against her, and its proximity inflamed her. She nipped lightly at his full bottom lip, at his jaw, his neck, swirling her tongue over his salty skin in the wake of her teeth.

He tangled one hand in her hair. "God, you excite me, Cicely." His fingers worked at opening the hooks on her gown.

"Hurry," she urged. "I need you *now.*" The memory of the delights he'd taught her gnawed at her mercilessly.

He bent to his task, scowling with impatience. "Steady, sweetheart. Let's make this worth waiting for."

One by one, the fasteners gave way before his determination. "What fiend stitched this thing?" His expression altered abruptly with success. "Ah! There we have it." Nimbly, he disposed of her corset and linen shift.

"Freedom at last," she muttered, and, naked, flung herself at him, tumbling him onto his back. She straddled his thighs as she made quick work of the few remaining buttons on the fall of his breeches.

Griffin folded his arms behind his head as he watched and grinned. "When I die, I hope 'tis with this view in my eyes."

A few flicks of her fingers, and the remaining buttons at the left knee of his breeches fell open. She tugged furiously to have them off.

His eyes widened in alarm, and he tried to sit up. "Gently, my love! You wouldn't wish to dispossess your husband of his manly attributes, would you?"

She paused in her struggle, the garment tangled around his hips. Her plan had worked! "So we'll marry?"

"I wouldn't be planning to make love to you now," he informed her indignantly, "were I not planning to wed you."

"We will wed tomorrow." She scooped a leg of the breeches over his bare foot. She liked being a woman of action.

"Tomorrow?" He kicked free from the clinging garment and clasped her hand to tug her back down to the blanket.

She closed her eyes as she brushed her breasts against his chest, luxuriating in the exquisite friction. "After tonight, I must make an honest man of you."

"Honest man, indeed," he murmured between kisses. "You just don't want gossip about me being a bit of used baggage."

Her giggle turned to a sigh as his mouth moved

down to her breast. His lips, teeth, and tongue tested the most sensitive areas, delivering intense flashes of pleasure that multiplied into a jewel-bright, throbbing haze.

She pressed his shoulders, guiding him to stretch out on his back. Kneeling beside him, she gazed her fill, dry-mouthed, at his powerful, long-limbed, smooth-muscled body that, even in repose, radiated potent masculinity. Starting at one knee, she traced her fingertips up his thigh. As she drifted over his flat belly, his muscles contracted sharply.

Abruptly, she swung her leg over and straddled his hips, feeling the need to capture some of his radiant virility for herself. He felt warm and smooth between her thighs. Leaning forward, she covered his lips with hers.

His hand softly traced the cleft between her buttocks. "Lift up, sweetheart. Ah, that's right." His fingers brushed against her, sending a deep quiver through her. Sharp and sweet, it sparkled through her body, jolting a surprised squeak from her.

A slow smile spread over his face. "Oh, I like that."

"So did I," she confessed breathlessly.

He reached up and wrapped her hair around his wrist, then drew her back down for another kiss. While his lips and tongue captured hers, scattering her wits before their heady foray, his masterful fingers pleasured her as she'd never thought possible. Higher and higher, she ascended up a coiling stairway that robbed her of articulation and thought.

Suddenly a white rainbow shimmered through her to burst like fireworks along her every nerve and muscle. When the last echo of sensation faded, she slumped against him in abject contentment.

He refused to let her rest. "Touch me," he whispered

into her ear, as she lay with her cheek against his chest. Still slightly dizzy, she sat up. He drew her hand behind her, and curled her slack fingers around his erect manhood.

She released him and wriggled back to a better position, where she could see and enjoy his pleasure. He jerked as the back of her thigh dragged against him. Instantly she apologized, afraid she'd injured him.

"No permanent damage," he assured her. "'Tis only that a man's . . . uh . . . manhood is vastly sensitive."

She gently curled her fingers around it. Again she was struck by its intimidating size. It heated her palm. "So large. So very hot." The long, hard length was flushed the delectable hue of a plum, and its tip possessed a voluptuous roundness that also reminded her of that treat. Without thinking, she lowered her head and swirled her tongue around the ringed top.

Griffin sharply sucked in his breath.

"Did I hurt you?" she asked anxiously.

"No," he croaked.

"What should I do now?"

"I would deeply appreciate more of what you just did."

She complied. Again, and again, and again, experimenting and elaborating with her lips, her tongue, and the edge of her teeth, until he grasped her wrist. Perspiration beaded his forehead and top lip. Lifting her by the waist, he lowered her slowly over him. As she felt the firm nudge against her, she realized what he proposed, and she stiffened with alarm.

"Ease yourself, sweetheart." he coaxed. "You'll like this, I promise. We'll ride together." He touched her again, stroking her back up to a peak.

Desperate for him, she followed his softly spoken instruction, astonished when he penetrated her with a long, breath-stopping thrust. A thrust that stroked new and delicious places in her.

From there, everything seemed so natural. Thrillingly, heart-poundingly natural. Her hips moved in a sensual rhythm, counterpoint to his. She closed her eyes and let the pleasure sing through her veins. The exquisite tension increased, yet denying her . . . denying her . . . His hands on her hips guided her into his thrusts, bringing her closer. . . .

With a cry, she arched her back and drowned in a torrent of pleasure. In the distance, she heard Griffin's hoarse shout and felt him shudder beneath her.

Moments later, she heard a soft whicker from the corner of the stables. "I think we woke Apollo," she mumbled.

Griffin settled her more closely against him. His lips moved against her temple. "He's just envious."

A contented moment passed. "I should return to the abbey," she murmured.

"Stay with me a little longer, sweetheart. There have been too many times when I feared I'd never hold you like this again."

She smiled sleepily. "The nights have been long and empty without you."

"Just the nights?" he teased.

"The days less so, for at least I could see you. Still, I've missed you sorely."

"Tomorrow we'll go to Mr. Joyes and say our vows."

Her eyebrows drew down over closed eyes. "What shall we do about poor Alasdair?"

"We'll discuss Alasdair tomorrow, shall we? Tonight I refuse to share my bride, not even with thoughts of a ghost."

She nestled against Griffin, slipping her arm across his chest. "All right then. Tomorrow . . . "

The cock's crow brought Cicely sitting bolt upright. Wildly, she looked around. This was not her bedchamber. A piece of straw dangled from her hair, in front of her nose, and she blew it away. She looked down. Dear God, she was naked!

Griffin stirred. His black hair was tousled and the dark growth of a night's beard shadowed his square jaw. He looked up. Immediately his eyes widened. "We fell asleep."

"We overslept! Benjamin will be here any moment to care for the horses!"

They scrambled around the stable box, gathering clothes and hastily pulling them on.

"I doubt we will fool anyone," Griffin said as he jammed the tails of his shirt into his breeches. "You've got straw in your hair and no shoes or cap."

The stable door swung slowly open. Digby peered around the edge. He grinned.

"Thought I'd protect the tender eyes of the lad," he said cheerfully, "and tend to the horses myself. No telling what state he might o' found you in." He eyed their rumpled, half-buttoned clothing littered with bits of straw. "Though I can guess."

Griffin glowered at him.

Digby closed the door and wandered over to lean his arms against the top of the stable box. "May I suggest a trip to the altar?" Clearly he enjoyed having the tables turned.

"We were planning to go this morning," Griffin said as he sat on the blanket and pulled on his boots.

"Ah. As you must have spoken all of twelve words to

each other yesterday, 'tis difficult for anyone to know you was headed for the vicar's today."

"Digby," Cicely said, her face burning, "will you please ask Hannah to bring me a cap, my stockings and shoes, and a hairbrush and pins?"

"Yes, m'lady," he said, doffing his hat. "And may I offer you felicitations?"

"Thank you, Digby, you're very kind."

Whistling a jolly tune, he let himself out of the stables, closing the door behind him.

Minutes later, Hannah slipped into the stables, a folded coverlet draped across her arms. She hurried to the stable box. Giving Griffin a cursory glance, she handed him a hairbrush. Then she turned to Cicely.

"I've brought you what you've asked for and a fresh gown besides," she said as she unfolded the coverlet to reveal, among other things, a trained sack gown of emerald green. "I knew you wouldn't want ter go ter your wedding in wrinkled clothes."

"Thank you, Hannah." Cicely was brought close to tears by Hannah's thoughtful gesture. She embraced her friend, whose eyes glistened with moisture.

Hannah helped her to dress, then brushed and styled her hair in a simple chignon high at the back of her head. Next came the lace cap, and over that a milkmaid hat trimmed with a fluttering green ribbon.

The door to the stables swung open, and Digby entered bearing a basin of steaming water and Griffin's shaving articles.

While Digby fussed over an impatient Griffin, Hannah and Cicely saddled Apollo and a mare named Bridgette, Octavia being in the dower house stables.

"I did send Benjamin ter tell the vicar you'd be ter see him for your wedding straightaway," Hannah said as Griffin assisted Cicely up onto Bridgette.

"Thank you, Hannah," he said. He bent to kiss her on the cheek, and she blushed a rosy hue. He rubbed a hand over his smooth, cleanly shaved jaw as he turned to Digby. "And you as well, Digby. Thank you." Then he set his booted toe to the stirrup, and in one graceful motion, he mounted.

As Griffin and Cicely guided their horses around the front of the abbey, Cicely turned to drink in the sight of the tall man riding next to her. She loved him more than she'd ever loved anyone, and sometimes it frightened her a little. Soon, for better or for worse, he would become her husband.

He turned, as if he sensed he was being watched. For a full moment, he solemnly met her gaze as they both swayed in their saddles. Then a tender smile curved his lips, and she knew she had made the right decision.

Together they cantered down the drive, on their way to their wedding.

As a beaming Mr. and Mrs. Joyes accompanied Cicely and Griffin Tyrrell, newly made husband and wife, from the old Norman church, a column of red-coated dragoons rode into Alwyn. With them rode two officers, who unsmilingly surveyed the medieval flint cottages and shops, and the residents who lined the narrow cobbled street to witness the unwelcome parade.

Cicely did not miss the concerned looks that passed among the village folk. Everyone here knew someone who had been sent to the hulks after a visit from the king's dragoons. A few men had even been hanged in chains. Children had been left homeless orphans.

And now the dragoons had arrived in Alwyn.

The only sounds to be heard were the ominous ring-

ing of horses' hooves against paving stones and the rattle of supply wagon wheels.

Like the other spectators, Cicely watched in silence.
Did that major know most of these people were starving? Because of Griffin, fewer people went hungry, but
he couldn't hire the entire parish.

Look at their faces! she wanted to cry. Would their
suffering persuade the major to leniency? She studied
his face. Here was a man who did his duty no matter
how unpleasant or difficult he found it. And everyone
in the village knew he had been brought here by the
duke of Marwood.

Griffin and Cicely were quiet as they rode back to
Cranwick. The arrival of the dragoons had robbed the
day of its sunshine.

Brewing trouble lay over the hamlet like a poisonous
fog.

19

At eleven of the clock that night, the dragoons thundered up Cranwick's approach. In the darkened manor house, Griffin watched from a mullioned window as they drew too close to the building, and well-trained horses shied or reared, throwing the neat formation into chaos. The major clipped off a round of sharp orders as he managed to calm his own beast and dismount. It took a few minutes, but the dragoons finally came to order and dismounted, leaving their horses well away from the abbey. More than a few men cast uneasy glances at the mansion. Straightening his shoulders, the major marched to the door and pounded on it.

Apprehension tight in his gut, Griffin opened the door. "Hello, Major Hornsby." The dragoons had been busy around the parish all day, tearing apart houses and shops in search of smuggled goods. It had not been difficult for Griffin to learn the man's name.

"I have orders to search your property for uncustomed items, Lord Griffin," the officer said stiffly.

From his use of his honorary title, Griffin knew the major had taken his instructions from Randolph. "Yes, I imagine you have. But before you start I think you should know that a ghost inhabits this place. Doubtless he'll object to your presence."

Major Hornsby stared at him, then drew himself up in indignation. "Really, my lord, if you desire to bamboozle me, you'll have to do better than that." He entered the abbey as Griffin stood aside. His men swarmed in after him. "Ha! A ghost indeed." He began rattling off instructions, assigning his men to search different portions of the house.

A cool breeze whispered through the crowded entry hall.

"Close the door," the major commanded.

"It is closed, sir," one of the dragoons answered.

Before men could move off to their assigned areas, a small *pop* could be heard even back by the door where Griffin stood. Visible above the heads of the king's men, a small ball of mist appeared. Rapidly it grew into a roiling, stormy-looking cloud, filling the area. The temperature dived.

Feet shuffled on the flagstones.

As Griffin watched the cloud gradually taking form, he had to admit Alasdair was getting more creative. Tonight the ghost was definitely playing to the audience.

The dragoons regarded the mysterious apparition with apprehension stamped clearly on their faces.

All at once, an enormous death's-head—complete with bits of decaying flesh—loomed over them. With a collective gasp, punctuated with cries of horror, they backed toward the door.

The death's-head's dripping jaws opened. "BE-GONE."

Its single word roared through the house like a gale, almost drowning out the shrieks from the dragoons as they tried to batter down the door by sheer weight. To avoid having anyone trampled, Griffin, almost crushed against the wall, managed to squeeze his arm through the press of bodies to the latch. The door swung open.

The dragoons tumbled out and ran for their startled horses. The hideous apparition slowly passed through the outer wall of the house, following the uniformed men.

Struggling with his rearing mount, Major Hornsby barked orders to his men to halt their mass exodus from Cranwick. They left him behind in their dust.

"Great God, man," he shouted to Griffin, "how can you live with that?"

"I don't have a choice," Griffin called back. "He won't go away."

The major spun his horse around and pounded down the drive after his disorderly dragoons.

When the last uniform had rounded the pillar and the hammering of the horses' hooves had faded from hearing, the grisly death's-head abruptly turned into Alasdair, standing a few feet away from Griffin.

"Bloody *Sasannaich*," he muttered, glaring in the direction they had retreated.

"I'm impressed, Scotsman," Griffin said, folding his arms over his chest. "I believe you've outdone yourself this time."

Alasdair smirked. "Aye, 'twas a brilliant performance, and no mistake. In two hundred years, a man has time to grow creative. Dinna often have such a fine audience, though." His smirk widened into a satisfied grin. "So much for England's finest."

All Griffin could feel was vast, luxurious relief at

knowing Cranwick and its residents had escaped the destructive search by the dragoons.

"Are they gone?" Cicely asked softly from the doorway.

Griffin turned to find her peering around the edge of the door. Honeysett's head popped into view just under her chin. He snuffled the door and the air, taking in the unfamiliar smells left behind by fourteen frightened men.

Behind Cicely bobbed another head. Cautiously, Kitty peeked around the side of Cicely's head, her sky blue eyes visible in the light of the candle now lighted on the table. Much to Griffin's surprise, Alasdair had offered no objection when Griffin had brought Kitty and her baby into the abbey, as soon as he and Cicely had arrived back from the village.

"Yes, they're gone," he said, striding forward to draw his wife into his arms, complete with puppy, who wriggled to be free. "Alasdair, the Scourge of Sussex, diverted them. Indeed, he brought entertainment to new heights. Oddly, they seemed eager to depart our hospitality."

Cicely put Honeysett down, and he streaked over to beg attention from the ghost.

"Aye," Alasdair said with obvious relish as he knelt to scratch behind the dog's ears. "Scared 'em near to death, I did. Och, and a fine sight it was, too! Their wee eyes grew *verra* large, did they no, Griffin?"

Griffin laughed. "Two of them swooned. Had their comrades not dragged them along and thrown them over their horses, they'd likely be here still, unconscious in the entry hall."

Kitty, cradling Janie, hesitantly stepped out the door, her wide gaze fixed on Alasdair as she moved toward Griffin and Cicely, her butter blond hair pale in the moonlight. "Is this the ghost?" she asked, her voice low-pitched.

Alasdair slowly rose to his feet, staring at Kitty as if in a trance.

Cicely held out an arm to her. "Come, Kitty. I would have you meet Alasdair."

He gazed long at her. His lips moved in a single word. Then, with a *pop*, he vanished. A forlorn sigh drifted through the night air.

Alarmed, Cicely looked at Griffin. "What did he say?"

Griffin hugged her closer to him, grateful he'd been given the chance to marry the woman who filled his heart. "He said 'Mary.'"

By noon the next day, everyone knew the dragoons had uncovered nothing in the parish, and that the duke of Marwood was in a rage.

A greater concern, however, was the advent of the black lugger. Winter was close, and without the silver to buy food, Cicely knew the few deaths hunger had hastened during the past several weeks would seem but a drop in the bucket to what the cold, bare months would bring. She wasn't surprised when, seven evenings later, Griffin kissed her and told her he had a meeting to attend.

Now she, Madge, and Hannah sat in the cozy, warm parlor of the dower house, applying their needles. By candlelight, Madge mended a seam in a pair of her son's breeches, Hannah darned Digby's stockings, and Cicely worked on a new shirt for Griffin. A fire crackled on the hearth while shadows danced in the corners of the room.

"What do you think they're talkin' about?" Hannah asked.

"About the black lugger," Cicely answered. What else was there to discuss that would require such secrecy? Tom and Mr. Coppard had returned with letters for Griffin, who had not made their contents known. She'd managed to refrain from asking, but she gathered that he was not displeased. For now she would abide with that. What concerned her more was Randolph's presence at Blekton. Just because the dragoons had been ordered to continue their mission farther down the coast did not mean Griffin was safe.

She wanted to be a good and dutiful wife to Griffin. Most of the time he made that almost too easy for her. She smiled to herself. Despite the danger that hung over them, the moments she shared with him were the happiest she'd ever experienced. His sweet words. His teasing. His kisses. Mornings she lay quiet, breathing in the warm scent of him as he sprawled next to her, his arm across her body, as if anchoring her to him. In the evenings, massaging his leg inevitably to led to hot, heady passion. The oil ended up smeared in the most interesting places. . . .

"I wish Will would tell me what they were planning," Madge said, frowning down at her needle as she placed a stitch. "I know he was shocked at how poorly so many Alwyn folk fare. He said as how only the silver the smugglers are willing to pay will get many through winter."

Hannah stabbed the heel of the stocking she mended. "And that Lord Marwood sitting in Blekton House like some nasty, great spider. Don't tell me he'd not love ter find out about the lugger. Oh, he'd have them dragoons back here in the blink of an eye, he would."

Cicely had to agree. "Well, our men are at Uriah Coppard's house for a reason. We don't know what reason, precisely, but I'd wager we can safely guess."

"The lugger," Hannah said and Madge nodded.

The door of the parlor opened, and Griffin, Digby, and Will entered.

"You've probably been wondering what was discussed at the meeting," Griffin said.

"Would it do any good for us to ask?" Cicely asked.

The men went to the fire to warm themselves. As Griffin passed her, she felt the night's cold emanating from his coat. He winked at her.

"You don't even have to ask," he said. "You see, all of us are part of the plan."

"What plan?"

"The plan to get the villagers their silver, while foiling Randolph's scheme to get rid of me."

A messenger from Barbara Rawle at Timsbley Hall arrived just before noon the next day, alerting Cicely to the fact that the duke of Marwood had accepted the invitation to the party. Now one must be staged.

Cicely rode Octavia over to help write the invitations that would go out this very day to what passed for persons of Quality in this parish.

Timsbley Hall was the perfect place to stage the fete. It was the closest manor house to the coast situated without a view of Maresmouth Cove or the beach, and, she'd heard that, unlike the master of Cranwick, the master of Timsbley profited regularly from the smuggling that had been going on for years.

By five o'clock she, Mrs. Rawle, and two ladies from other manors in the parish had finished with the invitations, which were given to twelve boys from the village for immediate delivery. Hot tea, hot soup, and a cold tray were set on the sideboard by Mrs. Rawle's footman while the ladies diligently worked on lists of supplies for refreshments, dinner, and entertainment, and inventories given of what each of the four households had in ready supply that might be used. Because time for preparation was severely limited, decisions were made regarding what dishes could be made elsewhere and brought to Timsbley Hall to augment what the kitchen staff there created on the day of the party.

The plan Griffin had explained to Cicely had sounded simple. A potion would be slipped into Randolph's wine. He'd sleep deeply for hours, giving the men of the village time to unload the black lugger and hide the goods farther inland. When the duke awoke, he'd experience the same effects as a hangover, and witnesses would claim he'd gotten foxed.

Cicely only hoped it worked.

Griffin arrived to accompany her back home. When the ladies finished their planning shortly before midnight, Cicely found him deep in discussion with Mr. Rawle. As soon as the men caught sight of the ladies, they broke off what they were saying and rose from their chairs.

As happy as Cicely was to see Griffin, she couldn't shake the feeling that he and Mr. Rawle had not wanted their conversation to be overheard. As he cordially greeted everyone, his smile was so easy and winning that she gradually relaxed into a haze of weariness and decided her imagination was getting the better of her.

"How did it all go?" he asked as they rode side by side across a field. The sky seemed to go on endlessly, black and cloudless. The moon and stars shone with piercing clarity.

"There will be a party," she said tiredly. "Despite the short notice on which the invitations went out, it should be quite grand. The resources of four manors, even in these times, are nothing to scoff at." A yawn overtook her. "Oh, dear. As I was saying, it will be a lovely party. Too bad it must be wasted on Randolph. No one likes the man, and everyone will be nervous. That will be the biggest problem, I think. We don't want him to become suspicious."

"No. Of course, he'll expect a certain unease. After all, at his behest a dozen dragoons have ransacked nearly every building in the parish. And, of course, he normally does not associate socially with those of the lower orders."

"I keep forgetting we're all peasants to him."

Griffin's teeth flashed pale in the dark as he smiled. "Sweetheart, to Randolph, *every*one else is a peasant, not just us."

Cicely took a deep breath of chill air and released it in a frosted cloud. "Well. And what did you and the other men plan?"

He shrugged. "Oh, how to move the contraband from the beach faster, and where to hide it. It will take all of us, but we'll manage. You look tired."

She suspected that he was changing the subject. "Are you hiding something from me, Griffin?"

"I'm simply not boring you with the details, sweetheart, that's all."

"Mmm." She studied his profile for a long minute, then sighed. She was tired. Perhaps she was seeing things that weren't really there. "Griffin, who were those letters to? The ones Tom and Mr. Coppard delivered?"

He turned to look at her. "Allies. A man in my position needs allies."

"Judging from the way people here act toward you, you have a whole parish full of them."

"You exaggerate."

"By little, I think. Perhaps you don't realize how unusual it is for a newcomer to be as accepted as you've been. In just a few months, you've gained their respect and trust."

"Randolph has come here because of me."

"But surely the soldiers were coming anyway. Why, 'tis nothing short of a miracle that they didn't come sooner. No one can understand why they didn't just march into Alwyn after they finished Cinderlea."

Griffin made no reply, and they rode in weary silence the rest of the way to the dower house. In their bed-chamber, he took her into his arms and, for a brave span of time, kept the world at bay.

"You go on to the party. I'll be there presently." Griffin refolded the square of foolscap the rough-looking fellow in seaman's clothing had brought, and slipped it into the pocket of his velvet coat.

Cicely studied the messenger, who nodded his acknowledgment of her, and she inclined her head in return. But she addressed herself to Griffin. "I'll wait for you."

With a light hand, he guided Apollo closer to her chaise. The hoop she wore beneath her rose-embroidered, silk sack gown prohibited another passenger in the chaise. Crystal beads stitched into the flower pattern winked in the light of the carriage's lanterns.

"Please go on, sweetheart," he coaxed. "You'll be safe at Timsbley Hall, and I promise I'll not be long."

"I'm not afraid for *me*," she replied, trying to fathom what was going through his mind.

Griffin smiled. "I'll be but a few minutes. This note requires a reply."

Mindful of the messenger, Cicely leaned closer to Griffin. "Who is it from?" she hissed. "What does it say?"

He bent in the saddle to brush his lips across hers. "A friend," he replied. "An unexpected friend who is taking a risk on our behalf. Now go."

"Oh, very well. If you insist. But it will cost you a kiss."

He chuckled. "Saucy baggage. What will this man think?"

She lifted her face to Griffin. "That your wife loves you."

"Most unfashionable," he murmured, then claimed her lips in a tender, lingering kiss that left her breathless.

Reluctantly, Cicely flicked the reins, and Octavia started down the road, toward Timsbley Hall.

"Cicely."

She halted Octavia and looked back at him.

"Whatever you do," he called, "don't leave Timsbley Hall before I get there."

"Come as soon as you can," she said, and flicked the reins again, sending Octavia on their way.

Frowning, Griffin watched her go. He disliked having her out of his sight away from the manor. She was safe for now, he knew. He had the roads being watched, as well as Blekton and the beach.

He turned back to the man who'd ridden hard to bring him the message, which read:

> *Sir:*
> *As you predicted, the duke of Marwood has contacted me. He desires that I alter my plans to have only half the cargo unloaded in the cove. The other half he wishes unloaded afterward on the beach just east of there, where a lantern will signal the spot.*
> *I much dislike being threatened, nor do I appreciate his interference in my enterprise. We have common*

*cause, you and I, and since you have dealt honestly
with me, I shall likewise deal with you. Therefore, I
await your word.*

    N

    *By the by, don't concern yourself with the informer
who led Marwood to me. The matter has been attended.*

"Thank you for waiting, Mr. Kinch," Griffin said.
"Won't you please come with me to Cranwick so that I
might write a response to Mr. Nodding?" he asked,
referring to the man responsible for the smuggling
activities in Maresmouth Cove. Henry had taken him to
the contact, who after careful investigation, agreed to
arrange a meeting between Griffin and Mr. Nodding.
Griffin had been surprised to discover the smuggling
mastermind a gently born man of education. But a man
didn't prosper as a smuggler unless he was also ruthless.

"Aye, sir." Mr. Kinch alertly scanned the area
around them. "Will it take long?"

"Minutes only. Those stone pillars mark the entrance
to Cranwick."

True to his word, minutes later, Griffin dipped his
quill into the pot of ink on his desk in the small dower
house library.

Everything was riding on how tonight went. He'd
done everything within his power to foil Randolph's
trap. Amazingly, the people of Alwyn had rallied to him,
even though Randolph was raging over having been
made to look a fool. Despite having turned the parish
inside out, no uncustomed goods had been found, but
neither the major nor Randolph had seemed to notice
the absence of almost every fishing boat on the beach.

Thanks to Will's warning, Griffin had managed to
convince the villagers to load the fishing boats with the

contraband. At no little risk, the fishermen had taken their boats out into the Channel and headed west along the coast. A mile up the River Arun, they had rendezvoused with the inland contingent of the smuggling gang. Through courage, sweat, and luck, payment was rendered to the Alwyn men and no one got caught. The angels had surely been with them that night.

Tonight they needed another angel. Despite the big show made of the dragoons withdrawing from Alwyn, word had come that they had not gone far. The curmudgeon who had been caretaker of Blekton so many years had surprised everyone by showing up at Mr. Ginger's shop and giving him a message to be conveyed to Griffin. The duke of Marwood was hiding the dragoons at Blekton. Tonight Griffin knew from his spies that the dragoons were posted at Maresmouth Cove.

Griffin had suspected that Randolph intended to use the cave and tunnels to engineer his death. This note proved Griffin's suspicions correct.

Well, there would be a small, but significant, change in plans. The ship would unload most of the cargo into the fishing boats at the mouth of River Arun, as already agreed, but now it would first go to the beach below the cave, hours before Randolph expected it.

Griffin would have to get word to everyone about the change.

With a grim smile, he scratched out his answer to his newest ally, Mr. Nodding.

Angels, it seemed, came in many forms.

Lights blazed in every window of Timsbley Hall as Cicely eased Octavia to a halt. A liveried footman appeared to offer his assistance, and she alighted from the chaise with a smile and a brief glance to him.

"Will you please see that Octavia is properly stabled?" she asked. "I wouldn't wish her to get cold."

The footman inclined his head in acknowledgment
of her request, and then summoned a groom, to whom
he repeated her instructions. As the groom led Octavia
and the chaise away, Cicely lifted her skirts and swept
up the torchlit path and past the front door held open
by another liveried servant. Still another servant took
her cloak and reticule, leaving her with only her fan to
carry.

My, she thought as she sought out the hostess, Mrs.
Rawle certainly had a great many people working here.
Many more than she remembered.

When she found Mrs. Rawle, Cicely inquired if the
dishes she'd sent earlier had arrived safely.

Mrs. Rawle's scarlet gown revealed she had not yet
recovered her figure after having her fifth baby. She
smiled, but its effect was ruined when her lips trembled. "Yes, they did. And I must have your receipts!
Your white veal escalopes quite put mine to shame.
And your orange cake. Superb, simply superb. You
used Portugal oranges, did you not?" Cicely nodded.
"You can always tell the difference between Portugal
oranges and Seville oranges, I always say. The flavor
of Seville oranges is very much sharper, don't you
agree?"

Cicely gently covered the other woman's fidgeting
fingers before they broke the delicate sticks of the
ebony fan they held. "Pray, don't be anxious, Mrs.
Rawle. 'Tis only a party," she said softly. "Tell yourself
that. Only a party."

Gentle brown eyes revealed naked fear as Mrs.
Rawle clasped Cicely's hands tightly between hers.
"Oh, how I wish I could believe that. If only that terri-
ble Lord Marwood were not coming."

"Our parts in this are the parts we've been trained all our lives to play and no more. It is not up to us to hand him the potioned wine."

Mrs. Rawle looked even more worried than before. "Our parts? What are our parts?"

Cicely pried her hands free, giving the hostess a reassuring pat on her wrist. With a leisurely flip, she opened her own fan. The faint scent of jasmine wafted up from the painted silk that spanned the ivory sticks as she delicately fanned herself—and Mrs. Rawle. She assumed a pleasant smile that revealed nothing of her own tension, and nodded to a passing couple. "Our part," she told Mrs. Rawle in a voice pitched only for that other lady's ears, "is to be the charming ornaments we were always told we were. But of course, we know that in reality, we are women of action."

Mrs. Rawle blinked. "Women of action?"

"Consider what we have done. In only a few days we have put together a party that should have taken weeks. We shall charm that snake Randolph into relaxing his guard. And when he wakes, we shall be the offended ladies his drunken behavior shocked."

"Yes. Yes, we are, aren't we? Women of action. I rather like the sound of that. And—and we *are* playing an important part in this scheme."

"We certainly are. Have you not worked your fingers to the bone to make certain this affair is so elegant that the scoundrel cannot compare it unfavorably with the gatherings to which he's accustomed?"

"Of course."

"Well, then." Cicely raised an eyebrow.

Mrs. Rawle rolled back her shoulders and opened her own fan. "Women of action. Yes, I quite like the sound of that."

"Remember. The perfect hostess," Cicely murmured.

She cast Mrs. Rawle a conspiratorial smile, then drifted away into the growing crowd. A widower in his middle years, who owned an estate in the far corner of the parish, politely offered to fetch her a cup of lemon brandy or milk punch and she accepted. While she waited she occupied her hand with her fan and fretted over Griffin's delay. It was so unlike him to let her out of his sight lately. And she was still beset with the nagging feeling that there was more going on than he was telling her. Absently, she watched Mrs. Rawle, who now possessed a more confident demeanor as she mingled with her guests.

"A fellow was bringing you this," said a chillingly familiar voice at her elbow. "I assured him I would deliver it."

It took more willpower than Cicely had ever imagined she owned to calmly turn and face the despised master of that voice. "Hello, Randolph." She accepted the glass cup he handed her, but made no move to sample it.

His wig was immaculately powdered white, and his suit of clothes and his waistcoat were made of the finest satin and trimmed with gold braid. Diamonds and rubies glittered on his shoe buckles.

His gaze raked over her from the top of her lunette comb to the pink brocade toes of her French-heeled shoes. "You look ravishing, my dear. For a provincial."

Where was Griffin? Suddenly that very question took on new, ominous meaning. She fluttered her fan in front of her face, hoping to distract from the fact that the thought had sent the blood draining from her face. "Your compliment leaves me breathless," she said coolly.

Randolph's carmined lips curled into a smile. "It should. All you need is a more sophisticated wardrobe and you could be a diamond of the first water even in London."

"And just what, pray, is lacking with my gown?"

The tips of his incisors showed beneath the red of his lips. "The neckline isn't cut low enough. The women of my acquaintance wear their gowns so that the edges of their nipples are revealed each time they take a breath."

She stiffened. "I am not a harlot, sirrah."

"I prefer to call them courtesans. You see, they're much more expensive than mere harlots." He shrugged. "Eventually, all women spread their legs. 'Tis only their price that varies."

Her palm itched to slap his face. Another time she would have. Tonight too much hung in the balance to indulge her revulsion. "As ever, our opinion differs."

"Only because you are so ingenuous. You've been twice married, yet you maintain this pink cloud of innocence around you. I find that interesting. Interesting and . . . exciting."

He eased the skirt of his coat back to his hips, revealing the bulge in the front of his breeches.

Outraged, she closed her fan with an audible snap. "Well, you're not in London, now. You're in the provinces. And provincial ladies, unlike the tarts you're used to, take exception to such vulgar displays. If you'll excuse me . . . ?" Without giving him a chance to reply, she escaped through the crush. When she was certain he wasn't following, she drew a deep breath and let it out. Only then did she realize her hands were shaking.

A second later, Mrs. Rawle appeared at her side. "What did you say to him?" she asked. "You should have seen him snatch up the glass of wine Benton brought him."

Not wanting to appear too obvious, Cicely refrained from turning to seek out Randolph in the sea of faces. "Is he drinking it?"

"No. No, he's talking to Mr. Patton. Wait, I can't

see . . . Yes. There he goes. He's drinking it. Drinking it all down at once."

"Excellent." Cicely hoped he slept like a rock and woke thoroughly sick. "What's he doing now?"

"He and Mr. Patton are leaving the ballroom."

"Where are they going?"

Cicely and Mrs. Rawle, and just about everyone else in the packed ballroom, rushed to the doorway to see where Randolph had gone. They saw the drawing room door close.

"Mr. Patton should be able to handle things," Mrs. Rawle said. Then frowned. "Don't you think?"

"I wouldn't trust Randolph any farther than I could throw a harpsichord," Cicely stated flatly.

"How long before the potion takes effect?" old Mrs. Grimble whispered.

"Ten minutes," Mrs. Rawle whispered back. "At least, that's what we were told."

Ten minutes later, they listened at the drawing room door. All was silent inside, save a soft snoring. Cicely eased open the door. Cold air from the open window greeted them as they looked into the room.

On the settee, Mr. Patton lay stretched out, sleeping soundly.

Randolph was gone.

20

Panic thundered through Cicely. Randolph had known—or suspected—that his wine was drugged and somehow switched it with Mr. Patton's. She ran to the window and leaned out just in time to hear the pounding of a horse's hooves growing fainter, but the dark concealed the rider from sight.

She whirled and began pushing her way through the crowded room. "Randolph's escaped. Let me through," she demanded, her heart pounding with fear for Griffin. If Randolph made good his escape, he would go straight to the beach, where likely Griffin and the other men were even now loading the fishing boats with the ankers of brandy and wine and parcels of tea and silk.

Griffin was in danger.

She ran to where the guests' wraps had been piled. She ransacked the heap until she found a hooded black cloak.

A large liveried servant stepped into the room. "What are you doing, Lady Cicely?"

Cicely's head snapped up at the familiar voice with its broad Sussex drawl. "Tom, I didn't know you were here."

"No, but I knew you were here. The cap'n a-sent me to watch over you, but every one o' the servants are in truth Alwyn men. Now, what do you think you're doin'?"

"Do you have a knife?" she asked.

Frowning, he pushed back the side of his ill-fitting coat to reveal his ever-present knife sheathed at his waist. He handed it to her and stared as she turned her back, rucked up her skirts, and sliced through the fabric tapes from which her oval hoop was suspended.

"Here, now," he objected. "Just what have you in your mind?"

The hoop dropped to the floor, and she kicked it aside, then set about cutting away a length of her white lawn and lace underskirt. "Randolph has got to be stopped, and it looks as if I'm the only one willing to do it."

"The cap'n gave orders for you ter stay put."

In the piece of lawn she cut two holes, then held it up to her face. Satisfied that she could see, she tied the ends of the cloth behind her head.

"What do you need a mask for?" Tom demanded, ransacking the garments on the couch, also taking a black cloak with a hood.

She donned the cloak she'd taken, and drew its hood over her head, effectively masking her identity. "Because I don't want to be recognized. Randolph must be stopped before he can get to the cliffs. He'll call the dragoons down on Griffin and the others unloading the black lugger. I can use your help, Tom, but if you don't wish to help, stay out of my way."

"I'm a-goin'," he said shortly.

In seconds, she hacked off another piece of her

underskirt and made another mask. She tied it on him, then hurried through the house with him right behind her.

"Here." Mr. Rawle handed Tom a pistol. "It's loaded."

Mrs. Rawle quickly embraced Cicely. "Good luck."

In the stable, the groom helped saddle Octavia and a big bay gelding. No sidesaddle was at hand, so two regular saddles were cinched into place. Tom managed to climb up on his own. He sat awkwardly, his shoes too deeply in the stirrups.

"I'm sorry about the saddle, m'lady," the groom apologized. "Will you manage?"

Cicely had never ridden astride before this moment. Her skirts hiked up to reveal a length of her pink, clocked stockings. The cold leather of the saddle in-truded rudely against her bottom and the inside of her thighs.

"I guess I'll have to," she answered, then dug her heels into the sides of her horse, sending Octavia into a fast canter, which, with Cicely's urging, developed into a flat-out gallop. Cold, sharp wind pulled at her hood and tugged at the cloak streaming back from her throat, pressing the frogged clasp into the tender skin. She leaned low in the saddle, hoping to reduce the wind's drag against her, which was certain to slow them down.

Suddenly, the big bay caught up with Octavia and pulled ahead. Cicely turned her head to see Tom clutching the narrow pommel for dear life. The gelding passed Octavia by, and Cicely realized that if she was ever to stop Randolph, her middle-aged mare must hasten her pace.

"Run, Octavia," she shouted over the roar of the wind in her ears, "run, girl!"

As if Octavia understood her words, she stretched out her legs even farther, coiled and sprang her great muscles more relentlessly in a heroic effort to please her mistress.

The mud brown mare caught up with the big bay and resolutely passed him. Ahead, Cicely spotted the shadowy form of a man on horseback.

"You're wonderful, my beauty," Cicely crooned, praying that she could catch that bastard in duke's clothing, praying that she could stop him long enough to save Griffin and the others. Praying that Octavia's heart did not burst.

Grunting with every breath, the mare pushed herself harder and harder, managing even greater speed, and, miraculously, she came up on the rider who had a head start on them.

Not to be outdone, the bay managed to stay close behind. Tom hung on with mute tenacity.

In the light of the stars and the crescent moon, Cicely saw that the rider ahead wore no hat or cloak. Jewels twinkled in the stirrup, and Cicely knew only one man in this parish could afford them on his shoe buckles.

"Halt!" she cried. "Halt, or be shot!"

Tom added his more intimidating male tenor to her soprano. "Halt or be shot!"

The rider obeyed. Hastily, Cicely tugged her hood back into place and twitched her cloak over as much of her legs and gown as she could conceal. As a highwayman, she knew her size made her less than intimidating, and her voluminous skirts and her pink brocade shoes likely did nothing to strike terror in Randolph's black heart.

Slowing to a walk, she guided Octavia around to confront the man in the windblown powdered wig. Under the cover of her white lawn mask, a smile of satisfaction curved her mouth as she saw his face. "Raise your hands in the air," she said gruffly.

Tom pointed the pistol at the duke as he managed to

direct the bay closer to the winded Octavia. "I say we tie him up," he said, his voice pitched for Cicely's ears only.

She regarded Randolph through narrowed eyes. He wanted Griffin dead, and as long as he lived, he would pose a threat to the man she loved. "Shoot him."

"Such a foul deed would plague you forever."

"Give me the pistol, and *I'll* shoot him."

"Taking a man's life is not a thing ter do lightly. Talk ter the cap'n someday, 'n' he'll tell you."

"All right, all right," she agreed sullenly. "We'll tie him up."

Randolph spoke up, snagging their attention. "I don't think you're highwaymen at all," he said. He began to lower his hands.

"Get 'em up," Tom barked.

Randolph raised his arms again. "Can you even use that pistol, I wonder?"

Both Cicely and Tom knew that neither of them had ever handled a pistol before.

"I would guess that you're Griffin's bumpkins. Or rather, *you* are," he added, looking straight at Tom. Abruptly, he reached under his coat.

Tom took aim and fired the pistol. Smoke billowed out and curled away on the night air.

Randolph fingered the ragged tear in the shoulder of his coat. He glared at Tom. "Not bad, for a peasant." Withdrawing a pistol from beneath his coat, he took aim at Tom. "I'll do better."

Cicely launched herself at Randolph. His pistol went off, and they both fell to the ground in a heap.

She staggered to her feet, and ran to Tom, who sprawled on the ground next to his stolid bay. In the gloom, she saw the dark stain on his temple. Her finger came away wet. She called his name and touched his shoulder. He didn't stir.

She heard a footstep behind her and whirled to find Randolph sneaking up behind her. "You killed him!" she screamed as loudly as she could, hoping someone might hear her.

Randolph laughed. "Of course I did, Lady Cicely. That was my intention. And you needn't bother to shout. No one will hear you out here." He plucked a watch from its pocket in his waistcoat. "I estimate that my dragoons will have rounded up your husband and his band of jolly clodhoppers by now. Imagine him colluding with a smuggler as notorious as Gentleman Jethro Nodding." He clacked his tongue in mock disapproval. "What will the judges think? Ah, well. It does save me some trouble. Now, instead of going to a prison hulk to await transportation, he'll go straight to the scaffold. It eliminates that final unpleasant step on my part, you see."

Cicely struggled to make some order out of her rioting emotions. *Distract him. Delay him as long as possible. He could be wrong about Griffin being captured. He could be lying.*

Randolph advanced on her. "You might as well give up. You're fighting a lost battle. Griffin is as good as dead." His mouth curved in an unpleasant smile. "You'll never see him again."

"*No!*" She scooped up two rocks in her hand and launched them in rapid succession.

One struck him on the forehead, the other on the chest. With a roar of rage, he charged her. She took flight, running down the middle of the road. Her feet battered the sandy dirt of the rutted track. Her breath labored in her lungs. She heard the pounding of his steps growing closer.

The French heel of her right shoe snapped off. Cicely stumbled.

Randolph caught hold of her cloak and snapped her

around to slam against his chest, jarring the little remaining breath from her body. In one bruising hand, he pinioned her wrists behind her. He jerked off her mask.

Grasping her chin, he forced her to look up at him. His fingers smelled of gunpowder. He studied her face a moment, then chuckled. "Griffin always got better than he deserved. But he'll have you no longer, my little hellcat. You see, dead men don't need women."

He kissed her with a punishing violence. Her stomach churned at the feel of his wet lips on hers, at the insistent spear of his tongue as it pried at her sealed mouth. She fought him with all her strength, thrashing in his viselike grip.

His lips curled up. "Good. Good. Fight me." He pressed her hips against his and she realized with horror that he had an erection. Fear lashed through her.

"One more kiss," he crooned, "then I'll show you how we do it in London."

He smeared his mouth against her. She felt soiled, violated, and her heart was breaking. *Griffin.* Capture would explain his absence.

She heard the thunder of hooves.

Suddenly, Randolph was jerked away from her. Her abrupt release sent her staggering back. Regaining her balance, she saw that her assailant had been whipped around to face an enraged Griffin.

"You dare touch her?" he ground out between clenched teeth. His fist connected with Randolph's jaw.

Randolph spun and fell to the ground. He sat there for a minute, stunned. Then he sullenly rubbed his jaw. "Bastard."

Griffin took a step closer, his hands still balled into fists. "Let's examine who the real bastard is."

Randolph scrambled to his feet and backed away. "Ah, but no one knows."

"*I* know."

"Who will believe the ravings of a lunatic? After all, the important witness is dead." Randolph clicked his tongue in mock dismay. "So unfortunate, the death of the duke of Marwood. Oh, and of course his beloved wife—a whore opera dancer."

"You arranged for that carriage accident, didn't you?" Griffin said softly as he advanced on his foe.

"Yes," Randolph hissed. "I killed them. He was going to see his solicitor in London. *He was going to disinherit me.*" He watched Griffin's every movement, sliding back with each step Griffin advanced.

Stunned, Cicely could only stare at the monster.

Griffin's nostrils flared with restrained fury. "You murdered your own mother."

"She talked too much!"

Griffin swung again, but, scurrying aside, Randolph managed to dodge. "Fight, you coward," Griffin growled. "Or are you only good at beating a man down when you can order someone else to do it?" His fist flew out in a jab. Blood spurted from Randolph's nose.

Randolph bellowed and clutched his wound. He swore, his words garbled and nasal. Finally he dropped his hands from his face, curling them into fists. He licked his lips, picked up his own blood, and spit. "You'll pay for this."

As the two men warily circled, Griffin's teeth flashed in a savage smile, reflecting the faint glow of the moon. "What are you going to do? Whistle for your dragoons?"

"Maybe." Randolph's gaze darted around.

"They aren't anywhere near here."

Cicely heard that news with a small sense of relief. But . . . how could he be certain? She kept her silence, unwilling to distract Griffin.

"Oh?" Randolph asked with patently false bravado. "And just where are they now?"

"Now? I'd say they're in your cellar, discovering all those tubs of uncustomed brandy and wine, and all those parcels of tea and silk. You know, the authorities might have been able to turn a blind eye to your smuggling activities, Randolph, if only you hadn't insisted on getting the dragoons involved. Major Hornsby wasn't happy over being made to look like a fool in front of the whole parish. I imagine the good major will be quite pleased to close the case on the smuggling going on in this area. It might even mean a promotion for him. I imagine they'll be along shortly to arrest you."

Randolph's hand darted into his lace-drenched cuff.

Cicely caught the glint of metal. "He's got a knife!"

A frenzied howl erupted from Randolph's throat as he charged Griffin.

With lightning speed, Griffin threw himself to one side, extending his leg low into Randolph's path. The armed man tripped, toppling headlong into the dirt. Griffin leaped to his feet. In an instant he brought a foot down across Randolph's wrist, pinning the hand holding the knife. With his other foot, he kicked the hand with the knife, effectively releasing the weapon and sending it skimming across the ground. Cicely ran to pick it up.

Griffin hauled Randolph up by his neckcloth. He retrieved Cicely's improvised mask from the ground. She passed him the knife, then gathered the two spent pistols.

"W-what are you going to do with me?" Randolph asked.

"Take your clothes off," Griffin said flatly.

Randolph blinked. "Clothes?"

"Take them off. All of 'em. *Now.*"

Cicely heard a soft moan from Tom and hurried to see to him as Randolph reluctantly stripped.

"This-this is an outrage!" he sputtered as he dropped his last garment onto the pile at his bare feet. "It's bloody cold!"

Griffin bound the naked man's wrists with Cicely's mask. "You'll live."

Cicely cheerfully handed her husband the other mask, then further reduced her dwindling underskirt by cutting a length of cloth long enough to bind Randolph to a tree by the side of the road.

"All done up like a Christmas goose," she said as Griffin tied the last knot.

He smiled at her, then bent to quickly kiss her lips. "Is that fair to the goose?" he asked as he strode over to Tom, who was sitting up.

"How are you feeling, Tom?" he asked.

Tom gingerly touched his temple, then winced. He gave Griffin a chagrined look. "Oh, I'll manage right enough. Sorry I let you down, Cap'n."

"It's my fault," Cicely blurted. "Tom told me to stay at the party, but I was afraid Randolph would find you and . . . and . . ." Her voice died away under Griffin's stern gaze.

He arched an eyebrow. "You and I are going to have to have a little talk."

As the three of them walked their horses by Randolph, who stood pale against the dark trunk of the sturdy elm, he shouted oaths at them. Griffin paused, and she saw the mouth that could be so beautifully sensual when he was kissing her became hard and uncompromising. He pressed the tip of the dagger into the soft underside of Randolph's chin until a single dark droplet beaded up.

"The next time you touch Cicely," Griffin told him,

his voice so dangerously soft, it sent a chill through her, "I won't have you strip and then tie you to a tree." He pressed a fraction harder and the droplet grew. "Next time I'll kill you."

Griffin said nothing more as he helped Cicely up onto Octavia. He gave Tom a hand up onto the bay, then swung into his own saddle. Without a backward glance, the three of them headed home.

It took a full five days for the dust to settle in the parish. In Mrs. Fullard's alehouse, at the village well, and in the shops, the villagers recounted with sideways glances and lowered voices how *three-quarters* of the black lugger's *largest cargo ever* had been loaded on the fishing boats and safely taken down the coast and upriver.

Alwyn men had carried the remaining quarter of the cargo up the rope ladder on their shoulders into the torchlit cave, then *into Randolph's own cellar*. Those ankers and parcels placed in the cellar had been donated by Gentleman Jethro Nodding himself. Insurance, it was speculated, that Randolph wasn't around to interfere should the smuggler wish to do business in the area again, though, Kitty confided to Cicely, who had come to present her finished mother-and-daughter portrait, that wasn't likely. At least, not for a very long time.

Everyone seemed pleased. The hungry had enough silver to see them through winter. The dragoons had gone. And Tom's temple, where the bullet had grazed it, was healing nicely.

"Ye should ha' stayed where Griffin told ye to stay," Alasdair scolded for what seemed like the hundredth time as he strode along beside her, Honeysett trotting at his heels.

"Yes, I know, Alasdair," Cicely said patiently, as she skirted the edge of a newly seeded field. She could not take her eyes from the sight ahead of her.

Standing on the boundary of Cranwick that faced the road, Griffin stood looking off into the distance. His face was turned into a brisk autumn breeze that bore the promise of winter. The wind tugged at the locks of midnight hair that had pulled free of the black ribbon that bound his queue. The sleeves of his white cambric shirt billowed back against his strong arms. Across his chest hung the cloth bag containing seeds.

Pride swelled within her breast as she watched him. Her eyes drank in the masculine beauty of his face. Oh, he still looked to her as if he belonged in silver mail, carrying a fabulous sword. And she could still envision him mounted on a high-stepping, fire-breathing stallion with ruby red eyes. But clearly she had been wrong about one thing. Magical warriors likely had been interested in being farmers. Hers certainly was.

"You should be wearing your coat," she admonished gently when she reached his side. Lovingly, she ran her palm up and down the side of his arm. "I wouldn't wish my husband, who has bested smugglers, dragoons, and his archenemy, to be brought low by a fever."

He took her hand between his and seemed to examine it for a moment. Then thick lashes the color of soot lifted to reveal his startling silver eyes. A smile curved his mouth. "You're just afraid you'll be deprived of your nightly amusements."

Aware of Alasdair's presence behind her, a blush heated her cheeks, but she couldn't deny the truth of Griffin's words. Their nights were spent in each other's arms, weaving wonder, pleasure, and joy. The en-